Instructions. Rose hadn't just written them, she'd followed them all her life. It was only when she realized she knew all too much about ceiling fans, curling irons, and cappuccino makers, and nothing about relationships, or life, for that matter, that is was time to move on. What she intended to do was just wing it for a while, make life up as she went along.... She'd written her last treatise on safety precautions.

Early praise

"Bonasia's portrait of a waterfront community's triumphs and squabbles is **as endearing as it is convincing.**"

—*Publishers Weekly*

"Lynn Kiele Bonasia's **hilarious and heartfelt** tale of redemption, romance, and mystery is an irresistible one. **I loved these people and this wise and humorous book.**"

—John Dufresne, author of *Louisiana Power and Light*

"An **intriguing** outsider's look at Cape Cod, jam-packed with 'trapezoidal,' as she puts it, or multisided, complex, **slightly askew characters, who will linger with you long after the book is closed.**"

—Sally Gunning, author of *Bound* and *The Widow's War*

SOME ASSEMBLY REQUIRED

Lynn Kiele Bonasia

A TOUCHSTONE BOOK
PUBLISHED BY SIMON & SCHUSTER
NEW YORK   LONDON   TORONTO   SYDNEY

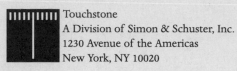 Touchstone
A Division of Simon & Schuster, Inc.
1230 Avenue of the Americas
New York, NY 10020

First Touchstone trade paperback edition July 2008

TOUCHSTONE and colophon are registered trademarks of Simon &
Schuster, Inc.

For information about special discounts for bulk purchases, please
contact Simon & Schuster Special Sales at 1-800-456-6798 or business@
simonandschuster.com.

Designed by Mary Austin Speaker

Manufactured in the United States of America

10 9 8 7 6 5 4 3 2 1

Library of Congress Cataloging-in-Publication Data

Bonasia, Lynn Kiele,
    Some assembly required / by Lynn Bonasia.
        p. cm.
1. Cape Cod (Mass.)—Fiction.   1. Title.
PS3602.06563S36 2008
813'.6—dc22

                                    2007033542

ISBN-13: 978-1-4165-5059-4
ISBN-10: 1-4165-5059-3

For my two: Jeff and John.

Thank you for purchasing this product.
Before connecting, operating, or adjusting,
please read these instructions completely.

CHAPTER ONE

Always maintain plenty of space around you in all directions.
—*from the Flexifoil Blade II Kite Instruction Manual*

Valeria Shimilitis is not a disease, though the name sounds like a mosquito-borne illness that might cause painful inflammation of the large intestine.

Valeria Shimilitis is not a dance. (*Come on, come on, and do the Shimilitis with me . . .*)

Valeria Shimilitis is not a shape, though this is what she claimed in those first moments.

"I'm a trapezoid," she said, so convincing Rose might have believed it had she been able to suppress her inner journalist, with an emphasis on *inner* since she'd yet to find work as such. Where are the edges? Rose wanted to ask. The angles and points? Had the woman claimed to be a circle, an oval, even a cone, Rose might have conceded. But a trapezoid? It seemed too far-fetched.

Valeria Shimilitis moved out of the doorway and onto the top step. Her bare legs were as white as the frost on the handrail. Rose backed down a couple of stairs to make room for her. The woman wiped her hands on her apron, then pointed to the edge of the yard.

"See, the property line comes in like this and then flares out down there, so you can park down by the fence." As she pointed, the loose flesh of her arm jiggled in front of Rose's nose.

The woman was talking as if Rose had already decided to take the apartment she hadn't even seen yet, a "waterfront one-bedroom" in her price range, according to the *Cape Gazette*. It was hard to believe anything in her price range could have running water, let alone be waterfront. Rose figured the ad had probably been a misprint, but decided to check it out anyway, desperate to escape the dark, musty room at the Ocean View Motel, which had no view unless one counted the sinkhole in the parking lot, no waves except the ones that had splashed from the toilet onto the floor the first night she was there. Rose had been almost ready to give up on Cape Cod. She wanted to live there but not enough to take that dingy basement room below the deli that smelled of cured pastrami and garlic pickles, or the shack that backed up to Route 6. All she wanted was something peaceful and clean, far from the city, and most of all, far from Martin.

Valeria Shimilitis pointed her thumb at a rambling, weather-beaten farmhouse visible through a leafless hedge.

"*She* says I'm a rectangle but I'm not."

It was too much to take in all at once, the elaborate anarchy of the woman's hair, the red terry washcloth that had been sewn into a rudimentary apron, and the way the flesh spilled out over the tight waistband of her madras shorts. And beyond her, the bay glittered like a box of diamonds.

A thick row of twigs ran along the front of the house. It was only the fourth of April, yet Rose knew they were hydrangeas. She pictured their soft blue pom-poms come summertime. Rose always loved hydrangeas, even as a kid when she used to come to the Cape with her parents. This place had always held happy memories for her, which is why she decided to come here when life took this turn.

Valeria Shimilitis's house was old, but had charm in the way old houses do, with its silver shingles, scrolled carvings over the front door, and dentil trim along the roofline. The house was situated high on a lot that sloped down to the water, offering a sweeping view of the harbor to the south, and the suede flats of the inlet beyond. From here it was just a short walk to the public beach. From these steps one could even hear the sigh of the incoming tide.

"Rose is a pretty name," the woman said. "I have a granddaughter named Rose. Come."

She waved Rose inside. Rose followed down the narrow hall, having to rely on other senses until her eyes had a chance to adjust to the dark. The house had decades of apples and onions baked into the walls. The uneven floorboards creaked beneath their feet. The hallway opened up to a bright and comfortable living room, with a picture window that laid out a panorama of the inlet.

"Have a seat." The woman pointed to a mission-style chair, its concave leather cushion cracked with age. All the furniture was faded and mismatched. Rose sank into the chair. Valeria Shimilitis sat on the mustard-print sofa. Rose could see she was somewhere in her mid-forties, though didn't know why she'd first thought the woman was older, something in how she carried herself and in the way she always seemed to be catching her breath.

"Your name is unusual," Rose said. "But pretty," she added.

"Valeria Shimilitis." The woman sang it like it was music. "It's Lithuanian. But call me Val. Everyone does. My father was born in the old country and my mother's family was English. My poor mother—imagine the leap of faith from Thayer to Shimilitis." She laughed.

Rose looked around the room. There were several portraits on the wall, accomplished oils that seemed out of place with the rest of the furnishings. To the left of the picture window was a painting of an old man with a long, narrow face and bristly hair.

He appeared sallow and sickly, and had that look of fear in his eyes that people get when they know they're going to die soon. Rose knew that look.

On the other side of the window was another painting, this one of a woman in her early sixties. She had a pink sweater over her shoulders and a beige purse in her lap that she clutched as if it might rise up and float around the room if she were to ease up on her grip. Something about that patent-leather bag with the gold clasp, the tightness of it, mirrored the woman's expression, the set of her jaw, and the way her thin lips pressed together. Whoever had painted this was a fine, intuitive artist, Rose thought.

Tucked in a dim corner between the bookcase and the fireplace was another portrait, this one of Val. It wasn't flattering. No imperfection had escaped the exaggeration of the artist's brush. She was seated in a chair by a window, staring at something outside the frame, as though she were waiting for someone. Her posture was rigid and her hands were folded in her lap. She seemed uneasy, or maybe just uncomfortable, as if the stool was too hard, or she'd forgotten to cut the tag out of her dress. Rose could see why the painting had been relegated to a dark corner.

Val obviously saw where Rose had been looking. "Noel did those. You'll meet him," she said. "That one of the gal with the purse is his latest."

Val pressed her thumb down to flatten the corner of a plastic doily that had begun to curl.

"I'd love to meet him," Rose said. Maybe there was a story here. Perhaps the best way to get her foot in the door at a newspaper was to write something speculative and try to sell it to an editor. There were just a handful of newspapers on the Cape and Rose's hope was to land a job at one of them.

The clock on the mantel chimed. It was a Howard Miller, the Lynton model that slightly resembled the kind of lantern one might find in the hand of someone riding through town on the back of a horse at the stroke of midnight, a square box with a brass handle at the top, finished in "Windsor" cherry with decorative corner spandrels and durable bronze bushings. Rose had written the instruction manual for it but had never actually seen one in person.

For clocks that have an operating moon dial, follow these instructions for setting the moon dial. For clocks that have a pendulum, follow these instructions for hanging pendulum.

This clock didn't have a moon dial or a pendulum.

One of the perils of writing instruction manuals for a living was that Rose couldn't go anywhere without seeing a fan or a vacuum or a VCR or a blender she knew intimately. She had become a repository of information on products she didn't own: *how to use a rubber spatula with your Sunbeam mixer* and *when to change the battery of the transmitter on your electric boat.* Her work was everywhere, translated into languages she'd never heard of, much less heard spoken. She'd become the go-to gal for instruction booklets, spoke at seminars instructing attendants on the how-tos of writing how-tos. She had more work than she could handle. The money was decent and the work, tedious as it sounded, was easy and even a little bit interesting. Rose had to admit she liked learning about how things worked in general. It benefited her from time to time, when the toast got stuck in the toaster or when she accidentally hit a button and the TV started speaking to her in Spanish. It wasn't a bad living. She could work from home, and on her laptop from Martin's apartment.

Even her ex-boyfriend had come with his own set of instructions. He couldn't be spoken to until he had his orange juice. Toothpaste had to be out of sight. At least once a week, Rose had to walk on his back in stockinged feet to relieve his sciatica. He couldn't sleep without a white-noise machine, which had to be set to "rain," and never "surf" or "wind." On Sundays, she was required to shave the hairs on the back of his neck. He was lactose intolerant and allergic to garlic. His feet blistered from walking on sand. To turn him on, Rose had to nibble on his ear or wear a tank top to bed. To turn him off, she had to leave her bra hanging on the shower rod, wear pink sweatpants, or talk about money. Large crowds made him nervous. He couldn't wear wool on his feet.

Instructions. Rose hadn't just written them, she'd followed them all her life. It was only when she realized she knew all too much about ceiling fans, curling irons, and cappuccino makers, and nothing about relationships, or life, for that matter, that it was time to move on. What she intended to do was just wing it for a while, make life up as she went along. At the very least, Rose intended to give a shot to her lifelong dream of becoming a journalist and following the path she'd set out for herself in college before getting seduced by the idea of making an easy buck.

After she and Martin split, Rose decided to throw out the rule book, the one that said at thirty-nine, she was probably too old to be switching careers. She'd written her last treatise on safety precautions.

Val got up and was rummaging through the top drawer of a writing desk near the fireplace. She produced a pad of paper and brought it back over to the sofa.

"Nice clock," Rose said.

"My daughter gave it to me," Val said. She studied the pad.

Rose noticed a stack of *Cancer Cell* magazines on the coffee table. An odd choice of reading material unless Val was caring for someone who was sick, or was sick herself. Rose had never thought to read *Cancer Cell* magazine, never even knew such a publication existed, when her mother was ill three years ago. Might it have made a difference?

"The cottage is out back. I'll take you to see it in a minute. First, my daughter gave me a list of questions to ask," Val said.

Cottage sounded a lot better than *apartment*.

"Let's see," Val said. She took a pair of reading glasses out of the ashtray on the side table and put them on. One side of the frame had been fastened to the lenses with tape so they sat a little crooked on her face. She ran her finger down the page. "Where are you from? What do you do? I'm supposed to ask for references."

"I can get a letter from my former landlord. I've lived in Boston for the last fifteen years, in an apartment in the North End. I'm originally from western Massachusetts. I'm a reporter," Rose lied.

Val's face lit up. "Have I seen you on TV?" she asked.

"No," Rose said. "Actually, I'm a technical writer but I want to be a reporter. I've been talking to one of the newspapers in town." *Harassing* was more like it. Rose got up and walked over to the window. "Incredible view," she said. "Have you lived here your whole life?" The place had a settledness to it, something in the collective weight of everything in the room.

"Not *yet*." Val laughed, maybe a little longer than the joke warranted. "Cape humor. You'll get used to it."

"My parents took me here when I was a kid. I always loved the beach but my boyfriend isn't—*wasn't*—much of a beach person. Type A. Couldn't sit still." Couldn't be happy with one woman.

Val's face dropped. "Did something happen to him?" she asked.

Rose tried to laugh but it sounded more like a choking sound. "He's fine. We just split up."

"How long were you together?"

"Four years."

"That's a long time," she said.

Please don't ask, Rose thought.

"What happened?" Val asked.

What would Rose tell her? The truth? "Irreconcilable differences," Rose said. She pretended to be enthralled with a framed snapshot on a table by the window.

"It's difficult starting over," Val said. "That's my daughter."

The photo was of a girl somewhere in her mid-twenties. She

had dark chin-length hair and enormous brown eyes. She was pretty. She also looked nothing like her mother.

"It was taken right before she knew she was pregnant with Rosie."

Rosie. To no one but Rose's poor dead father had she ever been a Rosie. Rosies were cute and round and Rose had never been either. She'd been a thin child with an angular face and straight hair that separated into blond ropes. When Rose hit her mid-teens, cheekbones emerged, giving structure to her face and her boyish figure took on some modest curves. It wasn't until the acne cleared in her early twenties that she began to enjoy some overdue male attention. But even then, none of her suitors had ever called her Rosie. Not even Martin. Not once. It didn't occur to people.

"How old is the baby?" Rose asked.

Val seemed to have to think a minute. "Thirteen months. I have some pictures upstairs. I'll get them down for you the next time."

At least Val was talking "next times." The two of them seemed to be hitting it off. Rose hoped she would like the apartment. No, *cottage.*

"Come, let's go see the place." Val rose from the sofa and set the pad of paper down on the coffee table. Rose saw there was no writing on it at all. No list of questions. Maybe she was just trying to look like she knew what she was doing. Maybe Rose wasn't the only one.

Though April, it was nearly freezing, certainly too cold to be wearing shorts, but Val didn't seem to notice. She didn't even bother to put on a jacket. She led Rose through the kitchen with its black-and-white-check vinyl floor and knotty-pine cabinets with old-fashioned wrought-iron hinges, past the gold stove and twenty or so orange prescription bottles lined up above the clock behind the burners. It seemed like a lot of medicine. Rose recalled the magazines on the coffee table. Before she had a chance to think about them, she and Val were out the door.

While the front of the house was shielded from the road by mature cedars and a tangle of underbrush, the back of the house was wide-open, with a lawn that sloped down to the marsh and the inlet beyond. At the end of the driveway, behind the main house, in the back right corner of the property, stood a small structure, a cottage. When Rose first drove in, she'd mistaken it for part of the main house. The cottage looked like a miniature of the original, with the same black shutters and silvered shingles. It was adorable, a dollhouse, and even closer to the water, presumably with a more spectacular view than the one Rose had enjoyed from Val's living room. She tried not to let herself get too excited. There had to be a catch.

"This is it," Val said. She took her crooked glasses out of her apron pocket, put them on her nose, and went through the keys on her ring, one by one.

Rose backed away from the cottage. She tried to picture herself living there. The forsythia at the side of the house was just starting to yellow. "It's nice," she said. She didn't want to seem too enthusiastic. Surely there had been others who had come to see the place.

"Here we go," Val said. She had found the right key and slid it into the lock. The back of her shirt was still bunched up from where she'd been sitting on the sofa, and when she jiggled the key, the loose flesh of her hips splashed up against her waistband like water up against a jetty. "Might be a little stuffy in here. I shut everything tight to keep out the critters. Last year I had bats in the attic. Oh, but they're gone, don't worry. Lou Tuttle from the Natural History Museum came and set traps. Actually, he's eighty-seven, so I was the one who had to climb into the attic, more of a crawl space, really. But I didn't have the heart to call an exterminator." Finally the tumbler gave way and Val pushed the door open.

She reached in and flicked on the light switch. Rose followed her inside, into a small living area that was sparsely furnished with two mission-style chairs, a lobster trap with a piece of glass over the top for a coffee table, and a small antique desk. Two windows on either side of the door held a generous swath of blue. Rose could see the mouth of the inlet to the north and the long stretch of dunes that ran the length of the outer beach. To the south, however, the pristine view was marred by a construction site, a large structure going up on a strip of land that jutted out into the inlet.

"Come see the rest," Val said. She tapped Rose on the arm.

"What is *that*?" Rose pointed.

"Ah, the *mystery mansion*," Val said. "That's what the locals are calling it this week, which is better than what they were calling it last week, trust me. No one knows who's building it." Val looked out the window herself. "It's gonna be something, huh? Don't know where these washashores get their money."

"Washashores?" Rose asked.

"Just means people from away. Not born and raised here," Val said. "No offense."

Rose could count at least six gables and the house possessed what had to be one of the most breathtaking views the town had to offer, encompassing the entire harbor, the inlet, the beach with its rolling dunes, and the ocean beyond.

"I'm hoping for a movie star," Val continued. "Could finally put my father's old telescope to good use. Oh, but I wouldn't just casually mention it to people in town or you'll get an earful. Most folks are opposed to the project and are looking for anything to raise hell about: pollution, runoff, encroachment on wetlands, endangering the horseshoe crabs, you name it," she said. "People don't like change, is what it is. Almost makes you feel sorry for those poor rich people who are going to try to live there. Come see the kitchen."

Poor rich people. It was funny, but Rose didn't think she meant it to be.

A low wall separated the living room from a tiny kitchen with pale yellow countertops and pine cabinets like the ones in the main house. The appliances were old but had been scrubbed clean. The burners on the electric stove were lined with fresh aluminum foil. There was a small fifties-style table with a Formica top and two metal chairs with matching red vinyl seat cushions. One had been repaired with duct tape.

"Sometimes the faucet drips a little," Val confessed. She started playing with the hot and cold knobs to try to stop the leak.

A leaky faucet is usually caused by a scratched or damaged cartridge, O-ring, or grommet. In most cases a cartridge repair kit or replacement cartridge will correct a leak.

"I'm pretty good with sinks," Rose said. "Is the bedroom back here?"

"And the bathroom. Don't think I could even squeeze into that shower stall anymore," Val said. She looked Rose up and down. "Of course *you'll* have no trouble."

Stress made you skinny, Rose thought. Then again, Rose had been skinny all her life.

Val stayed in the kitchen while Rose went to check out the other rooms. The bedroom was at the front of the cottage. It was a decent size and had three windows, two facing the hedges and the house next door, and one facing the driveway.

"What do you think?" Val asked from the kitchen.

Rose came out. She smiled. "It's perfect," she said.

Val clapped her hands. "You know, you never told me how you heard I was looking for a tenant. Just got the tax bill last week and hadn't even gotten around to putting a sign out front. Of course I'd mentioned it to Dorie Nickerson, and once you tell her something it's all over town. I just figured—"

"I saw the ad in the paper."

Val cocked her head to the side and squinted. "What ad?"

"In Sunday's paper. A 'waterfront one-bedroom—'"

"Uh-oh," Val said. The moment she said it Rose realized she'd been waiting for that "uh-oh" since she'd set foot in the place. It was all too good to be true. "Did it say three-fifteen?"

Rose nodded.

"That's Cooper. I'm three-nineteen. The cottage is three-seventeen."

"You mean I came to the wrong house?" And yet this whole time she'd acted as if she'd been expecting to show the place.

"Part of the nine on my mailbox is a little broken off. I can see how the nine might look like a five." Val put her hand over her mouth to try to hide the grin that had suddenly spread to her cheeks. "Cooper'd have a fit if she knew the ad she paid for got me a tenant."

"What's her place like?"

Val's smile disappeared. She shook her head. "Oh, you don't want to live *there*. Used to be a duck farm. She subdivided the old barn into two cramped efficiencies. The walls are paper-thin and the rooms all face the street, so you can't even see the water. And when it gets humid, the whole place smells like wet duck."

Great. "How much are you asking?" Rose asked. It had to be three times what she could afford.

"Well, I don't know. I hadn't gotten that far yet." She rubbed her chin. "What's *she* asking?"

"The ad said six hundred a month." Rose braced herself.

Val didn't answer right away. Rose stared out at the blue liquid backyard.

"Five seventy-five," Val said. "That's as low as I can go."

When life throws a pie in your face, you might as well taste it. It was one of Rose's mother's favorite sayings, and one that appealed to Rose's sweet tooth. As a kid, she couldn't wait for a little Boston-cream or cranberry-apple adversity. Now, suddenly, here it was. She'd been left with no choice but to try to see this situation as an opportunity, a clean start in a new setting. Landing this cottage was a lucky break, which was more than Rose's father got, thirty-five years as a bus driver for the Pioneer Valley, schlepping college students who reeked of pot and curry from one campus to the other, only to have his heart stop beating at sixty-two. Or her mother, who, four years after he died, found a lump on her breast that doctors said was "probably nothing." Only it turned out to be everything. In the end, dignity was the one thing life couldn't take from a person. Watching her mother die had taught Rose that much. Dignity was fuel. If you conserved it, there'd be enough to carry you through. Rose felt like she still had about a half tank left.

Martin and Rose met at the hospital during her mother's illness. He'd been visiting a friend's wife who was suffering from ovarian cancer. One day Rose saw him in the waiting room staring at a blank TV screen, apparently gathering the courage to set foot in the elevator and move on with his day. By then, Rose was good at spotting newbies. She understood how difficult it was making the transition from *in here* to *out there*. She got him a cup of coffee from the machine down the hall in a gesture that seemed to make her, if not the official goodwill ambassador, something of a cross between hall monitor and welcome wagon.

"Three kids," he had said. Those were the first words he ever spoke to her, though he probably would have spoken them to anyone who would have listened. "The oldest is six." His eyes were shiny and Rose wondered if he was fighting back tears or just one of those people with shiny eyes. Later she learned he suffered from chronic dry eye and had to apply drops three times a day. So on that day at least, his emotions had gotten the better of him. Rose suspected she knew it then too. She'd always been drawn to men who weren't afraid to show their feelings. Probably because she was the opposite.

Rose's mother had just finished up her third round of chemo after a radical mastectomy, and was suffering from a new set of complications, a case of neuropathy, which had left her without feeling in her legs and hands. She couldn't walk or feed herself. She couldn't brush what was left of her own hair. The doctors didn't know if the feeling in her limbs would ever return and they waited as with each day it became increasingly irrelevant.

Martin paid his friend's wife two more visits, both times while Rose was visiting her mother. Afterward, they had coffee and talked. When Rose learned the woman had died, she didn't expect to see Martin again. But a few days later, he showed up at the door to her mother's room and engaged the ailing woman in a conversation that lasted for hours. Later, Rose's mother told her daughter about the visit.

"I knew right away," she told Rose.

"You knew *what* right away," Rose asked. She adjusted the objects on her mother's bedside table, a blue plastic pitcher, a pack of mints, a small box of tissues, and a photograph of young Rose on her father's lap.

"I could tell as soon as he started talking." Her mother coughed.

Rose smoothed her mother's hair. It needed to be washed. She would tell the nurses. "You could tell *what?*"

"He's in love with you," her mother said. Apparently, the cancer had reached her brain.

"Oh, Ma." Rose dismissed her with a wave. Rose refused to entertain her mother's morphine-induced ramblings, though something inside her stirred at the idea.

"He asked all about you. He asked if you were seeing someone."

"And you told him my calendar was as 'barren as the fallow fields of Sunderland.'" Another of her mother's favorite expressions.

"I might have said something to that effect." Her mother smiled.

"And let me guess. You told him about my hula-girl costume, and my swimming trophies, and the time I drove Daddy's Pinto wagon into two trees in one night," Rose said. Rose couldn't think of a person her mother hadn't told those stories to at one point or another.

Her mother frowned. "And then you came home and said you

were sideswiped twice by two different cars and expected us to believe you. Honestly, Rose." She grinned. "There were branches lodged in the grille."

Rose felt a lump in her throat. Might this be the last time she and her mother played out this familiar exchange?

Her mother continued. "I didn't tell him about the car. But if he comes back, remind me." She adjusted her legs. Ironically, some of the feeling had come back to them in the last couple of weeks. "You know why I used to tell people that story?"

"To get even," Rose said. She reached for her mother's hand. Her mother's fingers were cold and her cuticles were dry as dust. Rose reached for the lotion on the dresser.

"Because I wanted people to know you weren't *all* Nowak. So even-tempered and well behaved like your father. There was at least a little wildness to you. A little *spunk*."

"And don't forget my vivid imagination," Rose added. She rubbed the lotion into her mother's hands. Her mother had always thought writing instruction manuals had been a waste of Rose's creative talent. "I mean it was a creative story as I recall."

Her mother coughed again. Her face reddened and the phlegm rattled inside her chest. It was as if there was nothing left inside the woman but phlegm and tumors. Rose drew her mother forward, then bolstered her back with pillows to let gravity do its work. When the coughing subsided, in a weak voice, her mother said, "If he asks, you go out with him. He's a nice man."

"Yes, Mother."

"You *will*." It wasn't a question.

"I will." Rose looked to make sure there was no one standing in the hall. Then she leaned in close, where she could already smell the decomposition that had begun in her mother's body. "He has to be better than the oncologist you tried to fix me up with who smelled like clove cigarettes and turned out to be gay." Rose leaned back. "And need I even bring up the orderly who carried Milk Duds in his breast pocket?"

Her mother raised her finger. "He had nice eyes." Her speech had slowed to the pace of a windup toy that had lost its juice. She tired so quickly now.

"You get some rest," Rose said. She stood to go.

"Promise." Her mother's eyes closed. The lids fluttered with current.

"I promise," Rose said. "I like him," she added.

A smile turned the corners of her mother's lips.

Before her mother passed, she'd had the chance to see Rose and Martin together. Their first date had ended at the hospital when Rose had been called by the nurses in a false alarm. Later Rose wondered if her mother had put them up to it. Rose knew seeing the two of them together had given her some peace.

Even to Rose, it seemed Martin was the man she'd been waiting for all her life. The *one*. His soothing voice over the phone, the cool, powdery feel of his hands, how he knew his way around a Thai menu, these were things that kept her sane through those early days of orphanhood.

Near the end of their first year together, they talked about getting married. Actually, Rose was the one who did most of the talking. Martin had been married before—two years, no kids—with financial consequences that made him reluctant to jump into it again. He didn't like to talk about it, but from what he'd led her to believe, his first wife had run off with a bartender. At the time she bought the story. Until she learned from one of his old friends that it was Martin who had done the running. Just one of the things she conveniently chose to overlook for the sake of love and momentum.

As far as he was concerned, Martin would say, they were as good as married. It was just a piece of paper, after all. Rose didn't press him, perhaps deep down fearing he might run from her too. She allowed herself to settle into a state of complacency. Marriage would happen for them sooner or later. After all, the stars had aligned to bring them together at her mother's death-bed. He had to be *the one*.

Though the initial transgression had taken place weeks earlier, the confession came on the Ides of March, a suitable day for betrayal, though Martin would never have deliberately planned this detail. He wasn't the kind who planned things. After working from her apartment all day, Rose had gone out for Chinese food to surprise Martin at his place. She expected he'd still be at work, so she used her key to open the door. There she found him standing in the shadows in the hallway, a stripe of light from the streetlamps bisecting his face. She heard the tinkle of ice in a tumbler.

"You scared me," Rose said. "For heaven's sake, turn on some lights."

She reached for the switch but Martin intercepted. He took her by the wrist. For a second, she thought she had walked into another surprise party, like on her thirty-seventh birthday, when their friends jumped out from behind the furniture. "Surprise!" This time Rose was in for a surprise. It didn't take her long to figure out something was wrong. Less than seconds.

All of it had happened less than three weeks ago. Rose had landed on Val's doorstep on Monday. By Thursday, she had moved into the cottage. After an exhausting day of navigating a rented U-Haul through narrow streets, lugging boxes and furniture, she'd fallen onto the mattress and slept like the dead. The next morning, as she peered out from the bedcovers at the strange room, she remembered something her mother had read to her once out of one of her old books, an essay by William Thackeray upon arriving in Boulogne from London. He'd written: "The morning comes—I don't know a pleasanter feeling than that of waking with the sun shining on objects quite new . . ."

This morning there was no sun, and even if there were, it

would have shone in a place that was quite new, but filled with objects that were quite old and familiar, and which now seemed strangely out of place. And so, rather than a pleasant feeling, it was one of dislocation. Rose was struck by the finality of the move and whirlwind of actions that had brought her there. How abruptly, if not impulsively, she'd called all of her clients and arrested her career. How she'd walked away from four years with Martin without so much as a definitive good-bye, just an unwillingness to pick up the phone ever again. All this had taken up residence in the room as well.

Rose stepped into the cocoon of a shower and was comforted by the smallness of it. This much she could absorb. She let the hot water run down her pale back and hamstrings, which were starting to ache from the previous day's exertions. When she got out, the porcelain tiles were cold on her feet. Rose dried herself and dressed quickly, before all the warmth from the hot water could escape her skin. She put on a pair of jeans and a turtleneck sweater, and was running her fingers through her hair when the doorbell rang. Through the peephole, she saw it was Val. She didn't need her landlady getting in the habit of dropping by unannounced. Rose would have to lay down the ground rules.

"Hi," Rose said, opening the door just enough to stick her head out.

Val smiled. "Hope I'm not bothering you. Just wanted to see how you're settling in." She strained to see in past Rose, apparently curious to see what her new tenant had done to the place. The room was still cluttered with boxes.

"I still have lots of unpacking to do, but thanks for checking up on me."

Val was shivering. A late season ice storm had hit last night and, once again, she wasn't wearing a jacket, just a thin cotton T-shirt that stretched tight across her belly and a maroon cardigan that had something heavy weighing down one of the pockets.

Rose was afraid she'd catch her death. "Want to come in?" She opened the door.

"Thanks," Val said. She stepped past the threshold.

Fine, but Rose wasn't about to invite her to stay for coffee. She had things to do, like find a job.

"Coffee smells good," Val said. She rubbed her hands together.

"Want a cup?" Rose asked.

"If it's no trouble." She followed Rose into the kitchen. "Clean mugs are in the cupboard."

"I found them," Rose said. She motioned for Val to take a seat at the little kitchen table. Rose took a mug from the cupboard and filled it with coffee, then handed it to her guest.

"It sure feels funny having someone living out here."

"Do you take it with anything?" Rose asked, hoping she'd say no because Rose had neither cream nor sugar.

"Just black," she said. "My father used this place to see patients when he *retired*." She made quotation marks with her fingers around the word. "Though he kept seeing patients till the end. He was an old-fashioned general practitioner. Last night I saw the light on and for a split second I thought he was still out here. The man's been dead for over thirty years. Can you imagine?"

"The mind plays tricks." Rose rinsed out the coffeepot in the sink, a Mr. Coffee, TR series, ten-cup.

A decanter-activated Pause 'N Serve drip-stop valve allows you up to thirty seconds to sneak a cup while the coffee is still brewing.

"That sink doesn't seem to be leaking anymore."

"I fixed it," Rose said.

"I think I'm going to like having you around." Val took a long draw of the coffee, then set it down. "I'll be honest. I really dropped by for three reasons." She touched her thumb. "*One* is to avoid Dorie Nickerson, who called to say she's dropping off a calendar list of things for me to do in the remaining two months before the Tri-centennial. As if I don't already know what they are. I'm afraid if she sees me, she'll add a few more for good measure."

Rose heard a car coming up the drive. Val stood up and peeked out the kitchen window.

"I've heard a little about that. When is it?" Rose had read a story in the *Cape Gazette* that laid out a brief history of the town of Nauset going back three hundred years to when it was first incorporated.

"June fourth. That's a Saturday. It's going to be quite a shindig, that is if we don't all kill each other before it rolls around, Dorie especially."

"Who's Dorie?"

"The town administrator's wife. She means well but she goes off full bore in twenty directions at once and thinks she can boss everyone around just because her husband's a bigwig. Lately, there's been no stopping her. I tell her she needs a hobby." Val stood up to look out the window again. Then sat back down. "The way she struts around town, you'd think we'd all forgotten how she and her scallop-shucking girlfriends came up in a carload from New Bedford one summer hell-bent on landing husbands. Dorie set her sights on Zadie Nickerson and that was it. He didn't stand a chance, poor fool. She's a handsome woman, least she was *then,* and pretty resourceful. Zadie's ancestors had come over on the *Mayflower,* by the way, and when you meet him, you'll know it in the first five minutes."

"Why's that?" Rose was thinking some obvious blue-blood pallor or protruding jaw like the Habsburgs.

Val sipped her coffee. "He tells you every chance he gets. Cooper's the only one who puts old Dorie in her place. See, Cooper's Portuguese too, and she won't let Dorie forget it, not for all the bottle blonde this side of Buzzard's Bay."

Rose laughed. It was good to get an insider's perspective. It might help with her reporting. "What's the second reason? You said there were three."

Val touched her index finger. "I wanted to invite you to dinner tomorrow night."

"Thanks, but—"

"You just moved in. You probably have nothing in that refrigerator yet. Am I right?"

Two cans of Coke, some packets of duck sauce, and a yogurt she'd had in a cooler in her hotel room for almost two weeks.

"I know what you're thinking," Val went on. "I'm going to be dropping by and bugging you all the time. I'm not. Let me just do it this once. I won't be a busybody landlady, I promise. I like my privacy too."

Rose had had her fill of iceberg-lettuce salads from Puritan Pizza. Plus she wanted to learn more about the people and the town, and about that artist.

"What can I bring?" she asked.

"Just yourself. Around six-thirty." Val stood and looked into the driveway again. "She's leaving, finally."

"What was the third thing?"

"The third thing." She reached into her sagging sweater pocket and produced a large Jimmy Fund can, the kind at cash registers encouraging people to drop in their spare change. "Raising money for cancer research is a pet project of mine." The cancer magazines. Was it her or someone close to her? "I'll be manning a booth at the Tri-centennial," she said. "Anyhow, I make a point of keeping a can around the house for when my wallet gets fat with coins. Every little bit helps."

She held out the can and Rose took it. There was a boy's face on the front.

Val continued: "You can just give it back when it's full. No hurry."

"Sure," Rose said. Maybe she'd lost her mother that way too. Maybe she was actually doing something about it. Rose felt guilty. She imagined their mothers up in heaven comparing daughters and her poor mother coming up short again. *No wedding. No grandchildren. And she didn't even raise a red cent to cure the damn disease that killed me.*

"I suppose it would help to know my daughter is a researcher at Dana Farber. I drive people nuts around here with my fundraising. Most know about Eve, so they don't mind. Gotta do what I can to help keep her in business, right? Just last night she called and told me they're onto something big, something to do with getting cancer cells to commit suicide."

Rose was impressed. Maybe Val wasn't such a kook after all, having raised a kid who was making that kind of contribution to society.

Val took the small gold cross around her neck into her hand. "Suicide is a sin but God would make an exception for cancer cells, don't you think?" She dug into her sweater pocket and pulled out a penny, a broken toothpick, and a couple of lint balls. She dropped the penny in the slot and shook the can. The lonely sound of it rattled in Rose's ears.

The streets of Nauset were deserted. Last night's freezing rain had glazed the roads. The tangle of vines and fallen branches near the street were weighed down with ice. It was hard for Rose to believe in a few short weeks they'd become scaffolding for a fresh green canopy. The soulless voice from the National Weather Service was forecasting high gusts and a marine advisory. It didn't feel like April, but half the time April never did.

Rose needed to go into town to drop off her résumé at the *Cape Gazette* before the weekend. She had finally gotten through to the editor over the phone and he agreed to take a look at her puffed-up, virtually nonexistent credentials. She knew she didn't have much of a chance but it was worth a shot.

As Rose pulled out of the driveway onto Sea View Drive, a beaten-up Volvo came flying out of the driveway next door, cutting her off. She jammed on the brakes and the car started to slide, eventually coming to rest against the curb on the wrong side of the road. The engine stalled. When Rose looked up, the Volvo was gone.

"Asshole." Rose started breathing again. She rolled down the window to get some air. It was so quiet she could almost hear her heart beating. She restarted the engine and crept down the street, which was in rough shape, with frost heaves and patches of cobblestone showing through the layers of asphalt. This town was behind the curve for improvements. Most Cape villages had already been gentrified, young families squeezed out to make room for deep-pocketed baby boomers approaching retirement. Schools were faced with dwindling numbers and some were on the verge of closing their doors. What tradesperson could afford to buy even a simple cottage? Property values had risen almost steadily throughout the eighties and nineties to the point where Val's land alone, without the house, would have to be worth millions. But she wasn't living like any millionaire. It was obviously all she could to do to scrape up the taxes. In the Boston papers, Rose had read stories about Cape Codders who had been forced to cash out and move to places like Maine and Florida, even descendants of the great Cape families, the very blood and bone, being forced into exile. And while one couldn't feel too sorry for them—after all they *were* now rich—one could certainly feel for the next generation, the kids graduating from high school who hadn't a hope of ever earning enough money to settle down in their hometowns.

Rose pulled into the lot behind the offices of the *Cape Gazette,* a community newspaper with a circulation of approximately thirty thousand. She checked her face in the rearview mirror and, in it, saw the green Volvo that had nearly killed her. She grabbed her folder of résumés and got out.

Rose approached the Volvo, which was less car than carcass. There was a dead Christmas wreath tied to the front grille, decades of dump permits affixed to the windows, and a bumper sticker that said *Plover tastes like chicken.*

She walked across the lot and entered the low brick building. Inside, there was a large wood counter and, behind it, a silver logo on the wall. A young girl with short hair and long earrings was busy with a customer.

"Think it's going to clear up, Cooper?" the girl asked.

"Always has."

Cooper. Wasn't that the name of the woman who was trying to rent the apartments next door? So she'd been the culprit. The woman had on a yellow rain slicker—regulation foul-weather gear—with thick navy corduroys tucked into moss green knee-high rubber boots.

"You want to run the same ad?"

"Don't know why I even bother. Last one did me no good."

The girl made eye contact with Rose and winked as if to say, *Bear with me.* When she moved, her earrings tinkled like wind chimes. "Any changes?" she asked Cooper.

"No changes. It's about the only thing around here that never changes, me wasting my time running ads in this crummy paper that no one reads." Cooper looked around to see if she had an audience. She was a tough-looking bird in her sixties, with thick bangs and straight white hair cropped just above the chin in a hard line. The skin on her face was ruddy and weather-beaten, and her hands were chapped. "If I don't fill up those rooms soon, your next headline will read, 'Landlord Takes a Swan Dive off the Sagamore Bridge.'" She closed her eyes, stuck her arms straight out at her sides, and held them there.

Rose smiled. "Excuse me," she said. "Did I hear your name is Cooper?"

The woman nodded, still in her crucifix.

"I'm not sure how many Coopers there are in this town but I think I might be your new neighbor. Rose Nowak. I just moved into the Shimilitis cottage."

The woman opened her eyes and let her arms slap the sides of her slicker. "See that, Alice? Shimmy does better than me and she doesn't even run an ad." She extended her hand to shake Rose's. Her skin felt like tree bark. "Cooper Almeida."

"I understand you rent out apartments?" Rose said.

"Need tenants to be able to say that," Cooper said.

"You have one," Alice said.

"Think that one's what scares away the others," Cooper said.

"He couldn't scare a fly," the girl said. The printer spit out a piece of paper. The girl named Alice took it and walked back behind the partition.

Cooper turned to Rose. "So how much she charge?"

The rudeness of the question caught Rose off guard. "Five seventy-five but—"

"A week?" Cooper whistled like it was a lot.

"A month," Rose said.

"What?!" Cooper shook her head in disgust. "That broad is nuts. The place is worth triple that."

"Do me a favor and don't tell her, okay?" Rose said, hoping to get the woman to crack a smile. She didn't.

"Don't have to worry about that. She never listens to me anyway." Cooper put her hands on her hips and narrowed her eyes. "I suppose she fed you that crap about her property line."

"She might have mentioned something about a trapezoid," Rose said. Suddenly she felt uncomfortable, like the temperature of the room had spiked.

"I'll tell you what. I've known that gal long enough to know she flunked geometry in high school. Fact is, she's a *rectangle*," she said. She drew it out in the air, in that way where one can almost see the lines connect.

Here we go again, Rose thought.

"And I got the deed to prove it," Cooper added.

Rose took a step back. "Well, it all sounds complicated," she said.

"You brought it up," Cooper said.

"Did I?" Rose felt the heat migrate up her neck. She started thumbing through the papers in her folder so she wouldn't have to talk anymore. She found a typo on her résumé.

"I gotta know something," Cooper said.

Rose looked up.

Cooper craned her head over the desk to make sure Alice was out of earshot. "Was Val yapping about that kid of hers?"

What kind of question was that? Did this woman have it in for Val or what? "If I had a daughter like Eve, I'd talk about her too."

Cooper slapped the counter. "Oh Jesus, here we go."

Just then Alice came back round the corner. "Here you go," she said. She handed Cooper a receipt. "Better luck this week."

"Better wish *her* luck," Cooper said. She nodded in Rose's direction. "She's gonna need it." She lifted the yellow hood up over her head and started for the door.

"I can see that," Rose said. Welcome to the neighborhood. She waited until Cooper was out the door. "What a piece of work," she said to Alice.

"Don't let her get to you. It's all an act."

Was she kidding?

"Sorry about the wait," Alice said. "What can I do for you?"

CHAPTER TWO

Do not immerse in water or other liquid.
—*from the Panasonic NB-G100P Toaster Oven Instruction Manual*

Simon Beadle awoke to the distant roar of a jet engine. He opened his eyes and saw a cloud shedding its lining, or was it just the silver skin of a plane flashing through layers of cumulus?

Where am I?

He could feel himself bobbing up and down. The skin on his face was so raw that it hurt just to blink his eyes.

What am I doing here?

Simon lifted his head and looked around. Nothing but shades of blue in every direction, not the deep bruise blue of the northern waters off Stellwagon Bank, but a brilliant turquoise. Understandable that he would be dreaming about the tropics, though it would be nicer if he weren't in his mascot costume, or, if he were, at least to be sharing it with someone of the opposite sex. It *was* a dream, after all. He closed his eyes and opened them. No dark cruise-ship cabin materialized. No bunk bed or porthole or tiny metal sink. He bit his lip like they do in the movies and, like in the movies, it didn't snap him out of the dream. The scenery didn't change, which could only mean one thing: Simon was adrift in the middle of the ocean. He felt his stomach flip.

"Help!"

He thrashed around and hollered at the top of his lungs. His throat hurt. *Knock it off,* he told himself. *All you're doing is attracting sharks. Sharks!*

Simon looked beneath him. He drew up his legs and hollered louder this time. Where had the cruise ship gone? There wasn't so much as a speck on the horizon. He screamed until the only sound he could produce was a dry, painful wheeze.

This wasn't getting him anywhere.

Take inventory. Feet, legs, arms. Aside from a general malaise and ache in his limbs, everything seemed to be intact, save for a small nick on his toe that must've happened during the fall. The only other appendage that was giving him trouble, depending on how one looked at it, was his right hand, which had cramped up around the neck of a half-full bottle of rum. Simon fixed on the amber liquid and it all started coming back: the booze cart, the lifeboat, the fall.

It was a miracle he was still alive. The black rubber bulb of his costume must have cushioned his landing and kept him afloat for however long he was out cold. Hours? Days? Now it was acting as a wet suit, absorbing sunlight, keeping him warm. Simon had underestimated the people at the nurse placement company, in particular, the costume engineers he'd initially scorned for having come up with such a stupid idea, a life-size blood-pressure cuff that no one, not even the nurses who wore them around their necks all day, could identify. The headpiece was a gauge with eyeholes at "110" and "120." The body consisted of a rubber bulb from which protruded a long black felt tube and, at its end, an arm cuff large enough to assess the vitals of King Kong. Yet, what the mascot development team lacked in style they'd apparently made up for in functionality, having the foresight to anticipate their sphygmomanometer apparatus might also need to serve as a flotation device.

Simon looked around. Which way was land? The sun's position was no help, considering Simon didn't know whether it was morning or afternoon. He looked up at the clouds again. They were drifting from left to right. Didn't clouds in the northern hemisphere generally move from west to east? Simon regretted that he hadn't paid as much attention to the Channel 7 weather girl's meteorology as to her "topography." *Let's see, if west is left and the sun is left, that would make it about midafternoon.* Damn. If his sophisticated calculations were correct, in a matter of hours it would be dusk, when the sharks came out to feed.

Simon felt something tickling his foot. He looked down. Through the water a cluster of thin, translucent fish had congregated around the cut on his toe. He shook his leg and they scattered, then one by one they returned. What harm could they do? Unless little fish attracted bigger ones. Barracuda. Makos. Hammerheads. He felt another wave of panic building.

"You," he said out loud to the bottle. "This is all your fault."

He told his hand to let go of it. His hand ignored the command. Then he used his other hand to pry each finger from the waterlogged label until finally they came unhinged. He opened and closed his hand to grease the joints and get the blood flowing again. The bottle began to drift.

Oh, no you don't, he thought. With all his might, Simon kicked toward the bottle. The costume wasn't streamlined. He tried making a sculling motion with his arms. This worked better.

He grabbed hold of the neck and held the bottle up under his chin while he tugged on the wet felt tube of his costume, which had undergone the transformation from tail to tentacle. He secured the bottle in the Velcro blood-pressure cuff, then let go. It floated within arm's reach.

He was exhausted. The sudden burst of energy had left him spent. He let his neck muscles go lax and the back of his head dipped into the water. His headpiece and booties were missing. And so were the gloves. What was he going to tell the agency? What difference did it make? He was through. Mascots for Jesus had a zero-tolerance policy for falling off the wagon, let alone cruise ships. So much for Christian forgiveness. He couldn't even bring himself to think about what would happen to his buddy Segundo, who'd recommended Simon for the job in the first place.

The sun was ferocious. Simon's lips were swollen and cracked. His eyes stung. His burgeoning bald spot was scorched. His only chance for survival was if he could swim to shore, or at least close enough to the international shipping lanes to be spotted and rescued. Simon oriented himself toward the clouds. He began to scull toward what he thought was the west. Simon sculled and sculled until it felt like his arms would fall off. Then he kicked for a while, but there was still no land in sight. Not even a boat. Was this how it was all going to end? Would they find his sun-bleached bones washed up on some remote archipelago, picked clean by blue crabs? Segundo had told Simon about the fins that encircled him in the days after his family's boat went down off the coast of Cuba. Simon stopped sculling. He put his hand to his brow to block the sun. He scanned the surface. No fins. Not yet. Maybe the smell of wet rubber would mask the aroma of the juicy, rum-infused morsel within.

Segundo used to say it was God's will that he survived the sharks, a hell of a fish story, though as an official best friend, Simon had little choice but to go along with the tale of how, at the age of eight, Segundo had landed on the shores of Miami clinging to a cooler filled with dead fish, the loan survivor of a boatload of Cubans who'd been caught in a sudden squall. They hadn't been trying to flee Castro but had just veered off course while trolling for dolphin, thanks to a Soviet-made compass. But no one in Miami believed Segundo's story. Who didn't want to come to America, after all? Rather than return the boy to his extended family in Cuba, the INS sent him to live with his cousins in Hialeah, a family of carnival workers who were scraping up the money to start their own clown school.

Segundo had always said it was the Holy Mother who'd kept between him and the fish, even as the rest of his family slipped beneath the surface and were picked off by hammerheads. *God's will.* Pretty presumptuous if you asked Simon, which no one ever did. Yet he had been compelled to voice his opinion numerous times anyway, on long, cold New Hampshire nights at the bar when there was little to do but drink, the amount of alcohol consumed determining the eloquence of Simon's argument.

"God's will my ass," Simon could recall it beginning one night.

"Believe what you will, my friend," Segundo replied, unshaken.

"God's got nothing better to do than to save a future drunk?" Simon asked. He went for his whiskey and missed his mouth. It spilled down the front of his T-shirt.

"That's all you see *now.*"

"What's that supposed to mean?"

"The Lord isn't through with me yet." Segundo handed Simon his drink napkin in slow motion.

"Oh, sure. The Lord's got *big* plans for you." Simon shook his head. He dabbed at the wet spot on his shirt and missed by inches.

Segundo clicked his tongue in disgust. "'Je of little faith,'" he said, pronouncing his *y* like a *j.*

"You mean *ye.* '*Ye* of little faith.'"

"I said '*ye.*'" This time he said the *y* like a *y.* "Get the wax out of your ears."

"You telling me I can't hear?" Simon asked.

"Jes. I know what I said."

"There you go again." Simon elbowed the guy next to him, who was passed out on the bar. "Didn't you hear him?" The guy snored.

"You telling me I don't know the Bible?" Segundo puffed out his chest like a pigeon.

"I'm saying why would God save someone who doesn't know *gee* from jack?"

"Ay." Segundo raised his drink to the ceiling and rolled his eyes. "Miserable *Jankees*."

Simon sculled and came upon a slick about ten feet wide. A pleasure boat must have passed that way, which meant he couldn't be too far offshore. Simon swam through the pink plastic tampon applicators and his spirits were lifted.

In hindsight, Simon had to admit, Segundo had turned his life around and maybe even saved a life or two, or at least made an effort. But that was Segundo's doing, not God's. People were always confusing hard work or even luck with divine intervention. Made them feel special. Trouble was, it made everyone else feel like crap. Ten people die in a plane crash, one survives. That one ends up thinking God likes him better, thinks his life is more worthwhile than the other ten. He spends the rest of his life telling his story on talk shows, telling people how blessed he is while they nod in agreement and wonder whether, if push came to shove, they'd be blessed too.

Simon had to believe the Almighty was above playing favorites. It was easier for him to believe God just sometimes fell asleep on the job or had bad days, particularly when God's will ran contrary to his own. Was it God who willed Simon's sister to fall for that bum who got her pregnant and then split? Was it *God's will* that her kid was born with troubles? Boy, that Iris must have been one hell of a monster for God to have *willed* that gasket to pop in her brain, leaving her dead on the kitchen floor. But Iris was no monster. She was just about the kindest person Simon ever knew, that coming from a *sibling*, which only served as further evidence that this divine intervention business was all a bunch of crap. God hadn't willed her to die. She just did, and when it happened, it shook up everyone, Simon most of all. Even the rabbi–turned–Unitarian Universalist–minister couldn't find words to comfort Simon after the funeral. He just tucked a copy of *When Bad Things Happen to Good People* into the pocket of Simon's borrowed black suit coat. Simon didn't need to read past the cover. Bad things happened to good people. The very fact that they happened at all sort of put God on the same level with people who kept fish tanks and ant farms.

One of the theories Simon kicked around for a while was that God, particularly that God of the Old Testament, had been abused as a child, like Hawk Morrows, who had lived three doors down from Simon and Iris when they were growing up on Cape Cod. Old man Morrows used to shave the hair on the back of Hawk's head into a target (before it was considered a fashionable thing to do) so he would have something to aim for with his empty beer cans. In turn, Hawk liked to ride his bike over frogs until their sides split open and poured salt on slugs until they shriveled into something resembling dried boogers. Abuse was a vicious cycle, everybody said so. But Simon's theory had no takers. Segundo just pinched his ears shut and chanted Hail Marys to drown out the blasphemy. Simon wasn't trying to be disrespectful. He was looking for some way to turn the Lord into a sympathetic character. He couldn't bear to go through life thinking God could be so mean and arbitrary. The more life Simon walked through, the more he was convinced God had deep troubles of His own.

Then one night on the jukebox at one of the bars, Simon heard Tom Waits sing the words: *Don't you know there ain't no devil, there's just God when he's drunk.* An epiphany. It opened up a whole new avenue of possibility, the idea of God as a drunk. It explained everything, why crazy things happened in the world, why people were born funny, with parts missing. It explained away the meanness. It explained why sometimes He was just plain missing in action, facedown on a cloud somewhere, letting down the masses the way Simon had let down everyone who ever mattered in his own life. If you looked back on history, you could see the times when God was on the wagon, times of significant human achievement: Egyptian times; the Roman Empire; the Han Dynasty; the Renaissance, when He was cranking out quality product like da Vinci and Michelangelo; or the sixties when he was sending men to the moon. And you could see when He was *off* during the dark times, the Middle Ages, the Spanish Inquisition, the Reign of Terror, the Hundred Years War. Hitler must have been one scary bender. And just maybe He was sleeping it off in a celestial gutter the morning the towers came down in New York.

Simon adopted this as his personal theology. If God was a drunk, at least there was hope. There was always the chance He could dry out. All drunks could straighten out if they really wanted to. The hard part was really wanting to. And hadn't God created Simon in His own image, after all? For once, Simon got to feel like the *chosen* one. The only two questions he had were: Where was the good Lord now, and was He planning to hit the sauce anytime soon?

All this thinking about drinking made Simon thirsty. There were two kinds of thirsty, and he was both. Even the seawater was starting to look good to him. But he knew drinking it would do a number on his kidneys. There was that leftover rum in the bottle, which might quench his immediate thirst but would dry him out in the long run. Kidneys or liver? Tough choice. But who said there was even going to be a long run? How long could he last out here? And if he was going to die, wouldn't death be easier to swallow with a buzz on? God would surely understand. Drunks had their code. They stuck together in times of need. It was probably *God's will* that Simon had managed to cling to that bottle in the first place, nothing short of a miracle when he thought about how far he'd fallen. Simon tugged on the tube and the bottle floated toward him. He unscrewed the cap, put the rim to his cracked lips, and drank. It stung like a son of a bitch. But the liquor soon passed his lips and coated his throat, then flowed down into his empty stomach. He felt a shudder from somewhere deep inside the bulb. The lightness came and then he had another problem. He felt too good to die.

So he did the one thing any man in his position could do. He started bargaining. He vowed if he made it through this, he'd never touch a drop of liquor as long as he lived. (He took another swig.) He'd never fake praying at AA meetings. (He took another.) He'd even check up on Iris's kid if he could just see dry land again. This was it. After *this,* he was done. He lifted the bottle out of the water and held it toward the sky. (Plenty left.) He savored the warm feeling radiating from his insides. One way or the other, he vowed—whether he quit because he quit or he quit because he died—this was it. In the meantime, he set his mind adrift on the waves and wound up somewhere he hadn't been in years.

"Something's wrong with him, Simon," his sister Iris had said. "I just know it. Mothers *know.*" She had cleared the lasagna-smeared plates from the table and set them in the old apron sink, then came back with a sponge to tackle the high chair.

Simon was stuffed. He pushed back from the table and stretched out his limbs, all four at once. "What do you mean? Isn't it good he keeps himself entertained?" He lit a cigarette and looked over at his nephew, who sat on the floor of the apartment with his back to both of them. Scattered around the toddler were tiny bits of paper, so much white, as if it had snowed inside the room.

"Ripping paper is all he ever does. And it's not even that." Simon heard the waver in his sister's voice. "It's that he doesn't *look* at me." If she was going to cry, he needed more wine. He reached for the bottle on the table and poured what was left into his glass.

"What do you mean he doesn't look at you?" He swirled the red liquid around like he saw them do on TV. Here his sister was coming to him for advice. He felt important.

"You know, the way he never makes eye contact."

Simon *didn't* know. He had never been around kids enough to know what they're supposed to do and not do. He didn't even see his nephew that often, maybe once or twice a month, mainly because he had more construction jobs than he could handle. And maybe too, he was still a little peeved at Iris for getting involved with that loser who got her pregnant in the first place. Hadn't he warned her not to? But she didn't listen. And now they were both paying the price, Simon by having to help with the bills and she by now having to raise a kid alone in the world.

"Sometimes I think he doesn't even recognize me," Iris said.

"That's ridiculous. You're his *mother*. How could he not recognize you?" Simon turned toward the boy. "Noel. Come here, honey."

Noel didn't turn. He picked up a long white strip of paper and began to shred it.

"Hey, Noel." Simon clapped his hands. He got up out of his chair and went over to the boy. "Hey, big fella." Simon tickled Noel under the chin like he saw them do on cartoons. Noel didn't respond. Simon looked back at Iris, who was watching with wide eyes, chewing on the corner of her dish towel.

"Wanna go for a ride on a rocket ship?" Simon scooped Noel up off the ground and lifted him high in the air. "Weeeee!" He "flew" the boy back over to his chair and sat Noel down on his knees. "Did you like that, little buddy?"

Noel looked down at his hands, only just noticing that the strip of paper was gone.

"Hey, looky here." Simon made a silly face. Then he snapped his fingers. The child blinked but otherwise didn't respond. Simon smoothed the hair on Noel's head. He gave him a kiss on the forehead. *Come on, kiddo.*

"You see?" Iris said.

"It probably doesn't mean anything," Simon said. But the

lasagna in his belly was starting to sour. What kid didn't squeal with delight at being flown around the room? What if Iris was right? What if something *was* wrong? No sense in getting her more upset. "He probably watches too much TV."

Iris buried her face in the towel.

"What? What did I say?" Simon asked.

The words came through the cloth. "We don't have a TV."

Simon put his face right up to his nephew's. Noel wrinkled his nose, probably from the booze on Simon's breath. At least his nose was working.

"Hey, Noely," Simon whispered.

The toddler examined his hands, turning them over, looking for the paper he'd dropped. The kid's lower lip started to quiver. For an instant, Noel looked up at his uncle. His big, beautiful eyes were overflowing tide pools. Simon froze. They were the eyes of the starving children he'd seen in those commercials on TV. They were asking for something the rest of him couldn't, begging even. *What?* And then whatever it was flickered out. Simon looked down and spotted the strip of paper on the ground. He handed it to Noel, who didn't show any emotion, just took it back to his corner.

"It's probably just normal kid stuff, Iris. You'll see. Why not take him to the doctor, just to ease your mind." *Mine too,* Simon thought.

Iris lifted her head and used the dish towel to wipe at the mascara that had pooled under her eyes. She put her hair back behind her ears. "I think I will."

Simon checked his watch. He was meeting some work buddies at the Barnacle and was already a half hour late. How many drinks would it take to make him forget those eyes? He kissed his sister on the forehead. "Just don't get yourself all worked up over this. I'm sure it's nothing. Whatever it is, we'll deal with it, you hear? I'm not going anywhere."

Iris looked up at Simon, who was a good three inches taller than she was. "I don't know what we'd do without you, Simon. Honestly." She nestled her head under his chin.

"What are big brothers for?" he said. Only he was really asking.

Simon gave his arms a rest. How many hours had he been swimming and still no land? The needlefish were keeping pace, still congregating around his big toe. He'd gotten used to them. He lifted his foot out of the water. The cut actually looked better. The salt water must be good for it, he thought. At least the folks at the morgue would have a pretty place to hang the tag.

Huge clouds hung in the sky like wet shirts on a clothesline, heavy at the bottom. If only it would rain, he could use the costume to collect enough water to ease his awful thirst. The effects of the booze had worn off and everything had hard edges again. It would be dark in a couple of hours.

The only thing worse than being sentenced to death was being sentenced to death with a hangover. How had he come to be thinking about Iris? He hadn't let himself think about Iris for ages. He had managed to drown her years ago. Speaking of drowning, where was that bottle? He sculled himself around in a circle. There had to be something left in it. Just a taste. But the cuff and the bottle were nowhere to be found. He tugged on the place on his costume where the tail attached and felt the weight of it beneath him. The bottle had sunk. Damn. He must have left the cap off and it had filled with water. Simon hauled it up. A tiny fish swam inside the glass. At least *it* looked happy. Simon poured the fish and water out. Maybe he could use the bottle to send a final message to his only living relation: *Dear Noel, Sorry I was such a shitty uncle. Love, Simon.*

No pen. No paper. Besides, Noel couldn't read. The doctors Iris brought him to had determined even at age three that the boy would never get along like a normal person. Iris had been right in her suspicions. Noel was severely autistic. The only thing he could do better than most people was draw pictures. When he was four, he stopped tearing paper long enough to scribble on a piece and, from that point forward, drawing was pretty much all he did.

Back then Simon couldn't bear to be around the kid for any length of time. It broke his heart, seeing the way Iris cared for him and how much patience she had with him. No mother should have to live like that, without hope. And then Iris died, and by that time, Simon had mapped out the trajectory of his own future, and it was less promising even than Noel's. By then, Simon had acquired a formidable disorder of his own. But the town didn't see it that way. No one had any sympathy for Simon. To them, he was no better than the scum who had knocked Iris up and dumped her in the first place. When the town rallied to take charge of the boy's affairs and keep Simon away, he didn't put up a fight. He wasn't in any position, financially or otherwise, to be taking care of a kid. They sent Noel off to a special school, and that was the last time Simon saw his nephew. The only consolation now was that Noel probably didn't have the wherewithal to hate Simon's guts. He probably didn't even remember his old uncle, and it was just as well. The kid was in good hands now. That's all that mattered. He had to be better off.

A vibration in the air crashed Simon's pity party. *Get ready, here comes the rain,* he thought. He sculled his way around three-sixty. But there were no really ominous clouds. Besides that, the sound didn't stop. The rumble just got louder. A helicopter.

"I'll be damned," Simon said. Could it be that someone was actually looking for him? Someone in the world cared whether he was alive or dead? He waved and hollered with everything he had.

CHAPTER THREE

*Due to the nature of the product, we cannot
accept a return on a unit that has been used.*
—*from the Solution ComfortSeat® Instruction Manual*

"Rose, sit," Martin had said. The liquor was heavy on his breath.

Rose dropped to the leather ottoman with the bag of Chinese food in her lap. Martin's leather chairs were so expensive. Even after four years, she'd never felt as though they were things one should actually sit on. "Did somebody die?" she asked.

"Not *yet*."

What was that supposed to mean? Martin fell back into the couch a little too hard and fast, so that some of his drink splashed onto his pants. He pretended not to notice.

"For God's sake, Martin." Rose reached into the bag, pulled out a wad of napkins, and handed them to him. "At least turn a light on in the kitchen."

"It's better this way," he said. "I have something to tell you."

That struck Rose as funny. He sounded so melodramatic. "Don't tell me . . . you took the last Sam Adams. Is that what this is about?"

He neither laughed nor denied it.

"Am I supposed to keep guessing?" The bag on Rose's lap was hot. In a minute it would start to leak.

"Don't even try."

But then he didn't say anything else, so Rose took it as her cue to start guessing. "You lost your job." No response. "You crashed the BMW."

"Remember that weekend you went to the Bahamas?"

Rose set the bag down on the floor. Back in February, an unlikable but wealthy client who manufactured ceiling fans had whisked a few of her favorite freelancers down to Paradise Island for a tax-deductible, collateral-planning boondoggle.

"Rose, listen to me." The ice cubes crashed against his teeth.

"Listen to you *drink?*"

"I went to Craig Elliot's bachelor party, remember?"

The fact that "Midlife Crisis" Craig was Martin's friend who had recently married Jennifer, a silicone-enhanced dumpling of a girl who was half his age, after walking out on his wife of twenty-six years didn't bode well. Rose remembered how hungover Martin had been that next day, so bad that he'd actually sent a car to pick her up at Logan. She'd been greeted by a man with a sign, *Novak* misspelled with a *v* like the movie star in *Vertigo*. Rose felt vertiginous herself. All kinds of things were swirling around in her head. Had Martin done something foolish? Had he been arrested for DUI, or gotten in some other trouble with the police?

"There were these girls there—"

Rose felt like a game-show contestant, like she was in a race to piece together what had happened before Martin could come out with the words, like if she did, she'd win something. "*Girls.* You mean *those* kinds of girls. *Bachelor-party* girls? Girls that jump out of cakes?" This all-important distinction needed to be made.

He mumbled something into his glass.

"What was that?" Rose said.

"Jennifer's friends."

"What were the bride's friends doing at a—"

"I slept with one of them."

Blood rushed to Rose's ears, and she remembered thinking what a bizarre physiological response, as if the body was trying to somehow flush out the hurtful words before they had a chance to alight in the mind and cause damage, as if blood was the mighty cure-all, the solution for everything. Got a wound? Send blood. Aroused? Send blood. Of course it didn't work. In this case, the blood had nowhere to go. It just built up and caused heat where there was too much already.

"What the fuck, Martin?" was the extent of her eloquence.

The bag of Chinese food bled moo shu onto the rug.

Val was expecting Rose for dinner. Rose was already late, but couldn't take her eyes off the seagull that kept dropping the same heavy clam onto the deck of a fishing boat moored close to shore. It was the sound of it that had her hypnotized, the persistent clunk against the hollow cabin.

Earlier, the editor of the *Cape Gazette* had told Rose he couldn't hire her without a single journalistic credential on her résumé. Besides, he said, all hiring was done through the parent company in Dedham. She also couldn't be sure he didn't notice the typo on her résumé, the three *c*'s in *accomplished*. From there she'd gone to the office of the *Nauset Oracle,* the smaller paper in town, an independent weekly that featured less day-to-day news in favor of more in-depth articles. The office was set up on the first floor of a Victorian near the ball field. There, Rose met Editor in Chief Calvin Christie, a small man with soft hands, who wore a suit even though there were only two other people in the office, both in T-shirts and jeans. Somehow, she liked him for it. He took his work seriously. Rose and Calvin hit it off, and she left with a formidable stack of obituaries to clean up. Rose saw the irony in how the ends of these people's lives seemed to spark a new beginning for her.

The *clunking* had stopped and the seagull was now pecking at the shattered bivalve on the bow, puffing his chest to intimidate another gull that was edging closer. The tide was coming in. From the old man who ran the Sea View, Rose had learned some things about this inlet, how the underwater terrain changed so frequently that no one even bothered to chart it. It was more dangerous to have a chart that was inaccurate than to have none at all. It was also one of the most heavily trafficked waterways on the Cape. When changes in the floor occurred, people shared the news at the local bait shops and marine supply stores, and with the harbormaster, who each day went out at dawn to check the shifting bars and reposition the channel markers so boats wouldn't run aground. It was also one of the hardest bodies of water to navigate because of the extreme tides. When it was dead low, the inlet was practically an expanse of beach with narrow rivers cutting through it, running from the harbor to the open sea. At high tide, the water filled in and those rivers became channels. Then most of the inlet was navigable, unless one had a deep hull or large fixed keel. It was navigating between tides that was most tricky, when the rocks, sandbars, and mussel beds lay just beneath the surface, hard to see until one was upon them, and then it was too late. Sometimes the current from an outgoing tide was even enough to suck small boats and kayaks out of the mouth of the inlet and into the open sea.

Now the inlet looked so peaceful. Color was beginning to drain from the landscape. Was it that Rose had mortality on her mind (Polly Snow, 81, homemaker, avid bowler, communicant of St. Mary's of the Harbor, leaves behind eight children and twenty-eight grandchildren) that made her, for the first time, see the sunset as a primer for death? (George Filmore Wilcox, 89, skeet champ and animal lover, born in Springfield, MA, worked in the laboratory of Chapman Valve Co. for forty-nine years.) A flash of color and then fade to black. (Love affair with Martin Blevins, dead after four years, no survivors.) If death was like a sunset, then some people got good ones and others got duds. This was something Rose had never considered.

Rose brushed a dead fly from the windowsill and slid the old mission chair back into the depressions in the braided rug, where it had clearly sat for decades.

As she took her jacket from the coat stand by the door, some movement caught her eye, and a flash of light against the hedges that separated Val's property from Cooper's. A white sneaker emerged from the bushes, then a leg, followed by the rest of a person. He was wearing a dark parka with reflective tape haphazardly applied to his back and arms. He stopped when he saw the light on in the cottage. Rose slid back behind the door. Horror films had taught her to be wary of strangers who came through bushes at night in rural towns. She was pretty sure he couldn't see her in the shadows. He came toward the cottage. His hair was curly brown and he was tall, about five ten, and slender. He looked young, somewhere in his late teens or early twenties. There was something flat and dark under his arm, a case of some sort. He came up to the window and pressed his forehead against it. Rose's heart was pounding. There was something off-kilter about his expression, or maybe it was that he seemed to lack one entirely, and his eyes, the color of sky as it darkens toward the horizon, so blue in the light thrown by the lamp, that they seemed unnatural on his face. The window fogged with his breath. He said something Rose couldn't understand, then turned and headed down the path that led to Val's house, leaving a forehead mark on the pane shaped like a butterfly.

Rose stood there in the shadows another minute, just to make sure he was gone. She had questions for Val. Who was this guy? What was he doing cutting through the yard, making butterflies on her window?

When Rose arrived at the house, the mysterious stranger was already inside. Rose saw his coat on the hook by the door.

Val greeted her and led her down the narrow hall to the living room.

"Noel," Val said, "I want you to meet someone. This is our new neighbor, Rose. Can you say hello?"

"Hi, Noel," Rose offered.

He didn't look up. Fiddling with the contents of his vinyl case, he actually looked much less threatening than he had back at the cottage. Rose might have thought him a moody teen if not for the way Val talked to him, like he was breakable, or already broken.

"Noel, come say hello to Rose," Val repeated.

The kid didn't budge.

"It's okay," Rose said.

"No, this is good for him. He doesn't meet new people very often. He needs the practice." She went over and gently lifted him by the arm. He rose up off the chair without a fight. The two of them came over to where Rose was standing.

"Noel, this is Rose. She's going to be living in the cottage. Can you say hello?"

The kid stared down at his sneakers. He seemed agitated. It pained Rose to put him through this. She had no choice but to trust that Val knew what she was doing.

Suddenly he snapped his head back and barked at the ceiling. "Belshazzar was the last king of Babylon," he said, his speech inappropriately loud and a little slurred.

Val's face lit up. She clapped her hands. "*Very* good, Noel. Very nice."

He walked back to his case. Rose looked at Val for some explanation. She gave none. "Keep me company in the kitchen while I get dinner ready?"

Rose followed Val out of the room. She'd dressed for the occasion, in a knee-length denim skirt and a slightly rumpled white short-sleeve blouse. Her hair had been swept up in the back and fastened in small strands with a mismatched assortment of clips and bobby pins, and Rose couldn't tell precisely what look she was going for. Her best guess was Cloris Leachman circa 1975. So much more work than running a comb through and pulling it back in an elastic band, Rose's hairstyle of choice ever since she'd retired the blow-dryer and the makeup, most of it anyway, to become a more believable Cape Codder, at least in her estimate of what a Cape Codder should be. So far, Rose had yet to meet anyone who fit her profile.

Val entered the kitchen, took up her red washcloth apron, and tied it around her waist. Rose took a seat on one of the tall stools near the kitchen counter. She noticed the Tri-centennial countdown calendar, the one the selectman's wife must have left, tacked to the fridge with a Jimmy Fund magnet. Fifty-eight days to go. It seemed like an impossible amount of time. So much could happen in fifty-eight days. So much had.

"Would you mind opening the wine, Rose?" Val rummaged through a drawer and produced an opener. She handed it to Rose along with the bottle.

"Is he a relative?" Rose asked.

"I hope you don't mind. I forgot to mention that Noel usually has supper with me on Saturdays."

"Of course it's fine."

"He's autistic," she said. She bent down and peered into the oven window. Her prescription bottles cast an orange glow on the white tile behind the stove.

"I'm sorry to hear that."

"We're not related, by blood anyway. But he's like family," Val said.

Rose had to ask. "What was he saying about Babylon?"

"He didn't speak until he was almost fourteen. Turns out he has a remarkable head for certain facts and figures. One of the things he squirrels away in that brain of his are *lasts*." She switched off the oven.

"What do you mean *lasts*?"

"'The last king of Babylon, last words of famous people, last lines of books and movies, lasts in sports, history, you name it. He gets them from TV, mostly. Biography, CNN, ESPN. It's tough sometimes when they come out of context." Val hit a button on the microwave, the only appliance under thirty years old in the kitchen. "Like the other day we were checking for mice in the cellar and he said, 'Monsieur, I beg your pardon.' No other clues. Drove me nuts for days."

Rose peeled the foil from the bottle and screwed the opener into the cork. "Couldn't he tell you where he got it?"

"Oh, he *could* have. It's just a little game he plays. I swear I think Cooper puts him up to it."

Rose remembered the girl, Alice, at the *Cape Gazette* had mentioned something about a person who lived in one of Cooper's apartments, the tenant who "scared people away" according to Cooper.

Val continued: "I was watching the Arts and Entertainment channel during a weeklong series on people who got their heads chopped off—I don't think that's exactly how they phrased it—and there they were, leading Marie Antoinette to the guillotine with a black hood over her head, a reenactment, of course. Well, not being able to see, she stepped on someone's foot and said, 'Monsieur, I beg your pardon,' and that was it." With her finger, Val sliced the air in front of her neck. "Her last words."

"That's unbelievable," Rose said.

"So the next day I see him walking to town—he loves to walk, walks everywhere, which is why I put the tape on his coat, so drivers see him—anyway, I pulled beside him, rolled down the window, and hollered 'Marie Antoinette!' Then I sped off. You should have seen his face." Val laughed. She got two glasses from the cupboard.

"Why *lasts*, do you think?" Rose had never heard of such a thing and wouldn't have believed it if she hadn't seen him do it herself.

"It's kind of a long story," she said.

"I'd love to hear it."

Val lowered her voice. "He never knew his father. Deadbeat *washashore*," Val said, as if that alone should explain things. She gave the cucumber on the cutting board a whack with a heavy knife. "Wasn't from around here. The creep left Iris before Noel was even born. She took an apartment in town, above the Landmark Gift Shop. By then, Iris's mother was gone and the old man had drunk himself to death, so everyone pulled together and did what we could to help out. We brought food and hand-me-downs for the baby. I even watched Noel a couple afternoons a week so his mother could get a part-time job. Other people took turns too."

"Small towns. I grew up in one too," Rose said. "Iris had no siblings?"

Val set down the cucumber. "A brother, but he had troubles of his own."

"What kind?"

"Booze."

"That's rough."

"Gets rougher. One day while she was making a grilled cheese for her kid, she just keeled over and died right there in front of the stove. Twenty-two years old. They said it was an aneurysm."

"What caused it? Had she been in an accident?" Rose asked.

"They did an autopsy. Doctors said it was a congenital defect. Anyhow, Noel saw the whole thing. He was five. People downstairs in the gift shop smelled burning cheese. They had to break down the door. It was just in time because the curtains over the sink had started to singe and the whole apartment could have gone up."

Val put down the cucumber, and took a covered dish out of the microwave. Rose recognized the model.

Liquids such as water, coffee, or tea are able to be overheated beyond the boiling point without appearing to be boiling.

"To this day, Noel can't stand the smell of burning cheese." She set the dish on the stovetop. "They couldn't do anything for her. She was gone. Then, of course, Noel became everyone's priority."

"The brother was too far gone to take him?"

"Sometimes I wonder whether we should have given him a chance. Most folks around here were dead set against it, Cooper especially. A kid like Noel needed special care and here was a fellow who couldn't even get through a day's work without a thermos full of schnapps."

"They were probably right."

Val sighed. She put another dish in the microwave and set the time. She talked over the fan. "I always thought he should have fought harder to prove everyone wrong. Fellow had no spine. Suppose that's why people drink, eh?" Val stopped and looked around as if there was something she was forgetting. Then she reached for the glass Rose had poured for her.

"Here's to new neighbors," Rose said.

Val raised her glass. "*Vallo,*" she said. She took a sip, then put the glass down and got busy pouring the drippings from a roasting pan into a glass bowl. "Lithuanian for 'cheers.'"

"*Vallo,*" Rose repeated.

"Anyhow, nobody wanted to turn Noel over to the state. Instead, the town created a trust in Noel's name. Zadie Nickerson set it up. Cooper drew the long straw and was named his legal guardian, but lots of us opened our doors to Noel. For years, just about every person who dropped dead in this town left a chunk of money to the trust. He was a cute kid with those big blue eyes of his. But his schooling didn't come cheap. A psychiatrist in town convinced Cooper it would be best to send him away to a special school where they could draw him out more. They thought it would be good for him to be with other children like himself."

Val screwed up her nose as if she still had a hard time believing it had done him any good. The timer on the microwave went off. Val punched the button, maybe a little too hard, and removed the covered dish.

"I missed him during those years," she said.

"Your daughter must have missed him too," Rose said.

"Oh, sure she did, you bet. Anyhow, when he was eighteen and done with school, the decision had to be made whether to let him stay here or send him off to a permanent home for autistics. There's a good one outside Boston. But Cooper and I fought like hell to keep him here. It's the one thing we've ever agreed on. In the end, she offered up one of her apartments. She gave up half her income for the kid."

"What about the cottage? Couldn't he have stayed there?" Rose asked.

Val looked out the window at the cottage. "I would have liked that but some people didn't think it was such a good idea."

"Let me guess. Cooper."

She looked at Rose and smiled. "You catch on quick. You'll do just fine here." Val pushed back her sleeves and stuck her hands in the sink. "She and my mother, Ann, were best friends, though I never understood what my mother saw in her, not until she took in Noel." She shook her head. "You know any people like that? Just when you think you have them pegged, they throw you a curve."

There was a fellow who came to Rose's mind. "So who cares for him now?" she asked.

"We all do. He has supper at the boardinghouse on Tuesdays and Thursdays. I feed him Wednesdays and Saturdays. Other days, he goes to other folks. I'd take him every day if I could. I'm crazy about that kid."

"But what about the *lasts*?" Rose asked. "How did that start?"

Val leaned her hip against the stove. "Give me a glass of wine and I forget what the question was." She blew a wisp of hair from her eyes. "When Noel was almost fourteen, someone at that fancy school of his got him to talk and the first thing out of his mouth was 'Want some goldfish till it's fixed?' He said it over and over. 'Want some goldfish till it's fixed?' They finally got him to talk and now they couldn't get him to shut up. Someone at the school called us and eventually Cooper and I figured out—actually *I* figured it out and Cooper took the credit. It was the last thing poor Iris said before she hit the floor. She had offered him some crackers while the sandwich was cooking. All those years he carried her last words around in his head. And then other lasts started coming out. It was as if he'd been accumulating them all his life."

Incredible. From where Rose was sitting, she could see into the living room, but not well enough to figure out what Noel was doing. It looked almost as if he were setting up a tripod.

"What's he up to?"

"He likes coming here 'cause I'm the only one who lets him paint in the living room. Dorie Nickerson sends him out to the garage. Even in winter. Says the turpentine gives her nightmares. I think it has more to do with her precious Karistan rugs."

"What does he paint?"

"They're all over the living room. Remember you asked about them your first day here."

Rose was expecting rainbows and stick figures. *Finger paints.* Val wanted her to believe this mentally challenged kid was the one who painted those portraits? The disbelief must have registered on Rose's face.

"Wait." Val wiped her hands on the red cloth. She hollered out to the living room. "Dinner's almost ready, Noel. Don't start a painting. Just use your pencils for now." Then she turned to Rose. "He pitches a fit if he gets started and then has to stop. Let me show you something." She led Rose down the hallway to her bedroom. They stopped at a large framed work. "I put this here because it still gets him worked up sometimes."

Val walked down the hall a little farther and flicked on the light.

It was a large canvas. The focal point was a woman curled into an S on the floor, her body soft and heavy against the hard gray surface, her face, peaceful like a child asleep in the middle of a good dream. She was wearing a brown bathrobe and white fuzzy slippers. Swimming around her were bright orange fish, the cracker kind, some of them crumbled, others whole, and shards of broken glass—incredibly, painstakingly rendered glass that reminded Rose of the still lifes done by the Dutch masters. She leaned in closer and in one of the shards saw the reflection of a child's face, a boy with wide blue eyes.

"He painted it twelve years after she died. Somehow he was able to remember every last detail," Val said.

"That's remarkable," Rose said. She couldn't take her eyes off the child's.

"There was a teacher at his school, an artist herself. She spent lots of time with Noel, working on technique. Guess it paid off, huh?" Val said.

"But how—"

"*Autistic savant* is what they call them nowadays. Just say *Rain Man* and everybody knows what you're talking about. They used to call them *idiots*. Show me an idiot who can paint like that," Val said. She walked out into the light of the kitchen.

Rose had heard of such people but never encountered their talent firsthand. She remained in front of the painting awhile longer. From the other room, Val said, "The Lord takes but He gives plenty in return."

In the dining room, Val struck a match and lit the two candles in crystal holders on the table. "Usually Noel and I just eat in the kitchen but tonight's a special occasion," she said. "Isn't it, Noel?"

The walls of the room were papered in an intricate white

snowflake pattern on a light green background. A long mahogany sideboard ran along the interior wall. The table was oval and covered with a crocheted tablecloth. It had been set with colonial-blue napkins in pewter rings to match the blue curtains on the window. Val slid the candles closer to Rose, she assumed so Noel wouldn't be tempted to touch them.

Noel and Rose were seated at the table across from each other. Val had left a place for herself at the head. Rose offered but Val wouldn't allow her to help, insisting Rose sit with Noel while she prepared their plates in the kitchen. Rose spooned the salad into three bowls. She'd never spoken to an autistic kid before.

"Your paintings are lovely, Noel," she said.

He spun his fork around on the table.

"How did you ever learn to do that?" she said.

He didn't respond. Rose sat back and finished off the last of her wine. She had to hand it to Val. This took patience.

Again. "Would you like me to pose for you someday?"

"On the contrary," he said.

The wine in Rose's mouth went down the wrong pipe. She started to cough.

"Ibsen," Val hollered from the other room. "I read him the last chapters of his biography last night. We get them at the library. The nurse at Ibsen's bedside was telling his visitors that he was improving. He said, 'On the contrary,' and then he kicked. Guess *he* had the last word!"

Val laughed as she came in, a plate in each hand. "Here we are." She set a plate down in front of Noel. "Wait until you see how he draws. Not that I know much about art but his technique is rather odd. You'd like to paint Rose, wouldn't you, Noel?"

Noel stared at his plate.

As she came around to deliver Rose's dinner, Val's hip bumped the table and some gravy spilled onto the tablecloth. She seemed too big for the room. "My daughter keeps telling me to go on a diet."

As Val set the food, Rose did a double take. Everything on the plate had been arranged into a face, with cod cheeks for the eyes, mashed-potato hair, carrot nose and ears, and spiced-apple mouth. The creamed spinach had been shaped into a rudimentary bow tie. A bit of a stretch, Rose thought. Val went back into the kitchen.

Noel's plate was exactly the same. He looked down at it, then up at her, right into Rose's eyes for the first time, and said, "The most popular last name in Korea is 'Kim.'"

"The most popular last name in America is 'Smith,'" Rose said. She winked.

Val came back with her own plate and Rose couldn't help but think it looked happier than hers, maybe the angle of the apple slice.

"Hope you don't mind," Val said. She sat down hard into the chair, and Rose could hear the plates in the sideboard rattle. "They say it's good for Noel to get as much human interaction as possible. Autistics have a hard time connecting with the human face. It's how they're wired. He seems to enjoy this."

Rose and Val both looked up in time to see Noel put a scoop of mashed potatoes into his mouth. Then he threw his head back to the ceiling and said, "Rocky Marciano was the last boxer to knock out Joe Louis." It wasn't pretty.

"You don't say." Val prodded the food on her plate with her fork, testing its consistency. "He loves mashed potatoes. Close your mouth when you chew, Noel."

For a while they ate in silence. The cod just melted in Rose's mouth. She hadn't realized how hungry she was. Val was a fabulous cook.

"This is delicious," Rose said. She took a sip of water. She still had a million questions about Noel but they'd have to wait. "Tell me about your daughter. And the grandbaby."

Val's face lit up. "If you saw us together, you'd never believe we were mother and daughter. Eve is the exact opposite of me."

Val reached over and wiped a clump of spinach off the tablecloth in front of Noel. "She's petite and has dark, shiny hair she wears short. She takes after her father. He was Portuguese."

Val wore no wedding ring. For some reason it was hard to picture her with a man. It would have been rude to ask. Not only that, it would give her license to start asking Rose personal questions.

"Eve's smarter than me too. She's always known what she wanted, never let herself get sidetracked by boys, even though they called all the time. She never seemed interested. For a while, I thought she might be a lesbian." Val popped a piece of tomato in her mouth. "That's why it came as such a surprise when she called and told me she was pregnant. 'I didn't even know you were in a relationship,' I said. 'I'm not,' she said. 'Then who's the father?'" Val lowered her fork and leaned over her plate. "You can imagine how confused I was."

"I bet," Rose said.

"The last episode of *The Waltons* aired on August twentieth, 1981," Noel said.

"'I used a sperm bank,' Eve said." Val dropped her fork and looked for Rose's reaction. Rose sensed it was supposed to be outrage, though truthfully, it didn't sound like such a bad idea. Less messy. Not to mention vials of sperm don't cheat.

"'Her daddy's in Mensa,' Eve said." Val picked up her fork and prodded her salad greens. "I say daddy's a squirt in a jar."

The mashed potatoes seemed to stiffen in Rose's mouth.

"And then it suddenly dawned on me that we'd been talking about a *her*, Eve already knew it was a girl. 'Be happy for me, Ma,' she said. 'After all, I didn't have a daddy, and I turned out okay.' Well, I couldn't argue with her there."

So Val had raised her daughter alone.

"Still, I had my mother to lean on. Here Eve is trying to do this thing on her own, working full-time. She's too far away for me to be of any help."

"It's a lot to take on. How's it working?"

"Fine, I guess. She makes good money at the clinic. They have a day-care facility. It's not an easy life but none are, I suppose."

"Here, here." Rose raised her water glass and Val did the same.

Then Noel raised his. "The last episode of *The Brady Bunch* aired on March eighth, 1974."

"We just avoid the topic of fathers and sperm banks. I figure it'll be a long time yet before little Rose starts asking questions."

Big Rose still had a few but Val had been talking so much there was still plenty of food on her plate and hardly any on Rose's. She thought she should give Val time to catch up.

"That's great you could get past your differences, for the baby's sake," Rose said.

"A couple of days after our argument, I got an envelope from Dana Farber with an article about a possible link between pancreatic cancer and a high-starch diet"—Val shook the potatoes off her fork and scooped up some spinach instead—"in overweight, sedentary women." Val set down her fork. She wiped the corners of her mouth with her napkin and pushed her plate away.

Sounded like Eve had an interesting way of showing affection for her mother. She could use a little sensitivity training. Still, Rose admired Eve's independence and how she seemed to have it so together at such a young age. She knew better than to allow her life to revolve around a man.

"When will I get to meet her and see the baby?" Rose asked.

"Soon, I hope," Val said. She pushed her chair back and got up. "I'll start clearing."

After the dishes were cleared and the pots were soaking in the sink, Val and Rose retired to the living room. Val brought out a couple of cold beers and Noel began to sketch her with a charcoal pencil.

"Are there any paintings of your daughter?" Rose asked.

"Not a one," Val said. She whispered behind her hand. "Noel was always a little jealous of Eve."

"The last dodo bird died in 1681," Noel said.

Val raised her chin a little. "Ten minutes and you have to go home, Noel." She turned to me. "Cooper gets her knickers in a twist if I don't get him home by nine."

Rose stood up and walked over to Noel. She watched over his shoulder. Val was right. His technique was unlike anything she'd seen. Rather than sketch the general shape of the head and then fill in the features, he began with Val's rather long earlobe, then captured an archless eyebrow, random details, which he rendered fully, and then proceeded to the next, eventually connecting them in perfect proportion.

"How can he do that?" Rose asked.

"Savants can draw things without interpreting, like they're seeing everything for the first time. I read their brains divide things like time, space, and even objects into equal parts. That's what makes Noel so good at spatial relationships, and why some savants are good with numbers."

"I heard about this kid who could tell you what day of the week it was by giving him any date," Rose said. "He could go back a thousand years."

Rose compared Val to the likeness on Noel's pad: the high cheekbones, her broad chin, the angle, the expression. It was her. Remarkable.

"Exactly," Val said. She was trying to be still, holding her head up high to minimize her double chin. Evidently, she was used to Noel's mercilessly accurate renderings. She wasn't going to like this one either. He was working on a detail of her sagging jowl.

"Imagine if everyone had this potential lock in our brains somewhere and all we had to do is figure out how to tap into it," Rose said. She was itching to get onto the computer.

"I think it's better this way," Val said. "Keeps Noel special."

As Rose returned to her chair, she noticed a photo on the end table next to the sofa that she hadn't seen earlier. Two women posing on the lawn with a split-rail fence between them, the same one that separated Val's property from Cooper's today, though in the picture, the hedges were still low enough to see over. The photo looked like it had been snapped in early spring, with forsythia in bloom and some daffodils pushing through the soil near the fence.

"The one on the left is my mother," Val said. She must have seen where Rose was looking. "Ann."

Ann was wearing pedal pushers and had her hair done up in a beehive. The other woman was Cooper. It was obvious. She hadn't changed her look in forty-some-odd years. Only in the photo her hair was still dark. Climbing the fence in front of her was a young boy around three years old. On the grass near Val's mother was a chubby toddler sitting cross-legged on a towel. She had a babushka tied under her chin. The baby's face was round and she was smiling a wide, toothless smile.

"Marilyn Monroe's last movie was *The Misfits*," Noel said.

"That was before my time," Val said to him.

"Is this you?" Rose asked. She held up the photo and pointed to the toddler so Val could see. Val broke her pose to look. Noel flapped his arms.

"Afraid it is." She sat back.

"You were adorable. And who's the boy?"

"Lino," Val said. She sighed.

"Lino?"

"Cooper's son. It'll be twenty-seven years this month."

"Twenty-seven years since what?" Rose didn't know Cooper had a son.

"Since he disappeared," she said.

"What do you mean, *disappeared*?"

"Just that. One minute he was here, the next he was gone. To this day, no one knows if he's alive or dead. I was pregnant when it happened. We were going to be married."

Val raised her chin a little higher. Her eyes were focused on the sky outside the window.

"Lino was Eve's father?" Rose set the photo back down, regretting that she'd ever picked it up in the first place. "God, that's awful."

"Seems like yesterday."

Val sent Noel home and Rose stayed to help finish in the kitchen. Val looked tired. Rose still had no way of knowing whether all those pills on her stove added up to something serious.

Suddenly Val flung her dish towel over her shoulder and leaned against the counter. "You're going to kill me," she said.

"Why?"

"I should have told you hours ago. I was just so busy I forgot. Somebody called for you today. He called here. Someone with a name like Mel or Maury."

"Martin?" Rose's heart jumped.

"That's it, *Martin*."

"What did he say?"

"He asked for you. I looked outside and saw your car was gone. I told him you were out and didn't have your phone hooked up yet. He was very polite."

"Listen, Val. If he calls again, tell him I moved. Tell him I died. I don't want to talk to him. Okay?"

Val's eyes widened. "The *ex*," she said. "I knew it."

Rose spent Sunday researching autistic savants at the library. Her phone wouldn't be hitched up for another few days, so she had to use the Internet there. The research so engrossed her, she probably thought of Martin only a half-dozen times. She learned that while Noel's abilities were rare, there were other autistic savants whose work commanded top dollar on the world market, including an eleven-year-old Malaysian boy and a twenty-one-year-old kid from Iran whose subjects included figures that resembled Degas' ballerinas. She learned other things too:

that most autistic savants can't read and have a hard time writing their own names,

that they're six times more likely to be male than female,

that there are several hundred of them around the world today,

that they tend to perceive the world with one sense at a time,

and that, to this day, no one knows the source of their talent, which can manifest in any number of ways, from mathematical capacity to memory feats to artistic abilities. Some scientists even believed that unlocking the mystery might change the way people used their brains, so that everyone might experience savant-like flashes of brilliance, just like Rose had suggested to Val the day before in jest. Only here it was becoming a real possibility. There was a doctor in Australia who was experimenting with something called "trans-cranial magnetic stimulation," where he used magnets to inhibit brain activity in a region called the fronto-temporal area, the centers for language and conceptual thinking. He believed this could bypass any kind of cognitive interference to get directly to the creative source. If his hypothesis was correct, there was a little Noel in everyone, the same technical genius that allowed one to see an object, process its form, and identify it in an instant, something Rose never considered, the amount of data that was assimilated in the simplest glance around the room. In the future, it wouldn't be unreasonable to imagine being faced with a monumental challenge and being able to whip out a kind of magnetic thinking cap that would deliver a brilliant solution.

How useful such a contraption might have been the night Rose stood in Martin's apartment and had to choose her course of action. The cap might have told her to clobber Martin on the head with the oozing bag of Chinese food, then stay and try to work things out. Instead, left to the machinations of her own meager brain, she'd stormed out and never looked back. Had she done the right thing?

It was almost dark by the time Rose got home from the library. She set her stack of books on the lobster-trap table and heard people arguing outside. She moved to the window. Cooper was out in the yard and Val was standing in her kitchen doorway.

"I *knew* it," Cooper said.

"You mind your own beeswax." All Rose could see of Val was her finger wagging out the door.

"*She* said you were talking about her." Cooper pointed her thumb in the direction of Rose's cottage. "And I see those darn *cans* everywhere again."

"I'm warning you, stay out of this," Val said. "And leave her out of it too."

"Believe me, I would if I could. As if I don't have a few hundred things to do to get ready for this damn birthday party as it is. If it were up to me, I'd get a cake with three hundred candles and be done with it." Cooper raised her fist in a histrionic gesture toward the sky. "This is the thanks I get, Ann."

"Leave my mother out of this."

"Your mother's the one who finally said it had to stop. She called Schmidt, remember?" Cooper said.

"She did not. *You* did."

"I dialed because she was too sick."

"It was you who put her up to it." Val's finger was visible again. She pointed. "It's *always* you. You're crazy. And, anyway, he said I could stop coming."

"Wait till he hears you're back to your old tricks." Cooper folded her hands in front of her chest.

"He won't," Val said.

"Oh, yes, he will. I'm calling tomorrow, and we're going as soon as he'll take us."

"The hell I am. Go away!"

The door slammed but Cooper wasn't about to leave it alone. She started ringing the doorbell, banging her knuckles on the windowpane.

The door opened again and Val's finger appeared once more, this time in a subtle but famously hostile gesture. "Forget your broomstick?" she said.

Cooper stiffened. "Listen, missy. We've been through this enough. I'll let you know when we're going and you be ready, you hear?" She turned and took off through the hole in the bushes. At the last minute, she looked back at the cottage. Rose ducked down so she couldn't be seen.

CHAPTER FOUR

We accept no responsibility for crash damage.
—*from the HeliHobby RC Nitro Powered Helicopter Instruction Manual*

The day of Simon's "downfall" had begun like any other. When the cruise ship wasn't at port, Simon had until 2 P.M. to be in costume. The early hours were his to catch up on sleep, work out in the ship's gym, or just hang out in the employee lounge. That morning, Simon had been awakened by a fragrant breeze funneling though his cabin porthole. The crisp air had beckoned him upstairs to the main deck, where he could enjoy the sun before people started spilling out of their cabins in search of food.

The cruise was part of a corporate incentive program for nurses, a reward for them having taken a certain number of temporary jobs at clinics and hospitals around the country. These were mostly hardworking women who relished the chance each April to leave the doctors and patients and husbands and kids behind to bask in the Caribbean sun. "Imagine a ship full of gorgeous RNs," Segundo had said, encouraging Simon to take this most coveted of jobs. Simon quickly learned "gorgeous" was a stretch. But it didn't matter. Simon was grateful just to be in the company of so many women, a gender with whom, up until very recently, he'd never enjoyed success. Men who overindulged on a nightly basis weren't much of a turn-on. Nor were men clothed in rubber bulbs, he feared.

Still, there were promising signs. Just the evening before, a woman, despite having shamelessly confessed she'd already been rejected by the ship's captain, an engine-room worker, and the lounge singer, had cornered Simon in a dark hallway. She'd pressed her body against his. Simon smelled the liquor on her breath, which alone had made her advances more appealing. He allowed himself to be manhandled until, in a huge breach of mascot code, she yanked off his headgear. She reached up and mussed his hair. "You're a lot better looking than I thought you'd be," she said. She flung her arms around his neck. At that moment, a room-service clerk rolled his bar cart around the corner and Simon panicked. He grabbed his mask and fled. The last thing he wanted to do was to be caught in a compromising position and jeopardize the recent uptick in his life's trajectory, something for which he knew he had his friend Segundo to thank.

A smile is my currency was Segundo's favorite saying, though one rarely appreciated by the bartenders. Segundo often talked about cleaning up his act and going back to Miami one day. He must have told Simon at least a hundred times how he had ended up in Hampton Beach, but always after they'd been drinking, and Simon's recollection of the story's details were sketchy at best. Eight years earlier, Segundo had come on tour with an aging heavy-metal band (or was it Southern rock?) that couldn't sell enough tickets to buy gas, let alone pay the clown they had settled on because the dwarf (or was it a midget?) they had really wanted had the business savvy to insist on cash up front. They eventually dumped Segundo at a rest stop outside Nashua (or it might have been Concord?). He came out of the bathroom with an Orange Crush and a bag of Fritos (Cheetos? Doritos?) in time to see the tour bus rolling out onto the highway. Segundo stuck out his thumb with the intention of hitchhiking back to Miami. In costume, it took him three days to land a ride as far south as Hampton Beach. *Close enough,* he'd decided.

Segundo always said he could never go home to Miami until he gave up drinking for good and could "return to the family with honor." Simon figured he was just chicken. Or making excuses. He lived in a trailer on the outskirts of town. One day, someone broke into his Airstream and stole his money jar and all his clown gear, his costume, makeup, everything. Segundo went on a fierce three-day bender, then just disappeared. No one heard from him for almost a year. Then one day, he returned.

That afternoon, Segundo walked back into the bar a changed man, with a new, poofy orange wig and a fresh pair of harlequin silk trousers.

"Hola," Segundo said, and ordered a Shirley Temple. He sat down on the stool beside Simon. "Simon, you look like *sheet.*"

Simon had always thought the way Segundo talked was funnier, even, than the clown getup. Simon laughed. He was already three "sheets" to the wind. He clapped Segundo on the back. "Where've you been, muchacho?" he said. Any Spanish words Simon knew came from watching episodes of Speedy Gonzales as a kid. At that time, where he'd grown up on Cape Cod, Hispanic people were a rarer sighting than the endangered right whale.

"Doing the Lord's work," Segundo said.

The grin fell off Simon's face. He cocked his head and squinted at his old buddy. He poked a finger at his enormous bow tie. "You an angel?" he asked.

"You a wiseass?" he said. "Take this." He handed Simon a business card.

Simon couldn't read it. He'd lost his reading glasses in a poker game months ago and, anyway, he was too drunk to focus at any distance. "What's it say?"

"Read it tomorrow." Segundo took the card out of Simon's

hand and tucked it into his shirt pocket. "Call when you're ready. Tell them I sent you." Then Segundo slid off the bar stool. "Adios and God bless you, my friend." With that, he vanished into the blinding glare of the late-afternoon sun.

Simon rubbed his eyes. He reached for his drink and, in a few moments, forgot all about Segundo's miraculous return. The next morning, he thought the whole thing had been a dream until the card fell out of his shirt pocket onto the floor. He picked it up and brought it close to his nose. It read, *Mascots for Jesus.*

Mascots for Jesus was a nonprofit job placement company for recovering alcoholics in the twelve-step program. Beyond caring what people thought of them, alcoholics apparently made great mascots. They found role-playing as animals and dinosaurs constructive ways of blowing off steam. What's more, alcoholics were used to being pointed to and laughed at, so they didn't take offense. By the time most drunks hit bottom, they were sufficiently alienated from friends and family so that they were free to travel at whim. They could tour with sports teams for an entire season, leave for extended gigs on cruise ships and resorts, even relocate near theme parks. Nobody missed them. Mascots for Jesus gave alcoholics something to work toward beside sobriety. Like everywhere else in life, there was an established hierarchy. Mascots began at the entry level, spending weekends as gorillas at used-car lots or working birthday parties. Simon had spent a few days as an owl for an Old-Timers' baseball team that folded abruptly when the only pitcher came down with diverticulitis. Then suddenly Segundo called with news of the cruise-ship opening (which he hadn't taken himself because as a professional clown, he felt it beneath him to perform any character other than the one he'd taken years to painstakingly develop). In the world of mascots, the only job more coveted was working for the Ice Capades, and that was just because it paid a little more and workers got to hang out with the ice queens, who, rumor had it, weren't nearly as frigid as one might expect. This was only

Simon's second tour of duty and already he'd reached the top of the mascot food chain.

That morning, Simon couldn't have foreseen his misfortune. He'd awakened to the sun rising off the bow. The sky was violet. Out on the Atlantic, the colors were all that ever seemed to change. Simon drew in a breath of fresh air. He couldn't wait to get upstairs. Technically, he was supposed to stay on the lower decks but who was going to report him? No one knew what he looked like.

Simon got dressed. He slipped on his one nice shirt, a Tommy Bahama button-down he'd bought with his first paycheck after learning his assortment of New Hampshire lumberjack flannels wouldn't cut it in the tropics. He left his room and made his way up the metal stairs to the level of the ship where the passengers slept.

He walked down the hall. A television was on inside one of the cabins. Newspapers had been placed at each threshold and outside one door sat a tray with dirty breakfast dishes. Outside another was a metal cart filled with empty liquor bottles, remnants of a party that had yet to be cleaned up. Simon walked by them and caught a whiff of liquor. He stopped and turned around. Where did it mention having to encounter carts of liquor in the Mascots manual?

Simon looked both ways down the hall to make sure no one was coming, then moved in, just to read the labels, just to see what was there, just to pay his respects to some old friends. Tequila. He grinned at the memory of those two-for-one margarita nights at the Piping Plover on Cape Cod. He picked up another bottle. Vodka. The Bloody Marys his old girlfriend Felicia had served with his eggs in the morning. A bottle of gin. Simon had never been much of a gin man but right now the smell of it buckled his knees. Next, Scotch, which conjured memories of the old-fashioneds his old man used to drink like they were soda pop, and how, even as the littlest kid, Simon used to pull out the cherry by the stem when his father wasn't looking and drop it in his mouth, careful to suck all the booze out before he swallowed. Simon moved on to the bottle of Jack Daniel's, an old friend, expecting it too to be empty. Instead, about a half finger of golden liquid glowed at the bottom. He swirled it around, then closed his eyes and brought the bottle up to his nose. Why did it have to smell so good, like home—not the place but the feeling. He swooned and put a hand on the wall for balance. Why was it that some people could enjoy this while others drowned in it?

Simon looked down the cruise-ship hall again. There was no one around. He heard snoring coming from the room across the way. On a ship full of nurses, where was a damn health-care professional when you needed one? He raised the bottle to his lips and threw his head back, letting the warm fire coat his tongue, then his throat. He shuddered, held in the embrace of a long-lost pal, a war buddy, a mother, a lover. It felt so good. Too good. He got scared. He put the now-empty bottle down and his hand was shaking so bad he knocked three others over. The snoring inside the cabin stopped.

Simon ran down the hall to the stairway that led to the upper deck. *It never happened,* he told himself. *It didn't count. It was nothing.*

It was *everything,* a voice somewhere inside of him shouted.

Upstairs, blinded by the light of day, he stepped onto the cruise ship's jogging track, where a nurse was power walking at a fast clip, swinging her tiny purple hand weights. A yoga class was in progress by the pool. Simon noticed a woman on a mat who had her legs over her head. *Why can't this be enough?* He took a deep breath to clear his head. He could still taste the liquor. He started to walk.

When he got close to the lounge where an enormous Polynesian-style breakfast buffet was being laid out, Simon veered off the track.

"The omelet station will be up and running in a few minutes," said a kitchen worker. Simon took an apple off the fruit display and polished it on his sleeve. "Coffee?" she asked.

"Can you make that an *Irish* coffee?" He took his apple and sat down at one of the tables.

"With *whiskey*?" The woman wrinkled her nose.

"I'll take it in a to-go cup if you don't mind."

Simon lay in a hospital bed with cool bandages on his face and neck. Though some things had come back to him, most everything that had happened after the Irish coffee was a blur. Simon remembered putting on his costume that afternoon, and some difficulty to do with getting the bulb zipped. But he had no recollection of ever actually reporting to work. Where had the bottle of rum come from? How had he ended up in the lifeboat?

He remembered waking up on that moonless night with a dull pain at the back of his skull. The dance music had stopped. The ship was quiet. All Simon wanted was to go back to his room and sleep it off. The next day he would call Segundo and apologize for blowing it.

Simon remembered the red digits on his watch that displayed the time: 4:20. It was too dark to tell how much booze was left in the bottle; he might as well take it back to the room. There was no telling how bad tomorrow was going to be. He didn't even want to think about tomorrow.

Simon recalled peering out from under the heavy tarp, then climbing out of the boat. And while he remembered something of that split second when he realized he'd stepped out the wrong side, he had no memory of actually hitting the water.

As it turned out, no one had been looking for the mascot who'd fallen overboard. Instead, Simon had benefited from a drug bust that was going down about a mile off Miami Beach. On his way to the Turkish freighter, the police chopper pilot spotted something odd flailing on the surface, a manatee in distress or maybe that elusive giant squid he had learned about on the Discovery Channel. Or just maybe it was a person. He radioed back to Miami and a Coast Guard cutter was dispatched to investigate.

By nightfall, Simon was pulled from the water and transported to Jackson Memorial Hospital, where the rubber bulb had to be surgically removed from his body. Simon was treated for dehydration, first degree burns to his face and scalp, and circulatory problems in his legs. As for the cut on his toe, it had miraculously healed.

Simon was given intravenous fluids and observed until his burns showed enough signs of healing that he was past the risk of infection. The cruise ship had initially decided to press charges for breach of contract, which they retracted almost immediately to avoid negative publicity when it was brought to the attention of the police that the cruise ship never had actually bothered to report Simon missing. By then, Simon's picture, a dramatic rescue photo of him being pulled out of the water by four beefcake Coast Guard workers, had been plastered on the front page of every local paper. The Fox Channel even had one of its reporters climb into a makeshift replica of Simon's costume and jump from a cruise ship docked at the Port of Miami to simulate the fall for the cameras, which they ran on the six o'clock news, minus the Coast Guard rescue that ensued when the reporter hit the ship's rail on the way down and broke his own shin. The next day, the *Miami Herald* printed scientific diagrams drafted by a retired NASA engineer showing precisely how the costume had cushioned Simon's fall and enabled him to weather the elements for thirty-six hours. However, by the end of the fourth day, the story of Simon's survival was usurped by that of a feisty grandmother who had survived three days on nothing but rainwater and a roll of Life Savers in the murky swamp beneath a highway cloverleaf after her car had been sideswiped by an eighteen wheeler and catapulted over the guardrail. Simon was old news.

Nine days after he was pulled from the Atlantic, he was

released into police custody. With no one pressing charges, he was free to go. Free to go where?

"Got any relatives in Miami?" the cop asked.

"No." Simon had no relatives anywhere, except for Noel.

"You must know someone. Everyone knows *someone* in Miami."

Everyone except Simon. He thought hard. Then he remembered. Segundo's family. They still lived in Miami. Simon hoped they might see it as God's will to help him get back on his feet.

"Have you heard of the Martinez family?" Simon asked the cop.

"You've got to be kidding." The police officer reached into a drawer, pulled out the four-inch-thick Miami White Pages phone book and dropped it on the counter. Simon looked under M. Marino. Martin. Martinelli. Martinez. He ran his finger down the column until the tip turned black with Martinezes. There were hundreds, maybe even thousands. What was Segundo's uncle's first name? It didn't matter, there were at least twenty of every first name imaginable.

"Got the Yellow Pages?" Simon asked.

The cop dropped another thick volume onto the desk. Simon looked under C. There were eight ads under *Clown*, only three of them Martinezes and only one offering free cotton candy, which Segundo had told Simon was his family's marketing ploy. (When the carnival came to Hampton Beach, Segundo earned drink money working the cotton-candy concession and would show up at the bar at night with pink in his hair.)

The rest of the ad was in Spanish, so Simon asked the Cuban police officer to make the call for him. Simon didn't understand what was being said, but at the end of the conversation, the cop nodded and told Simon to wait for Señor Martinez on one of the benches in the waiting area. Simon took up his new duffel bag filled with old clothes given to him by a Miami Red Cross worker who'd paid him a visit in the hospital. He sat down on a hard wood bench. The air conditioner blew down the back of his shirt. It felt good.

Simon thumbed through some of the old newspapers piled onto a side table. He was looking for one of the articles on his ordeal that he might save for posterity. He found a three-day-old *USA Today* in which he appeared in a small thumbnail on the front. *See Lifestyles, E-1.* He found the section but forgot all about his own story when another caught his eye, one that had him swimming again. The headline said: "Art Genius Tucked Away in the Dunes."

CAPE COD, MA—He walks alone at a fast clip, in a navy parka marked with reflective tape, past the weathered, two-hundred-year-old homes and scrubbed pines on Nauset's cobblestone streets, a seemingly ordinary young man, young for his twenty-two years. But Noel Beadle is far from ordinary. Orphaned at five and severely autistic, he is the talent his former art teacher, Beth Philp, at the Pond School for Autism in Auburn, MA, heralds as a "pioneer" whose work is "devotionally intimate" and "culture-pastiching."

Culture-pastiching. Simon's fingers clenched the placket of the slightly worn lavender polo. He read on.

"We always knew he was good. We just didn't know how good," said Cooper Almeida, custodian and owner of the apartment where Noel lives.

"*I* knew," said another caretaker, Valeria Shimilitis.

And there was a photo. Simon brought the paper closer to his nose. Only then did he realize how much his hands were shaking. There was Noel, all grown up and flanked by three women. He knew two of them. One was Val "Shimmy" Shimilitis, who'd been a senior in high school when Simon was a freshman. She looked the same, only older and wider. The other was Cooper Almeida, the mother whose kid disappeared almost thirty years ago and for all Simon knew had reappeared since. And there was a third woman, someone he didn't recognize. He read the caption:

From left: Caretakers Cooper Almeida and Valeria Shimilitis, Noel Beadle, and Nauset Oracle *reporter and family friend Rose Nowak.*

Rose Nowak. And there were two other photos, those in color. One of a painting Noel had done. It was the figure of a woman curled on the floor. Simon felt the sweat squeeze out of his pores. God, the auburn hair, it looked like Iris. He even recognized the gray linoleum from Iris's old apartment. But how could Noel remember any of it? She had died when he was only five. The other photo was a close-up of Noel at work on a canvas. Simon was suddenly very thirsty, more thirsty than he had been since he polished off the last of the rum at sea. He looked at his nephew and saw something painfully familiar, himself at twenty-two.

"Señor Beadle?"

Simon looked up. Before him was a man in his late sixties, about the same stature as Segundo with the same white cast to his face from the stage makeup that was never as easy to get off as the package made it seem, so Segundo had always complained.

"*Hola,*" he said. "*Me llamo Jesús.*"

CHAPTER FIVE

Once the knife has entered the shell, twist like a screwdriver.

—*on opening oysters from colchesteroysterfishery.com*

During the night, a nor'easter swept through Rose's sleep. In the dream, the level of the inlet began to rise. From the cottage, she watched as the tips of the eelgrass sank beneath the surface. The black water lapped up the grassy bank like a tongue, moving closer. At first, she was worried about Val. But as the harbor swelled, Rose could see Val's home stood on an island of higher ground. She was safe. It was the cottage that was under siege. Salt water started seeping through the closed windows, until they gave way and the sea began to gush in. Rose ran to the bedroom, the only room that was still dry, and closed the door. The cottage began to list and groan, and, with a jolt, broke free of its stone foundation, setting her adrift. And the strange part is, she wasn't afraid.

Wonderful smells wafted through the hall of Val's house: fresh brewed coffee and melted cheeses, pastry, and something sweet, like anise. Tinny music was coming from the old hi-fi in the living room, a chorus of children singing in another language, a boys' choir, with a few changed voices scraping along in a lower octave. Val was humming. Rose entered the living room and saw Val barreling toward her, head down, an orange Crock-Pot in her hands.

"Hot. Hot. Hot," she said. She came at Rose full speed.

Rose swung the stuffed monkey she was holding out of the way and jumped back to avoid a collision.

"Rose!" Val sidestepped her and jogged to the table to catch her balance. The back of Val's blouse was dark with sweat. "I'm sorry I didn't see you there. Did I get kugalis on you?"

"Not a drop."

Val caught her breath and shook out her hands. They were bright red.

"Let me turn down the music," she said. "Who's your friend?"

Rose looked around, then realized she meant the toy.

"It's for the baby." There Rose had stood in front of the stuffed-animal display at the Wooden Boat, trying to decide which creature might appeal to a toddler, finally settling on the chimpanzee with the mischievous smile. "Every kid likes monkeys, right?" Rose sat him on the radiator cover. "Sorry I'm late. Are they here yet? I didn't see a car."

"You're not going to believe it." Val blew a strand of hair from her face.

"What?" Rose said.

"The last Model T Ford rolled off the assembly line on May twenty-sixth, 1927," Noel said.

Rose hadn't seen him there in the shadows. He was sitting in the understuffed wingback. "Hey, Noel," she said.

"Car trouble," Val said. "Bad brakes. And it's a brand new car."

"Bad brakes on a *new* car?" Rose said.

"Can you believe it?" Val said.

"The last passenger pigeon died in captivity at the Cincinnati Zoo in 1914. Her name was Eve," Noel said.

"That isn't nice, Noel. People can't help it when their cars break down." Val turned and pointed toward the fireplace. "And now I've got enough food to feed the Lithuanian army."

Rose's attention was drawn to the elaborate banquet set up on a large folding table in front of the hearth. There were baskets of fruits, muffins and pastries, the still-steaming orange Crock-Pot, a silver coffee pitcher, cups, plates, dishes, and utensils, not the everyday stuff, but family silver, and a plate of finger food, chopped cooked carrots, and crackers that must have been intended for her granddaughter.

"You went to a lot of trouble," Rose said.

Val shrugged. "These things happen," she said. She seemed to be taking the news well. "Please, eat. Eve said she'd call this afternoon when she hears from the mechanic."

"I doubt I can make a dent in all of this. Noel, help me out." Rose grabbed a plate and started filling it up. Val poured herself a cup of coffee, sat down on the sofa, and picked up a *Cancer Cell* magazine.

May had ushered in the first truly balmy day of the year, the first morning they could open the windows and feel the heavy breeze flush past the sill. Rose imagined the moisture from the April rain wicking up from the ground through the joists of the house, swelling the shingles and floorboards, softening the wood for the fat, black ants that she was beginning to see crawling up the cottage walls.

Rose sat with her plate of food. Val was looking down through her reading glasses at the magazine on her lap, the soft light trapped in the folds of her face, illuminating her plump cheeks. Val's eyes glistened as if the moisture had begun to wick up her as well.

She had taken extra care choosing her clothes this morning, a crisp blue sleeveless cotton blouse with an enamel forget-me-not pinned to the Peter Pan collar, a khaki skirt and white tennis socks with baby blue around the ankles. Val had on lipstick for the first time since Rose had met her.

"So what did your fellow have to say?" Val asked.

"How did you know Martin called?" Rose asked. "And he's not my *fellow*," she added.

"There's a funny click on the old phone in the study whenever a long-distance call comes into the cottage. I just guessed it was him."

Rose stuffed something delicious into her mouth that oozed a creamy filling, which backed up to her ears, leaving no room for thoughts of Martin. "I didn't pick up," she said with her mouth full.

"The last wolf in Great Britain was killed in 1743," Noel said. He'd taken the plate intended for baby Rose, bit a smile into a Ritz cracker, and constructed the rest of a face out of carrots.

"Don't you wonder why he's calling?"

"Probably just to congratulate me on the *USA Today* article. Let's talk about something else."

Val tossed the cancer magazine onto the coffee table and picked up a *Yankee.* She licked her finger and began to page through it. "I once knew a man with size EEEEEE feet," she said. "They were like dinner plates." She held the magazine under her chin and used her hands to show how wide. Noel turned to see. "He wanted to join the army but they wouldn't take him. He was one heck of a swimmer, though. He could paddle clear across the bay to the jetty and back without stopping. Believe it or not, he was a shoe salesman. Married a girl from France."

Val set down the *Yankee,* got up, and headed to the table of food. Rose happened to glance down and there in the bottom right-hand corner of the page was an ad for extra-wide men's shoes. She was about to ask if Val was pulling her leg.

"Cottage-cheese dumpling?" Val brought a plate of golden balls to the coffee table. "Family recipe."

Rose took one and, in the process, knocked her knife from the edge of the plate onto the floor. "Sorry." She picked it up and wiped filling from her shoe.

"We're going to get a male visitor!" Val said.

"What?"

"The last Olympic tug-of-war was held during the 1920 summer games," Noel said.

"A knife or spoon means male. A fork means female. One of my father's old superstitions. Never fails. You wait."

If there was one thing Rose wasn't, it was superstitious.

She ate her way through the plate of cottage-cheese dumplings then moved on to the Crock-Pot and pastries for seconds, which she washed down with Val's strong black coffee. Such a shame all Val's hard work had been for nothing. Why couldn't her daughter have just rented a car? To cancel at the last minute seemed cruel. She must have known what lengths her mother would go to in the kitchen. In spite of the day's bad news, Val seemed to be enjoying watching Rose gorge herself.

Rose undid the top button of her jeans and leaned back. While she had been busy eating, Noel had returned to his painting. Val was peering over his shoulder.

Rose closed her eyes. Strange, but it was as if she had spent every morning of her life in this house. The simple dignity of the place reminded her of her childhood and the town in rural western Massachusetts where she'd grown up, where tobacco fields and weathered farmhouses stood in place of the ocean and the Cape's gray-shingled cottages. After living in the city for so long, Rose had forgotten the lovely parts of rural life, the pops and creaks of an old house, the smell of the soil as it thaws.

In one month's time, Rose had gone from instructing people on the art of inserting AAA batteries into their new nose-hair trimmers to writing a story about the art of a twenty-two-year-old savant. She'd gone from cleaning up obits to having her story about Noel published and picked up in papers around the country. This life of reporting seemed to suit her. In fact, she was almost happy. Rose closed her eyes and, to her surprise, Martin was there behind her eyelids as he had been for days, this time, in a replay of what was truly her first experience as a gatherer of information.

REPORTER:

For the record, you had sexual intercourse with another woman?

MARTIN:

You don't deserve this.

REPORTER:

. . . the kind of woman who has sex with men at bachelor parties.

MARTIN:

I don't know what I was thinking.

REPORTER:

And then you came home and had sex with your girl-friend, who, for all anyone knows, could now be infected with a host of STDs.

MARTIN:

I thought about killing myself.

REPORTER:

Let's put that aside for the moment. Did you know this woman before the party?

MARTIN:

Of course not.

REPORTER:

And did you have sex with her more than once?

MARTIN:

You mean *that* night?

REPORTER:

(Saliva goes down the wrong pipe, followed by a fit of coughing.) Well, let's start there.

MARTIN:

Twice.

REPORTER:

Twice, as in *two* times.

MARTIN:

Yeah.

REPORTER:

And *after* that night?

MARTIN:

I told her I had a girlfriend. (Sound of ice cubes being crushed between molars.)

REPORTER:

How old is she?

MARTIN:

I don't know.

REPORTER:

Ballpark it.

MARTIN:

Midtwenties.

REPORTER:

Do you wish to pursue a relationship with this *girl?*

MARTIN:

God, no. (Eight-million-year pause.) I don't know.

REPORTER:

How can you *not know*? (Clears her throat to regain professional demeanor.) You mean you may have *feelings* for her?

MARTIN:

I love you, Rose. But I can't stop thinking about her. I try not to but I can't help it. I don't know what's wrong with me.

REPORTER:

I see. There's just one more angle I'd like to cover.

MARTIN:

Stop sounding like a reporter.

REPORTER:

Did you have sex with this woman because your girlfriend was somehow inadequate?

MARTIN:

Don't be crazy. I was drunk.

REPORTER:

(Reporter leans in.) Did this happen because your girlfriend is almost forty? Think carefully before you answer.

MARTIN:

It's not you, Rose. Things haven't been easy for me lately.

REPORTER:

And this makes *things* easier?

MARTIN:

Rose. (Interviewee breaks down. Interviewer hands him his own fine, imported cashmere throw to wipe his face.) I don't want to lose you over this. (Reporter heads to the bathroom, collects her toothbrush and hair dryer.) Please, Rose. Don't go. We can work it out. Four years has to be worth something. (Reporter leaves her Connie Chung mask in the bathroom. Comes out with her junk.)

ROSE:

That's what I'm thinking too.

Somewhere around two years into their relationship, Rose had learned more about the woman Martin had been visiting in the hospital when they first met, including the reason why the husband, Martin's "friend," had never been there when he came to visit. Martin's explanation that the guy—a man whose wife was dying in the hospital—somehow "couldn't get away from work" never did sit right. It was a lie, of course. The husband was never there because he and his wife were estranged. Martin and the woman, that married mother of two—that part was true enough—had been having an affair. Rose knew this two full years before he cheated on her. And yet, she'd trusted him.

Noel had returned to working on a painting he'd begun the day before, a vase of red and yellow tulips Val had on the mantel. Rose got up and took a closer look at his work. In just a few loose strokes, he'd managed to capture the essence of the flowers.

When she was researching the article, Rose had called Noel's former art teacher at the Pond School in Auburn, just to see what light she could shed on Noel's talent. As far as Beth Philps was concerned, Noel was a legitimate phenom.

"At the Pond School, we promote neurodiveristy," she'd said.

"*Neurodiversity?*"

"There are people out there who consider what Noel and others like him are able to do as somehow inferior because of their . . . deficits," she said. "*Outsider artists* is a term they use. It's really a matter of whether you look at autism as a pathology or simply an alternate wiring of the brain." She'd said *pathology* as if it had tasted bad. "What makes an artist interesting is the passion he or she brings to the subject. You'd say that about any artist. You can certainly say it about Noel."

"You said 'Noel and others like him.' *Are* there others like him? I mean savant artists who are that good?"

"I've seen work from autistic savants in other parts of the world that are *that* good. A few years back, I had a student who did magnificent pencil drawings of clocks."

"Clocks? That's it?"

"Just clocks. I liked to think he was somehow fascinated with the concept of time but he may have just liked the face and the numbers. He was never able to articulate the reason. But they were glorious," she said. "Noel's more diverse in his subject matter."

He could go from people to flower petals with equal proficiency.

Now Noel closed his eyes and turned his head to the side to signal that he was about to speak. He never could say anything without this deliberate ceasing of one activity in preparation for the start of another, in this case, the shift from drawing to speech.

"Scarlet Baby," he said.

Rose looked to Val for interpretation.

"Iris had a small garden behind the apartment where she grew tulips. Scarlet Baby. That was the variety. When we cleaned out Iris's place, Cooper picked one of the flowers and pressed it into the Beadle family Bible. Now it's framed behind glass in his room."

"He said 'Scarlet Baby.' That's not really a *last,* is it?" Rose asked. "I mean, technically." It was as though she was looking for Noel to have points taken off.

"His mother's last flower, I suppose."

Rose felt like an ass. "Of course."

This was how he kept his mother alive, through the smallest details. The more specific, the more real she became. Not flower, not tulip, but *Scarlet Baby.*

"I guess it's true how you wind up talking to *them* the rest of your life," Rose said.

"Who?" Val asked.

"In an interview I read once, an actor said, 'When you lose people you love when you're young, you wind up talking to them the rest of your life.'"

The sun that had been on Val's face all morning seemed to pass beneath a cloud. "Maybe so," she said. Val looked out her window, then suddenly jumped out of her chair and started clearing the buffet.

Rose had never seen her move so fast. "What is it?" Rose asked.

"A toad."

"Really?" Rose looked around her chair. "Where? I didn't see—"

As Val filled her arms with serving dishes and brought them to the kitchen, Cooper exploded through the front door.

"You," Cooper said. She pointed a thick finger in Rose's direction. "This is all your fault. I got so many busybodies pulling into my driveway I can't get a minute's peace. Finally had to get Mike Eldridge over here to divert traffic."

From the kitchen came the sounds of opening and closing cabinets, plates being scraped.

"How'd you manage that?" Val said from the kitchen.

"I asked him to. With all the taxes we pay, we should each get our own personal cop," Cooper said.

Val came out of the kitchen. She went to the window, wiped her hands on her apron, and drew back the curtain. "Wouldn't mind having Mike Eldridge as *my* own personal cop," she said. "Rose, come look."

"No thanks," Rose said. Bad guys were more her speed.

"Think he should come cart this one away in cuffs for the trouble she's caused," Cooper said. She crashed down on the sofa, her back to the buffet.

Val let the curtain drop. "We haven't had any trouble, have we, Rose?" Val looked at Rose and shrugged. Rose shook her head innocently.

"The paper didn't say Noel lived *here*," Cooper said.

"We didn't print an address," Rose said. "Paper policy." She was a reporter now. She worked for a paper. That paper had a policy.

"You printed my *name*. You said he lived with me. Anyone could look it up."

Rose frowned. She hadn't considered that.

"People come to the door looking for autographs from a kid who can barely write his own name," Cooper said. She folded her arms across her chest.

"How does it feel to be famous, Noel?" Rose asked. She was determined not to let Cooper get to her. Rose tried to remember how Alice at the *Cape Gazette* had said it was all an act. If so, Cooper had an Oscar coming.

Noel put down his paintbrush on the lip of the easel. He pressed his eyes shut. "The last great auk was killed by collectors on Eldey Island in 1844." He picked up the paintbrush again.

Val winked at him and smiled, as though she understood perfectly. She pushed aside the curtain and looked out the window again, then jumped.

"He's coming!" Val said. She shot away from the window, smoothed down her apron, and checked her teeth in the tiny mirror beside the door. She caught her breath in her hand and smelled it.

"What the hell is he doing? He's supposed to be at his post," Cooper said.

The doorbell rang. Val opened the door. The uniformed cop stepped into the room.

"Mrs. Almeida, I didn't know you were here," the cop said. He seemed a little flustered, like a kid who'd been caught skipping school. "Morning, ladies, Noel." He was average height and solid, built like a fieldstone wall, his eyes hidden behind a pair of aviator sunglasses that were a little too big for his face. He looked at Rose and took off his police hat. "We haven't met."

"She's the one who wrote the dang article," Cooper said. "And stop calling me Mrs. Almeida. Makes me feel old."

"Thought you looked familiar," he said to Rose. "Must've been your picture in the paper."

"Who ever heard of reporters appearing in their own articles? Think that reporter from *USA Today* had the hots for her," Cooper said.

Rose turned to Cooper. "The only reason they printed my photo is because when they picked up the story, they found out I was living here, and that I was more than just a reporter. I was Noel's friend."

"With friends like *you*—" Cooper started.

Rose got up and extended her hand to the cop. "Rose Nowak," she said.

"Mike Eldridge," he said. They shook. "With an *i*," he added.

"I beg your pardon?" Rose said.

"Lots of Eldridges on the Cape. Some with an *e*, some with an *i*," Cooper said. "Ones with an *i* come from a long line of mooncussers. Somehow he's proud of that."

"That's not why—" he started.

"What's a mooncusser?" Rose asked.

"In the old days, on moonless nights, they set out decoy lanterns that looked like lighthouse beacons from offshore. They tricked the ships into coming close to the rocks. Once they ran aground, mooncussers killed the crew and looted the ship," Val said. "They were *pirates*."

"Lazier, but the same idea," Cooper said.

"Mooncusser," Rose repeated. The word had its own sinister rhythm. "Why *moon*cusser?"

"'Cause when the moon was out the captains could see. Had to be dark so the mooncussers *cussed* the moon. Get it?" Cooper said. She rolled her eyes like it was so obvious.

"I just tell people that so they don't confuse me for Mike Eldredge with an *e* who works at the dump," Mike said.

He took the black aviators off his nose, carefully checked them for fingerprints, and slipped them into his front shirt pocket. He had dark, deep-set eyes with sleepy lids and a strong jawline, a little gray at the temples. Rose could see why Val might find him attractive.

"Sure you do. So what are you doing in here when you're supposed to be out there?" Cooper said. She motioned outside with her thumb.

He seemed contrite. "I was just . . . I caught a whiff of something good." He winked at Val. "Thought I'd better investigate." His gaze landed on the table with plenty of food left on it. "Skipped breakfast."

"Please, Mike. Help yourself," Val said.

"Yeah, what is all that?" Cooper turned and saw the buffet.

"Val was expecting—" Rose started to tell her about Eve and her car trouble.

"I just had a little brunch planned. Nothing fancy," Val said.

"On his last voyage, Sinbad was taken a slave by pirates," Noel said. "But he escaped."

Cooper stood up and looked at the table behind her.

"You got enough food here to feed the firehouse," she said. She looked at Val. "And you're wearing *lipstick*."

"As if I *never* wear lipstick." She blushed.

"You don't," Cooper said.

"How come people always bring food to the firehouse and not the police station?" Mike said. His mouth was full. He'd discovered another plate of cottage-cheese dumplings. Rose thought she'd finished them off.

"People don't like cops. They're scared of 'em," Cooper said. She sat back down.

"Shouldn't be unless they got a reason. So where are you from, Rose?" He filled a plate and sat down on the sofa.

"Originally western Massachusetts. Recently Boston."

"How do you like it here so far?" Mike asked.

"Feels like home. Much of that is thanks to these guys." Rose included Cooper only out of kindness.

"You're working for old Calvin, I hear." Mike smiled at Val like they were in on some joke. Val ran back out to the kitchen.

"Let me get some soda," she said.

"Calvin's a peach," Rose said, almost defensively.

"Bet he is," Cooper said. Cooper turned around and looked at the table. "So, Val, why the heck did you need to make so much food for a few—"

"The last king killed by a monkey was Alexander of Greece," Noel said. "In 1920."

Rose turned and saw he was staring at the stuffed animal she'd brought.

"Where did the monkey come from?" Cooper asked.

"Mike, you know about the Tri-centennial planning meeting tomorrow morning? It's here at ten A.M. It was supposed to be at the Nickersons' but the toilet downstairs at their place is busted again or so Dorie claims. You're welcome to join us," Val said. Her voice came out a few octaves higher than normal.

Mike looked at Rose. "You covering it?" he asked.

"I didn't even know about it." Rose turned to Val. "Would it be something interesting for me to cover?"

"I don't know about newsworthy but it sure is fun to watch Cooper and Dorie go at it," Val said.

"Never mind," Cooper said. It looked like her rain slicker was squeezing the blood out of her arms.

"You should come and hear about what we're planning," Val said. "This is your home now too."

"I'm off duty Monday," Mike said. "Might swing by. Got a few choice words for our beloved selectman."

"You off duty now?" Cooper said.

Mike had another pastry in his hand and was about to take a bite. He set it back down on his plate.

"I suppose I'd better get back to my post," he said. He brushed the crumbs off his hands. "Thanks for the food, Val. It was great."

Val's mouth twisted into a goofy smile.

"Nice to meet you, Rose," he said.

"Same here," Rose said.

As soon as the door closed behind him, Rose got up and started to clear the table. From the window she saw Mike walking up the driveway. He pulled a comb out of his wallet and ran it through the stubble of his crew cut, then put on his hat. He slid the aviators out of his top pocket and put them back onto his nose. He sure looked the part.

Rose lifted a platter off the table and brought it into the kitchen, which smelled like Crisco. There were burn marks on the Formica and places on the refrigerator where the enamel was chipped. On the Tri-centennial countdown calendar there was a big circle around Monday to remind everyone of the planning meeting. Rose set the platter down on the stove.

She heard Cooper in the other room, talking through her teeth. "You better not be pulling any of your nonsense."

"I don't know what you're talking about," Val said.

"Like hell you don't. All that *food*."

"People have to eat—"

Rose tried to hear the rest but Cooper lowered her voice. Whatever they were arguing about, it sounded like more of what she'd heard at the side of Val's house the day after she moved in. Perhaps it had something to do with those orange bottles on the stove.

With those two busy snarling at each other, Rose had her chance. It was really none of her business except if there was something wrong with Val, it might be important for her to know

Val's condition. If, God forbid, she ever had to call 911. Could be a matter of life or death, Rose rationalized. She leaned over the stove and examined the closest bottle, read the word: *Risperdal*. It had been filled in March.

"Rose, dear," Val called out.

Rose jumped back and almost knocked a saucepan off the stove.

"I made extra of everything for the meeting tomorrow. The Tupperware is in the bottom drawer next to the fridge. I'll be there in a minute," Val said.

Rose had a minute.

Risperdal. She'd never heard of it before. The rest of the labels were turned around. Were they the same or something else? Rose reached toward the back of the stove and picked up a vial. Same drug, only this one had been filled in February. All the bottles were full. Whatever it was, Val wasn't taking it.

"Did you find them?" she said. She was coming.

"Find? Oh, the Tupperware, right here." Rose opened the bottom drawer and pulled out a handful of plastic containers.

Apply gentle pressure around the edge until completely sealed. Listen for the "burp."

After the food was put away, Rose offered to take Noel with her for a walk on the outer beach. She'd driven them to the parking lot and now the two of them walked in silence. The sand was soft and their feet sank inches with every step, making it tough going. Noel's legs were long and muscular and Rose had to struggle to keep up with him. She focused on each step, one at a time. It felt good just to fill her head with steps, sand, and salt. There were some big waves breaking on the bar offshore.

Rose was beginning to see how when you lived near water, you tended to exist in a state of quiet anxiety. She was thinking of the way Cooper and Val were always at each other, all of their emotions so close to the surface. Last week, a late-season storm had swallowed up several feet of shoreline. It had temporarily broken through a thin slice of outer beach, exposing the homes on the inlet to the full driving force of the surf. A few days later, it closed up again. But after that, the people building the house on the Point had decided they needed a larger seawall, which had everyone in the town up in arms again. Apparently, for most, it was bad enough they'd gotten approval for the first one.

Cooper wasn't happy about the big house. At first Rose just thought Cooper was being selfish. It was fine for the locals to stake their claims by the water's edge, but when someone else tried to build, there was always some reason why they shouldn't be allowed. There were always a handful of people trying to push through a moratorium on construction, seemingly unconcerned by what it would do to the local economy and the ones who relied on new construction to feed their families. Cooper's beef was less about the house being waterfront and more about the rules that appeared to have been bent in order to get the house built. She was a stickler for justice.

Rose was starting to soften toward her a little. Sometimes when Cooper was stirring up trouble, setting off fireworks with her caustic tongue, Rose had to stop and think about what the kind of loss the woman had experienced might do to a person, what it might be like to raise a son and one day have him just disappear, then to continue living alone as the days and months ticked on, staring out the window, wondering where he was, the only answers coming in the form of hollow waves breaking on the outer beach. Maybe Cooper found comfort in those rhythms. Maybe they were more soothing than the *nothing* some got when they posed their questions to a higher power.

The outer beach was deserted now, though, it being Sunday, just a few hours earlier had likely been crowded with four-wheel-drive vehicles and sunbathers out for their first real taste of spring. There was a family in sweatshirts flying kites. From up the beach came the smell of meat grilling on a barbecue. Summer was just around the corner. Now the sun was going down and the temperatures were cooling off again. The tide was high and a few small waves were hurling themselves lazily onshore. The dunes cast long shadows in the sand and damp air was rolling in on a heavy cloud that could be seen just above the horizon.

"Noel, stop a minute. I need to catch my breath," Rose said. She stood with her hands on her hips.

Noel picked up a dead crab and examined it from all sides. Rose looked back toward the parking lot. Down the beach a good twenty yards was a man she had seen as they started their walk. When they stopped, he did too. He had on a baseball cap and his hands were stuffed inside the pockets of his red jacket.

"Let's head back. Cooper wants you home before dark."

"All my possessions for a moment of time," he said. Queen Elizabeth. After a month, Rose was getting good at it. Noel flung the crab out into the ocean and started walking back toward the parking lot at the same pace as before.

"Wait for me." Rose jogged to catch up.

Now the man on the beach had decided to head back too but Noel's gait was too quick. They were gaining on him. As Rose and Noel approached, the man tucked his chin down so that they couldn't see his face. If it wasn't for Noel's recent celebrity, Rose might not have thought anything of it. People on the beach respected one another's privacy. For all she knew, with his head down like that, he was praying. Then again, maybe he was a pedophile, a kidnapper. Rose started to feel uncomfortable. As they passed, she decided to look him in the eye. As she turned and lifted her head, so did he. The appearance of his face shocked her. He had obviously been involved in some kind of accident. His skin was almost black in places, and peeling like a charred marshmallow. His lips were blistered.

"Afternoon," he said, not to Rose, but to Noel.

Noel heard his voice and looked up. He usually never

responded to strangers, so Rose was surprised. Even so, Noel kept on walking back toward the lot, maybe a little faster than before.

"Hi," Rose said.

The man tipped his cap at Rose and she got a better look at him. There was something familiar about his face, his blue eyes. He brought his hand up to his chin. He seemed nervous. He nodded, then turned toward the surf.

Rose broke into a jog to catch up to Noel, a little afraid to turn around and find the man would be following close behind. But when she finally reached the lifeguard stand, Rose looked back and he was right where she had left him, staring out at the horizon.

When she got out to the parking lot, Noel was leaning against the car.

"I have a terrific headache," he said.

"Who's that, Noel?"

"FDR," he said.

CHAPTER SIX

Risk of entanglement: Keep hands away from moving parts. Tie up or cover long hair.
—from the Global Machinery Company Finishing Nail Gun Kit Instruction Manual

It had taken Simon three days to get to the Cape. He probably could have made the trip faster but the closer he got, the more nervous he became. By the time he reached the bridge, he was barely pushing fifty miles an hour. What if he wasn't welcome? What if Noel hated him? Once he arrived, Simon hunkered down in a local motel room living on stale crackers and Cheez Whiz for three days until he finally had to venture out for food. He bought himself a sub at Puritan Pizza. That proceeded without incident, so he decided to take a walk on the beach. An hour later, he was back in his room with the dead bolt latched and the *Do Not Disturb* sign hanging on the outside knob. His hands were shaking. *Calm down,* he told himself.

Though it was the middle of the day, the motel room was pitch-dark, save for the glowing numbers on the push-button phone. Simon threw the key down on the dresser, turned on a lamp, and sat down on the thin, floral chintz bedspread. His heart was thumping like a rabbit in his chest. How had he even managed to walk home?

Simon had chosen the Governor Higgins Motel because it was in town, near the shops and walking distance to the beach, and because it was cheap, at least relatively speaking. Here it was the beginning of May and they were still offering off-season rates. Of course "cheap" meant being awakened in the middle of the night by headlights from cars barreling up Main Street. It meant smelly soap and towels that were too small to make it all the way around his waist.

Simon laid his head down on the hotel pillow. It smelled like potato chips. He closed his eyes and saw the kid again. It *had* been him. There'd been no mistake. He'd heard the woman call him by name, "Noel." How many Noels could there be in this town? And even if she hadn't used his name, it was so obvious. He had the Beadle family nose, long and narrow, and freckles under his blue eyes, just like Iris. And the kid had recognized Simon. He knew that much. He'd responded to Simon's voice. But how could a kid who'd been just six remember the voice of someone he hadn't seen in over fifteen years? Then again, this was no regular kid. Just how much did he remember about his uncle Simon? That his breath always smelled like booze? Did he remember the time Simon broke into Iris's apartment one night after he couldn't find the car keys in his pocket, passed out on the floor, and slept through the night in a puddle of his own pee? Did he remember the last card Simon had sent to his nephew for his ninth birthday, *Happy Birthday* scrawled on the back of a bar napkin with a twenty taped to it, or how it had arrived a week late? Would Noel say anything to Cooper or Shimmy about whom he'd seen at the beach? *Could* he, even? Hell, Simon didn't even know if the boy could talk. And what about the blonde who'd been with him? She looked familiar.

Simon got up off the bed and went to the dresser in search of the newspaper clipping from the police station in Miami. He found the crumpled paper in the drawer and pressed it flat on top of the dresser, held it down with his palm, and examined the photo. Rose Nowak. That was her name. She was the one who'd written the story. Simon owed her a debt of gratitude. It if weren't for Rose Nowak, he might not even be here. Still, Simon hadn't missed the way she looked at him, like she thought he was some kind of predator. So much for his warm welcome home.

Three days ago when he arrived, things hadn't gone much better. Simon had rolled into town in a rented economy-size car, short on legroom, so that after his 1,570-mile trip from Florida with his knees jammed up against the steering wheel, he got out at the gas station and crumpled to the ground, realizing too late that his left leg had fallen asleep. On the other side of the self-service pump, an old woman saw what happened. She bent down presumably to make sure he was all right. Then she seemed to recognize him. She squinted, cocked her head and sniffed, then shook her head in disgust.

"*You* again," she said. Then she got in her car, slammed the door, and drove off.

Little had changed about the place. The trees were bigger. The street signs were nicer. The buildings were still there, though many of the businesses had changed. There were hordes of daffodils pressing up through the ground on the sides of the road where there used to be weeds. There was a new, modern library where the old one had stood. One of the one-way streets was now one-way in the opposite direction, so that Simon nearly ran head-on into a garbage truck before he realized his mistake.

Out of habit, he had driven straight to his old house in the center of town, across from the ball field, and had to stop himself from entering the driveway. How many nights had he made that drive on automatic pilot? He pulled over in front of the mailbox, brand new with a lobster painted on it. He couldn't believe his eyes. Whoever had lived there since had painted the house, restored the gingerbread and the shutters. They'd taken off the aluminum siding, dented from where Simon used to kick the basketball into it, and replaced it with new wood clapboard. The sagging roof of the porch had been fixed. The old tire swing had been taken down and a prettier wood one hung in its place. This wasn't how it was supposed to be. You were supposed to come home after sixteen years to find the place had fallen to ruins. Instead, Simon's earwig-infested, musty old rattrap of a house had been lovingly restored. In fact, the whole block of run-down Victorians had been transformed into painted ladies, including one farther down the road, the Christies' old house, which was now a newspaper office. It didn't seem right. The improvements only served as proof that at least one American town was better off without Simon Beadle.

Well, whether they liked it or not, he was back and ready to settle down, find some steady work. As for Noel, the plan had been to learn what he could and take things slow. He'd had no intention of blowing into town and busting up the kid's world. But all that had changed now. Noel knew he was here. Simon couldn't just fall off the face of the earth again. But he couldn't very well show up on Cooper Almeida's doorstep either. She would toss him out on his ear. She and Val would think Simon had come back to cash in on Noel now that he was a famous artist. They'd think Simon had come back for the wrong reasons. Who could blame them?

Simon needed a chance to prove himself to the women and earn their trust. He wanted to do right by Noel, his only kin, and by his late sister. To do that, he needed to stay sober, this time for good. Simon closed his eyes and tried to banish the negativity that had somehow snuck past the bouncer in his brain.

In the end, all Simon knew was this: he and Noel were damaged goods. Two peas in a pod. They needed each other, even if it had taken Simon over a decade and a half to come to that realization.

Somehow, in spite of everything, Simon had managed to sleep through the night. He dreamed he was back in the Martinez household, being spoonfed by Señora Martinez her magical soup made from cured beef, pork, and vegetables—cassava, plantano, malanga—while outside the window, coconut palms clacked and scissored in the breeze.

Jesús and his wife had been gracious hosts and their Miami home had provided a warm, peaceful place where Simon could recuperate after he was released from the hospital. Señora Martinez attended to Simon, bringing him cool glasses of lemon water and applying steroid cream to the blisters on his sunburned face, and when she leaned close, Simon caught the scent of dry leaves and nutmeg on her skin.

By the third morning, Simon finally felt strong enough to begin his journey back to New England. He got up out of bed and found his clothes in the closet. Hanging above the dresser was an ornate wooden crucifix. Simon inspected it closely. Christ's face had been carved into a smooth, peaceful expression despite the blood dripping from the wound in his side and the nails protruding from his palms. Perhaps through all of his ordeal, Simon had come to understand a little more about Segundo's faith, something to do with exhibiting grace under pressure.

Jesús helped Simon secure a car rental for the trip up north. Simon tried to repay them for their kindness but they wouldn't take a penny. All Jesús asked was that Simon keep an eye out for his nephew, who he had reason to believe had lost his job and started drinking again, and was on his way to Cape Cod.

When Simon awoke from his Miami dream, he'd felt better about having seen Noel on the beach. It was destined to happen sooner or later anyhow. Simon finished brushing his teeth and caught his reflection in the narrow motel mirror. A long strip of dead skin was hanging off his face. He yanked it and let it drop into the sink, leaving a tender square of pink on his chin. At least the blisters were healing. How long before his face stopped looking like a wet paper bag? He rubbed his hand over the stubble on his scalp. In the hospital they'd shaved his head to treat the burns. Now, he decided, the short hair suited him. It was more in keeping with the new Simon. His days of hiding were over.

He stepped out into the morning sun and walked past the blue motel-room doors to the office, where he got himself a cup of coffee in a Styrofoam cup. The Styrofoam brought back the night Simon had fallen off the ship. How many Irish coffees had he had that morning? What had gotten him started in the first place? The tray of empties? When would he be able to get through a day without thinking about booze, when an empty vessel—a cup, a glass, a mug, a bottle, a vase, a bowl, a rowboat, a swimming pool—wouldn't trigger the longing for it to be filled with something from a package store.

With his coffee in hand, Simon started for the corner store, where he picked up a local newspaper for the want ads, then headed to the Point off Sea View Drive, an old haunt. He would take the sandy path through the tall grass that, when he was a kid, he used to tiptoe down, pretending it was the part in a giant's hair. He'd follow it to the top of the dune, take off his sneakers, lie back, feel the contours of the sand under his back, and watch for the faces in the clouds to tell him how he should proceed with Noel. But when he got to the place where the path opened up from woods to open sky, he saw even this had changed. A house was going up on the Point. He could hear nail guns firing and there was a Bobcat down on the beach. It didn't seem right. This had been a spot that had belonged to everyone. Now it belonged to *someone*. Simon walked up to the site, up what would be the long private driveway. It was going to be one hell of a house. Foundations always looked small before the rest of the house was framed out but this one was already enormous.

"You lost?" a voice behind him asked. The guy was wearing a black hard hat and an orange zip-up sweatshirt.

"Whose house?"

"You fall off a fish truck, pal?"

No. Just a cruise ship, Simon thought. The guy yelled something to another guy in the foundation hole. Then he turned back to Simon.

"No one knows," he continued.

"What do you mean, *no one knows.* Who signs your paycheck?" Simon asked.

"State Street Realty in Boston. What do you use that newspaper for? To wipe your ass? Might try reading it."

Simon tightened his armpit around his *Cape Gazette.* "I just got into town."

The guy squinted at Simon. "You look familiar."

He took off his hard hat. Simon recognized him straightaway. Chris Sparrow. He was a couple years younger than Simon and had beaten the crap out of him at a party once. Funny, how you don't forget a face.

"Class of '81." Simon mumbled the last digit. Then he stuffed the paper under his other arm and stretched out his hand. "Name's Beadle."

"Hell, yeah," the guy said. He smiled like maybe a bloody face splattered on beer-soaked pavement was suddenly coming back to him. "Chris Sparrow." He shook Simon's hand. Then he said, "Something different about you, though. You look . . . striped."

"You the foreman?" Simon said.

"Yep."

Chris Sparrow puffed out his orange chest. With his big schnoz, Simon thought he looked like an oriole.

"Need a hand? I'm looking for work."

"What can you do?"

"Sheetrock, framing, general carpentry, a little masonry," Simon said.

"Don't take this the wrong way, man. But are you off the sauce? If I remember right—"

"You remember right. And I'm off it."

"What the hell," Chris Sparrow said. He led Simon down into the hole.

Simon reemerged onto Sea View Drive from his detour, having forgotten all about his disappointment over the trophy house. Rather, he was elated. A job had fallen into his lap. He started Wednesday.

Up ahead, a young girl approached. She wore a backpack and her hair was pulled into loose braids. Probably a chambermaid for one of the fancy inns up the street. There were headphones coming from her ears, and something on her forehead, a smear. Hadn't Ash Wednesday come and gone? Then he saw it wasn't a smear, but writing. Was this something new the kids were doing? Stenciling their foreheads? Maybe it had something to do with a rock band, or a cult. Simon was hopelessly out of tune with what kids were into these days.

As the girl got closer, Simon tried to read the black letters without being too obvious.

"Morning," she said.

She stopped and lowered her head so he would have a better view. Simon felt a little embarrassed but there was nothing he could do now but read the words: *Nauset has a secret*. He scratched his head and looked around. Was this some kind of joke? One of those TV shows where they tuck a camera into the bushes? He looked into the rhododendron hedge to his left. When he turned back, the girl had already moved on.

"Hey," he said.

She kept right on walking. She probably couldn't hear him with the music playing in her ears.

Had it come to this? People selling body parts as billboards? What kind of nut had come up with a crazy idea like that? Crazy, but in a way, also, sort of brilliant. Simon shrugged and turned back around when he felt a sharp blow to his elbow. His coffee cup sailed to the ground and splashed the bottom of his pants. There was a kid in his face.

"Tell me you didn't do that on purpose," Simon said. He shook the now-cold coffee off his fingers. Then he recognized that parka from yesterday, and that hair, those freckles. It was Noel.

They stood eye to eye. Simon felt light-headed until he realized it was because he had stopped breathing. He sucked some cool air into his lungs. Noel cast his eyes down to his shoes.

"Noel," Simon said.

The kid kept his head down and turned it a little sideways, as if he was only willing to listen with one ear.

"Do you know who I am?" Simon asked.

"Hello, Uncle Simon," Noel said.

He looked up and stared Simon straight in the eyes, raised his hand to Simon's face and tugged at a strip of dead skin, and set it free in the breeze. Then he bent down and picked up the empty cup at Simon's feet and handed it to his uncle.

"Good-bye, Uncle Simon," Noel said. He started walking off toward town.

"Wait, Noel." Noel stopped without turning. "Don't you want to know how come I'm back? Or where I've been, or where I'm staying? We have a lot of catching up to do. I heard you're a famous artist now. I'd like to see your paintings. I really would love that. You know your mama was a good artist too." Simon had just suddenly remembered the cards Iris used to make for birthdays, anniversaries, how she used to copy the animals out of the *National Geographic* so that they looked better in pencil than in the actual photographs.

Noel turned around. There was a look of curiosity on his face, like Simon was some rare species of insect that he had never encountered, and if Noel had a stick, he might poke Simon to see what else he could do.

"I'd like to have the chance to spend a little time with you,

Noel. I'd like to make up for missing so much of your growing-up years. I want to be a part of your life from now on if that's okay with you. I could take you places. We could do stuff together. It'll be just like old times."

So much for not coming on too strong. Simon had promised himself he wouldn't mention Iris until the boy had gotten used to him, and now here he was, spewing his guts like a car-sick three-year-old. Old times. What old times? When had Simon ever done *stuff* with Noel? There was the one time Simon could think of, when Iris had left Noel with him so she could earn a few extra bucks shucking scallops. That day he took Noel to a bar with him and Noel sat on the floor and played with the sawdust in the corner while Simon drank himself into a stupor. As if he had been reading Simon's own mind, Noel started to walk.

"Where are you going? Can I call you sometime? Noel? Would that be okay?"

Noel turned around. "What is the question?" he asked.

"I said, 'Can I *call* you sometime?'"

Noel didn't reply. He just walked away. Simon was left in the middle of the sidewalk, unable to move. Across the street, he heard voices, then a door close. He turned to see where it had come from. No wonder he had literally bumped into Noel. He was right in front of Shimmy's property, the house blocked from view by a tangle of bushes. He was right near the place where Noel lived. There was the old farmhouse and set back to the right, the old green barn Cooper Almeida had turned into apartments. Some of the shutters on the main house were missing, and it was in dire need of a paint job. There was an enormous half-dead spider plant hanging from a hook on the porch and a 1970s-style brass eagle hung crooked above the entrance to the apartments. Cooper's crushed-shell driveway ran parallel to Val's, though a row of hedges ran between the properties. Simon saw Val's driveway was lined with cars, including a police cruiser.

"Hey. Wait there." It was a woman's voice. She'd appeared

from around the back of Val's house and was coming up the driveway toward the street. "I saw you talking to Noel. And I saw you on the beach yesterday. I don't mean to be rude, but I'd like to know who you are and why you seem to be following him around. What did you say to him?"

Simon was still standing on the sidewalk across the street. He considered making a run for it but there wasn't time. The woman stopped directly in front of him. She kind of looked like Jane Goodall, but hotter. A tall, hot Jane Goodall with thick blond hair pulled back in a tight ponytail, only she had missed a strand in the back entirely so that she seemed to Simon a tall, hot, messy Jane Goodall, which by his estimate was a good thing. Except that her being Jane Goodall, and his having been observed by her, seemed to relegate him somehow to the kingdom of the chimp. She put her hands on her hips and waited for Simon to say something. Only then did he notice her eyes. They were the kind of eye color you couldn't pin down, a little green right now, but if the sun passed beneath a cloud, all that could change. They were the kind of eyes that could get a man in a heap of trouble when asked by a third party "what color are her eyes" and then unable to think of any one way to answer the question. They were mood-ring eyes, in this case, green, which said to Simon that she wasn't quite at ease but she wasn't afraid of him either.

She bunched up the sleeves of her brown cardigan to her elbows. Simon figured he'd better say something quick or she might hit him. "I used to live here," he said. "I knew Noel years ago." *Oh, what the hell,* he thought. "I'm his uncle."

"The drunk?" She pressed her hand to her mouth. "I can't believe I said that. I'm sorry. It's just—"

"Guess my reputation precedes me." Simon winked to let her know it was okay.

"I'm sorry. It's just that I heard you left town years ago. People thought you might be dead." She stuck out her hand. "I'm Rose Nowak. I'm renting the Shimilitis cottage."

"Simon Beadle." He shook her hand. "And I did leave, years ago, but now I'm back." He shuffled his feet, opening his palms and stepping forward as if to say *ta-da*.

Rose Nowak didn't laugh. "Did Noel recognize you?"

"I think so."

"What makes you think so?" she asked.

"He said, 'Hello, Uncle Simon.'"

Rose Nowak folded her arms and squinted at Simon, the same reaction he got from women in bars whenever he tried to talk to them. "That's impossible," she said. "He only speaks . . . he only says *certain* things."

"He also said, 'Good-bye, Uncle Simon.'"

"You need to come with me." She stepped off the curb and headed across the street toward Val's. She motioned for Simon to follow. He obeyed.

"And then he said, 'What's the question?'" Simon said. "I didn't know what he meant."

She turned around in the middle of the street. "What was that?" she said.

"The last thing he said before he took off. I asked him if I could call him sometime and he said, 'What's the question?' I repeated what I had said but then he just kept going. I thought that was kind of strange."

A car was coming. Rose and Simon jogged to the sidewalk. Rose stopped. She snapped her fingers like she was trying to remember something. Then she clapped her hands and pointed to Simon like she was guessing at charades.

"Gertrude Stein!" she said.

Simon knew he didn't look his best but to be compared to Gertrude Stein was truly a blow, particularly coming from a hot Jane Goodall. Maybe he'd heard her wrong.

"Come again?" he said.

"It was the last thing she said before she died."

"What was?"

"'What's the question?'" Rose said.

"What was the last thing she said before—"

Rose shook her head.

Simon was lost.

"No, no. 'What's the question?' Those were Gertrude Stein's last words. First she asked, 'What's the answer?' When no one answered, she said, 'In that case, what's the question?' And then she died, according to her lover. I guess people thought it was kind of profound."

Simon scratched at a scab on his scalp. "Was it?"

"Was it *what*?"

"Profound."

She cocked her head and looked at Simon like she was scanning his retinas, hunting for gray matter.

"I don't know," she said. She seemed to be thinking. Then it was like she shook it off. "You must think I'm crazy. The thing is, Noel only speaks in *lasts*. It's complicated. Once you're around him for a while, you get used to it. He sort of uses the same facts and phrases over and over. But sometimes he'll come up with one that's totally new, and then Val and I have to try to retrace his steps to figure out where it came from. Val usually gets them. She's been doing it a long time."

"But why would he do a thing like that?" Who had ever heard of such a thing? The article hadn't mentioned anything about speaking in *lasts*. "How does anyone know what he wants?" Simon asked.

"Like I said, it's complicated. Anyhow, that's why I know you're full of it when you tell me he said, 'Hello, Uncle Simon.' Come on," she said.

They were in front of Val's house, in front of the thicket of locust trees and pricker bushes.

"Where are we going?" Simon said. Who did this woman think she was? And why was it that Simon seemed so amenable to following her? "But he *did* say it." She started for the driveway again. Simon chased after her like a kid in a playground. "He *did*," Simon said. "Why would I make it up?"

They stopped at the top of the driveway. She turned and looked into Simon's face. (Her eyes had softened to a shade of blue. Kettle-pond blue.)

"Everything all right out there?" A guy's voice came from a window of Val's house.

"I'm fine, Mike," Rose called out. "I'll be back in a minute."

"Who's that?" Simon said.

"Mike Eldridge." Rose said. "With an *i*."

"With an *i*?"

"They're wrapping up a Tri-centennial meeting at Val's house. Cooper's there too. I was going to bring you inside but—"

"Went to school with a Mike Eldridge." Simon rubbed the back of his neck. Seemed like everyone had stuck around here but him.

"He's a cop," Rose said.

"I'll be damned," he said. "Must not be the same Mike Eldridge." The Mike Eldridge Simon remembered wouldn't have been cop material. "You said *Tri-centennial* meeting? What's that about?"

"The town's three hundredth birthday party," Rose said.

Three hundred years. This was one hell of an old town, Simon thought. His family went way back here too, probably all the way to the beginning if the stories Simon's father used to tell were true. According to him, Simon's great-great-great-great-grandfather had come on a boat from England.

"At least it started out that way, but then Mike and Zadie Nickerson—he's the selectman—started arguing about the house going up on the Point."

Simon thought better of mentioning that this was his new place of employment, at least until he found out which side Rose was on. She sat down on the curb behind the brush so that people in the house couldn't see them. Simon sat down next to her. Not too close. He was still a little afraid of her.

"So you mean to tell me Noel really did speak to you without using lasts?"

"Cross my heart."

Rose shook her head. "That's remarkable. We didn't think he could do it."

Simon tried to fight back the feeling of pride. He didn't want to appear to gloat. Less than five minutes with the boy and already he was working miracles. He had done the right thing, coming back. He knew it now. "Are you sure you want to tell Val and Cooper I'm here right away?" he asked.

"Why not?"

Simon crushed a clump of dried dirt with the toe of his secondhand sneakers. "It's been a long time," he said. "But if memory serves me right, Cooper is a bit of a hothead."

Rose Nowak seemed to think. Then she said, "Maybe you're right. Maybe I can sort of feel them out first. Where are you staying?"

"At the Governor Higgins."

"Okay. In the meantime, I'd appreciate it if you'd steer clear of Noel, just until I can see how he's handling all this."

"Is he really as good an artist as everyone says he is?"

Rose's eyes (hazel) snapped up to meet Simon's. Her look was hard, suspicious, then it softened. "He is."

A breeze picked up and Rose must have felt the stray hairs against her neck because she pulled out the elastic and redid her ponytail. Her hair was a pretty color. Sort of like wet sand. "If you don't mind my asking, why did you come back *now*?" Simon noticed when she spoke, the tip of her nose moved. Simon had had a crush on an elementary school librarian with a nose that did that too. Like it was on a little string.

"Never should have left in the first place," he said. "But I went through some stuff that made me realize that. And I saw the article about Noel."

"You did, really?" Rose seemed tickled. "Where did you read it?"

"Florida."

"Florida." She took a deep breath and seemed to hold it for a while. "Isn't that something?"

"It was a great article," Simon complimented. "The writing was very good." As if he had even paid the slightest attention to the writing or was in any way qualified to judge.

She smiled. She had the kind of smile that made you want to smile with her. "Have you quit drinking?"

Simon stopped smiling. "I have." Three weeks, three days, seven hours.

She seemed to be deciding whether or not she believed him. "Have you been in a fire or something?"

Simon had almost forgotten about the burns. He brought his hand up to his face, rubbed his chin, watched the flakes of dead skin drift to the gutter.

"I'm sorry. It's none of my business." Rose looked down at her feet. Simon was fast realizing she could ask him anything and he'd probably tell her.

"It was a boating accident," Simon said.

"Really? That's terrible."

"I'm just grateful to be alive." And he meant that last part, maybe even a little more now, for knowing Rose Nowak.

CHAPTER SEVEN

For most stains . . . there is a solution. If your
stain persists contact a professional.
—*from the Wear-Dated Carpet Stain Removal Guide*

Calvin kept a toothbrush and a plastic razor in a glass on the sink in the bathroom of the *Oracle* office, and an inflatable mattress in the hall closet, just in case there was a need for him to pull an all-nighter, though as far as Rose could tell, no news for a weekly paper on the Cape ever warranted round-the-clock reporting. If red tide was contaminating the shellfish beds in the harbor, chances are it would be around for weeks or even months. If a group of beach shacks were threatened by the sea, it might take years for the various governing bodies to decide on a course of action, decades for a nor'easter to actually come and snatch one off the sand. The *Oracle* stayed away from accidents, robberies, and domestic violence, stories that ran in the dailies and would be old news by the time Calvin's paper hit the stands on Friday.

Calvin's background was a bit of a mystery. Back in the eighties, he'd worked as an administrative assistant for an attorney in town. Then he'd undergone a transformation—that's what he called it—which Rose took to mean a kind of mind shift or epiphany over what he wanted to do with his life, a moment of clarity like the one that had come to Rose, only later in life and as a direct result of her having been cheated on. Calvin took his life savings, bought a few PCs and some printing equipment, hung up his shingle, and he was in business. *Founded in 1992* it said on the newspaper masthead.

But a lot had changed since 1992. Thanks to the Internet, the newspaper business was a dying industry. Even so, Calvin's numbers were up. He seemed to have carved out an audience of like-minded locals and summer tourists who flocked to the newsstands for something easy to read on a windy beach. (Laptops and sand don't mix.) The *Oracle,* in its compact tabloid format with splashy four-color front-page photo, made it the paper of choice.

The Tri-centennial lent itself to Calvin's brand of in-depth reporting, where, over the course of months, he could dig in and talk to people, drawing out stories about their ancestors and providing background on the history of the town. Circulation had picked up even further in recent weeks. The town's biggest bank had stepped up and bought six months' worth of back-page advertising. Rose liked to think some of it was her doing. Calvin said fate had brought her to him. Her story on Noel was the first ever to be picked up by the newswires. She'd helped put him on the map. There were now five of them on staff, including Rose and Calvin, his girlfriend, Mona, who was from Taos, and two recently hired interns from Cape Cod Community College.

Since the story on Noel, Rose had written others too, about the guy in the cowboy hat and Truman Capote glasses who manned the booth at the town dump (Mike Eldredge with an *e*) who made planters out of old automobile tires in his spare time and sold them in his front yard, much to the chagrin of his neighbors, who only put up with it because Mike was independently wealthy and gave every cent of the proceeds to charity. Rose had written a story about a woman who, for decades, placed anonymous personal ads from her cat, Truman, in the *Cape Gazette,* as a way of poking fun at local politicians. She'd written reviews for a couple of amateur theater productions and eateries, and a story about a band called Tilt & Grind that had been playing the same songs at the same local bar for over thirty years.

Calvin also sent Rose to the library and the historical society for nuggets that would bring the history of the town to life. There, she learned some interesting things. Like she was amazed to discover that most of the Cape had been entirely deforested just a hundred and fifty years back. They ran a pictorial of "then and now" photographs, including shots of the grand buildings that had once lined the streets of Nauset's town center that had either burned down or been demolished in the name of progress. (Upon seeing these pictures of how Main Street once looked, eighty-nine-year-old Johnny Newcomb went on a hunger strike and called for the razing of everything that had been built post-1950 on Main Street. He got some of his neighbors at Senior Housing to join in and pretty soon the local Meals-on-Wheels group had to call in the authorities over the number of untouched trays for fear that a generation of locals were starving themselves.)

But the big story, the one most everyone from around here knew, was how Nauset had actually been attacked by the British during the War of 1812. A squadron of British ships had been sent to block trade in and out of Boston Harbor. With their ports controlled and no access to food and supplies, all of the Cape felt the squeeze. Meanwhile, Nauset had earned a particularly bad reputation with the British, first for refusing to pay a thousand-dollar ransom in exchange for protection of the town's saltworks and then for serving as a haven for ships attempting to run the blockade. On December 19, 1814, the frigate *Newcastle* sent four barges to attack Nauset Harbor. They managed to set fire to the pier and the saltworks. But the locals fought back. They fired their weapons from behind trees and stood their ground even while enemy shells were falling around them. They even managed to kill one British marine, prompting the British to take leave. It was a proud moment in Nauset history that still captures the spirit of the locals, which is why, every few years, the town of Nauset celebrates the event in the form of a lavish reenactment. Generations of local families have taken part in the pageantry, with the lead role going to a "British marine" who takes one to the chest and tumbles into the drink amid an uproar of applause.

"Hey, boss," Rose said.

Calvin looked up from his computer. He was wearing his reading glasses up on his head. The office smelled like cream-of-chicken Cup-a-Soup. "Morning, Rose," he said.

"There's a Tri-centennial meeting at Val's this morning. Think it's worth sitting in on?" She eased into the creaky director's chair across from his desk.

"Who's going to be there?"

"The town administrator and his wife, Val, Cooper, Eldridge the cop."

"Doubt they'll get much done," he said.

"Why's that?" Rose pulled the pencil from behind her ear and opened her notepad.

"Yesterday, the selectmen granted permission for an extension of the seawall at the Point. For some reason, Nickerson's been issuing permits out there like they're beach stickers."

"Why?" She started writing.

"Wish I knew. It's not like him. Means more dredging at the site, disruption of the shellfish beds, plus people are afraid it's going to look ugly. It'll be in the *Gazette* tomorrow. Meanwhile, Eldridge is one of the most vocal opponents of the project, even though he's a cop and not supposed to have an opinion."

"Maybe I should sit in and see what happens," Rose said.

"It's worth a try. But Nickerson's been pretty tight-lipped." He reached for his mug filled with thick yellow sludge. "Oh, by the way," he said. "Some guy called here looking for you. I took the message." He set the mug down and tore a pink slip of paper from a "While You Were Out" message pad. "Martin Blevins." He handed her the message.

"What did he say?" Rose asked. She feared she'd turned the color of his soup.

"He said he'd try again later. Everything okay?"

"Just an old beau," she said. She tucked the pink slip into her notepad.

"Probably just wanting a piece of the action now that you're *famous*," he said. Calvin smiled. "Make him suffer." He winked.

That was the thing about Calvin. Rose barely knew him, and yet they talked like old girlfriends. He always knew what to say.

It was 10:16. Cooper pulled the shredded toothpick from between her teeth. "Let's get this show on the road," she said. "Only four weeks left and I feel like we've been sitting here for one of 'em."

"Patience, dear," said Clara McGregor, the only one in the room who was older than Cooper and could thereby get away with calling her "dear." Minutes earlier, Rose had been introduced to the high school drama teacher, who, she had the feeling, would be in her element this morning. Tension was crackling in the air. Until Cooper broke the silence, the only sound in the room had been the steady whistle from one of Zadie Nickerson's nostrils.

"We can't very well start without Dorie," Zadie said. He wiped the corners of his mouth with a napkin and set his grease-stained paper plate down on the coffee table.

"Why not?" Cooper said.

"Zadie likes us to think he's fearless but his wife really runs the show," Val whispered to Rose.

"I heard that, Val," Zadie said.

Val shrugged.

Zadie was thin, fair-skinned, and had a full head of blazing white hair. He was somewhere in his early sixties and had spent a lot of time in the Cape Cod sun, as evidenced by the amoeba-like blotches on his forehead and the spongy flesh on his cheeks. He wore an American-flag enamel pin on the lapel of his blue blazer.

Rose counted seven more nose whistles and couldn't stand it anymore. "Is it true your ancestors came over on the *Mayflower*?" she asked Zadie.

Cooper rolled her eyes. Zadie sat taller in his chair. "Why, yes it is. Ebediah Nickerson. He was a farmer and traded with the—"

There came a knock on the door.

"I'll get it," Cooper said. When she saw who it was, she let go of the knob and let her hand drop to her side.

"Just Eldridge," she said. "With an *i*."

"Morning, Mrs. Almeida," Mike said. He looked down at his shoes like a schoolkid. Cooper had the power to reduce even the toughest law enforcers to putty. She seemed to relish it.

Mike was wearing civilian clothes, if one could call them that. Camouflage pants and a military-issue T-shirt, tight around his impressive biceps. His body type was the opposite of Martin's, who was impossibly lean and long-limbed, and whose friends had nicknamed him "*Lean* Martin" because of his build and because he liked to croon when he had a few, which suddenly made Rose wonder whether he had crooned to the girl he'd had sex with that night. And now here Martin was calling, leaving messages all over town. Rose looked down. Her fists were white knots.

"Mike, come in. Glad you could make it," Val said. She was wearing lipstick again. Mike Eldridge clearly had a way with the ladies. "Help yourself to some food."

The table was set up again just like the day before. Mismatched chairs had been gathered from around the house, set up in a circle in the living room. Val had vacuumed the carpet for the occasion. There were fresh stripes in the pile.

Mike went straight for the table, filled his plate, and took the empty seat beside Rose.

"We're waiting for Dorie," Val said. "But we can at least start talking about the Jimmy Fund booth. Nauset Printers is making up a sign. I've ordered a hundred cans and five hundred brochures. Think that's enough?"

No one said anything. Mike chewed. Cooper rolled her eyes. Zadie's nose whistled and this time he must have heard it. He sniffed and checked his watch. Val must have hit them up for money one time too many. No one seemed enthusiastic about her fund-raising efforts.

Val was unphased. "I was hoping I could get a good location, nothing too close to the road. I'd like to be near the food concessions so people already have their wallets out."

"Sure, Val. That makes sense," Zadie said. There was a gentleness to his voice.

"Have you heard from Eve?" Rose asked. All heads snapped in her direction. "About the car, I mean."

Val smiled, almost triumphantly. She opened her mouth to speak.

"Here she comes," Cooper said. "Finally." Cooper flew up and opened the door.

Val looked at Rose and mouthed behind her hand, "Timing belt."

On a new car? It didn't make sense. Besides, yesterday she had said it was the brakes. Rose was starting to wonder whether the daughter was just making excuses. Before her mother's illness, Rose had become an expert at it herself. But Val didn't seem the overbearing type. So what was keeping Eve away?

An attractive woman in her sixties sauntered through the doorway. She had wide-set brown eyes and a pucker of wrinkles around her mouth, her lips held tight as if about to utter the words *what* or *why* or *would you?* Her short hair was done up in that beauty-parlor way that created a cloud of blonde. She had well-manicured pink fingernails that stood out against her dark tan skin. She was long-waisted and heavy in the hips but hid it well beneath tailored black slacks and a Burberry raincoat, open to show off the signature white, tan, and black tartan lining. Rose recognized the woman from Noel's painting, only she looked better in person, as was to be expected. .

Cooper didn't see the man who was following behind, and nearly closed the door in his face. He was short and slightly pudgy, soft around the edges, and dressed in black from head to toe, presumably to hide the fact. He wore a black button-down shirt, black jacket, black shoes (*expensive* black shoes), skinny black tie, and a rather bad rug. His complexion was pale and his face was broad, emphasized further by the tiny rectangular glasses on his nose.

"Sorry I'm late, everyone. This is Milo Vanderloos. He's an art collector." She pronounced it "Mee-lo."

Milo nodded at the group, with an expression as though he'd just bitten into a pickle.

"Morning, Milo," Zadie said.

"New coat?" Cooper said. She felt the fabric of Dorie's plaid cuff. "I've seen these around only usually just on rich tourists."

Dorie's face reddened. "This old thing? I've had it for ages." She gave Cooper the evil eye and turned down the cuffs. "Anyway, Milo is here because he has a wonderful idea for the Tricentennial. Isn't that right, Milo?"

Milo ignored Dorie and the rest of the group. He walked directly up to one of Noel's paintings on the wall.

"I know that guy from somewhere," Mike whispered to Rose. .

Milo studied the painting of the old man to the left of the picture window. Rose imagined it must be exciting for an art collector to encounter such talent. Dorie peered over his shoulder, practically resting her chin on Milo's lapel. Rose looked over at Zadie, who didn't seem at all bothered by it.

"Isn't that one something, Milo?" she said.

"Malcolm Mayo. Owned the cranberry bogs north of here till he sold out to land developers," Zadie said.

"Been dead three years now. So are the cranberries," Cooper said. "Can we get on with things? We're behind as it is." She glared at Dorie.

"Dorie, this is Rose Nowak," Val said. "She's covering the Tricentennial for the *Oracle*. She wrote the article about Noel."

Dorie turned. "Good to meet you, dear."

"Just remarkable," Milo said.

For a split second, Rose thought he was talking about her story. But no one else had made that mistake. Their eyes had turned to the subject of Milo's admiration. Noel's painting. Rose looked at Val's face. It was filled with pride. Even Cooper's eyes seemed to glisten a little.

"Milo wants to bring all of Noel's works together for a one-man show at the town hall. He's generously offered to lend his creativity in helping us determine how the works should be displayed. He thinks the show might even draw some out-of-towners. We could charge admission, maybe raise some money for the boy's trust," Zadie said.

Maybe living in the city all those years had jaded Rose some, but she thought it wouldn't hurt to at least check out Milo Vanderloos before they trusted him with Noel's work. "Are you affiliated with a particular art organization, Mr. Vanderloos?" Rose asked.

"Francesca Wentworth," Dorie said, like it was the name she always wished she'd had. "It's a famous gallery in New York City, dear."

Rose wrote it down in the margin of her notes.

"Good idea. All in agreement say aye. *Aye.* Done. Now, Mrs. Town Administrator, would you please take your place beside your *husband*," Cooper said.

Dorie plopped down next to Zadie, her back to the window.

"And let's get going," Cooper continued. "We've got the reenactment and a budget to go over . . ."

Milo had moved on to the painting of Val in the corner by the fireplace. Val and Cooper ignored him, as though they'd already written him off as the kind of artsy kook people had to tolerate as part of the price of living where they did. Rose, on the other hand, wanted to know what he was thinking. Had he seen savant work before? Did he consider it "real" art or "outsider art"? He must consider it important or he wouldn't be there.

"I swear I know him from somewhere," Mike said. "Think there are Vanderloos in Chatham."

"Milo used to vacation there as a boy," Dorie whispered. She made the money sign by rubbing her fingers together.

Zadie elbowed her.

Mike sat with his legs apart so that everyone in the room, willingly or not, was drawn into the vortex of his crotch. His thigh was resting against Rose's. She thought of Martin, who used to sit with his legs crossed like Jack Benny.

"Let's talk about the reenactment," Zadie said. "Where should we have it?"

"On the Point. Where else?" Cooper said.

"It's a mess, with all the construction going on," Zadie said.

"No thanks to you," Cooper said. *Here we go,* Rose thought. "The invasion happened on the Point and that's where the reenactment should take place, mess or no mess. Isn't that right, Clara?"

It was Clara McGregor and her high school troupe who were in charge of the performance.

"I should hope so, though I have a student whose father works on the site. He said they keep digging things up, pieces of metal, bottles. Last week, the boy brought in a compass, probably off a boat," Clara said.

"See? This is *exactly* why I don't think it's a good idea," Mike said. "Poses a health risk."

"A health risk?" Cooper said. "Since when is a compass a health risk?"

"There's all the equipment and the debris, all the sand that's been moved around. It might collapse," Mike said.

"The sand might collapse?" Val said.

"Like a sinkhole. With all those people out there. Remember the kid a few years back who dug a hole too deep in the sand and got crushed? It could be dangerous," Mike said.

"That's crap," Cooper said. "Just get them to stop digging that day and clear everything out. The whole reason we chose June fourth is so the tide would be right. There won't be a problem."

"There is something to be said for tradition. I'm not even sure there's another place in town where we could do it," Clara McGregor said. "Of course, if you really think people would be in danger—"

Rose watched Milo as he moved on to the portrait of Dorie. "My *God*," he said.

Cooper snapped her head around. "Could you stop doing that, please? We're trying to have a meeting here."

"What is it?" Dorie asked. She shot up to Milo's side, as if she just realized she'd been neglecting him. Then she gasped.

Cooper snickered.

"Didn't you know Noel painted your portrait? We must've forgotten to tell you," Val said.

"None of us escaped. Why should you?" Cooper said. "You ought to see the one he did of me. I look like a troll."

Rose had an idea what everyone in the room was thinking at that moment but no one had the courage to say it.

"Let's have a look," Zadie said.

He got up and stood beside Milo. He slipped on his glasses and looked at the portrait, then to the real Dorie. "You don't look well, dear."

Rose wasn't sure if he meant in the painting or in real life.

"When did he do this?" Dorie asked.

"About a month ago. Isn't that right, Cooper?" Val said.

"'Bout that," Cooper said. She folded her arms in front of her.

"Remarkable how he captures the tension on the face and mirrors it here in the purse. And his use of pink, so disarming. Very important piece," Milo said. Rose had thought so too.

"Like hell it is," Dorie said. Her fists were clenched. "I never even posed for it."

"All the more remarkable," Milo said. That he could manage such a likeness from memory. But then, Noel's capacity for memorizing things was beyond remarkable.

"How come no one told us he did this? We'd love to have this portrait in our home, wouldn't we, dear?" Zadie asked.

"Meeelo, how much you think it's worth?" Cooper said.

He rubbed the stubble on his rounded chin. "Hard to say," he said. "Thousands. Maybe *ten*."

Mike whistled.

"No, we don't want it in our house," Dorie said to Zadie. She took her seat beside Zadie. She flattened her palm and pressed on her husband's thigh, a signal that the discussion had ended. "And it's not going into the show either. Now where were we? The reenactment."

"Nonsense," Milo said. "This one *must* be in the show."

"We'll discuss it later, Milo," Dorie said. Her voice was arctic.

"Lotsa luck, Milo," Zadie said. He shook his head.

"Another thing to consider about having it at the Point . . . the fact that it's being developed. People are angry. When people get angry, bad things happen," Mike said. He looked at Zadie. It almost sounded like a threat. But then he quickly softened it. "Might pose a security threat."

Cooper kicked the leg of her chair. Mike cringed a little. "A health risk. A security threat. That's the place where the Brits landed and that's where the reenactment has taken place for the last two hundred years. We just need the rich bastard who's building the house to give us permission, which, as far as I'm concerned, is the *least* he can do," Cooper said.

Zadie flinched.

Dorie cringed.

"Now, now. No need to be calling people names," Zadie said.

"Oh yeah? I'll call him worse once I find out who he is. And don't even start with me, mister. This whole thing is your fault. *You're* the one who ushered all the paperwork through without batting an eyelash, before anyone had a chance to do anything about it. And now this monster of a seawall. What about 'preserving our fragile coastline'? If I recall, that was part of your campaign speech," Cooper said.

"You're overreacting," Zadie said.

"What about the revetment wall? All that dredging at the shoreline?" Mike said. "Where do you draw the line? You think money's gonna hold back Mother Nature?"

Mike's ears were crimson. Rose looked over at Val and she was staring at Mike, clenching the neck of her sweater in her fist, obviously flustered by this surge of testosterone.

"Now, Mike, Cooper. Let's all just calm down," said Clara.

Dorie took Zadie's hand and gave it a squeeze.

Mike apparently wasn't about to mind the schoolteacher. "What about the damage down the beach? You think it's fair to the people on the southern shore?"

Zadie remained calm. "You don't know what you're talking about. The builder hired engineers. They spent weeks out there and concluded nothing down the beach would be compromised," Zadie said.

"And since when did you become such an activist, Mike?" Dorie asked. "I was just wondering since I never once saw you set foot in a conservation hearing until this project came along."

He did seem impassioned. Maybe that was just his personality. Maybe he was just a passionate cop.

"Do I need a reason? You get older, your priorities change," he said "This isn't about me. It's about the Point," Mike said. "It's about doing the right thing." He thrust out his chest a little. Rose felt his thigh press harder into hers. What confidence, she thought. What swagger, to further expose one's greatest point of vulnerability in the midst of a heated debate as if to challenge everyone in the room. *Go on. Just try to mess with my manhood.* Rose crossed her legs.

"He has a point, Zadie. You did let the ball drop on this one," Val said.

"I suspect it's even worse than that," Cooper said.

"What's that supposed to mean?" Zadie said. He took off his reading glasses and tucked them inside his jacket pocket.

"I'll give you a hint. Word starts with a *k*," Cooper said. Her eyes narrowed.

"Cooper!" Dorie slapped her palms on her thighs.

"It's okay," Zadie said to his wife. "Let it go."

Rose was still trying to think of a bad word that began with *k*.

"How dare you even imply—?" Dorie stood up.

Rose got it. *Kickback.*

"You with your *designer raincoat.* Never have been the brightest bulb, Dorie. If I were you I'd shut my piehole," Cooper said.

Cooper had the bully market cornered. Wait until Calvin got a load of this. Rose looked up at Milo and even he seemed amused.

Mike raised his hand. "I vote we move the reenactment down the shore and closer to the harbor. Just makes sense. Plus you'll never get permission to have it at the Point. There are liability issues for the homeowner," he said.

"The homeowner isn't liable for what goes on below the high-tide mark," Val said. "That's where we'd be. Technically, we don't even need permission."

Rose looked at Zadie. She thought if she were him, on a town administrator's salary, she'd tell them all where to go. But he seemed to be an extraordinarily patient man. Either that or Cooper's accusations were warranted.

"I bet Zadie could get the mystery homeowner to cooperate, couldn't you, Zadie? By the way, did you know a town official accepting bribes is a felony?" Cooper said. She tried to stare him down.

Zadie looked away. "I doubt he'd—" Zadie said.

"So you *have* met him. And it's a *him*. Is it someone famous? Is it a movie star? Why doesn't he want anyone to know who he is?" Val asked.

"Some folks are just like that," Zadie said.

"Well who is he?" Mike asked.

"I'm not at liberty to say," Zadie said.

"Let's go," Dorie said. She stood up. Zadie tugged on her arm and she sat back down.

"But I might be able to get him to cooperate. Perhaps it'd make his life easier in the long run," Zadie said.

"But—" Mike started.

"But *nothing*. The reenactment will take place on the Point. Get back to us on it, Nickerson. What's next?" Cooper asked.

Clara McGregor took a handkerchief out of her dress pocket and wiped her pink forehead.

Rose looked beyond Cooper to the window facing the street. Noel was on the sidewalk talking to someone.

"Has anyone seen those people walking around with words on their foreheads?" Val asked.

"I have," Mike said.

"What words?" Rose asked.

"They say 'Nauset has a secret.' Wonder what it means and who put them up to it?" Mike said.

Zadie leaned back in his chair and grinned. He stuck his thumbs in the waistband of his pants. Dorie wasn't paying attention. She was looking over her shoulder at Milo, who wouldn't stop staring at her portrait. Rose could see it was driving her nuts.

"I see that smirk on your face. Spill it," Cooper said.

"I was getting to it. We found a time capsule," Zadie said.

"A what?" Val asked.

"The boys were digging up the foundation at the corner of the town hall for repairs and they came across a sealed-up metal box, an old one. It had a year etched into the top: 1879. A long time ago I'd read something about a time capsule that had been buried in the new foundation after the old town hall burned down. This is it. Thought the Tri-centennial would be a great day for its unveiling," Zadie said. "Anyhow, I got wind of how these people were selling body parts as billboards on the Internet and I got to thinking, why not pay some of the kids in town a few bucks to walk around with words on their forehead, drum up a little publicity, build the momentum? Clara talked to some of her kids," Zadie said. "Now, Ms. Nowak, all this is strictly off the record. We don't want to spoil the surprise."

"Sure," Rose said. "As long as you let us break the news ahead of the *Cape Gazette.*"

"One day before the Tri-centennial," he said. "Not a minute earlier."

"Deal," Rose said.

"I gotta hand it to you, Nickerson. It's brilliant," Cooper said. The room fell silent. Rose assumed no one was used to Cooper doling out compliments. "What better way to distract people from the shady business going down at the Point? Just throw them a new mystery, a red herring."

"Oh, for heaven's sake," Dorie said.

Here we go again, Rose thought.

She leaned left to get a better look at who Noel was talking to and accidentally brushed Mike's shoulder. He pressed his thigh into hers even harder than before. She shot up to escape and get a better look out the window. It was the man they'd seen on the beach the day before. Noel was walking away.

"I'll be right back," Rose said. "Need to call the office."

"Certainly, dear," Val said.

"Remember our deal," Zadie said. He put a finger to his lips.

"Sure, don't worry," Rose said. She hurried through the kitchen and out the back door. She wanted to get there before the guy got away.

Nauset had a secret all right. Simon Beadle was back. What did it mean for Noel? Would it be a good thing to have this link to his past all of a sudden just reemerge? Being family, might Simon draw Noel out somehow, maybe help the boy connect with people in a more meaningful way? How would Simon's return affect Noel's art? And all that aside, could Simon be trusted? Could any man, for that matter?

After talking to Simon on the street, Rose returned to the meeting and was nearly trampled by Zadie and Dorie, with Milo in tow, as they came busting out the front door, apparently in too much of a hurry to say good-bye.

Rose slid past them and went inside. "What happened?" she asked.

But before she could get her answer, Rose saw Cooper sitting right where she'd left her with a grin from ear to ear. On her forehead in crooked letters were the words: *Zadie's an ass*.

"Is *that* why they left?" Rose asked.

"What do you think?" she said. She seemed pleased with herself.

Val had Mike cornered by the food table. They'd both turned when Rose entered the room. Mike's shoulders dropped a little. He seemed relieved.

"Well, I guess I'll be going, ladies. Lots of work—" he started.

"But you said it's your day off," Val said. She looked crestfallen.

"You know, stuff around the house," Mike said. "Rose, can I talk to you outside for a minute?"

"Thanks for the steady hand, Mike," Cooper said. So Mike had done the writing for her.

"Sure, Mrs. Almeida."

Rose followed Mike out the front door.

"Did you write that on her forehead?" Rose asked. "What were you thinking?"

"She asked me to," he said. He shrugged. "What was I going to do?"

Rose rolled her eyes. "You just do what people ask, no matter what it is—"

"*Some* people," he said. He smiled. This was a different Mike Eldridge from the one who'd been in the room with Cooper a minute ago. "Look, Rose." He took a step closer. Rose could see Val was watching through the narrow windows alongside the door. Rose took a step back. Mike continued, "I saw you talking to that guy outside. Who was he?"

What business was it of his? "Friend of a friend," Rose said. "Not a boyfriend."

"What?" Was he about to hit on her? How long had it been since Rose had someone hit on her? She laughed. Some of it was nerves. The laughing must have thrown him off.

"I'm sorry. I know this must be strange." He rubbed the back of his fingers along his chin. "It's just that since we met yesterday, I've been thinking about you. I was just wondering if you might want to have dinner with me sometime."

Those bedroomy eyes. And he was very smooth. Good cop bad cop rolled into one. He was close enough now that Rose could smell his cologne, some kind of musk that she remembered a guy in high school wearing. Mike had probably worn it since high school too. Was this how it was for guys? See someone you think is attractive and immediately put the moves on her? Four years was a long time to be off the market. Was it just guys or were women like this nowadays too? Was this how the girl came on to Martin at the party, dripping sex, full of confidence? Maybe she'd tested the waters first, pushed her thigh into his leg just to see what he'd do. It must have been a turn-on for him, Rose had to admit. Her heart was racing a little now. She knew she should probably be savoring it more.

He nodded toward the house. "Inside, I kind of thought you were sending me a vibe, you know?" he said.

"A vibe? You mean when I got up and accidentally brushed your shoulder? You took that as a vibe?" Rose had broken the mood.

"Look, if you're not interested . . ." he said. Rose doubted he had any intention of finishing off the sentence.

Martin's girl had had better success. Now that Rose was out of the way, was she still pursuing him? Had they hooked up again? Were they seeing each other? Was it serious? Was that why he was calling, to tell Rose they were serious before one of her Boston friends did? Was that the secret reason Rose was afraid to answer his calls? Because she didn't want to hear something she didn't want to hear?

"Rose?" Mike said.

"I'm sorry. I'll be honest with you, Mike. I'm coming off a bad relationship and it's going to take me some time. But thanks. I'm flattered. Really," Rose said. Not a yes. Not a total shutdown. She'd left the door open. She'd given his ego some wiggle room.

"Hey," he said. He threw up his hands like someone being frisked. "No problem. Another time, eh?"

As soon as he said it, Rose regretted turning him down. There were things she could have learned from him. She could have found out what it was like to have casual sex with a stranger. Maybe even back-to-back sex. Rose bet Mike would have had the stamina for that.

"Sure, Mike."

"So long, Rose," he said. It was a movie-star moment as he

walked to the cruiser, got in, and reached for the sunglasses in the visor. He slid them on, taking his time starting the car. *That's right, let her see what she turned down. Give her time to wallow in regret.* Rose felt like she should be taking notes. Then he put it in reverse and backed down the driveway. No peeling out. No flying dust. Very dignified.

Rose went back inside. Val was in her face.

"What did he say?" she said.

"He just wanted to make sure I wouldn't write about Cooper's forehead. He was afraid he'd get in trouble with the police chief."

"I don't know how you get him to do what you want all the time, Cooper," Val said. She seemed frustrated and even a little sad.

"So what was that about anyway?" Rose said.

Cooper started. "Everyone was bickering about the house and the seawall and that Milo fellow disappeared and all of a sudden we heard a squeal from down the hall."

Val took over. "Dorie, Zadie, and I ran to him, thinking he might have fallen and broken something, and there he was, standing with his hands on his hips in front of Noel's painting of Iris and the goldfish and I'd had enough. 'That's it, Mr. Vanderloos. Show's over,' I said. I ushered him out of the hallway and then Dorie got angry at me for being rude to her friend, who, by the way, had just shown up uninvited and was roaming around my house, squealing and doing God knows what else, and I told her maybe she and Mr. Vanderloos should come back another time. Then we all returned to the living room to find Cooper with the words on her forehead, and that was the last straw. They left."

Cooper beamed. She was so proud of herself.

"Hope Mike didn't use a permanent marker," Rose said. She knew Val kept them in her kitchen drawer.

"Just that gray one over there," Cooper said.

"Uh, Cooper. I think you'd better try to wash that off," Rose said.

Cooper went up to the mirror by the door. She licked her thumb and rubbed at the letters. Nothing smudged. *"Filho da puta!"* she said. She tried again. Nothing. Her face turned red.

Val laughed.

"I gotta go," Cooper said. She flew out the front door.

Val laughed so hard she had to sit down. Rose was glad she wasn't sad anymore. "You don't seem too upset about the meeting falling apart," Rose said.

"They'll cool off. Happens more often than you think," Val said.

"I'll find out what I can about Milo Vanderloos," Rose said.

"I'd love for Noel to be able to have his show. He'd be so proud. You know, before the whole marker incident, Dorie had a change of heart and actually offered me *money* to take the portrait home. 'Not a chance,' I told her. 'This is not about *you,* Dorie. It's about Noel.'" Val got up from the chair. "Help me clear?"

Rose picked up an empty platter.

"Just hypothetically speaking, what if Noel's uncle ever just showed up at your door. What would you think?" Rose asked.

"Ha. That'll be the day," she said. She disappeared into the kitchen. Rose followed.

"Seriously," Rose said.

"Seriously, that's one heck of a long shot. Let's see. Given the choice between his father or his uncle, I'd guess I'd pick the uncle."

"Well, that's good to—"

"Of course, that's *not* much of a choice. I'd have some major reservations about letting Simon back into Noel's life. I'd want to know his motives, like why *now* all of a sudden, and why he hadn't been able to find it in his heart to so much as drop the kid a note in all these years."

"Well, that's understandable."

"I'd have to know he's off the booze. I'd need proof, and even then, I doubt I'd trust him to be alone with Noel. I'd want to know what he'd been doing the last fifteen years, and whether he had a record with the police."

Val let the platter in her hands drop onto the kitchen counter with a crash. She put one hand on her hip. "I'd want to know what made him think he had the right to just come waltzing back into our lives."

"Fair enough—"

"I mean, it isn't always a matter of being related by blood. It's about love and how much you're willing to sacrifice. Families come in all shapes and sizes."

"Sure, but—"

Val's eyes narrowed. Her cheeks got flushed.

"And if he ever tried to take Noel away from us, there'd be hell to pay. If he thought he could disregard all we've invested in that kid, all the sleepless nights when he was away at school, wondering if he was being treated well, if he was happy and making friends."

"Val—"

"Whether he was being teased or bullied or—"

"Val!" Rose finally shouted, just to get her to stop.

"I'm sorry, what were you asking?"

This was it. Either Rose told her or she didn't. Either she got involved and tried to help Simon Beadle, a complete stranger, or she let him fend for himself. But it was only a matter of time before word got around town, and her telling Val now might help her friend prepare herself for the reality that he was back. Val's knowing now might even help Noel. So there it was.

Rose looked up at the Howard Miller clock on the mantel.

To start clocks with a pendulum, reach through the front door of the clock and place your hand on the side of the pendulum disk. Move the pendulum to the far left of center and release. Let the clock operate a few minutes until the pendulum settles into an even swinging position.

"Simon Beadle is back."

"Beadle? You saw him?" She groped for the counter behind her.

"I saw him on the beach the other day but didn't know who he was. Noel recognized him. And that's why I left the meeting today, because I saw him outside talking to Noel. I interrogated him for a while, and I get the sense he's here for the right reasons. I don't know for sure but I'm usually a pretty good judge of people." She'd done such a stellar job with her own boyfriend, hadn't she? "I believe him."

Val let herself drop onto a kitchen stool. She fanned her face with her hands. "Wait till Cooper hears."

CHAPTER EIGHT

*Before each ride, check to make sure all latches
and quick releases are properly secured.*
—*from the Citizen Folding Bike Instruction Manual*

It was six in the morning. Simon drew back the motel curtains. The clouds looked like hair combed thin across an old man's scalp. He cranked open the windows to draw fresh air into the room. He had to be to work by seven.

Simon threw on his work clothes, a T-shirt, and a pair of old jeans. He brushed his teeth. The water tasted like old pipes. She'd woken him up and said she'd be there in five minutes. That was five minutes ago. He smoothed down the bedcovers and tucked the bedspread under the mattress. *That isn't how it's done,* he thought. It would have to be good enough.

He filled the miniature coffeepot with water from the sink and poured it into the machine. As per the instructions, he opened what looked like a powder puff and dropped it into the filter chamber, then hit the on switch.

Simon ran around the room collecting empty soda cans and cartons from last night's Chinese dinner and threw them into the trash. He stuffed whatever clothes and dirty underwear he could find into a drawer beneath the TV. He scanned the room.

Decent enough. Then he ran back into the bathroom and examined his face. Needed a shave but the skin actually looked better this morning. Still splotchy, but better.

Then came a knock on the door.

Simon looked through the peephole and there were at least twelve Roses kaleidoscoped into the broken lens.

"Coming," Simon said.

His fingers fumbled with the latch. Why was he so nervous? Finally the door swung open and there was Rose, just *one*. One was plenty.

"I'm sorry to bother you so early like this," she said.

"No bother, I was up," he said.

"I just wanted to talk to you in person before I go in to work."

"You go to work at six in the morning?"

"Six-thirty. Calvin gets there at five. It's just until this Tricentennial is over with. We're doing a special insert, which means twice the writing. Plus I sort of lost Monday to that meeting at Val's."

She was wearing a sleeveless turtleneck and a silky knee-length skirt. She smelled fresh, like soap bubbles.

"Come in," Simon said. Without thinking, Simon offered Rose a seat on the bed. She took a chair by the window.

"This is fine, thanks," she said.

"Would you like some coffee? Just the motel stuff."

"Whatever is fine."

Simon went into the bathroom and slid two paper cones into the brown plastic holders.

"She's decided to see you," Rose said.

Already? Simon thought it would have taken more days, weeks, even months of convincing. Instead, here it was only two days since he'd met Rose on the street in front of Val's. He thought that he'd have had more time to prepare. What would he say to Val?

He poured two cups, carried the plastic bag filled with packets of nondairy creamer, sugar, stirrers, and napkins in his teeth, and brought it all out to Rose. She reached up and took the plastic sleeve from his lips. Her sudden proximity made him nervous. He set her coffee down on the table beside her, spilling a little on the rug.

"Thanks," she said. She smiled.

Simon took a sip. The coffee was vinegary. It scorched his mouth.

"What made Val come around?" he asked.

"Actually, it was Noel's doing."

"I don't follow you."

"He did a painting."

Simon ran his hand through his hair. He sat down on the bed. Rose struggled to open the creamer packet. "Of what?" Simon said. "May I?" He took the packet and tore at a weak spot in the cellophane, something that had taken him days to figure out himself, then handed it back to Rose.

"Thanks," she said. "Not *what*, you."

"Noel did a painting of me?"

"Of you a long time ago."

"I thought you said he did it since Monday?" Simon scratched his head.

"He did. The painting is of what you looked like years ago. How you looked when you left."

How could Rose know what Simon looked like when he left?

"Did I know you then?"

"No." She laughed. "Don't get me wrong, you're not a bad-looking guy, but you're not exactly in your twenties."

"That's how old I look in the painting? In my twenties?"

"Your hair was longer and there was more of it, for one thing."

Simon got up from the bed and walked to the back of the

room. He was letting it all sink in. "That's something, isn't it?" he said. He was touched that his nephew would do a painting of him. Even more touched that Noel remembered him from all those years ago. He felt a welling up inside like he could cry if he let himself but of course there was no chance of that. Not with Rose in the room.

"Once Val saw that, she knew how much you meant to Noel, and how you being here could turn out to be good for him. She felt she had no right to stop the two of you from developing a relationship. Her biggest concern is that you'll hurt him. But she talked it over with her daughter, Eve, and they agreed the two of you should meet—"

"Shimmy has a daughter? I didn't know that."

"And a granddaughter too. They live up around Boston. Eve works for Dana Farber. The cancer institute."

If she'd had a kid, it was after Simon left, which would make the girl no more than sixteen or seventeen, and too young to be working at Dana Farber. Maybe Val had adopted. Or maybe it was a stepkid.

"So Val's married?"

"Actually she never got married. It's a long story."

"Guess I *have* been away awhile." Simon scratched his head. "I don't remember any daughter. Actually, I don't remember lots of things."

Rose got up from the chair. "Well, I'd better be off. I'll see you later, then? At Val's, about four-thirty? Is that too early?"

"Four-thirty's good," Simon said. "Oh, and one more thing. Has anyone mentioned anything about me to Cooper yet?"

"Val didn't think that would be a good idea."

"I imagine that's going to take some planning."

Simon arrived at the construction site and the crew was already fast at work. It had rained last night and the ground was a squishy mix of mud and sand. Three pickup trucks with oversize tires and beach stickers on the windows sat at the end of the driveway. One had a galvanized box that took up half the cab.

"First day and you're late," Chris Sparrow said. He didn't look up. He was sitting on a new stone wall with pieces of a dismantled air compressor scattered around him.

Simon looked at his watch. It was six minutes after seven. "I'm sorry. Family stuff. It won't happen again," Simon said.

"Better not," he heard Sparrow say under his breath. "Grab a gun."

Simon picked up a nail gun from the cab of one of the trucks and headed to the side of the house where some guys were already busy on ladders.

"Hey," Simon said. "Need a hand? Name's Beadle."

One guy was on the saw and the other was nailing panels to the studs. The saw guy made a cut and Simon stood there until he was done.

The guy took off his glove, raised the goggles over his head. "Joe Higgins," he said. He shook Simon's hand.

Joe Higgins looked to be in his early fifties. He was a solid, barrel-chested guy with a rod-straight back and dark hair jutting out in all directions from under his tattered Red Sox cap. Higgins was an old Cape family name. Simon had known plenty of Higginses from school and around town. One branch of the family used to run the clam shack down at the beach. Simon didn't know Joe right off but he was sure Joe knew who he was.

The other guy on the ladder didn't say anything. He just nodded. Simon noticed he had an incredibly round head.

"Those over there need to be measured," the orbed one said, pointing to a pile of wood fresh from the lumberyard.

"Didn't catch your name," Simon said.

"Didn't throw it," the guy said. Simon thought a guy with such a round head shouldn't be making ball jokes. "Daryl Cummings. We worked together a long time ago." Cummings grinned. "Think it was a job on Weeset Road."

Great. There was no escaping his past. The only way he was going to prove himself now was to keep his mouth shut and put in a hard day's work. By the time they broke for lunch, he'd measured and cut the entire pile of wood for the north side of the house and framed out three of the upper windows.

Simon joined some of the guys down in what would one day be a large bathroom.

"What kind of house needs nine bathrooms?" Simon asked.

"People who have so much shit they don't know what to do with it," Cummings said.

"Last year we did a house with two huge full baths off the master. *His* and *hers*," Chris Sparrow said.

"People are fucked up," Cummings said.

"So how does it feel to be back after all these years?" Sparrow asked.

"Town's actually nicer than when I left," Simon said. He took a bite of the ham sandwich he'd picked up the day before at the convenience store.

"Berry, toss me your chips," Sparrow said.

Daryl Cummings rifled a bag of Fritos past Simon's ear. Simon guessed the nickname had to do with the shape of his head, which was outlined in a layer of dark fuzz.

"Hey, Beadle, that your nephew who's the artist?" Berry asked.

"Yeah," Simon said.

"You better stay the hell away from him," Berry said. He took a bite of his sandwich.

Simon felt like he'd been kicked in the stomach.

"Why's that?" Higgins asked.

Berry finished chewing. Here it came. Now Simon would be humiliated again, told he was a worthless drunk. Simon braced for it. "'Cause one look at you and he'd wanna break all his paintbrushes in half. You are one ugly son of a bitch with that shit all over your face. What the hell happened? You fall asleep in front of the sunlamp?"

Simon shook his head and laughed. He looked out at the harbor, at the tide that was coming in so hard it was slanting the channel markers. Simon had the sudden urge to dive into the water and wash off the last two decades.

"My wife did that with a sunlamp once," Sparrow said.

"That explains the blisters on her lips," Berry said. "Thought they were from giving me a blow job."

A thermos whizzed by Simon's ear and Berry grabbed it out of the air.

"You. You don't even have a wife. Who the hell wants to marry a fucking Ping-Pong head," Sparrow said.

Berry raised his middle finger while he stuffed the second half of a Twinkie into his mouth.

"Actually, it's just a bad sunburn I got down in Florida," Simon said.

"That where you were living?" Higgins asked

"Most recently," Simon said.

"Why'd you come back?" he asked.

"Can't wait to leave, then they can't wait to come back," Berry said. "Hear it all the time."

"Came back for my nephew, mostly," Simon said.

"He still living at the Almeida place?" Higgins asked.

"Uh-huh," Simon said.

"Cooper know you're back?" Higgins asked.

Simon shook his head. "Uh-uh."

"Shit," Higgins said. "That ought to be some good fireworks."

Simon could already tell he liked Higgins. He seemed a straight shooter.

"Hey, I'm assuming you know most of what goes on around here. What can you tell me about Val Shimilitis's kid? I don't remember her having any kid."

"She don't," Sparrow said.

"I heard she had a daughter," Simon said.

Higgins moved the ball of food in his mouth from one cheek to the other. Berry took the opportunity to jump in. "Shimmy popped a gasket after Lino Almeida disappeared."

Lino Almeida. There was someone whose name he hadn't heard in decades. "That was more than twenty-five years ago," Simon said. So he never did come back. Simon felt a pang of sadness for old Cooper. Must've been rough for her. Simon knew there'd been something between Val and Lino before he disappeared, but they were upperclassmen and Simon had just been a freshman when they were all in school together. He'd never paid much attention.

"It all came out like ten years later," Sparrow said.

"What all came out?" Simon asked.

"I guess Val told Lino she was pregnant the night he disappeared. Who knows if it was true but some people thought that's why Lino left," Higgins said.

"No kidding," Simon said. "Didn't really know the families till years later when they got involved with helping my sister. But I don't remember any kid."

"That's because there wasn't one," Berry said. "Pay attention. She lied and tried to trap him. He got scared and bolted. Who could blame him? If someone told me I was gonna be a daddy, I'd have been on the first bus out of town too."

"Don't worry. You'll never get close enough to a girl to find out," Sparrow said.

"People who knew Lino don't think he could have done it. Some of us think something else must have happened to him. Like an accident. He'd gone out in his boat but they never found a trace of him or it," Higgins said.

"I remember that." It was coming back in bits and pieces. By the time Simon was fourteen, he was already sneaking booze out of his father's liquor cabinet, so even at that age, things were fuzzy. "So people just assumed he'd run off? How come they didn't keep searching?" Simon asked.

"Someone came forward and said they saw him after that night," Higgins said.

"At the bus station," Berry said. "It was old man Bassett."

"Cops pretty much called off the whole search after that," Sparrow said.

Higgins spit into the dirt.

"Anyway, this is the part that didn't come out until later. After Lino disappeared, Val started showing . . . six month, eight months, nine, *ten, eleven, twelve* . . ." Higgins said.

"Huh?" Simon said.

"Parents must have thought she was giving birth to a fucking elephant," Sparrow said.

"Then I guess she was walking around the house with a baby carriage and you know what was in it?" Higgins said.

"A salami," Berry said.

"*Nothing.* It was empty. She just pretended like she'd given birth to a baby girl. Her parents took her to doctors and shrinks. They tried to keep the whole made-up-kid thing quiet and did a good job for years. It wasn't until the mother died that it finally came out. No sooner was the mother in the ground than Val was out talking about her ten-year-old daughter, celebrating birthdays, showing pictures around town."

Simon had left Nauset by then.

"Creepy shit," Sparrow said.

"Where'd the pictures come from?" Simon asked.

"Magazines, I don't know," Higgins said. "Guess she's kept the damn thing up for more than twenty-five years."

"If you're gonna have a kid, might as well have one that cures cancer," Sparrow said.

"Imaginary kids are great. Don't piss their pants. Don't mess up your stuff," Berry said. "Cheap as hell."

Higgins took a huge bite of his sub to make up for all his talking.

"So she's nuts," Simon said. He felt even worse now, finding out he'd left his nephew in the charge of someone who was crazy.

"Actually," Higgins swallowed. "It's not like she's totally looped or anything. Some people think it's just a little game she plays to keep Lino alive. And she doesn't do it all the time either. Just every now and then. When she does, everyone just goes along with it."

"When you see the Jimmy Fund cans around town, that's how you know," Sparrow said.

"So *everybody* in town knows about it?" Simon asked.

"Pretty much," Sparrow said.

"They just put up with it. Doesn't hurt anyone. I guess folks figure deep down we're all a little nuts," Higgins said.

Quitting time was three-thirty. By then, the north side of the house was three-quarters of the way covered in plywood. Simon was physically spent. He hadn't done a day's work like this in years, and he was miserably out of shape. Every muscle in his body tingled with the promise of tomorrow's pain. His back was stiff and his forearms ached from holding the nail gun. He almost wished he hadn't agreed to be at Val's by four-thirty.

"Good work today, Beadle," Sparrow said.

"Thanks. Hey, been meaning to ask you. You don't know of anyone who's got an apartment to rent. Just a studio, nothing fancy. It's for a friend."

Simon had finally tracked down Segundo, who would be arriving in less than a week. Simon figured it was important to set up his friend with a place first. He could worry about where he would live later.

"There's Cooper's place," Sparrow said. He grinned.

"Yeah, right," Simon said. He took the bandanna out of his pocked and wiped the dust off his face.

"I'll ask around," Sparrow said.

• • •

"And that's how I wound up coming back," Simon said. His whole spiel had taken less than twenty minutes. He looked from Val to Rose, who gave him an encouraging smile, then back to Val again.

"I see," Val said.

Not once had she done or said anything to make Simon believe she was a nutcase. He got up and stretched his stiffening legs. He'd only had enough time to shower, throw on a clean pair of jeans and his best shirt, the Tommy Bahama he'd finally gotten back with the rest of his stuff from the cruise ship, and get over to Val's. Now he was wishing he'd thought to pop a few ibuprofen.

Simon walked over to the mantel, where the painting Noel had done of him was propped up and still drying. He'd been a handsome SOB. At least *then* he had. Simon was surprised Rose had even known whose likeness Noel was trying to capture.

Simon thought it best to give Val a few minutes to let it all digest. He'd told them both about his cruise-ship ordeal, an abridged version, at least, and focused on how, while he was out there waiting to be rescued and facing his own mortality, all he could think about was Iris and his nephew, and then when he'd finally gotten out of the hospital and was waiting for his friend's uncle to come pick him up, he'd seen Rose's article.

Val had asked Simon for some assurances that he was off the booze for good. Simon had been honest and told her he had none to give. He told them this week he would start attending AA meetings in town and how this time something inside him just felt different. But that was all he could promise. A true drunk would promise the world. The fact that he knew better than to try seemed like a first step.

Next to the window was a framed picture of a pretty young girl. Simon recognized the image from a liquor ad. Supposed to be Eve, he guessed. And here was the next challenge: telling Rose her new friend was deceiving her. He didn't look forward to that.

And yet he knew it was the right thing to do, before she had the chance to embarrass herself. People around here weren't always so forgiving.

While Simon's back was turned, Rose had come up behind him and given his shoulder a squeeze. It sent white stars firing through his body. She left her hand there.

"Well, I thank you for being so honest, Simon," Val said. "It must have taken a lot of courage to come back here and I believe you when you say you have Noel's best interests at heart. Rose told me something about Noel, about how he was able to speak to you without using lasts."

"That's true," Simon said. Her hand was still on his shoulder.

"Well, if it is true, and I'm not entirely sure I believe it, I think that's another good reason for you to have contact with the boy. I think it would be great if Noel could find other ways to express himself," Val said.

"Speaking of Noel, where is he?" Rose asked. Her hand slipped off his shoulder and she walked back toward the sofa.

"Cooper took him for chowder at the Legion Hall," Val said.

"Any thoughts on how to handle this with her?" Rose said.

"She's never been one to let go of a grudge," Val said. "I'd be careful. And if she ever does talk to you, I wouldn't bring up the thing about him not speaking in lasts. She'll never buy it."

Val had insisted on giving them dinner. Simon stuck with water, but Rose had had a little wine, which probably explained why she had agreed to walk with him. By the time they left Val's, it was close to eight o'clock. The sun had already gone down. For early May, it was atypically warm, and early enough in the season that there weren't any mosquitoes or gnats buzzing around their heads. Simon and Rose walked down the sidewalk, staring at their feet as they grew darker and then lighter with each streetlamp they passed. Simon's legs felt like lead and he had to be careful not to trip on the uneven concrete that had been pushed up by tree roots and frost heaves. He didn't know how much farther she'd walk with him. He thought about ways he might keep her at his side awhile longer.

"He *did* say it," Simon said. "You still believe me, don't you?"

"I do," she said.

Simon stopped walking and kicked at some uneven concrete. "How come?" he said.

"How come I believe you?" She laughed. Her laugh was creamy, like butter left out on a picnic table. "Still haven't figured that one out yet."

They started walking again.

"I wonder what seeing me means to him after all these years," Simon said. "I wish there was some way to know exactly what goes on inside his brain." *I wish there was some way to know what goes on inside yours too,* he thought.

"He seems to like having you around," she said.

Simon smiled. Then the smile faded. He gritted his teeth. Who was he fooling?

It was the dark voice inside Simon that said, "I don't deserve it."

"What do you mean?" Rose said.

As if it wasn't obvious. Did he have to spell it out for her? "He was just a little kid, for chrissake," Simon said. "I left him."

Rose rested her hand on his forearm. "From what I gather, you wouldn't have done him any favors sticking around."

Simon understood. "You know the worst thing about drinking is that when you finally snap out of it, you expect to be able to pick up where you left off. But it's not like that. The whole world has moved on. You arrive at the party, and it's over."

"I know how that feels," she said.

"You do?" Simon asked.

"Not in the same way," she said. A breeze came up. She moved the hair out of her eyes. "But I know what if feels like to lose years of your life."

"To an addiction?" Simon was hopeful. Perhaps they could conquer their demons together.

"To a relationship," she said.

Not the response he'd been hoping for.

They were approaching the break in the shrubs that marked the path Simon used to take to the Point, legendary in the old days as a place to bring girls or shoot back beers with the guys.

"Want to see where I work?" Simon asked.

"What do you mean?" Rose said.

"My new office," he said.

Simon took Rose by the wrist and pulled her toward the path. He could have taken her down the driveway too but this was more fun.

She stopped. "I'm not going in there," she said.

He smiled. "Where's your sense of adventure?" he said.

"It's dark," she said.

Simon could tell she was weighing whether to go off into the woods with someone she barely knew.

"It's okay, and not that dark with the moon. Grab my arm," he said. He reached for her hands and put them on his forearm. When he did, all the achiness in that limb seemed to vanish. With his other arm, he lifted a low branch and nodded for her to duck under it.

"Where does it lead?" she said.

"You'll see," he said.

She ducked and they started down the worn dirt trail. Simon could feel the roots through the soles of his tennis shoes. A breeze rustled the tops of the trees, the sound mingling with the distant waves breaking on the bar offshore. The tree canopy darkened the path. Up ahead, Simon anticipated the clearing. Soon they'd come upon the silhouette of the house bulging over the dune.

Rose stumbled. Simon caught her around the waist.

"Ouch. This better be good," she said.

"It will be," he said. "Trust me."

Simon's heart swelled with bittersweet memories of the path that hadn't changed in all these years, just as narrow and steep, generating the same fresh scent of earth and the sound of his feet crunching on dried leaves and sticks, then giving way to loose sand. The path hadn't changed, only what it led to had.

"I can hear the water," Rose said. "I can smell it."

Simon stepped on a beer can that wrapped itself around his shoe. "What the—"

He bent down to extricate the can from his insole and Rose went off ahead of him.

"It's the house! I can see this from the cottage," she said. "It's massive."

"Watch your step. There are nails and stuff," Simon said. He pried off the can and caught up to her.

"So this is *your* house?" Rose teased. "What a surprise. You should have told us, Simon. *You're* the mystery man."

"Not *the* mystery man. But a mystery, to be sure," Simon said. "Even to me."

Rose, who had been walking toward the house, suddenly stopped and looked back at him. "You're less of a mystery than you were that first day."

Simon didn't know if that was a good thing or a bad thing.

"Let's go this way," he said. He led her around the foundation, to the top of the dune that would one day sit below the first tier of an expansive deck. "Glad to see they haven't leveled this dune. Used to come here as a kid," he said.

"Used to bring girls here, I bet," she said.

"Nah, never," he lied.

"What did you mean about your office?"

"I'm working the site," he said. "Framed those windows up there today." Simon pointed to one of the gables.

"No kidding," she said. She didn't say anything for a while. "Must have been beautiful here when there was no house." She looked down to the beach, toward the pile of boulders and the tractor in the sand. "And all that mess."

"Still is if you just pretend it isn't there, if you stand right here and look out toward the inlet."

The moon was a silver hammock above the harbor, reflecting off each blade of eelgrass. The boats had become just the shadows of boats. From down the shore came the muffled sound of someone's television that made everything ordinary seem so far away.

Simon turned to Rose and saw the moonlight on her skin. She looked about sixteen, and despite the deep ache in his bones, and the stiffness, Simon felt like a kid again too. If only he could turn back time and start over. If only he could forget all those wasted years. There were so many things he'd have done differently. So many things.

"You okay?" Rose said.

"I was just thinking."

Rose sat down on the top of the dune. He lowered himself to the sand like an eighty-year-old man, a respectable distance from her.

"Building a house is hard work, huh?" she said.

"Just have to get my legs back," he said.

"So tell me something about your past," she said.

"Haven't you heard enough for one day?"

"Tell me how you wound up in New Hampshire."

"Seems like all my stories are ugly and twisted out of focus, like I'm seeing them through an empty bottle of whiskey."

"What was her name?"

"Huh?"

Rose laughed. "I *knew* it. Who was she?"

Simon smiled and shook his head. "Felicia. She was a hairdresser from New Hampshire. I met her at one of the bars here in town."

"*Felicia*. That's a pretty name. How old were you?"

"Twenty-four. She was almost ten years older, but by then I had enough wear and tear on me that you probably couldn't tell the age difference," Simon said. "She liked her booze too, so we hit it off. When it came time for her to go back to Hampton Beach, I decided to go with her. There was nothing keeping me here. Iris was gone about a year then."

As soon as he said it, he realized how callous he sounded.

"What about Noel?" she asked.

"I didn't mean *he* was nothing. I mean I just couldn't seem to do anything right by him. Folks in the town had stepped in and collected all this money to send him off to a special school. What could I do for him? He *was* better off without me."

"You still think that?"

"Those folks did a damn good job with him. But Felicia and drinking weren't the only reasons I left."

Simon ran his fingers through the sand. The heat of the day was still trapped beneath the surface, making the ground seem like a living thing. He grabbed a handful and let it sift.

"Why else?"

"This is going to sound awful."

"Try me," Rose said.

She leaned in a little closer. Simon could smell her shampoo.

"There was something about Noel that spooked me. It wasn't just his autism, or that he spent hours tearing paper to shreds, or that he didn't talk. He had a way of *looking* at me."

"What do you mean, *looking*?"

"It was like he could read through all the bullshit with me. It was like that boy had a main line to my conscience. It was something I couldn't live with. Not then."

"What about now?"

"He did it Monday, when he said hello, and even earlier, on Sunday, when I saw you both on the beach. It's like there's some kind of wise man trapped inside of him, like he knows more than he lets on. But he can't, right?"

"Who knows what he really knows?" Rose said. "The question is, does he still spook you?"

"No. I mean, not really. Guess I'm older and wiser myself. And maybe my conscience is a little clearer lately. I used to read him differently. Maybe the drinking clouded my perceptions. I don't think he's judging me anymore. It's just how he is."

On the water, a channel marker was rocking side to side in the wake of a passing boat. "So what happened with you and Felicia?" Rose asked.

Simon's legs were starting to cramp up. He stretched them out in the sand. He put his hands behind his head and lay down on his back. Stars were popping through the sky like holes in a colander.

"She broke my heart," he said. "She did right by leaving me, though. I was a mess."

"Well, give yourself some credit, Simon," Rose said.

She lay down on her elbow facing him. "You quit drinking, didn't you? That can't be easy. It's something to be proud of. How long has it been now?"

Simon sat up and sidearmed a smooth stone over the dune. He wasn't going to lie. Not to Rose. "Three weeks, six days."

Rose shot up. "That's *all*?"

"Before that, three weeks and two days." And eight hours.

"Jesus."

"You asked."

She sank back down and lay flat on her back and didn't say anything for a while. Simon was afraid she wouldn't want to trust him anymore.

"Did you really care about Felicia?" she finally asked.

"Enough to wallow in it a few years. And use it as an excuse for the booze."

"You think she was the great love of your life?"

Simon felt like Rose was trying to get at something that had nothing to do with either himself or Felicia. "You believe in such a thing?" he asked.

"Nah, probably not," she said.

Simon felt like he was losing her to this sudden sleepiness, to the warmth and contours of the sand or, even worse, to someone else. He felt the panic rise up in him and rather than keep cool, he blurted out: "Men are dogs, mostly."

"Amen," she said.

"I mean, for all you know I could be a liar and a cheat. I could be nothing more than a good-for-nothing alcoholic." What the hell was he saying? He was self-destructing, blowing himself up before she had the chance.

She didn't even open her eyes. "You're none of those things," she said. Her face was serene. *Who is this woman?* he thought. *Where did she come from?*

"I'm at least one of those things," he said.

A smile crept onto her lips. "Good for nothing?" she said. Her voice was pebbles in the surf.

"Alcoho—" he said.

But before he could finish the word, she was up in his face, her lips on his. She kissed him. Simon pulled back. He looked in her eyes. She seemed far away. She didn't apologize or kiss him again. She just looked at him. Simon didn't much like the look in her eyes, so he fixed on her lips, the shape of them, the tiny lines that ran through them, the divet at the top and the slight pout to the lower. The moon was bright enough for him to see. He traced their curves with his eyes and then, like the kid who can't control himself, who has to reach out and touch whatever catches his eye, he leaned down and kissed her. His cheeks burned. He started to pull away. She put her hand on the back of his neck and pushed his mouth down on hers again. That was all the encouragement he needed. Simon felt her come alive. He felt her mouth open like doors to the inner sanctum, like doors to a church. She was all religion.

As they kissed, he sensed the hunger in her, the need to be close. It came down to spaces, the ones between their lips, their tongues, the hollow of her neck, the peaks and caves of her face. If he could only fill them, press himself there, make them smaller, fill them with something, his face, his mouth, his hands, his soul, that thing he'd never believed in. Though as long as he was with her, anything seemed possible, each kiss bigger than both of them, the dizzying scent of her mixed with the damp musk coming off the ocean, the organic stew of salt and life and death, so powerful in its subtlety, elusive and ethereal.

She trusted him. For some goddamn reason she trusted him and he wasn't about to betray that trust.

"Wait," he said. He pulled away.

"What is it?" she said. "What's the matter?"

"Are you sure this is what you want?"

She laughed. "I'm not sure of anything. That's the only thing I'm sure of." Then she put her hands up under his shirt and drew her nails lightly down his back. Simon closed his eyes, and the Simon he'd been for the last twenty years rose off his skin and evaporated into the night. He could be anyone now.

"So that's what it's like," Rose said. They'd been lying there for at least ten minutes before she spoke.

"Hmm?" Simon said. He was drowsy. "Don't tell me that was your first time?"

She groaned and tugged at the hair on his chest.

Simon pulled up his shirt to cover her bare shoulder. "You warm enough?"

She nestled into him closer. "Think we could sleep here?"

"Think we'd be eaten by crabs and coyotes before dawn," Simon said. "Poor Calvin would have a news story on his hands and no one to report it. Two sets of tangled bones found at the Point."

"Did you know Calvin from before when you used to live here?"

"I knew Karen Christie. I grew up on that block."

"Which house?" she asked.

"One with the lobster on the mailbox."

No need to tell her that the mailbox back then had been a rusted, dented hunk of metal covered in *Keep on Truckin'* and *Sex Wax* surfer stickers, and that it wouldn't close, so that late-payment notices addressed to his father would always come into the house too wet to read.

"No kidding," she said. "He has a sister Karen?"

"So you haven't figured that one out yet," Simon said.

"Figured *what* out?"

"Ever notice how Calvin's voice is kind of high for a guy, at least it was. Maybe he's been taking hormones."

"What are you saying?" Rose sat up and the shirt fell off her.

Simon looked at her. He grinned. "Sorry, what were we talking about?"

Rose snatched the shirt off Simon and covered herself. "Are you trying to tell me Calvin Christie used to be a *girl?*"

"Not that there's anything *wrong* with that."

"Get *out,*" Rose said. Simon waited as she seemed to be reliving her encounters with Calvin in a new, informed light.

"Karen was a miserable, depressed kid and, from all indications, Calvin seems to be a happy, well-respected pillar of the community. It was obviously a good move. Shame about those boobs, though, 'cause Karen was, you know." Simon put his hand out in front of his chest. "As the adolescent boy next door, I can attest to that."

"That's not funny," she said. She slapped his hand down and laughed in spite of her protest.

"No, but I guess it's better to know than to not know, right?"

"I guess so," Rose said, begrudgingly. She lay back down and nestled into the crook of his arm.

He'd been waiting for the right time to tell her about Val. Now Simon was feeling confident. If this thing he felt for her was going anywhere, he had to be open. About *everything*. No more secrets. He would come clean. He'd done it twice so far tonight, first when he told her how long he'd been sober and again with Calvin, and the results had been better than he ever could have hoped.

"And on the topic of things you should know—" he started.

"Good Lord, what else could there possibly be?"

"This one's about Val," Simon said.

"What about Val?" she asked lazily.

"Actually not so much about Val as about her daughter."

"There's someone who seems like she has it together. Haven't met her yet. She was supposed to come down Sunday but she had car trouble and canceled at the last minute," Rose said. "But you must've seen her around when she was a kid, right? Tell me about her."

Rose sat up, covering herself with the shirt.

Simon saw her face. This wasn't going to be easy. He'd better just say it. He sat up too. "Well, see, the thing is, *technically,* Eve doesn't exist."

Rose looked at him like she hadn't heard what he'd said. "What are you saying? What do you mean she doesn't exist?"

Maybe this wasn't the best timing after all. "See, when you mentioned Val's daughter, I didn't remember Val having a daughter."

"Yeah, well, we already established a perfectly good reason for that," Rose said.

"That's why I asked the guys who were on the job with me about it."

"And . . ."

"And they said everybody knows Val doesn't have a kid, and they just go along with it."

"That's the craziest thing I ever heard."

"I thought so too—"

"Did it ever occur to you that just maybe they were goofing on you?" Rose asked.

"Well, no, that actually hadn't occurred to me but you're right. It probably should have," Simon said. He panicked. *Could they have been? No,* he decided. The guys were being straight with him. Higgins wouldn't do that. "But one of the guys said Val snapped after Lino Almeida disappeared. And I did remember them being together in high school."

Rose was flustered. Simon realized his mistake. He shouldn't have rushed to tell her. He should have guided her to the conclusion herself, let her be the one to figure it out.

"You saw her today. Did she seem like someone who's *snapped*?"

"Did you notice that photo in the frame on the mantel?" Simon asked.

"What photo? You mean the photo of her daughter?"

"I mean you've seen that photo in magazines, right?"

"What are you talking about?" Apparently, she hadn't. She fished around in the dark for her clothes.

"It's from an ad." Hennessy. Or was it Dewar's. "Val just cuts out pictures from magazines. She puts them in frames. She takes them around town and shows people. That's what one of the guys said."

"Simon, that's nuts." Rose found her shirt and threw it on over her head.

"That's what I'm trying to tell you."

"You're saying Val is nuts," Rose said.

"Not *nuts,* just—"

"What about the *Cancer Cell* magazines and the Jimmy Fund? What about the sperm bank and her granddaughter, Rose?"

"*Rose?* There! Doesn't that sound like a coincidence?" Simon said.

It came out mean-sounding. He hadn't meant it to. She was just being stubborn. She slipped on her underwear. Simon found his boxers. They were full of dried seaweed.

"You know what, Simon? No one's that good a liar." She

turned her back to him. Rose struggled to zip up her jeans. She stuffed her bra in her pocket.

"I *like* Val. I'm not saying it's her fault." It was too late. Simon had blown it. The night was a beer can kicked over the dune.

"Sorry, Simon. This was great but I gotta go. I just need some air."

Was there anywhere in the world with more air? They were on top of a dune overlooking the ocean. She got up. She was actually leaving him there.

"Hell, Rose. Let me at least help you find the path." He just needed to find his shoes.

She didn't wait.

CHAPTER NINE

> *To disconnect, grip plug and pull from wall*
> *outlet. Never pull on cord.*
> —*from the John Lewis Built-In 1400 Spin Washer Dryer*
> *Instruction Manual*

REPORTER:

So what's it like to have casual sex with a stranger?

REPORTER:

I'm sure it depends on the stranger.

REPORTER:

You know what I'm asking. Did it feel dangerous?

REPORTER:

Not as dangerous as it would have been if I were still in a relationship. Maybe not as thrilling as it must have been for Martin, I don't know. I did get a little charge out of being the aggressor. At first, I imagined I was Martin's girl.

REPORTER:

Did you stay "the girl" throughout?

REPORTER:

No. Sometimes I was the girl. Sometimes I imagined I was Martin. Then, eventually I was just Rose.

REPORTER:

Was that part of the plan?

REPORTER:

No.

REPORTER:

Was *he* ever Martin?

REPORTER:

No. The way he touched me was different. And the way he looked at me . . . he was never Martin.

REPORTER:

Did you want him to be Martin?

REPORTER:

At first, maybe a little.

REPORTER:

Were you let down when he wasn't?

REPORTER:

Not really.

REPORTER:

What does that mean?

REPORTER:

I guess it just means that it was different. It'll be interesting to see if I find myself thinking about Simon the way Martin found himself thinking about the girl, his fixation on the casual-sex partner.

REPORTER:

For you to even entertain being "fixated" means it couldn't have been too disappointing.

REPORTER:

I never said it was disappointing.

REPORTER:

Would you say it was good?

REPORTER:

Good, *different* good.

REPORTER:

This isn't providing much insight. What exactly did you learn from this experience?

REPORTER:

How much I like having sex outside. I'm kidding. I don't know. The experiment was ruined.

REPORTER:

Because of what he told you.

REPORTER:

About Val. And that's really where my head's at now, to be honest. How could someone make up a daughter? People don't make up children.

REPORTER:

That isn't what this interview is about.

REPORTER:

No, it isn't.

REPORTER:

Do you plan to repeat the experiment?

REPORTER:

Not with Simon. He's not a stranger anymore. Besides, the guy's an alcoholic with fewer than four weeks of sobriety under his belt. He's Noel's uncle, for Christ's sake. I'm feeling bad enough about that as it is. I don't want to mess with his head. I should have gone out with Mike Eldridge with an *i*.

REPORTER:

Do you really mean that?

REPORTER:

Probably not. It's just that now everything is a mess.

REPORTER:

Do you think Martin must've felt that way too, afterward?

REPORTER:

Interesting. I'm sure he must have.

REPORTER:

Do you think you'll ever be able to forgive Martin?

REPORTER:

I don't know.

REPORTER:

If he's calling because he wants you back, will you consider it?

REPORTER:

Maybe I'll at least answer the phone.

On Rose's desk there was a Bunn-O-Matic cup warmer, a gift from Calvin that had come with a box of Asian Beef Noodle Cup-a-Soup. On the side of the appliance, there was a sticker Rose thought she might have written: *Do not touch hot surfaces. Do not use outdoors. Do not operate if damaged. Allow all parts to cool.*

Why had it taken her so long to see the wisdom in her precautionary statements? Perhaps she'd been an instruction "savant" all along, able to write brilliant directives without understanding their full implications. Perhaps she shouldn't have been so hasty to quit her old job. Clearly, Rose had been kidding herself about being a journalist. Journalists were supposed to be sharp, intuitive. They were supposed to pick up on clues, challenge the status quo. What kind of journalist worth her salt could miss the fact that her landlady's child happened to be made up? Rose still wasn't convinced, so she called Dana Farber.

"Hi. I'm looking for a researcher named Eve Shimilitis, That's S-H-I-M-I-L—No? Can you try the last name Almeida? That's A-L-M-E-I—are you sure? I see. Thanks, anyway."

Then she did an online search for *Risperdal,* something Rose should have done when she first learned about the prescription. She'd just been so busy and it hadn't seemed all that dire. If she had done it earlier, she would have known something was up.

Risperdal. A popular antipsychotic drug that adjusts the imbalance of dopamine and seratonin in the brain.

And the bottles had all been full, hadn't they?

What about that very first day at the paper when Cooper had asked if Val had been talking about her kid? Especially later when Rose found out the question had come from the woman who was supposed to be the girl's *grandmother.* Then there had been the bickering between Val and Cooper on the steps at Val's and again in the living room while Rose was clearing away dishes the day Eve supposedly had car trouble. Rose had just assumed Val had covered up the reason she'd prepared all the food because she hadn't invited her neighbor. And what about that guy Cooper had threatened to take Val to see? Schmidt. A doctor? Rose should have looked him up earlier too. She would have learned there were just three "Dr. Schmidts" on Cape Cod: an English professor at Cape Cod Community College, an equine veterinarian, and a psychiatrist. Val wasn't taking night classes, and she didn't have a horse.

And there had been more clues staring her in the face. Like Cooper's reaction at the Tri-centennial meeting when Val had started discussing the Jimmy Fund booth, how she'd rolled her eyes, and how everyone had seemed uncomfortable when Rose had asked about Eve's car trouble.

Cooper. If Rose had a list of people she was upset with, Cooper was right there at the top, above Val, even, and just a notch below herself. How could she have kept something like this from Rose? Could the woman really be so malicious?

On her way into work, Rose passed the mailbox with the lobster on it. She parked in front of the house where Simon had said he grew up, an idyllic Victorian with a painted front porch and a swing in the yard. Rose looked at the upstairs windows and tried to imagine which might have held the face of a little blue-eyed boy who didn't know what the future had in store for him or his sister, two kids with time bombs in their bodies, hers, the slightest weakness in her cerebral artery, and his, a gene that would eventually cause him to lose everything and everyone that mattered. As she looked at the house now, the morning sun flooding the front yard, such a menacing future for its former inhabitants just didn't seem possible.

"You okay?" Calvin stuck his head in Rose's cubicle. His voice was no higher than it had been yesterday.

"Sure. Fine. Have a seat," Rose said. She pointed to the small Windsor beside her desk.

"You were staring at your noodles. Never been much of a fan of Asian Beef, to be honest."

Rose looked at him. She tried to picture him with breasts. *Stop it.* "I've been wondering about something. Whatever happened to that kid who disappeared? Lino Almeida?" she said.

"There's a name you don't hear every day. Went to school with him, as a matter of fact. He was a bit older."

"I've just been spending time with Cooper because of Noel, and I'm trying to make sense of what happened. I mean I know he disappeared twenty-seven years ago, and no one's ever heard from him since. And that part about him and Val Shimilitis being sweethearts before, and that she might have been pregnant."

"You mind?" Calvin asked. "Actually smells pretty good." He reached over and took Rose's mug off the warmer. He took a sip. After he drew from the mug, there was a greenish foam mustache on his upper lip. "You won't make sense of this one. Cooper, the police, journalists, private investigators, everyone tried. For *years,*" he said.

"Do you think he left or did something happen to him?"

"I don't know." He picked up one of Rose's pens and twirled it in his fingers.

"Let me ask you this. Do you think Val was ever pregnant?"

"Think we *all* know the answer to that, don't we? I mean it's pretty obvious," he said.

Real obvious. Great. "Sure. Of course."

"If you want to do some poking around on his disappearance after the Tri-centennial, I'm fine with it. It's one of our greatest unsolved mysteries. People never get tired of it. Talk to Cooper. She might be ready to revisit the whole thing again. I know she never appreciated rumors that her son had just checked out. Think she's always believed he died out there on the water. I'm sure she wishes she could clear Lino's name once and for all."

"Good idea. I'll talk to Cooper."

Now Rose had no choice.

"*After* the Tri-centennial, though. Okay?" he added. "There's just too much going on right now."

"You got it."

Ten minutes later, Rose was locked in the upstairs bedroom-turned-conference-room dialing Cooper's number. Rose knew she should have gone to see her face-to-face, but she just didn't have the stomach to be looking into those positively charged ion eyes of hers this morning. Someone had opened a trapdoor beneath Rose's feet and she was dangling. Just hanging on. She felt betrayed and she was angry. Cooper owed Rose some answers. Rose thought she might have a better chance of keeping her cool if she wasn't in the same room with the woman.

"Saw a clown this morning," Cooper said. "He was snooping around the barn."

"Clown as in *funny-looking character*?" Rose asked.

"Clown as in red nose and a clown suit," she said.

First Val, now Cooper was cracking up. Maybe there was something in the water.

"Look, I want you to level with me. What's the story with Val and Eve?"

Rose wanted to hear that Eve was the daughter of Val and Lino, just like Val had said, and that she was working toward finding a cure for cancer and that her baby, Rose, Cooper's granddaughter, was as cute as a button. Instead, Cooper's voice was sharp like broken glass. It punctured the air.

"Finally, the great reporter puts two and two together."

Rose's stomach sank. "What's that supposed to mean?" she said.

"It means you *know* what it means. I don't know if someone told you or if you finally figured it out for yourself, but there is no Eve. Never has been. Sometimes, when Val gets lonely or chooses to go off her meds or makes friends with someone new and gullible, we get *Eve*."

Rose tasted bile.

Cooper continued, "There was Baby Eve and then Toddler Eve, think that one came off a box of disposable diapers. Then we were good for a few years until precocious Five-Year-Old Eve, who played the violin. I know she's supposed to be my granddaughter but I really couldn't stand that one. Spoiled rotten. Then Fourth-Grade Equestrian Eve, who came with a complete set of horse figurines and Misty of Chincoteague books. She came after Ann died. Then there was Brilliant Eve, around fifth or sixth grade, who was off the charts with her test scores. Always thought she must've got it from me because Val and even

Lino—God love him—weren't exactly Mensa material. Then, in high school, there was Cheerleader Eve, Prom Queen Eve, and Valedictorian Eve. Then came Vassar Eve, and MIT Grad School Eve, which brought us to Cancer-Curing Eve, and now, since you've arrived on the scene, Single Mommy Eve, which comes complete with Baby Rose and a broken-down car. That just about covers it."

Rose tried to speak but her throat was as dry as an August lawn. Finally, the words came. "Why didn't you tell me? Why did you let it go on?"

"Aside from the laughs?"

"Cooper—"

"I had bigger things to worry about, dearie. I tried to nip it in the bud and get her to the doctor, but I couldn't very well carry her there. She wouldn't go. Once Val knew she had you, I had to be careful. She doesn't take it well when confronted about Eve. She gets upset and defensive, and then, sometimes—not often but sometimes—she falls into a depression that can last for months. When that happens, it doesn't just affect her, but it affects Noel, who knows something's wrong and withdraws. I just wanted to avoid the whole mess, especially given that the Tri-centennial is a month away. I thought if we could put it off a little while, it might even go away on its own. It does sometimes. Usually comes and goes in waves."

Rose wanted to blame her for perpetuating the lie and making her look like a fool, but she understood. Cooper cared about Val and Noel, and was just trying to hang on, protecting the people in her life, the few she had left. Rose couldn't fault her for that. She didn't envy her.

"So I'm just supposed to keep up the charade?"

"Like everyone else in town. Congratulations, you've passed the hazing. You're a local."

Rose knew she was supposed to wait until after the Tri-centennial but she just couldn't. "Cooper, what do you think happened to your son?" Rose said. Fatal Boat Accident Lino, Runaway Lino, Expectant Daddy Lino. Cowardly Lino. "Do you think he's still alive somewhere? Do you think Val does this because she can't cope with being abandoned?"

"Let me tell you something," Cooper said. "My son would never have walked away from a pregnant girl. Sal and I raised him to be a decent human being. I know some people think he ran off, but I can't worry about them. I knew he was a good boy." Her voice wavered and she paused for an instant. "Other people who knew him would say the same. That includes Val. The reason he never came back is because he's dead. It isn't an easy thing for a mother to say, but I know it in my heart. It's how I manage to get myself up in the morning, how I get dressed and face the day. If I thought he could come walking through that door at any minute, I'd be in the nuthouse by now. I've come to accept that I may never know what really happened. But he's gone."

"I'd like to help you learn what happened," Rose said.

"No offense, honey, but you can't tell the difference between a photograph and a gal in a booze ad."

The photo of "Eve" on the table by the window. No wonder Simon had recognized it. Simon. Rose felt a sudden pang of guilt over last night. He'd just been trying to help her.

"That may be true, but I'd like to see what I can uncover."

"It's a free country," Cooper said. "Just be careful around Val. She doesn't need to be burdened by this. None of the doctors agree with me, they just feed her pills, but I think the reason she creates a life for Eve is out of guilt for telling Lino she was pregnant the night he disappeared. She blames herself for his death. She was just a kid. They both were."

"*Was* she pregnant?" Rose asked.

"Years later, Ann, her mother, told me she'd miscarried. Nobody knew."

"I'm sorry," Rose said.

"After the baby was gone, she couldn't let go. You think I don't wish there'd been a baby, someone to carry on my son's legacy? It would have changed everything. Instead, we have a ghost that likes to rattle around Jimmy Fund cans. Life is something, eh?"

"I'm sorry, Cooper. For *everything*. Thanks for being straight with me. I won't let Val know I know."

"One other thing. What do you make of this Meeeelo Vander-*loser* fellow?"

Rose had almost forgotten about Noel and the show. "I did a search on him right after the meeting on Monday. He seems to check out. He's a reputable collector and has even overseen a number of auctions at Christie's in New York. His gallery checks out too. I think we can trust him."

"If you say so," Cooper said.

If Rose could find out what happened to Lino, she might find a way to forgive herself for being duped by Val. She went to the library and pulled microfiche on the coverage of the disappearance in the *Boston Globe* and the *Cape Gazette*. She found out that Lino Almeida had grown up around boats, son of the late Sal Almeida, a Portuguese fisherman, one of the last of a dying breed. Lino had played soccer and hockey in high school, and pumped gas at one of the stations in town on weekends. In one of the articles, Cooper said he had no plans for college but that his dream had always been to run a boatyard, that he had been good with his hands and liked to tinker with outboards.

Rose looked up his senior photo in the yearbook at the library. He had his mother's eyes, only they were dark, like his complexion. Except for a bad case of acne, he was a handsome kid. Rose looked up Val, who was no beauty even in high school, with her heavy features and her fine, blunt-cut hair parted in the middle and anchored behind her ears. She'd had kind eyes then too. Rose was about to return the yearbook to its slot on the shelf when she remembered Simon had said he'd been a freshman that year. She flipped to the underclassmen pages, under *B*, and there he was, top row, two photos directly above Karen Christie, a mousy-looking girl with long stringy brown hair who bore barely any resemblance to Calvin. Simon's snapshot wasn't the best picture either but it stirred something in Rose just the same and was pretty close in likeness to Noel's rendering. In fact, he looked a lot like Noel himself. His long hair was mussed and made his head look lumpy. He had a piece of rawhide tied around his neck. But the school photo captured his tentative smile and something else, a hopeful look, like he had the whole world laid out ahead of him. Rose suddenly wished she'd known him then. She might have been able to save him. It was a childish thought. She snapped the book shut and slipped in into its place on the shelf. That was the beauty of books filled with the past. They could be snapped shut.

Later that night, Rose was getting out of the shower when the phone rang. This time she answered. It was Martin. He said he'd been leaving messages, trying to reach her for weeks. He said he was coming to town the next day and wanted to take Rose to dinner. She thought he was surprised when she accepted. In forty-eight hours, she'd gone from being asked out by Mike to sleeping with Simon, to accepting a date with Martin. The image held in her mind before sleep, though, wasn't of Martin. It was the picture of Simon from his school yearbook. Fixation on the casual-sex partner. It was happening. Rose wondered if it was happening for Simon too.

CHAPTER TEN

Just point and shoot right where you want.
—*from the Presto SaladShooter® Electric Slicer/Shredder*
Instruction Manual

Simon came home from work to the pile of clothes he'd left by the door the night before. He picked up the pants and sand sifted from the pockets. He picked up the shirt, held it up to the light, and recalled the way it had looked next to Rose's skin.

All day long his mind had generated images from the night before. He'd eaten his lunch alone at the top of the dune. He'd run his fingers through the sand and this time the surface was warm, the sand below, cool. His lips on the coffee mug became his lips on the warm hollow at the base of her throat. A strand of spiderweb fastened to a piece of Sheetrock brushed his forehead like the soft curtain of her hair and gave him a chill. And when Berry called it quits and headed down the path with his lunch pail, Simon thought of Rose's retreat and it made him feel thirsty, the most thirsty he'd been since the ship.

Did he have to tell her? The answer, he knew, was yes. He only hoped that what he'd told her last night had been corroborated by Calvin or someone else today. He'd tried to call her.

He'd used Sparrow's cell phone around eleven, but he'd gotten her voice mail and hung up.

Simon drew the curtain closed. He went to the bathroom, got a white hand towel, and laid it over the bedspread for a place mat. He removed the white carton of Chinese food from the bag by its metal handle and opened the flaps. He lifted out the wax-paper bag of egg noodles, the packets of soy sauce, and the fortune cookie in plastic. He clicked on the Red Sox game and fished around the inside of the carton for something he could skewer with his chopsticks. (He always forgot to ask for a knife and fork.)

There came a tapping on the glass from behind the drawn curtains.

Segundo wasn't coming till tomorrow. It could be the desk manager looking for this week's rent. Or it could be Rose. The excitement he felt at this prospect quickly gave way to mortification over the idea of being caught in his motel room eating Chinese food over a bath towel, just as he'd done most nights since he'd arrived.

He got up and peeked behind the curtain. There, separated only by a thin layer of glass, was Noel's face, his forehead pressed to the surface. Simon jumped. At close range Noel's forehead resembled an ant farm, the furrows in his brow for tunnels. Simon craned to see if anyone else had come with Noel. It was just him.

Simon unlatched the dead bolt.

"Hey, little buddy," he said, sounding avuncular and too much like the Captain on *Gilligan's Island*.

Noel slid past him and spotted the plastic-wrapped fortune cookie on the bed. He looked at Simon.

"Go on. Take it," Simon said. "Never been a big fan of fortune cookies." Simon sat down in the chair by the door. "Sweets. I can take 'em or leave 'em. How about you?"

Noel bit through the plastic and spit the corner out onto the rug. He slid the cookie out of its wrapper and popped the whole thing into his mouth.

"Watch out for the paper inside, son."

Did Noel not know there was paper inside? Had he had fortune cookies before? Was he not able to remember stuff like there was paper inside of fortune cookies? One of the last times Simon had seen his nephew, he'd been on the floor at Iris's, surrounded by shreds of torn paper. Was that something he still did? Had he graduated to eating them too?

Noel didn't say anything. He just ate. Would he swallow the paper? Guess it wouldn't hurt him too much. Maybe there were no fortunes in those cookies. Maybe they didn't do that anymore because some public-safety group decided fortunes pose a choking hazard.

"Have some water," Simon said. He handed Noel the glass on the bedside table but Noel shook his head. "So what brings you here, pal?"

Noel threw back his head and howled, "The last bare-knuckled fight in pro boxing took place in 1889," spitting cookie everywhere.

Simon nearly fell off the chair. Maybe he liked Noel better when he didn't speak. He was so loud Simon worried that the people in the adjoining rooms might call the front desk, or even the cops. That was all Simon needed. And the reference to the fight. Was that supposed to mean something? Did he want to fight Simon? Was there meaning to these "lasts" or were they randomly generated, only occasionally serendipitously.

Before Simon could ask, Noel stuck two fingers into his mouth and pulled out the fortune, completely intact. Somehow he'd managed to chew around it. "You will achieve great happiness in this life," Noel said, without looking at the words on the paper.

That wasn't a "last." It was a fortune. "What's all this business about *lasts*? Either you can talk normal or you can't. Seems like you can read pretty good," Simon said.

"The last fortune printed by the Hong Kong Fortune Cookie Company, Teaneck, New Jersey," Noel continued.

"Let me see that," Simon said. He got up from the chair and took the damp fortune out of Noel's hand. It said: *Pray for what you want, but take what you need.*

Noel flapped his arms. Simon was startled by the sudden gesture. What did it mean? Did he think he could fly?

"I'm glad you came to see me, Noel. Is there something you want to talk about?"

Noel flapped faster. Simon didn't know what to do.

"I mean I want us to spend time together but I have to make sure it's okay with Val and Cooper first. Otherwise, they'll worry. They'll get mad at me. You don't want that, do you?"

Noel's flapping slowed until he finally came to a landing on the corner of the bed. Simon went to him and put his arm around his nephew's shoulder.

"What do you say you and me take a walk?"

Noel nodded. Simon slipped on his loafers and jacket, stuffed his room key in his pocket, and clicked off the TV.

"If things go like I hope, maybe we can spend more time together real soon. Maybe we can go to a movie or go fishing. You like fishing?"

Noel threw his head back. "Last call at the Barnacle is two A.M.," Noel said.

Simon walked Noel back to his room at Cooper's. Over the course of the walk, he learned the last men's-only Olympics was in 1908, that the last cigarette commercial ran during *The Tonight Show* on December 31, 1970 (for Virginia Slims), and that *amen* was the last of the 773,692 words in the King James version of the Bible.

Simon gave Noel an awkward hug at the top of Cooper's driveway and watched the spindly kid cut across the grass, descend the stone steps, and disappear through the door below the crooked eagle. Poor Noel, Simon thought. Autism was a cruel affliction, getting in the way of the one thing human beings needed most: contact with other human beings.

Simon was about to leave. He noticed the light was on in Rose's cottage. He could see through the bushes. She was home. His brain told his legs to go but they revolted. Simon moved down Cooper's driveway. He slipped through an opening in the hedges near the farmhouse and came out just a few feet from Rose's bedroom window. Just for a minute, he told himself. Just to make sure she's safe.

What are you doing? Are you out of your mind?

The window was open a crack. She was on the phone but the other person was doing most of the talking. She was wearing a yellow bathrobe and her hair was still wet from the shower. She was wearing glasses. Simon didn't know those kinds of things about her: how she liked her eggs, what she wore to bed, whether she wore glasses. Of course he knew the last one now. Those were things a guy should know before he jumps into bed with a woman. They hadn't even jumped into *bed,* had they? What the hell *was* that and what had it meant? That was the question he'd been asking himself all day. He just wanted to know.

Leave now.

Rose headed toward the window and Simon ducked down, not before catching that cute wrinkle between her eyebrows and the way her robe fell away a little as she reached for a hairbrush on the table beside her bed. She turned toward the door leading out of the room. With her back to him now, he could see her spine stiffen. She paced. Simon strained to hear.

"I'm not sure that's such a good idea . . . I not saying you *shouldn't* come . . . You can do whatever you want . . . of course I still care about you, Martin, but . . ."

Simon felt his stomach ball up in a knot. He had a feeling this was nothing he wanted to hear.

"Tomorrow night, fine . . . *Just* dinner . . . You know what I mean . . ."

Simon heard slow footsteps coming up the crushed-shell driveway. The hedges blocked his view. Noel must have been spying on him while he was spying on Rose.

"Noel, that you? Just dropped my room key in the bushes. Here it is." He bent down and pretended to pick up his key. He gave it a jingle. "I'll be off now."

He turned and found himself staring into the barrel of a shotgun poking through the hedges.

"Nice and easy," the old woman said. She slipped through the opening in the bushes. It was Cooper. She hadn't changed in seventeen years. Same chopped hair, same scowl. Only there were some marks on her forehead but it was too dark to make out what they were. She motioned with her head for Simon to move away from the cottage and up Val's driveway.

Simon put his hands up in the air.

"So you changed your costume, eh?" she said. "The other one was better."

Who did she think he was? "It's not what you think," he said.

What was it, then? he wondered himself. And why did he seem to care more about getting caught by Rose than getting his head blown off? A bead of sweat trickled down his neck. When the sound of a blow-dryer came from inside the cottage, he started to breathe again. He started back through the bushes.

"That's it," Cooper said. "Nice and slow."

"I can explain," Simon said. He whispered.

They came to a stop beside Val's house.

"One word out of you and I'll pull the trigger," Cooper said.

"For heaven's sake, Cooper. Put down that gun," came another voice. It was Val. Had she seen Simon spying on Rose too? Couldn't a guy get away with anything in this town?

"Get back in the house, Shimmy. He might be packing," Cooper said.

"'He might be packing.' No more *Matlock* reruns for you,"

Val said. She was standing in the shadows. Simon couldn't see her face.

"I said get back in the house. Go call the cops," Cooper said.

"Don't you recognize him?" Val said.

Cooper lowered the barrel a little and squinted.

Simon was heartsick. It wasn't supposed to happen like this, him getting caught sneaking around. She was supposed to learn what an upstanding citizen he'd become. He'd wanted to impress her.

"*Filho da puta*. You!" Cooper said.

"Amazing, isn't it? How much he looks like Iris? And Noel too. I'd forgotten." Val turned to Simon. "Don't worry, Simon. She doesn't keep the gun loaded."

"Now why'd you go and tell him that for?" Cooper said. She put the gun down at her side. "What the hell are you doing here, Beadle?"

"I came back for Noel," he said. He realized how it must have sounded. He didn't mean it that way. Cooper raised the gun again. "I don't mean I want to *take* him anywhere, I just mean I want to be something to him. An uncle."

"Shimmy, go to the apartment and see to it Noel doesn't come out here. I don't want him to see this—"

"Too late," Val said. She sang it.

Cooper swung her head around.

"I mean Noel's seen him," Val said.

Cooper's face and neck reddened. Simon thought she might be having a stroke. "You've got one hell of a nerve," she said, firing the words through her teeth.

Simon noticed the eyelet of her nightgown sticking out from the bottom of her yellow rain slicker.

"But Noel was thrilled to see Simon. He even painted a picture of him," Val said.

Simon wished Val would just be quiet. She wasn't helping. Cooper turned to Val. She pointed the gun at her.

"I'll deal with you later," she said. Her voice was January cold.

"If you'd just give me a chance to explain," Simon said.

"Explain what you were doing prowling around like some kind of reptile?" Cooper said. "Doubt there are many explanations worth hearing,"

"He's snookered with Rose," Val said.

Simon wanted to shrink down into the dirt and slither away. Had he been that obvious at Val's yesterday?

"I suggest you take those keys and go back to wherever you came from," Cooper said.

"But—" was all Simon could get out.

"And so help me, if I see you around here again, I'll have you arrested," she said. "And next time the gun'll be loaded, trust me."

"You don't even own bullets," Val said.

Cooper ignored her and held the gun steady, pointed at Simon's nuts. It was enough to get anyone's point across, bullets or no bullets.

"Can't we just talk this out like reasonable—"

"You want Nowak to know what you were up to?"

It seemed as though Cooper had found her ammo.

"You'll have to forgive her, Simon. She's been trying to break up love affairs for as long as I've known her," Val said. "She can't stand to see anyone happy."

"That's enough out of you. Get back in the house," Cooper said. She stomped her foot. The nightgown rustled beneath the foul-weather gear.

"Just like poor Lino and me. She's never accepted her grand-daughter, just because she was born out of wedlock," Val said. "One day soon she'll have to answer to Lino at the pearly gates. You remember poor Lino, don't you, Simon?"

The conversation seemed to be headed in a dangerous direction. Cooper's face had hardened to stone. Simon felt another drop of sweat run down his neck.

"Sure, I remember Lino," he said. Simon said it in a voice so low he doubted anyone could hear.

Cooper didn't say anything. She just put down the gun and waved for Simon to go. He obliged. He started up the driveway.

"Don't worry, Simon," Val said. Simon turned around. "Neither of us will say anything to Rose."

Cooper shot another icy round at Val.

"I'm sorry about tonight. I truly am," Simon said. And he left.

By the time Simon got to the sidewalk, his hands were shaking. Any chance he had of winning Cooper over was gone now. And if Rose got wind of what he'd been doing, she'd be gone too, if she wasn't gone already. Who had she been talking to? Some guy named Martin. Last night, Rose had referred to a relationship that had gone sour. Martin must be the old boyfriend. What if she was still in love with him? What if they got back together? Where would that leave Simon?

Same place he was about this time last night, he thought. He checked his watch. Twenty-four hours ago, she was fleeing down the path. It hadn't taken long for the luck of the old Simon to return. In some ways it felt good for the bad luck to be back. It was familiar, at least. In fact, everything had been going too well for him lately. It had made him a little uncomfortable. Tonight, maybe even at the tail end of last night, the planets had slipped back into their *unalignment* and Simon was back to his old bumbling mess of a self. Who had he been kidding?

Simon went back to the motel. The red light was flashing on the phone. He had a message.

"*Hola,* muchacho." It was Segundo. It sounded like he was in a bar. There was music in the background. "Where are you? I come all this way and can't find you. I even wear my costume for you. Aye." He'd been drinking. "Well. I'll keep looking. Martinezes never give up."

When had he called? Simon packed up the Chinese food, put it in the minifridge, and he was back out the door.

Last call at the Barnacle is two A.M.

Noel had ambushed Simon with that one. Vintage Simon Beadle, to be sure. Simon had always had a fondness for last call. The last drink at the bar put a cherry on the night, a drunk's punctuation. And then a new sentence would begin: a party back at Segundo's trailer, sloppy sex with Felicia or someone else, a lonely trek through empty streets. That last drink at the bar, though, that was magic. Made the girls prettier. It was a warm coat on a cold night. An hourglass turned upside down.

Simon felt a yearning in his gut and a chalkiness at the back of his throat. God, he was thirsty. He was coming up to a tourist bar, the kind filled with fishing nets and plastic lobsters. The kind of place that served fried seafood on paper plates and charged a bundle. Simon cupped his hands around his eyes and looked in the window for his friend. The place was almost empty. It was still too early in the season for there to be more than a few out-of-towners.

A young guy was coming out the door.

"Hey, you see a Spanish clown in there tonight?" Simon asked.

"Dude, that's not cool," the guy said. He did a little two-step.

"What's not cool?"

"Calling Spanish people *clowns,* man."

The guy's eyes were swimming in his head, coming up for air, then dunking back under.

"I didn't mean it that way. I mean I'm looking for a . . . never mind," Simon said.

The guy was already stumbling toward the street.

"Hey, you're not planning to drive anywhere, are you?" Simon asked.

"Fuck no. I live up there."

He pointed up the street and staggered off in a zigzag. Simon watched. That zigzag walk pretty much summed up the experience of being a drunk. You take twenty steps to get to the same place you could've gotten in two. Simon shook his head. He watched the guy until he turned the corner.

There was another bar on Main Street. The Fore and Aft was a locals' joint, one of those places from which Simon had been barred from "for life." He wondered how they kept track of a thing like that. They must have a bulletin board out back by the time clock covered with photos of the bar's notorious "unwanted" drunks. He imagined each new bartender got a set of "alcoholic" trading cards, each featuring a photo and listing the stats: number of arrests, DUIs, hospitalizations. Number of people hurt. Number of remaining friends. Number of falls off a cruise ship. The good thing was they'd never recognize Simon. His card would be seriously out-of-date.

The window on the outside was too high for Simon to see through, so he'd have to actually set foot in this one. He pushed open the heavy wood door and saw a party in progress. The tables were mostly full and it was standing room only. J. J. Cale's original rendition of "Cocaine" was blaring out of the jukebox, welcoming him home in a dangerous way.

There had been music in the background when Segundo called.

Simon thought he'd be okay, but when he actually got inside, he swooned. Someone near him was drinking bourbon. He didn't even like bourbon. Now, suddenly, he'd sell his left testicle for a glass of the stuff.

Simon scanned the room. No sign of his friend. He headed for the bar. There were some women he thought he recognized from a long time ago, pretty girls back then. Now one had blotchy skin and deep lines running down the sides of her mouth. Her hair was thinning at her temples. The other had better hair, all done up in curls, but her face looked bloated and tired. Simon just needed to talk to the bartender and get the hell out of there.

"What'll it be?" the bartender said. He put a white napkin in front of Simon.

"I'm looking for someone," Simon said. "Guy about this tall." Simon held his hand in front of his nose. "Dark hair. Spanish accent. Dresses kind of funny sometimes."

"What kind of funny?" the bartender asked. He was looking at Simon like maybe he recognized him from a trading card.

"Like he wears clown stuff sometimes," Simon said.

"And he's got a weird name," the bartender said.

Simon lit up. "Segundo!"

"That's it. Yeah. He was in tonight."

"How long ago did he leave?"

"Fifteen, twenty minutes."

The bartender flipped a couple pilsner glasses onto the bar and started pouring beers into them. Simon watched the foam rise. *Wonder if it counts if you just drink the foam,* he thought.

Simon knew he needed to get out of here fast. Too much temptation. Too many people having a good time. And just the thought of his old friend bellying up to this bar like they used to in the old days put Simon in a perilous place. Forget about finding Segundo tonight.

He started to walk out.

"Hey," someone said.

Simon turned. It was Higgins. At first Simon thought he was swaying to the music.

"Hey, Higgins."

Higgins didn't say anything. His eyes were almost closed. He just stood there with a grin on his face and listed side to side. Simon couldn't believe his eyes. At work, Higgins seemed like such a solid guy. Here he was drunk off his ass in a bar.

"Buy you a beer?" he offered. The words slurred together into one, "bayoubeer."

"No thanks, pal." Simon said. He clapped him on the shoulder and Higgins teetered. "See you tomorrow."

Simon left Higgins and pushed his way through the crowd to the door. He stepped outside and his heart was pounding. Seeing Higgins there like that. It wasn't right. He looked up to Higgins. Higgins was a family guy, had a wife and kids. No one was safe from it. There was no escape. If the booze wanted you, it would get you, sooner or later.

Simon started walking fast, back to his motel. A car passed with the radio blaring and the bass thumping. Someone waved a beer out the window and hollered at Simon.

Were they calling to him? Did they know who he was? Or was it just the bottle of beer that recognized him. It seemed like no matter how hard he tried, there was no escaping his urge to drink. His hands were shaking. It was everywhere and it always would be. It never got easier. Never. One week, two weeks, three weeks. No easier. He thought about the gun Cooper had pointed to his head earlier and wished it had been loaded. She'd have done him a favor by pulling the trigger. To think of going through this forever, it was too hard.

Simon felt lower than the worms living under the cobblestones.

He made his way around the corner to Main. Down the alley to his right, some Chinese kids in white aprons were smoking outside the Wonton Abandon. They were passing around a bottle of something. Scotch. Simon knew them from the restaurant. He turned down the alley, just to bum a cigarette, he told himself. Just to see if the kitchen was open. Just to ask what time it was, even though the bank with the sign that gave the time and temperature was just across the street. One of the kids was wearing cool boots. Simon just thought he'd ask the kid where he got his boots.

"Looking for something?" said the kid with the boots. He had no accent.

Minutes later, Simon walked back up the alley with a three-quarters-full bottle of Scotch tucked under his arm that he'd bought off the kids for thirty bucks.

There was no weight or indecision to his steps now. On the contrary, there was enormous relief. The deed was done. Simon made a dash for his room at the Governor Higgins Motel. "Here's to Great-Great-Great-Great-Grandfather Higgins," he said, raising the bottle to the motel sign, a logo that featured an old-fashioned hat from the Puritan days, and took a swig. *Ugly fucking hat,* he thought. The alcohol burned. He tried to imagine Higgins in a hat like that. The alcohol coated and soothed. Simon slid his key in the lock.

Only a few hours till morning and miles to drink before I sleep, Simon thought. He went straight to the bathroom, where he grabbed a cup. He took the plastic wrap off it, then sat down on the bed and filled it with Scotch.

"Is this the lovely Rose?"

"Who is this?"

"Did you know the name *Rose* is Latin and was brought to Great Britain by Normans?"

"What?"

"And *rose* is a Christian symbol. Rosa mystica"—*mystica* had five or six syllables. "It means the Virgin Mary." Simon was glad he'd been drinking Scotch. Scotch never made him stupid-drunk. It made him sound smarter.

"Simon?" Her voice was filled with sand.

"Am I calling at a bad time?"

She didn't answer right away. "It's four in the morning." Had he really been drinking that long?

"And it can be traced to an old German word for 'horse.'"

"What?"

"*Rose.* It also means 'horse.'" After work, while he was waiting for his takeout (which he'd never gotten around to eating but now remembered was waiting for him in the fridge), he'd gone for coffee at the Internet café next to the restaurant. There, he'd done an etymological search for *Rose*.

"Are you alone?" he asked.

"What?" There was a pause. "Simon, are you drunk?"

Simon let the pause answer. He had to wait until the pauses finished talking to each other.

"Not *drunk*. Just happy." It was true. A wave of pure happiness had come over him.

"I thought you were serious about quitting. God, I should have known."

And then that wave of happiness passed. Simon panicked.

"I *was* happy, last night. I want to be happy again. Will you make me happy again, Rosie?"

"I don't even know what *happy* is." She sounded more disappointed with him than even he would be with himself tomorrow. "Simon, it's late. I've got to be at work early. Don't call again, okay? Good night." She hung up.

The alarm bled into the room. It gushed. Simon had to stop the bleeding. He reached out and smashed the clock with his palm. The plastic in front of the numbers popped out.

He opened his eyes. With the curtains drawn, it was pitch dark, except for the glow of the six and the two zeros, even brighter now, which shone through the thick glass of the empty bottle.

What have I done?

CHAPTER ELEVEN

Unhinge the body shell from the body.

—on *"How to Eat a Lobster"* from the Lobster Dock Restaurant Web site

Val, great news! My mother's not dead after all. She was spotted with Elvis at a Laundromat. I plan to stake out the peanut-butter aisle at the supermarket in case she and the King turn up. Let's just pray I get to her before the aliens do. In any event, I'm afraid I'll have to cancel our coffee date this morning. Of all people, you understand. Rose had spent the early-morning hours penning excuses that would allow her to cancel her coffee date with Val—a last-minute invitation to the White House, emergency cosmetic surgery. She wanted to see what it was like to just make stuff up and, she had to admit, rather enjoyed being free from nagging truths, unburdened by such petty things as the laws of nature.

Maybe whether or not a person was labeled crazy depended on how many others were willing to go along. Just about everyone in town had made the deliberate decision to support Val in her *untruth,* out of pity or loyalty or something Rose just might never understand. In the end, could Val even be held accountable? Could her fantasies even be called lies?

How could Rose be mad at someone for wanting something

so badly she risked everything—even her sanity—to have it be true? The more Rose considered this, the less crazy it seemed, the more commendable.

When Rose arrived at the house, Val's front door was unlocked. She let herself in.

"Val, it's me," she said.

"I'm in the kitchen," Val said.

Rose started down the hall. The painting of Simon was still propped up on the mantel in the living room. Rose stopped to look at it. *Simon doesn't drink. He's not an alcoholic.* What if Rose just wished it to be true? But that would be crazy. There was no one to go along with it, especially around here. Three weeks and six days had been the extent of his sobriety. For some reason, Rose had believed him when he said he was through with booze. She should have known better. Her instincts should have kicked in. Her instincts were clearly subject to random power outages.

Did Rose have an obligation to tell Val and Cooper he was drinking again? She imagined Cooper would find out he was back and learn the whole story soon enough. Word traveled fast around here. When Cooper did, she'd have her excuse to keep Noel away from him. But what if his uncle really had the ability to help Noel in ways the others couldn't? Rose didn't want to be the one to take away that chance. The time had come for Rose to extract herself from the middle of this mess, even if some of the mess was her doing. The best she could do was keep her eye on Simon, for Noel's sake.

As the hall opened up to the kitchen, Rose was greeted by the smell of fresh-ground coffee and cinnamon, and by Val's formidable behind sticking out over a cardboard box. Styrofoam packing peanuts were strewn over the table and floor. Val lifted a mound of white cloth out of the box.

"Hey," she said. There were peanuts stuck to her forearms. In her hands were at least twenty T-shirts. She shook the top one off the pile and handed it to Rose. It was a Jimmy Fund shirt. "These came yesterday. I'm trying to get people to wear them the day of the Tri-centennial. Would you mind?"

Rose took the shirt and slung it over her shoulder. A wave of anger percolated and died back down. She took a deep breath. The Jimmy Fund was a good cause whether Val had a meaningful connection to it or not.

"You look tired," Val said.

"I woke up and couldn't get back to sleep," Rose said.

"So you heard it?" she said. Val brushed the peanuts off her arms, went to the coffeemaker, and poured out two mugs of coffee. She set one in front of Rose. "Here. This will help." A Styrofoam peanut was floating in it.

Rose plucked it from its black sea. "Heard what?" She sat down at the table.

"All the fuss last night," Val said. She pushed the box aside and sat across from Rose. "You mean to tell me you didn't hear it?"

"Hear *what*?" Rose asked. She poured some cream into the mug and stirred.

"Cooper saw Simon. He was here."

No wonder he'd hit the bottle. "What was he doing here?"

"You're not going to like it," Val said. "Then again, you might. I don't know." Rose got the sense that Val was trying to stir up more than her coffee.

"Out with it, Val," Rose said. She was in no mood for games.

"Cooper found him pulling a Peeping Tom outside your bedroom window."

"What?" Rose dropped her spoon. "What time was that?" she asked.

"A little after nine. I'd been watching the news and they said it might rain, so I went outside to put the hammock in the shed—of course, *did* it rain? Not a drop. They always get it wrong. Anyway. I came outside and heard voices. I walked over to the driveway and there was Simon facing into the barrel of Cooper's shotgun."

"Cooper has a shotgun?"

"It's just for show." Val blew on her coffee.

"And he was really looking in my window?"

"That's what Cooper said."

Was Val even telling the truth? Rose didn't know what to believe. She hadn't heard anything last night. Nine o'clock was around when Martin had called. And then she had gone into the bathroom to dry her hair. Could that be why she didn't hear?

Rose felt sick. "Val, do you have any crackers or anything. I just need to put something into my stomach."

Val got up and came back with a fat slice of Boston cream pie. It helped.

The inside of the Barnacle was smoke-stained and dark, with wood floors and rows of wobbly tables steadied by matchbooks left over from the days when people could light up in restaurants. Behind the long oak bar lived a burly barkeep with a handlebar mustache. There was sawdust on the floors, piled up in corners, representing decades of sopped-up overindulgence.

Rose had chosen the Barnacle because pubs were more her speed, fancy restaurants were Martin's, and she wanted the territorial upper hand with this encounter. It had taken her six outfit changes to finally settle on a pair of jeans, a camisole, and a white blazer. At the last minute, she'd kicked off her flats and slipped on heels. *Make him suffer,* Calvin had said. On her way over, Rose passed by the Governor Higgins Motel. The only good to come out of Simon's misstep was that it simplified things.

Martin was sitting at a table, his head directly beneath a Mississippi license plate that said STOLEN. His hair had grown longer and he looked too thin. When Martin lost weight, his cheeks hollowed. He'd also cut himself shaving. There was a spot of dried blood on his chin. Rose felt the urge to lick her finger and wipe it away but she caught herself in time. There were rules now, certain lines that weren't to be crossed. In spite of the lost weight and the blood on his chin, he looked handsome in the black turtleneck Rose had given him for Christmas, though that he should still be able to wear clothes Rose had picked out for him seemed like a breach of the new rules.

As Rose approached, he stood up and pulled out a chair for her. "Thanks," she said instead of hello.

Martin gave Rose a hug. She went limp. He was wearing a new brand of cologne. She was relieved. For Rose, emotions triggered by smell were the strongest. She pulled away and sat across the table from him.

"You look great, Rose."

Not great enough, Rose thought, or he never would have needed to chase "twentysomethings" in the first place. It hadn't taken long for the anger Rose had been repressing for weeks to bubble up.

"Thanks for meeting me here," he said. "I just ordered a beer. Can I get you one?"

Before Rose could answer, he flagged the waitress. When she came over the words "Whiskey and soda, make it a double" came out of Rose's mouth. It was what her father used to order. She never drank hard liquor.

"You sure?" Martin said.

"What's that supposed to mean?" Rose could be as self-destructive and immature as she liked.

"The last time you drank hard liquor, you had your head over the toilet for two days."

"As a matter of fact, I drink hard liquor all the time now," she lied. "That's all anyone does around here." Simon. "Besides, you're one to talk. What happened the last time *you* drank hard liquor?"

Rose flicked at a crumb that was embedded in the threadbare tablecloth. They both watched as it bounced off the table and onto the floor. After what seemed like an hour, the waitress came back. She brought Rose's drink and put a draft down in front of Martin. He raised his glass, "Touché."

Rose took a gulp. The whiskey seared her throat the whole way down. In a good way.

"Remember the time we came down here and wound up at that bar in Wellfleet?" Martin said.

"The oysters," Rose said. She rolled her eyes. She'd written a pamphlet that accompanied a shucking knife and couldn't wait to try out her newfound skills, how you weren't supposed to chew but just sort of press them into the roof of your mouth with your tongue, then let them slide down your throat. Martin had gagged and almost gotten sick. Rose had felt sorry for him then. That was then. "Your face got all purple and people at the tables around us were staring, and you were making these ridiculous choking sounds. It was so embarrassing."

"I've been practicing," he said. "Think I finally got the hang of it."

Of course that sent Rose's mind to wondering with whom he had been practicing. Why *oysters*? Why not littleneck or cherrystones? Why not shrimp? Did Martin need a little help getting his new girlfriend turned on?

The smile slid off his face. "The thing about the oysters is, I didn't give up. I got right back on the horse."

What was that supposed to mean? Rose had given up on them too easily? Some mixed metaphor to do with swallowing and riding. She should have sucked down a plate of oysters and gotten on a horse?

The waitress came back. "Do you know what you'll have?"

"I'll have the lobster," Rose said. "The two-pounder." She was in the mood to rip something apart, not to mention Martin was paying and it was the most expensive thing on the menu.

"Let's start with some oysters?" Martin said.

Rose shrugged.

"A dozen, please?" he said to the waitress. "And give me a minute on the rest?"

"Sure," she said.

He didn't even flirt. He'd just pointed to the menu. In the old days, Martin always flirted with the waitresses in front of Rose. He did it so heavy-handedly that Rose had always known it was for her benefit. The fact that he wasn't doing it now sort of stung.

Rose took a sip of her drink. In no time, she could feel the beginnings of a low comfortable vibration, a buzz, a hum, a groove. She drank some more.

"Slow down there."

"You're not allowed to say that anymore." New rules.

Martin rolled the edges of his drink napkin. "So you're just going to bust my balls for the rest of my life?"

Rose put her hands down in her lap and looked him in the eye. She'd forgotten how one of his eyes was bigger than the other, in a handsome way. "No. I'm going to bust your balls *tonight,* then send you on your way."

Martin looked hurt. What did he expect?

"Does it really make you feel any better? If it does, go right ahead. I deserve it," he said.

"See, that's the thing. It really doesn't. It's not even the slightest bit fun being mean to you. I can't seem to hate you. I try and I try," Rose said.

"That's a start." He grinned.

"It's one lousy step above *hatred,* Martin, and about twelve billion steps below *like.*"

"I'll take what I can get."

The waitress arrived with the oysters and set them on the table. They seemed to quiver in their shells.

"Another round, please," Rose said. If she had looked up, she'd have seen Ward Cleaver across the table reacting to her request with fatherly disapproval. So she didn't look up. She looked at the oysters.

"No problem," the waitress said.

Rose picked up an oyster and heaped on the horseradish. She

wanted to feel something. The drink had her coasting when what she really wanted was to feel the bumps.

Martin slurped an oyster from its shell. Then he chewed and some oyster juice slipped out of the corner of his mouth. Rose shook her head. He wiped his chin.

"Tell me about the people you've met here. Tell me about your new landlord, Valeria with the last name that sounds like a disease, and her family."

"She's a trapezoid," Rose said. She thought about that first day she'd shown up on Val's doorstep, how Rose had immediately taken a liking to the woman and how Val had told Rose about Eve. And in some way Val had lived up to her proclaimed shape, hadn't she? Multisided, complex, slightly askew.

"Did you say *trapezoid*?"

"That's what she said when I met her. She was talking about her property lines. I didn't get that at first. I just remember thinking, *I'm sorry but I just don't see it*."

"When I called once I talked to her. She said something about a daughter who works at Dana Farber. I know some people there—"

"Do we have to talk about this?" Rose said. Did she have to be reminded of what a fool she was?

"Sorry, just wondering about your life and who's in it."

Rose felt bad for snapping at him. "There's this autistic kid, Noel, you know, the kid from the article. The one who paints." Noel made Rose think of Simon. She took a sip of her drink to swallow him back. Maybe she could meet Simon halfway. She could become an alcoholic too. How hard could it be? She took another sip. "He's not actually her kid but he might as well be. Gives Lucien Freud a run for his money."

"His story's fascinating. I was going to ask you about him. I tried to call you a bunch of times after the article came out in the *Globe*. I'm really proud of you, Rose." That made Rose feel good. She was surprised at how good. She spread cocktail sauce over an oyster with the wooden fork. She could feel Martin's eyes on her.

"Forget about me. Tell me about you. How's work?" Rose asked.

He shook his head. "Well, if you really want to know, someone found a finger in some chili in a restaurant in Ohio and the whole campaign we were working on for four months got axed. Everything had been shot, edited, the works . . ." Martin took a breath. He put his face in his hands. Rose thought he was having a finger-in-the-chili meltdown. When he moved them away, his face was red. Neat trick.

"I need you, Rose," he said, all of a sudden. There it sat on the table, between the ketchup and the salt. Like a finger in the chili.

Rose hiccuped. The waitress came back and set down round number two.

"Do you have some rolls or something?" he asked. "Or some oyster crackers?" He looked at Rose. "You need to get something into you."

"Do you have any Boston cream pie?" Rose asked. "Just kidding." She had to watch those inside jokes.

"I'll bring some bread sticks. Know what you'll have for dinner?" the waitress asked Martin. She was a really cute girl, blond hair, blue eyes, curvy, with a beauty mark near her mouth. Rose couldn't believe he wasn't flirting.

"Steak, medium rare."

"Fries or baked potato?"

"Baked, thanks." He didn't even look up from his menu.

"You hypocrite," Rose said when she left.

"What?"

"People always order steak but they could never kill a cow."

Rose slurped another oyster out of its sanctuary. She was the beast. This was good, the way she was talking to him, rather than getting all tongue-tied and defensive. It was the booze giving her strength. It was like slipping into a mask and acting. She was pretending to be someone else. No wonder people became drunks. Rose took a deep breath, adjusted in her chair, and got serious. "Can I ask you something?" she said. She folded her hands in front of her.

"No," he said. He started shaking his head.

How could he possibly have known what Rose intended to ask? "I'm serious," she said.

"I am too."

"I need to know—"

"It's really not going to help make anyone feel better. It's not going to change anything."

"I haven't even asked the question."

"I *know* the question."

Rose said it fast. "Why'd you do it?" There. At least it was out.

"Ugh." He pushed himself away from the table a little. He wiped the corners of his mouth with the napkin. "You deserve an answer. I wish I had a good one. It had absolutely nothing to do with us. I know that's hard to believe."

"Everything was perfect but you just wanted to have sex with someone else." The waitress brought a basket of bread. Rose took a bread stick and started gnawing on it. This was easy. It was like talking about the weather.

"Just this feeling of what's it all about, you know?"

"Not in the least. Go on."

"I felt like life was slipping away from me. I still do. There are these kids at work, and I see it in their eyes sometimes, the fire, and I know I've lost that. You reach a certain age and everything just starts falling away, your drive, your looks, your hair—"

"Your girlfriend," Rose said. "Besides, you're not losing your hair *and* you can still hit a golf ball."

"Oh yeah?" He pulled his hair back off his forehead. Sure enough it was receding a bit. You just couldn't tell the way he wore it. "And I meant *sex* drive," he said.

"I see." Rose smoked her bread stick, exhaled. She was a stitch.

"I'm not going to sit here and blame anyone but myself. I knew exactly what I was doing."

"Well, that's more than I can say for you when we had sex," Rose said. She was a riot. A freaking riot. "Just kidding," she said. Sort of. Rose thought Simon *was* better in some way. Better lips, hands. Might have just been the illicit nature of the act. Might have been that for Martin and his girl too.

"Very funny," he said. The skin on his forehead was loose, which made him look his age. It struck Rose as such a letdown to think one's handsome, brilliant boyfriend could fall victim to something as pedestrian as a midlife crisis. It was such a turnoff.

"Let me ask you something," Rose said. Might as well put it all out there. She was fearless. "Is it better with her?"

"You mean *was* . . ."

"So you were seeing her," Rose said. The fixation.

"Briefly."

"When did it end?"

"What difference does it make? Did you think a thing like that would last?"

"I think *you* did," Rose said. "Or at least you hoped it would."

"Rose," he said, like he was admonishing a six-year-old.

"Come on, answer my question. Was it better?"

"Why go there?"

"If the tables were turned you'd need to go there too, trust me."

"You want the truth?"

"Probably not," she admitted. "But go on."

"I can't even remember what she looked like with her clothes off. When I was with her, I was drunk. It was dark. I mean if I'm going to lose my girlfriend and have my life change forever over some stupid affair, I'd at least like to know whether I enjoyed it."

Rose didn't buy it but she admired his quick thinking. "The Lord works in mysterious ways," she said.

Rose excused herself to go to the restroom. She was about to walk through the door labeled *Gulls* when she spotted a pay phone. Who used pay phones anymore? She fished in her jeans pocket for some coins, walked over to the phone, and deposited two quarters. She called information, for the number of the Governor Higgins Motel. When she got the office, Rose asked them for room number seven. They put her through. It rang once, twice, five times, six, seven. An answering machine for the hotel picked up and Rose hung up. She had no idea what she might have said if Simon had answered.

By the time she returned to the table, the lobster had arrived. Rose became lost in the ritual of eating it, in tearing apart the body and sucking the meat out of its crevices. A couple of times she caught Martin cringing when she splattered him with lemon juice or when gobs of white blood dropped to the tablecloth. Rose held the torso in one hand, tail in the other, and twisted the lobster as if it were a dishrag. It snapped apart to reveal its prize, the thick, rich, green tamale, the liver, which she smeared on a piece of roll and ate like it was pâté. "Want some?" She held out a green slice to Martin.

He had barely touched his steak. "No thanks."

After dinner, they ordered another round of drinks. They mostly sat without talking. Rose noticed the chairs and tables started to move around them. The staff was rearranging the floor for a folk band that was setting up in front by the jukebox. Even better. Rose and Martin wouldn't have to talk at all.

They stayed through the first set, then through the second. By last call, Rose was in no condition to drive home. She left her car in the parking lot and let Martin take her home. Once they got to Val's, he shut off his lights, cut the engine, and rolled down the driveway in the dark, stopping within feet of the cottage.

"This is weird," Martin said.

"I know."

"How about I just see you to the door. You never know what kind of weirdos are out here in the sticks." Rose thought of the way Noel had come through the bushes that first night, and how Simon had been hiding beneath her window the night before.

"Okeydokey," Rose said. She started to get out. She didn't want to wake up Val. "Don't slam the door." As they got out of the car, Rose noticed there was still a light on in Val's bedroom. When they got to the front steps of the cottage, she stumbled. "Shhhhh," she scolded herself. Rose tried to keep from laughing while she looked for the key. She couldn't find it. "I need a light."

"Use the moon," Martin said.

He was staring out over the water, which seemed to glow from underneath. He stepped aside and there it was, practically the same moon as with Simon on the dune, a little less round maybe. Rose thought it could have at least changed a little more, just to help her keep things straight. She found the key in her purse, unlocked the door, and pushed it open.

"I suppose you can go now."

"Let me just make sure it's safe. You never know what—"

"What kind of weirdos, I know," she said.

Rose went inside and he followed. She didn't think he would try anything, though she might have been drunk enough to let him have his way with her, slut that she'd become. He checked the bedroom for robbers and monsters. While he was doing that, Simon crept into Rose's head again and this time she let him stick around. She sat down and the ceiling became a spinning flower, then morphed into the spinning dial from the game of Life. If it ever stopped, she'd know her next move.

"Looks like we're the only weirdos in here," he called from the other room. Rose heard the bedspring creak.

He was in there waiting for her. All of a sudden she felt something bubble up from her gut. She put a hand up to her mouth. "Simon, you've gotta go," she called.

"You called me Simon. Who's Simon?"

"Did I?"

"You did."

Rose laughed. She couldn't help it. Then she felt sick.

"Who's Simon?" Martin asked again.

"I'm serious." Rose did a zigzag to the bathroom and closed the door. "*Simon says go,* okay?"

He came close to the door. "Are you all right?"

"Sure."

It was the messy, clipped "sure" of someone who was drunk.

"I just miss you, babe. I want us to be together. How about I make us some coffee, and we'll talk about it?"

Rose sat on the toilet to see if the queasiness would go away. The bottom half of the walls began to writhe. They were papered in a burled wood pattern that allowed only the most inebriated to see beyond the wood, to the sad, hanging faces trapped inside, as the knots became eyes and howling mouths in the agony of Dante's hell, the old people, the babies, the skin melting right off of them. Eve. Lino. Baby Rose.

Rose slid off the toilet, put her head over the bowl, and threw up.

"Rose? It'll be like it was." He must have had his mouth pressed to the door. The words sounded like they'd been squeezed through pursed lips. "Rose?"

"It wasn't that great," Rose said into the bowl. Never too drunk to miss a jab. "Go home, Martin. Go home. Go home."

Rose sat there another few minutes until it became obvious she was going to be sick again. For what seemed like an eternity she knelt over the toilet and heaved, until she heard the front door close, and Martin's car pull out of the driveway. Until it was just the faces watching her. They didn't say anything. They didn't have to.

CHAPTER TWELVE

To change the dryness level, press DRYNESS
until the desired selection is made.
—*from the Electrolux Dryer Operating Instructions*

Friday night, about nine. The Barnacle was dark but even so, Simon could tell little about the place had changed in all the years he'd been gone. In fact, it looked just like it had the last night Simon had been there, the night he met Felicia. There were the same creaking floorboards and the same wood tables covered in faded red-and-white-check tablecloths. Could they even be the same tablecloths, Simon wondered, and the same stains, the same yellow cardboard menus slipped between the ketchup and mustard bottles? No chance of that, Simon thought, the way prices had gone up here and everywhere else. But the food offerings hadn't changed. Fried clams. Fish and chips. Broiled swordfish. Roast beef au jus. The rafters were filled with hundreds of license plates from around the country. Simon had stared at them many a night, trying to decipher the messages in the letters and numbers. From Iowa: IDH82BU. From Connecticut: F8SKS. From Broward County, Florida: KYHONEY. And from here in Massachusetts: MTBRAIN. All hanging right where they used to.

Simon slipped off his windbreaker and hung it over the back of a bar stool. He sat down and rolled up his sleeves. Segundo had given him the place to meet but forgot to say what time.

"What'll it be?" the bartender asked.

Simon scanned the colorful display of bottles behind the bar, the intricate labels and elaborate shapes. There were bottles that looked like women. Bottles that looked like oversize gemstones, shards of glass, and hunks of wood. Bottles that looked like musical instruments. Bottles that looked like bottles.

"Soda water with lemon," Simon said.

The bartender filled a glass with ice, fired into it with the rubber hose gun, stabbed it with a swizzle straw, and tossed in a wedge of lemon. He set it down in front of Simon.

Simon leaned back and brought his elbows together, stretching his back muscles, which after a week on the job seemed to be aching less. Maybe he was getting stronger. This morning, after a few cups of coffee at the site, the queasy stomach and the throbbing pain between his eyeballs had dissipated. If Higgins remembered seeing him at the Fore and Aft last night, he hadn't let on. After work, Simon had gone straight to his first AA meeting at the First Encounter Coffee House in what used to be the old Baptist church. He didn't dare tell anyone at the meeting about his plans to set foot in a bar tonight. He hadn't said much except "My name's Simon and I'm an alcoholic." He thought he had recognized a few of the people there from the old days, one of Iris's old girlfriends and a guy who used to separate glass bottles by color at the recycling station out behind the liquor store.

Simon had gone to the meeting despite the fact that he'd never been able to buy into the whole concept of AA. He'd always stumbled on the second step, the one where you have to surrender yourself to a higher power. Simon understood the need for humility but thought it downright irresponsible in light of his personal theory about God and His long-standing ambrosia-abuse

problem. In that case, handing yourself over to God was like putting your kid in a car seat and leaving it on the hood. Like building your dream house on Krakatoa. It was like laying your beach
blanket on the sands of Iraq.

What Simon liked about AA were the stories. He liked to
hear about people who struggled with the same things he did.
As unkind as it was, he liked to hear about people who were
more messed up than he was. For an alcoholic, AA was "base"
in life's game of hide-and-seek. It was a safe haven. Simon
found it useful, the peer pressure among perfect strangers
who, for some reason, didn't want to let one another down. It
reinforced his ideas about how all people are connected, that
in the end, we're all here to prop one another up, something
that had appealed to him about Mascots for Jesus, in theory,
at least.

Simon also liked the AA's "take it one day at a time"
approach, which allowed him to worry about today and pro-
crastinate away the rest. And so Simon had gone to AA to
repent and fortify, even though he didn't really need it, seeing
as it was always easier to lay off the booze when some of the
effects of the drinking still lingered. Simon had all the lingering
effects from drinking that he needed in the hazy recollection
of his phone call to Rose. In that one enormous lapse, he'd
proven to Rose that she *had* been right. She couldn't believe in
him. He couldn't believe in himself. All he could do was not
drink today.

If there was any silver lining to Simon's fall off the wagon,
something positive to be had in the way he'd handled this misstep, it was this: he'd found the wound, applied the tourniquet,
and stopped the bleeding. He hadn't let everything spiral out of
control the way he had in the past. He hadn't used one slip as
an excuse to keep sliding. Instead, he'd gotten himself back on
track, showed up for work on time, gone to a meeting, ordered
club soda. He hadn't lost his focus entirely. One day soon, he

might even be able to forgive himself and put it behind him. One day maybe Rose would too. In the meantime he'd leave her be.

Simon heard groans. He looked up at the TV. Someone had turned off the Red Sox game and there now appeared a woman with pink hair swirled into a confection, dabbing a hankie to eyes raccooned with makeup. There was a microphone in her hand, a Bible on her lap, and a toll-free number at the bottom of the screen along with MasterCard and Visa logos. Someone in there had requested the Christian Network and Simon had an idea who that someone might be. He turned around and there, leaning against a column with a drink in one hand and dabbing his eyes with a bar napkin, was Segundo.

"Muchacho!" Simon said. "Over here."

Segundo dropped the napkin and threaded his way through the crowd to his friend. They embraced. Simon noticed a smudge of white makeup behind Segundo's ear.

Segundo held Simon's face in his hands and squeezed. "So good to see you, my friend. It's been too long." Segundo's breath was enough to sedate a house pet.

"Me too," Simon said. "Settle down there, friend."

"It's a wonder you survived the accident. It was a miracle," he said. "The Lord answered my prayers."

"Thanks but you didn't even know I was out there until after I was rescued," Simon said.

"I had a feeling." Segundo patted his chest.

The man in the seat next to Simon had already discreetly moved one bar stool down. Segundo sat. He was dressed in layman's clothes, a pair of black pants and a blue denim button-down shirt. In spite of his tasteful attire, an exuberant Hispanic in this bar was about as exotic as it got.

"Yeah, well, it was really your aunt and uncle who came to the rescue. And they're worried about you. They want you to come home," Simon said. He frowned. "So what's this about?" Simon flicked Segundo's drink with his finger. It made a *ping*.

"It's a long, sad story," Segundo said, "beginning with when I was tragically wrenched from my homeland." He cast his eyes down and shook his head.

Simon couldn't help but smile. Segundo had to be the best shit slinger he'd ever known. "What does Cuba have to do with you drinking?"

"I've been getting signs from the Blessed Virgin."

"What kind of signs?" Simon said.

"Something is about to happen."

"Happen where? In Cuba?" Simon asked.

Segundo looked around to make sure no one was listening. He nodded. "I need to return to Florida," Segundo said.

"Your family will be glad to hear it but I don't follow you."

"*Signs*. Like yesterday I was walking on the beach and there, just sitting on the sand, illuminated by a single ray of sunlight, was a piece of driftwood shaped like my beloved country."

"You found a stick shaped like Cuba," Simon said. He scratched his head. "Aren't all sticks shaped like Cuba?"

"*Then* in my tea this morning—"

"Since when did you start drinking tea?" Simon said.

"Since I found out it goes good with rum," Segundo said. "You want to hear the story or not?"

"Sure, sorry."

Segundo set down his drink so he could use two hands to tell his story. "Fidel appeared. Right there in the tea leaves. As I live and breathe, it was Castro himself."

"If that's not enough to make a man switch to coffee, I don't know what is."

"I'm serious," he said. He gripped Simon's wrist. "The signs I'm getting are from the Blessed Virgin."

"How do you know?" Simon asked.

"I just *know*," Segundo said.

He waved his hand, which Simon knew meant he'd heard enough from the heathen.

"Where are you staying? I found a place for you."

"I'm at the Sea View Inn," he said. "But there's no sea view."

"That doesn't surprise me. Tell me what you've been doing since, you know, the mascot thing went sour," Simon said. He looked down at his club soda and watched the bubbles rise to the top.

Segundo stared at him. Simon could feel it. Segundo waited.

"All right. I know I messed that up for you. I'm sorry, I really am," Simon said.

"As long as you're sorry," Segundo said.

"I am." Simon buried his face in his soda glass. The soda bubbles spit at him.

"Let me tell you something about this place. No one likes funny," Segundo said.

Simon laughed. "What do you mean? I like *funny*—" he said.

Segundo was serious. "All day, I look for work. No one wants to hire a clown. Not for parties, not for picnics, not for grand openings. No one here likes to laugh. It's not like New Hampshire," he said. Segundo looked hurt. Perhaps there was some truth to his observation.

"I guess Cape Codders just aren't big on clowns," Simon said.

"They're frightened of us," he said.

"How do you mean?"

"Today, I go out on the street. I juggle. I do mime. Put out a hat. Nothing. People go out of their way to step around it. Then this afternoon, I get an idea. I change my smile."

"Change it how?" Simon asked.

"From a smile like this—" Segundo pulled up the corners of his mouth. "To a smile like this—" This time he pulled down the corners of his mouth to create a sad, almost sinister expression.

"Hell, that's no smile. No one likes a sad clown," Simon said.

"No, but they're *afraid* of sad clowns." Segundo smiled. He wagged his finger. "And that's how I make money."

"People pay a sad clown not to hurt them?" Simon said.

"I would never hurt them. But they don't know that."

"That's crazy," Simon said.

"It's true. You locals are, how you say, *uptight*."

Segundo flagged the bartender for another drink. Simon ordered another soda water. He looked down the bar. There had to be at least fifteen people with *Nauset has a secret* on their foreheads. Come to think of it, even Cooper had writing on her head last night, though it had been too dark to see what it said. This thing, whatever it was, had taken on a life of its own. So what was the big secret? That someone famous was building at the Point? That the doctor's daughter had a made-up kid? That Simon Beadle was back in town? No secret anymore. Maybe the secret was that Cape Codders were afraid of clowns.

"Take that lady at the place where your nephew lives," Segundo said.

"You saw Cooper?" Simon slapped his forehead. "Now it makes sense. She thought I was *you* last night. How did you know Noel lived there?"

"Jesús told me about the story in the paper. So I ask someone where the painter kid lives and he tells me. It's no big secret."

"So you went there looking for me," Simon said.

"She sees me and tells me she's getting her gun," Segundo made a pistol out of his finger. "If that's not afraid, I don't know what is." He slapped the bar.

"Did you see my nephew?" Simon asked.

"No-el." He said it like he was talking about Christmas.

"Noel," Simon corrected.

"Handsome like his uncle," Segundo said. "Now *him*? He's not afraid. I talk to him and he tells me, 'The last time whiskey outsold vodka was in 1972.' He's the only one who talks to me like a regular person," Segundo said.

Simon laughed. "Look, pal. I might be able to scrape up

enough dough to get you back to Florida if that's what you want. I'm working now. I got a construction job."

"No. I don't take your money," Segundo said.

"Segundo, I *cost* you your last job. You can take my money," Simon said.

"I *earn* the money," Segundo said.

"But how? Scaring people on street corners?" Simon said. Then Simon had an idea. Of course, why didn't he think of it sooner? "There's a big celebration coming up the beginning of next month. It's the town's Tri-centennial. I bet they're hiring clowns."

"Tri-who?" Segundo said.

"It's like a big birthday party the town is throwing for itself."

"I'm good at birthday parties. I make balloon animals."

Segundo put the glass to his lips and skimmed off the top third of his drink. "I make a good balloon vagina. Have you ever seen me do that?" he asked.

"No balloon vaginas. This is a birthday party for everyone, kids, adults, old people, get it? I know some people who are involved with the planning. I'll bet I can work something out."

"*Bueno, gracias.*"

"Well, okay then. Here's the deal. No more drinking."

Segundo looked at him wide-eyed. "After this one," Segundo said. He started gulping.

"Okay, after this one. Then that's it for the next four weeks. At least we'll have some time to hang out together. But right now, I'll show you your new place and we can call your uncle, tell him your plans. Tell him that you're coming home in a month."

"I'll tell him about my visions."

"Just tell him you're coming home to Florida. You can worry about Cuba and the Virgin later."

Simon and Segundo clinked glasses. Simon looked out over the restaurant floor. Being there reminded him of Felicia. Simon tried to pick out the table where they had been sitting that first night he'd met her.

There, Simon thought. Right in the center, a few rows back from the jukebox. A man and a woman were sitting there now. The woman had her back to the bar. The man was tall and lean. He had dark wavy hair. And the woman . . . funny but from the back, she looked just like Rose. Simon knew his eyes were just playing tricks on him. What would Rose be doing in a bar with another man? Then he remembered last night, the phone call, the conversation he'd heard from the bushes. Someone had invited her to dinner. The boyfriend. Could it be? The woman who looked like Rose was smoking a bread stick. She turned to blow out the smoke. Simon saw more of her face. It *was* Rose.

Simon turned toward the bar. He felt his back grow hot. He hunched over his seat, tried to become small. After last night, the last thing he needed was for Rose to catch him in a bar.

"What is it, amigo? You look like you've seen a ghost?" Segundo said.

"Just thought I saw someone I knew," Simon said.

"*Lots* of ghosts for you here." Segundo was working out a magic trick, pretending to stuff a bar napkin into his ear and pulling it out of his sleeve. He sucked down the last of his drink. He took out the straw and let the ice hit him in the teeth. "A whole *town* full of ghosts. Like Miami for me."

Simon turned back again and saw Rose was getting up from her chair. The guy jumped up and pulled out her seat the rest of the way, then placed his hand on her back. She leaned in to him a little. She seemed a little wobbly. Had she been drinking? She cut a slow, deliberate path to the restroom, her head down, apparently watching her feet. Now was Simon's chance to get out of there.

"Segundo, let's go." Simon dropped some cash onto the bar.

"But the ice hasn't melted," Segundo said. "The ice still counts as part of the drink."

"It's melted enough. Let's go. I gotta get up early for work tomorrow," Simon said.

"But tomorrow's Saturday."

Simon looked up at the TV. The Red Sox game was back on. "Okay, gotta get up early for *Mass*. Come on, friend. Let's call Jesús."

"There!" Segundo said. He pointed to his glass. "Right there!" he said, raising his voice. People turned to look at the two of them, including the guy from Rose's table.

"What *is* it?" Simon said through his teeth. He looked over toward the bathroom door. She was already inside. He could feel sweat breaking out on the back of his neck.

Segundo lifted his glass. "Right there." He pointed with the swizzle straw. "Elian Gonzalez. In the ice cube. See him?"

Simon took Segundo to the house Sparrow had found. It was on the historic register and had once belonged to a frigate gunner named Joshua Crosby during the War of 1812. There was a plaque to the left of the front of the door, and a brass bell. To enter the walk, you had to pass through a pair of enormous bleached whale jawbones that rose out of the ground to form an arbor. Segundo would be sharing the place with three young waiters from Ukraine. Not only was the place cheap, but Simon had been assured by Sparrow, who knew the owner, that the kids didn't party. Simon knocked on the door and Segundo met his new roommates. Simon asked to use the phone, then waited with Segundo for what seemed like forever until one of the roommates finished talking to his girlfriend in Odessa. Then Simon dialed Jesús and handed the phone to Segundo, who handled it like something that might blow up. He put his ear to the receiver and pushed out a high-pitched *hola* and that was the last word Simon understood. Gradually, the wrinkles smoothed out of Segundo's brow and a light came into his friend's eyes, warming them. He'd be okay. Simon waved before he left but Segundo didn't see. He was talking to his aunt and weeping.

Simon thought Segundo was pretty lucky to have people like the Martinezes in his life. Out here on the street in the middle of the night, he'd never felt more alone. His feet were headed in the direction of the Governor Higgins, but he wasn't ready to face that tiny room with those four dingy walls, where the aloneness would have something to bounce off of and come back and hit him in the face over and over. Soon he needed to find himself a decent place to live. His rent was paid through the middle of June. After that, he'd look for something where a little light actually came in through the windows and the furniture wasn't chewed-and-glued wood.

It was a beautiful night, clear with a big moon like when he'd been with Rose on the Point just two nights earlier. What a difference a couple of nights could make. Simon got as far as the motel and kept on walking, past the convenience store and old rose-covered capes on Sea View Drive, past the road to the Point and the path he'd taken Rose down. He kept walking, toward the old duck farm where his nephew lay sleeping and Cooper lay waiting for the next clown she might take out with her shotgun.

Suddenly a black BMW came down the road and turned in to Val's driveway. Simon ducked into a cluster of old rhododendrons in front of Cooper's place. When he thought they were gone, Simon inched back onto the sidewalk. He could see through the hedgerow between the two properties that the driver had cut the lights and the engine, the only sound being the shells crumbling under the weight of the tires as they rolled forward, as if they were trying to be quiet on purpose. The car came to a stop in front of the cottage.

Shadows emerged. Simon heard laughing. Two people walked to the front door. He should leave. He'd done enough spying in the last two days. For all he knew Cooper might be watching from her window right now, this time loaded for bear.

Still, something wouldn't let him leave. He wanted to run down the driveway like a crazy man. He wanted to stop them. She hadn't even gotten the chance to know what kind of good things Simon was capable of. He didn't really know what they were either, but at least until Thursday, he'd felt like a man on the verge of doing good things. In time, he hoped that feeling would return.

Simon listened as the front door to the cottage opened. He counted off the seconds before the headlights would come back on and the car would pull out. Seconds became minutes. He saw the lights switch on in the hallway, and an instant later, the bedroom. They weren't wasting any time. Simon inched closer, just enough to see the face of the man who was now testing Rose's bedsprings. The guy from the Barnacle. Martin.

He didn't need to see any more. Simon returned to the motel and crawled into bed feeling more sober than he had ever felt in his life.

CHAPTER THIRTEEN

If pressure is too high, slowly release.
—*from the National Highway Traffic Safety Administration*
Tire Safety Brochure

Rose had almost gotten used to the sounds of the fishing boats leaving the harbor at dawn's first light, and the saws and compressors out at the construction site. Now there was a different drone, tractors down on the beach that had started at five in the morning. Rose attributed the ungodly hour to their having to work with the tides, with only a window of time each day to push sand and move boulders before the waters rose again.

The first morning Rose had heard them, almost three weeks ago, she'd thought the sounds were coming from inside her head. It was the morning after she and Martin had dinner. Rose had been a fool to think she could handle that much liquor, just grateful when she awoke that it was Saturday and she didn't have to go in to work. Maybe Rose knew she couldn't handle the booze and that's why she'd drunk so much in the first place, so she wouldn't have to deal with Martin. If that was the case, the night had been a success. They had managed to get through the entire evening without resolving anything. The next day Martin called from Boston.

"How are you this morning?"

"Horrible," Rose said. It was as if someone had wedged a spatula between her eyes. "Look, I'm really sorry about last night—"

"We've *all* been there," he said. "Look, I was wondering if you wanted to come to town next week for a Sox game."

Then, as if someone had taken the fishbowl off her head, there was the clarity Rose had been seeking all the days since she'd left Boston. She knew what had to happen next. "Martin, I just don't think I can do this right now. I'm up to my ears with work on this Tri-centennial thing and—"

"No problem. I get tickets all the time."

"That's not it, Martin," Rose said. She took a deep breath. "What I mean is, I think it's better if we just leave things as they are. I'm here. You're there. It didn't work out. We have our own lives now."

Rose heard him hit something. "For crying out loud, Rose. What do you want from me? Can't you just *accept* my apology?"

Rose thought he had a right to be upset but not *angry*. "I can't get past it, Martin. I've tried. It's a matter of trust. Our foundation is cracked. It's beyond repair. That's just how I feel."

There was a long silence. "I'm good with a caulk gun."

There was a little of the guy she'd fallen in love with. Rose had to fight to keep it together. "I'm sorry, Martin. I hope you find what you're looking for."

"Rose—"

"Good-bye, Martin."

That morning after she'd hung up, Rose realized some of her hangover wasn't actually *hangover* at all. Some of that sick feeling lifted right away.

It wasn't that the tractors bothered Rose as much as how the sound of them carried her to the Point, where Simon was. Three weeks had gone by since the night he'd called her drunk and Rose hadn't heard another word from him—no apology. Nothing. Her own experience with overindulgence allowed her at least to sympathize with the humiliation he must have felt as bits and pieces of the broken night came back. He'd made a fool of himself, just as Rose had a night later with Martin.

Still, it was a small town. They were bound to run into each other sooner or later. And since Rose hadn't said anything to Val or Cooper about his transgression, she still owed it to them to keep an eye on Simon so that Noel wouldn't get hurt. That was the rationalization she used to ask Calvin to see what he could find out. He was a distant cousin to someone in the Higgins family who was working the site. The cousin told Calvin that Simon was showing up every day and that he appeared to be fine. In fact, an old friend of Simon's had come to town and it was *Simon* who was helping the *friend* stay sober and find work. Simon had even gone to Val about getting his friend a job at the Tri-centennial. He must have chosen the time carefully, going out of his way to avoid Rose. Just because she'd told him to leave her alone didn't mean he actually had to. Since when did people ever follow her instructions? Martin hadn't left her alone despite her initial pleas. Clearly, what had happened out there on the Point hadn't meant much to Simon, and whatever post-casual-sex fixation had caused him to come back and spy on her in her bedroom must have lasted only a single night. Otherwise, nothing could keep him away. Maybe Simon just didn't like what he saw through the window. There was always that possibility too.

In the end, as long as Simon was sober, that's what mattered. For Noel's sake.

The wind whistled through the rusty hole in the floor of Mike Eldridge's pickup as he and Rose ambled down Main Street toward the beach, whipping by silver cottages. Soon the canopy of oaks and locust cleared out to a big sky filled with clouds. They passed a sign with an arrow that said *Nauset Beach,* but rather than follow it, Mike suddenly took a left, then another sharp right down a dirt road. They came to a sandy clearing and stopped. Rose presumed the tracks ahead led through the dunes to the beach. Even with the windows closed she could hear the surf.

"Why are we stopping?" Rose asked.

"Have to let some air out of the tires," he said. He tossed a penlike object at her, a tire gauge. "Fifteen pounds is good."

He got out of the truck and Rose did the same, too proud to admit she had no idea how to work a tire gauge. A second later, Rose heard hissing from Mike's side of the car. She could see his knees in the sand from beneath the truck. *I can do this,* she told herself. In fact, she had some sketchy recollection of having written something a long time ago to do with tire pressure for a government Web site. Rose unscrewed the cap on the right-front tire valve, then pressed the nub on the top of the gauge onto it. Air that smelled like the inside of a mechanic's garage gushed from the narrow chamber.

Earlier, she had been the one to call Mike.

"I was wondering when you were gonna call," he said.

"I beg your pardon?"

"What'll it be? Dinner? A movie? Both?"

"Actually, I was just looking for some information," Rose said. She could feel her ears heat up. "A question about some police records."

"Ever been driving on the outer beach?" he asked.

"Me? No," she said.

"I'll make you a deal. Come with me for a drive this morning and we can talk out there."

"But—"

"That's the deal. Take it or leave it," Mike said.

If Rose turned him down, she wouldn't get his help. Besides, a relationship with an insider on the police force was worth cultivating. The final pre-Tri-centennial issue of the *Oracle* was almost put to bed, which was why, for the first time in three weeks, she finally had time to get back to her investigation of Lino's disappearance. So for these reasons and because Rose had always wondered what it was like to drive out on the beach, she'd accepted.

Now the hissing stopped on Mike's side of the truck. Rose took that as her cue to stop also. She pressed the gauge into the tire valve and the red arrow shot to twenty, then fell. Rose released another five pounds, screwed on the cap, then moved on to the back tire. When both were done, Rose got into the cab, where Mike was waiting. She handed him the tire gauge, proud of her ability to improvise.

"Why did we do that?" Rose asked.

"So we don't get stuck." He clipped the gauge to his sun visor. "Gives the tires more traction."

He started the truck. Rose rolled down her window. Once they broke through a clearing in the dunes, Mike slipped into the tracks above the high-tide mark and the ride smoothed out a little. They were on the beach cruising parallel to the surf. Rose checked the speedometer and they were going no more than thirty miles per hour but it seemed so much faster. The wind was whipping the hair around her face and it was too bumpy to talk, so Rose just settled in, enjoying the scenery as they kept pace with the birds flying low over the water. Rose watched a tern as it dove into the surf and came up with a flash of light in its beak.

"Pretty nice, huh?" Mike raised his voice to be heard over the wind and the engine.

Rose held the hair back from her face. "It's incredible."

"Just a little further," he said.

Rose nodded. She didn't want the ride to end. The sun was starting to wear through the cloud cover. "Mike," she said. They hit a bump and she flew off the seat a little. "Did you know about Val's daughter?"

"Eve?" He turned to her, dropped his sunglasses below his eyes, and smiled. "Always thought Adam was supposed to come first."

Rose shook her head and looked out the side window.

"I thought she might have had you going," he said.

"For a little while," Rose said. She wondered how long it would have taken her to figure it out if it weren't for Simon, how much more of a fool she might have made of herself. She owed him for that.

Mike took a hard right out of the tracks, stepping on the gas to get the truck up and over the soft sand. For a second, Rose thought he was taking them right into the ocean. Once they were facing the surf, he cut the engine. Without the wind and the truck noise, it was suddenly quiet.

"Wow," Rose said. She attempted to smooth down her hair. "That was something."

Mike smiled. "So what did you want to ask me about?" He got out of the truck, pulled a couple of beach chairs out of the back, used his foot to kick them open, and set them up facing the waves. He did it fast, in one graceful series of movements, as if he'd done it a million times. "Not exactly beach weather but we can hang a little while. Should have brought my pole."

Rose got out of the truck and her feet sank in the course sand. Everything was so vast and gray. She'd never been down to this part of the beach. It was so deserted. In the distance, she could see smaller waves breaking on the bar near the mouth of the inlet. It was easier to breathe out here. Rose dropped into one of the chairs. Suddenly a beer appeared over her shoulder. This was getting less professional by the minute.

"I shouldn't. I'm working," Rose said. "Sort of." She took the beer anyway.

"Me too," Mike said.

Rose turned in her chair and looked at him.

"I'm *kidding*. Cheers." He raised his bottle and took a swig.

"What made you become a cop, Mike?" Rose asked. She dug her toes into the sand.

He sat and stretched out his thighs. He took another swig of his beer. Rose watched his Adam's apple bounce. "Nothing so noble."

"What do you mean?"

He hesitated for a second, like he was trying to decide whether to tell her. "All this is off the record, right?" he said.

"This isn't an interview," Rose said. "I'm just curious."

Mike got up and went to the truck. He pulled a blue Red Sox cap from behind the seat and put it on, smoothed it flat over his head, then sat back down. "Grew up hating cops," he said. "My dad hated cops and that's how I was raised." Mike twisted the beer into the sand. "He was in prison till I was four. Armed robbery."

"No way," Rose said.

"That was the *first* time. Second time he went away for longer. I was sixteen."

"That must've been horrible."

"All those years growing up, he told me he'd been framed. He said the cops set him up. Hell, no kid wants to believe his dad's a crook, so I didn't question it. I just grew up hating cops." Mike pedaled the sand, grinding one heel, then the other. "When I was sixteen, a few of my father's old friends showed up at the door. A couple days later, my old man just disappeared. He was gone two weeks before the cops came looking for him. Wouldn't say what they thought he did. My mother and I didn't know where he was, and even if we did, I wouldn't have told. Then, in the middle of the night about a week later, he just shows up at the back door looking like hell with his face all cut up, no money, smelling like booze, wanting me to hide him in the basement. 'Don't tell your mother,' he said. Up until that moment, I'd believed every word he ever told me. Right then, I knew it was all lies. He was a crooked piece of crap."

"What did you do?" Rose asked.

"I told him to go to the basement while I gathered up some food, blankets, whiskey. Then I used the phone in the upstairs hall and called the cops. They came and took him away." Mike lowered the brim of his hat over his eyes.

"And you became a cop."

"Soon as I was old enough. I didn't want to be like him and being a cop in my eyes was the farthest I could get," he said.

"How'd you get through those days? I mean, it must've been hard. You were just a kid," Rose said.

"*That,*" Mike said. He pointed to the water. "Spent a lot of time fishing out there on the bars. Was the only thing that could clear my head. Still is. I come out here by myself when I need to think."

"I bet most people who grow up around water have a kind of therapeutic connection to it," Rose said. She felt a twinge of jealousy having grown up around tobacco fields. "What happened to your father? What did they arrest him for?"

"Those *friends* had talked him into trying to hit an armored car." He laughed and shook his head. "One of the guys got busted at the scene and ratted out the others. They all got hard time. My father did another thirteen years. Heard he died a couple years after he got out. My aunt was the one who called and told me."

"You never reconciled."

"He used to write me letters from prison till he found out I was a cop." Mike laughed in a way so forced it looked like his face might crack.

"I'm sorry," Rose said.

"Yep. So, what did you want to ask me?" Mike pulled the cap from his eyes and got up from the chair with his empty. "Want another beer?"

"No thanks."

He reached into the cooler in the cab and cracked open another one.

"Actually, this goes back to when you were a kid too," Rose said.

"Oh yeah?" He sat back down and adjusted the chair to recline.

"I'm trying to find out what I can about an old case," she said. "Did you know Cooper's son, Lino?"

Mike's beer bottle hit his teeth. A little stream of beer trickled down his chin. He sat up and wiped his neck with his sleeve. "You gotta be kidding. You mean that kid who ran away almost thirty years ago?" he asked.

Rose leaned forward in her chair. "Did you know him?"

"A little," he said.

"I was hoping I could access the old files. Do you know if the case was ever officially closed?"

"Had to be. But I wouldn't know where to begin. I wasn't even a cop yet then." Mike took off his hat, ran his hand through his hair, then put it back on.

Rose traced her fingers through the sand. "But surely you guys keep your old records somewhere. Can you check into it for me?"

He took off his sunglasses and looked at her. "You realize this is a pretty painful subject for some folks in town."

"I talked to Cooper. Val and she both believe Lino's dead. Cooper just wants closure."

"They're so sure, huh?" He sat back in the chair.

"You're not?"

"Think it was old Avery Bassett who saw him at the bus station a day or two after he *disappeared*." Mike made finger quotes around the word.

"Somebody *saw* him?"

"That's how come the investigation got called off, as I recall." He pulled at a thread on his cap. It started to unravel.

"Cooper didn't tell me that," Rose said. Kind of a large detail to leave out. She was famously adept at keeping Rose in the dark.

"She and the Bassetts haven't spoken since."

"Is this Avery Bassett guy still around?" she asked. If so, Rose wanted to talk to him. She lay back in the chair and closed her eyes.

"He and his wife live out near the Point," Mike said. "He's kind of a kook."

This town had no shortage of them. "I did find out something about Lino from the papers. How he once got in trouble with the cops for racing his boat in the channel. Think that's import—" Rose was hit in the mouth with a spray of sand. Mike had gotten up and was folding his chair. She wiped her mouth with her hand and spit out the sharp grains.

"Did I do that? Sorry. Was thinking we should head back."

"Already?" Rose asked.

"I just remembered some paperwork I was supposed to do this morning. Guess I spaced. And then I have to get out to the Point too. Been some suspicious stuff going on out there."

"Like what? I thought you were off today."

"Just ramping up security for the Tri-centennial. Want to make sure there's been no more mischief out there, broken windows, spray paint, that sort of thing."

Rose was about to ask how come he couldn't just have one of the other cops take a look when she realized Mike was standing near her chair like he was waiting for her to get up. She obliged. Ten seconds later, the chairs were back in the bed of the truck and they were on their way back. Once they got to the parking lot, Rose waited in the cab while Mike used the community air pump to refill the tires. Before he dropped her off at the cottage, she reminded him about the records. He promised to look into it.

Rose had said she was conducting an *Oracle* poll on the location of the reenactment, whether it should take place in the spot where the clash between the British and the militia actually happened, or, in light of the construction, at a new location farther down the beach? Even with the Tri-centennial just days away, everyone still had an opinion on that. Seventy-two-year-old Prudence Bassett, wife of Avery Bassett, was no exception.

When Rose arrived, Pru greeted her at the front door. She was wearing a snap-front housecoat with embroidered owl pockets, and nylon socks rolled down to the base of her thick ankles. On her head was a large straw hat with a band of pink polka-dot fabric around the brim. She smelled like cigarettes and Jean Naté, and had a scar on her cheek, just below her left cheekbone, from where Rose had learned her husband had hooked her while surf casting off the outer beach more than two decades earlier.

According to Val—unreliability of the source duly noted— the story went that Avery had gone four weeks straight without catching a single striper while everyone else in town, even the tourists, were having a great season. This wouldn't have mattered much except Avery earned his living selling pogies in the shed out behind his house. People started to wonder if there was something wrong with his bait. Avery knew the only way to prove them wrong would be to catch the mother of all fish. One late June day, he brought his wife out in the Wagoneer, set his pole in the sand at eight, and when he still hadn't caught anything by noon, descended into a funk and started drinking whiskey out of a thermos. Pru had wanted to pack sandwiches but Avery wouldn't hear of it. He was going to catch a bass and they were going to fire up the grill right there on the beach in front of everyone. Pru had made some potato salad and she had been fishing a piece of hard-boiled egg out of the bowl with her fingers when all of a sudden a hook came flying out of nowhere and snagged her on the cheek. By that time Avery was so drunk he didn't know which way the water was. He just felt the pull on the line and knew he had to start reeling it in.

Pru was screaming her head off but Avery thought it was just because he'd finally caught a bass. He reeled in as fast as he could.

When his catch got close, Pru hauled off and knocked him out cold with the bowl of potato salad.

That day—Val had slowed down mercilessly for the punch line—*Avery didn't land a bass, but a Bassett landed Avery.*

Pru led Rose around to the back of the house, to a small patio shaded from the sun by an overhang that sagged at one end, a bird's nest tucked into the crook of one of the fallen supports. Tall weeds grew up from between the uneven bluestones. There were a couple of wicker chairs with soiled, makeshift pillows and a rusted tray table that held a sea-clam shell overflowing with cigarette butts. Pru sat in one of the chairs with her back to the water. From the Bassetts' backyard, the construction site to the north was hard to miss. With the wind coming out of the northwest, Rose had to raise her voice to compete with the tractors.

"Lovely spot," Rose said.

"Was before *that* monstrosity," Pru said. She didn't turn around, just pointed over her shoulder with her thumb.

"Maybe it won't be so bad when it's done," Rose said.

Pru raised an eyebrow.

"I just mean houses always look worse when they're first going up, when the wood is new and stands out from everything around it. Maybe when the trees grow and the shingles gray up a bit, it might not be so bad." They were close enough that Rose could see some men working on the roof. Simon was probably one of them.

Pru's eyes narrowed. "Where'd you say you're from?" she asked. Rose wasn't about to tell her she came from somewhere other than the Cape, let alone the city.

"As I explained over the phone, the reason I'm here is that the *Oracle* is taking a poll on where people feel the reenactment should take place—"

"Should happen where it happened, house or no house,"

she said. She clicked her tongue and folded her arms across her chest.

"So you don't think it would be more practical to move it down the beach?"

"If washashores are going to be allowed to build houses in places that matter to us, then there should be conditions. Things are gonna change, you can't stop it, but you can't change what happened two hundred years ago and you can't change *where* it happened either. Deed or no deed, the Point is a part of our heritage. That pinhead Nickerson should have thought about that before he allowed *this*." A thin blue vein pulsed at her temple.

About fifty feet behind her, Avery came out of the shack. He was tall and skinny, and was wearing orange rubber overall waders. He stretched and reached under the bib to scratch his belly, squinted in Rose's direction, then slipped back inside.

"Well, thanks for your opinion, Mrs. Bassett. It's one shared by my many folks around here. I was hoping to talk with Mr. Bassett too, if I may."

She waved her arm like Rose had told her a joke. "That'll be the day," she said.

"What do you mean. I just saw him go into the—"

"That man hasn't talked to a soul 'cept me in a decade. Besides, his opinion is the same as mine. After you been married fifty-one years, you got two brains but just one opinion." She laughed and at some point it segued into a phlegmy cough.

It looked as though Rose had no choice but to ask her about Lino. "There was something else I was hoping to ask you if you don't mind. This one goes back a bit."

"These days I'm better with what went on back there than with what I had for breakfast," she said.

"You remember when Cooper Almeida's son disappeared?"

Her shoulders slumped and she seemed to age another decade right before Rose's eyes. "Who forgets a thing like that?"

"I read in an old newspaper that your husband had seen Lino at the bus station in Hyannis," Rose said.

"Shoulda kept his trap shut."

"Why is that?"

"Folks didn't believe him. Accused him of stirring up trouble. Some even stopped buying bait from him, just because he stuck to his guns, stubborn fool. To this day, when Cooper sees me comin' in the supermarket, she starts wheeling the other way, as if *Avery* had anything to do with her son running away."

"He's sure it was Lino he saw? I mean, did he know Lino?"

Pru took a cigarette out of the pack and lit it. She drew the smoke deep into her lungs, then let it out through her nose.

"Know how many people lived here year-round back then? About a tenth of what's here now. Of course he knew Lino. Used to sell bait to Sal. Everybody knew everybody," she said. *"Cops believed him anyway."*

"In the paper, it said Avery had been at a donut shop across the street from the bus station," Rose said.

"He'd been to the auto supply next door for some parts for the old Wagoneer. That was when you had no choice but to drive a half hour to that congested godforsaken hellhole for certain stuff. Now you can get just about anything you need right here. Haven't had to leave Nauset for twenty years, which is fine by me."

Pru dislodged the ash at the end of her cigarette by touching it to a butt in the shell. Rose looked to the shed for signs of Avery. When he'd come out earlier, hadn't he squinted in this direction? And the fishing story. No matter how drunk, how could a fisherman catch his wife on the line and not know until she was practically on top of him?

"Is that all?" Pru said. She started to get up.

"Mrs. Bassett," Rose said, "does your husband wear glasses?"

"Not a day in his life," she said.

What if that had been the answer when the cops asked too?

What if they didn't ask the next most obvious question. "Has he ever been to an eye doctor?"

She sat back down. "Been trying for thirty-five years to get him to go, the stubborn SOB," she said. She cussed under her breath, picked up the pack of cigarettes, and tossed it into her lap. At that moment Rose knew Pru didn't believe her husband had seen Lino either.

"Didn't he need an eye test to get his driver's license?"

"I do the driving," she said. "I drove to Hyannis that day."

"But why did you let people believe he'd really seen Lino if you knew his eyesight was bad?"

Pru mashed her cigarette into the mound of butts.

"You *married*, Ms. Nowak?" Her eyes looked like gray stones at the bottom of a tide pool.

"No," Rose said.

"Didn't think so," she said. "Go on and marry a proud man someday. Then come back and we'll talk."

Down the hill from the town hall, the police station was an unsightly structure, the kind of building someone might go on a hunger strike to have torn down. It had been built in the seventies with just a few windows, faux-brick siding, and an asymmetrical roof pitched at a steep angle. The inside was nearly as dated with rustic barn-wood paneling. There was a waiting room with benches, and a Plexiglas window behind which the officer on front-desk duty sat.

Rose hadn't heard from Mike in the two days since their beach outing, so she thought she'd catch up with him on her lunch break. With four days before the Tri-centennial and three to go before their last issue hit the stands, things were finally winding down at the paper and focus was shifting toward coverage of the big day itself.

Rose walked up to the window. "I'm looking for Mike Eldridge," she said.

The cop behind the counter had freckled skin and a layer of baby fat around his cheeks. He looked less like a cop than a kid playing dress-up. He turned around and asked someone behind him. "Hey, Eldridge on duty today?"

"Check the Point," the voice behind the wall said.

"You want me to try to reach him over the radio?" the kid asked.

"Maybe I'll just go down there myself," Rose said.

She hadn't seen Simon or even been to the Point since the night they were together almost three weeks ago. Rose figured she was bound to run into him at the celebration on Saturday, so what was the big deal if she saw him a little sooner? *I can do this,* Rose told herself. She was a reporter. So what if the last time she'd been there, she'd had her clothes scattered to the wind? Just because Simon happened to be there now wasn't reason enough to shy away from her journalistic duties. Rose was a professional.

For about an eighth of a mile, she clung to that.

Rose headed down Main Street, passed the Governor Higgins Motel, then took a left on Sea View Drive. The construction-site entrance was easy to spot for the mud and sand that had been tracked onto the street. She passed the old cottages and slowed as she approached the wide entrance to the driveway. Rose put on her blinker and pulled in, stopping at the top. Her hands were sweaty on the steering wheel. She looked down the driveway. The trees and undergrowth had filled in since their night in the dunes. It was harder to see to the house but it was also harder to be seen, which was good. Rose could make out three or four guys sitting on a new stone wall. They had lunch pails beside them. Mike's cruiser was parked at the end of the drive. His uniform made him stand out from the others. He was there talking to the guys on the wall. All Rose had to do was go down there.

She looked in the mirror and checked her face. She smoothed back her ponytail and took a deep breath.

One of the guys on the wall hopped off. Rose couldn't tell for sure but it looked like Simon. She panicked. It was all she could do to stop herself from stepping on the gas and backing out onto the road. Rose closed her eyes and took another deep breath, trying to find some reserve of inner calm.

When she opened her eyes, the workers had scattered and Mike Eldridge was walking out toward the dune. The guy who Rose thought might be Simon lifted a heavy toolbox and slid it onto the bed of a pickup truck parked beside Mike's cruiser. Then he jumped up onto the back of the truck—*jumped,* which made Rose think there was a chance she had the wrong guy; after all, Simon had barely been able to walk after his first day on the job. He took a bandanna out of his back pocket and wiped his neck. He stood on the truck and seemed to be watching Mike as he climbed the dune. Rose saw him shake his head and kick something in the back of the truck. Then he hopped out of the bed and disappeared around the side of the house.

Rose sat there staring at the house for a few minutes. These past weeks, she'd had to work to keep him off her mind. She'd done a good job of it.

Rose took out her cell phone and dialed the nonemergency police number, though the thumping in her chest had her wondering whether she should really be dialing 911.

"Nauset police," the voice said.

"I'd like to leave a message for Mike Eldridge. This is Rose Nowak. Please ask him to call me. He has my number. Thanks."

Later that evening, just before dusk, Rose pulled out of the driveway and headed into town to pick up dinner. With pizza on her mind, she noticed the orange sky dotted with gray mushroom-like clouds. She was so busy constructing her metaphor—the anchovy slivers at the horizon and the sun itself that could be likened to a big juicy yellow pepper—that she nearly clipped a jogger who was coming up the street at an impressive gait. Rose was almost upon him before she recognized the ebbing hairline and the line of his shoulders. His hair had bleached lighter and his face had healed, his skin was smoother and shoulders tan, no doubt, from being out all day in the sun. He seemed younger and more muscular. How was it that a person could change so much in a few weeks?

He saw Rose and raised his hand in a little wave. He smiled. She gave him the thumbs-up sign. The thumbs-up! What did it mean? *Nice going? Looking good? Bygones? Better keep right on running, pal?*

The next morning, after being unable to get the jogger off her mind (POST-post-casual-sex fixation? Something else?), Rose overslept. When she finally got into the office, she saw the message light flashing on her phone. She half expected it to be Simon. It was Mike.

Hey, Rose. Mike here. Sorry I haven't gotten back to you on those records but I haven't had a spare minute. Been out at the Point. Last night someone took a hammer to a rain gutter and then we found someone spray-painted "Nauset has a secret" on the seawall. Looks like Nickerson's little diversion brought the attention right where he didn't want it. Thought you might want to know, maybe send someone out to snap a photo before they clean it up. You got about an hour. If anyone asks, you didn't hear it from me.

According to Zadie Nickerson, the seawall was going to be about five hundred feet long, running the perimeter of the Point. It was about two-thirds of the way finished, with a large stretch still under construction at the south side. Each day, the tractors worked to set the eight-to-twelve-foot stones until the tide came in and filled the excavation site with water. Then the equipment had to be moved to higher ground. At high tide, the coast became a navigational hazard with underwater boulders that posed a danger to small boats and kayaks. When Rose saw the writing on the seawall from the photographer's skiff, she thought of the Bassetts, who were now looking directly upon an even more offensive mess. At least she was banking on Pru's being able to see it. The graffiti spanned five large stones to the south, one word on each: *Nauset-has-a-se-cret* with *se* and *cret* taking up the last two. The graffiti was big enough to be seen from anywhere in the harbor and probably even from the outer beach beyond.

By the time the *Cape Gazette* got wind of the vandalism, the words had been washed away with acid. Thanks to Mike, the *Oracle* had a great front-page photo for the final pre-Tri-centennial edition on Friday, the one where the paper would finally be allowed to break the story of the time capsule. It was perfect. Mike Eldridge with an *i* might have come from notoriously bad stock, but as far as Rose was concerned, he was one of the good guys.

CHAPTER FOURTEEN

*Switch on to prevent undesired response when
you accidentally press buttons.*
—*from the Panasonic Digital Audio Player Model SV-
SW30V User Manual*

He didn't let himself think about her all the time. He put her
on a shelf in his mind. He convinced himself he wanted what
was best for her, even if what was best was some good-looking
guy in a flashy car. He just wanted Rose to be happy. He figured
it was only a matter of time before she'd move back up to the city
to start a new life. Or pick up on an old one. So seeing her pass by
in the car this evening had taken him by surprise. And she'd given
him the thumbs-up sign, at least that was the sign he'd hoped she
was giving him.

Simon hadn't allowed himself to dwell on Rose all these weeks
because he'd been busy working on himself. The one good thing
about construction work was that it whipped you into shape. By
the end of week one, he was coming home tired but not broken.
And by the beginning of week three, he'd even added a short jog to
his evening routine, no more than a mile or two but it was something. Simon was feeling better than he had in years. Sometimes
he walked by the mirror in his motel room and didn't recognize

the guy who was looking back at him. Except for a lingering rud-
diness to his complexion, his burns had all healed. He had a nice
even tan over his back and shoulders, which he could feel getting
stronger each day. His hair had grown in some since they'd given
him a buzz cut at the hospital in Miami, and it had lightened from
being outside in the sun. He was getting himself together, prepar-
ing for the next battle, which would be over his nephew. Simon
didn't know what Rose had told them about his drinking. Cooper
had made it clear she had no intention of letting Simon back into
Noel's life. This time Simon wasn't about to slink away. He would
stand up and fight for the right to be a part of his nephew's life. As
for getting in shape, he couldn't deny that just maybe he wanted
Rose Nowak to feel a little sorry for what she'd passed up.

That's how he'd felt up until seeing her drive by this evening.
(Hadn't she come awfully close to hitting him, and wouldn't it
have been nice if she'd clipped him a little, maybe just broken
a couple of toes so she would have had to stop and take him to
the emergency room, then help nurse him back to health, as it
would have been the least she could do.) It was as if seeing her
had somehow tossed him off his high road and onto a lower one.
If he was being honest with himself, he didn't necessarily want
what was "best" for Rose Nowak. He just wanted Rose Nowak.

If it wasn't for good-natured Val, Simon had a feeling selling
Segundo the Clown to the town of Nauset for the Tri-centennial
would have been tougher. One afternoon, the sky had opened
up in a downpour and Sparrow sent everyone home early. Simon
paid Val a visit.

"Simon, so good to see you," she'd said. "Come in. I was just
giving Noel a snack."

Noel was at the kitchen table, eating off a plate of food that
looked like Bette Midler. Wild orange mac-and-cheese hair. Half-
circle black olive eyes. Slice of red beet for the lips and a long
celery nose.

"Hey, pal." Simon came up and put his hand on Noel's shoulder. He gave it a squeeze.

Noel bit off some of the nose and the face changed to Meg Ryan.

"I have to hand it to you, Simon. You do have a way with him. I don't know many people who could come in here and lay a hand on Noel without having him try to fly away."

"The last *H* in 4-H stands for *hand*," Noel said.

"Can I fix you a plate?" Val said.

"No thanks," Simon said. He looked out the window, just to make sure Rose wasn't coming up the walk. He knew she'd be coming home soon. "I can't stay. I was hoping you could help me. I have a friend who's come to town. He's a professional clown by trade—"

"What an interesting thing to do. Noel, wouldn't it be fun to paint a clown?"

"The most popular last name in France is Martin," Noel said. He was looking out the window.

Martin? Had he done that on purpose? "Anyhow," Simon said. He looked over at Noel again to see if he was smiling. He wasn't. "His name's Segundo. I've known him for a long time, great guy. Makes all kinds of things with balloons. Has his own helium tank. Anyway, I was wondering who I might talk to about setting him up with a job for this weekend."

Val looked at him stone-faced, like she might be reliving some bad clown experience.

"Can't have a Tri-centennial without clowns, right?" Simon added.

Simon was banking on the fact that after all these months of planning, her biggest fear would be something important that they'd forgotten. She turned away from the sink and set her dishcloth on the counter. All he needed to do was convince her this was a detail they'd obviously overlooked.

"A clown," she said. "Do you really think we need one?" She fussed with a clip in her hair.

"Of course. For the kids, I mean," Simon added. "Remember how we loved to see clowns at birthday parties when we were kids?"

"You remember seeing them at birthday parties? I actually can't recall a single party where there was a—"

Come to think of it, Simon couldn't remember a single party where there had been a clown either. "Segundo's not just any clown. He's the best. Kids love him, especially the little ones." Simon felt a twinge of guilt. "Wouldn't be fair to deprive a generation, now, would it?"

Val picked up the dishcloth again and started wiping the counter in broad circles. "I suppose you're right. In fact, my daughter was just telling me how much my granddaughter *loves* to watch reruns of *Bozo*," Val said.

Simon smiled and wondered if he'd be able to look himself in the mirror again.

"I'll speak to Dorie about it. I don't know what we have left in the budget to pay your friend but I'm sure we'll scrape it up from somewhere. We have to have a clown," she said.

"After all, it *is* a birthday party," Simon said.

"You're absolutely right," Val said. She tossed the cloth in the sink and dried her hands on her apron. "It's settled."

"Noel, you must be getting excited about the exhibit. Can't wait to help you set up," Simon said.

"'Tis the last rose of summer, left blooming alone; all her lovely companions are faded and gone," Noel said.

Simon looked at Noel. The last *Rose*?

"'The Last Rose of Summer.' It's a song or a poem, I don't know which. Don't know where he got it," Val said. "Cooper keeps a lot of musty books around."

Noel loaded up his fork with noodles and stuffed them into his mouth. Simon was reluctant to look away, like he might miss something if he did.

"Does Cooper know you're planning to go?" Val asked.

"Go?" Simon turned to Val. "You mean to help set up? Sooner or later, Cooper's going to have to realize I'm here for the long haul. This show is a big deal for my nephew, and I'm going to be there."

"I'm sure Noel wants you to be there," she said.

She went over to Noel and rubbed him on the back.

"The last public execution by guillotine was in France in 1939," Noel said.

A lone elbow of macaroni shot out of his mouth and landed in a potted African violet at the center of the table. Val scooped it up with her fingers and threw it in the sink. She wiped her hand on the red dishcloth tied around her waist. She would have made a good mother, Simon thought. She sort of wound up being one anyway.

"Wait, Simon," Val said. "I want to give you something. I'm asking all my friends to wear these on Saturday," she said.

She reached into a box and pulled out a white T-shirt. She handed it to Simon and he held it up by the shoulders. It was a Jimmy Fund T-shirt. It had a picture of a kid on the front.

"Thanks, Val," he said. "For everything, I mean."

For the last few weeks, there'd been a cop at the construction site. In general, cops made Simon nervous. Something akin to the fear of clowns Segundo had talked about. During his New Hampshire years, blue uniforms were something to be noted and avoided. Now there was no rational reason for his discomfort. He wasn't being disorderly or drinking behind the wheel. He wasn't drinking, period. He wasn't breaking a single law he could think of. And still, he didn't like cops. Even ones he knew.

At first he didn't recognize Mike Eldridge, who had been scrawny as a kid. Couldn't say that about him now. He was a few years older than Simon and, when they were in school, had been pegged as wild man for antics like blowing donuts in the beach parking lot and drag racing in the inlet. Simon thought Eldridge had seen trouble from the cops himself back in those days.

Something to do with his old man. So the idea that he'd turn to law enforcement as a career was something no one would have foreseen. But by now, everyone in town was used to it. People changed. Simon just needed to catch up.

Eldridge had been assigned to the construction site over what, to Simon, seemed like pretty insignificant acts of vandalism, especially given the general controversy over the building. It could have been a lot worse. On every site, there were always kids coming around at night and popping out windows, making off with tools that had been carelessly left around, and carving their initials into two-by-fours. So what was the big deal? Most days, Eldridge stationed himself up at the top of the seawall and watched the tractors pick up and lay down rocks. He paced the length of the wall. He claimed he was providing a "police presence" to ward off the riffraff. But the way he just sat on the boulders and stared at the Bobcats all day, Simon wondered if there was anything going on under that police hat at all, whether he'd burned a few too many brain cells in his younger days. The guy seemed restless. Sometimes he'd come down and try to shoot the shit with the crew. They all knew one another but Simon saw how Eldridge made the guys feel like he was better than they were. He had an air about him that way, how some people do, almost always not because they really think they're better but because they think just the opposite. The guys on the site just put up with it.

It was Berry who had the balls to occasionally sling some abuse Eldridge's way. To him nothing or no one was off-limits. "Hey, Ponch, don't you have crooks to chase on your bicycle?" he said.

"Got some crooks to chase right here. They broke another window last night," Eldridge said.

"Nah, that was Beadle. He was looking at his reflection and the damn thing cracked," Berry said. Berry was squatting on the ground, loading his nail gun. He had a red bandanna around his head that made him look like the planet Saturn.

"Don't know if you can get away with that shit anymore. These days he's looking better than you, Berry boy," Sparrow said. He was up on a ladder.

"Eldridge, who's the fairest of us all?" Berry said. "Besides yourself."

Simon laughed. Eldridge seemed like the kind of guy who spent time catching his reflection in the mirror.

Sparrow didn't give him the chance to answer. He said to Eldridge, "I don't know how you do it, man." He turned to Higgins. "You see the chicks he still gets?"

"Saw one in the truck with him this morning," Higgins said.

"Goddamn," Sparrow said. He came down the ladder and spit in the sand.

"That reporter from Boston," Higgins said. "One living with Shimmy."

Rose? Simon looked up from the flashing he was installing at the base of a door. Eldridge was grinding his coffee-cup lid into the dust with the heel of his shiny black boot. His mind seemed somewhere else.

"The one who wrote the story about Beadle's nephew?" Sparrow asked.

"Rose Nowak is her name," Simon said. He couldn't expect to be the only one in town who'd noticed how attractive Rose was. Could she really be interested in Eldridge?

"Not bad," Berry said. He tested the gun and it fired a nail close to where Eldridge was standing. "Kinda old, though."

"Not for a fossil like Eldridge," Sparrow said.

"Fuck you I'm a fossil," Eldridge said. He puffed out his chest and his arms hung loose like they were attached to an ape. "I could kick your ass across the harbor."

"Probably could," Sparrow said.

"Not that who I'm banging is any of your business," Eldridge said.

Simon felt his face go dark. He wanted to rip Eldridge's head off. He had a crowbar in his hand. It suddenly got lighter. "Watch your mouth," he said. It was a different tone than anyone had been using up to that point. They all turned around. "She's a friend of the family."

Berry couldn't resist. He just didn't know when to shut up. "Oh yeah? How good a friend?"

"Think Beadle's been smelling the *Roses* too?" Sparrow said.

"Think Beadle got *pricked*?" Berry said.

"That was stupid," Sparrow said. He threw a piece of foam insulation at Berry and missed.

"Fuck off," Berry said.

The exchange gave Simon a chance to cool off. They were like kids in a school yard. "She's just been good to my nephew is all," Simon said. He turned to get back to work.

Eldridge took a few steps closer to Simon. "How *good*?" he said.

Simon felt the hairs on his neck stand on end. He swung around with the crowbar in his hand, felt his grip grow tighter around the metal, so tight that his hand started to hurt a little. He saw stars behind his eyes.

"Hey, Simon. Chill out," Sparrow said.

"Why don't you go back to your post, Ponch. I see some bogeymen coming out of the sand."

Eldridge's face turned white. *Must've scared the crap out of him with the crowbar,* Simon thought. *Asshole wasn't so tough.*

"Plus your fucking tan is fading," Berry said to Eldridge.

Eldridge turned and started walking up the dune.

Higgins came up to Simon, took the crowbar out of his hand, and led him back around the house. "You okay?" he said.

"He can be a son of a bitch," Simon said.

"Everyone knows it," Higgins said. "Don't let him get to you."

With Eldridge gone, everyone got back to work. Simon loaded some stuff into the truck and watched Eldridge as he climbed up the dune. A few minutes later, though, Eldridge came back.

"Come get a load of this shit," he said.

"Now what?" Sparrow asked.

"Someone vandalized the seawall," Eldridge said.

"Bogeymen," Berry said.

"What'd they do?" Sparrow said. Finally he was acting like a foreman.

"Had a little fun with a spray can," Eldridge said.

"What'd they write?" Higgins asked.

"'Nauset has a secret,'" Eldridge said.

"What the hell is all that about?" Sparrow said.

"The secret is Eldridge is a homo," Berry said.

"I'm betting we'll find out next Saturday," Higgins said. "Gotta have something to do with the Tri-centennial."

"*I* know," Eldridge said. "Can't tell you, though. You'll just have to wait and see."

"Bullshit," Berry said.

"I've got a call to make," Eldridge said. He walked back toward his cruiser.

"Higgins, got any acid in the back of the truck?" Sparrow asked.

"I'll check."

"You want to burn him alive? Count me in," Berry said.

"Just hold off for about an hour or two," Eldridge hollered.

"How come?" Sparrow asked.

"He has to secure the crime scene," Higgins said. It was the first wiseass thing he'd said all day.

There was a good chance Simon would see Rose tomorrow night when he made an appearance at the town hall, where Milo Vanderloos would be hanging Noel's paintings for Saturday's big show. The idea of seeing Rose again made him nervous. After the crowbar incident last week, Eldridge hadn't said another word about her. But that didn't keep Simon from wondering what was going on between them. In fact, it was all he could think about.

On the way home from the site, Simon decided to swing by to see how Segundo was doing. So far, his friend had been keeping up his end of the bargain. To Simon's knowledge, Segundo hadn't had any liquor since that night in the bar.

Simon walked through the whalebone entrance to Segundo's cottage and knocked on the door. The windows were open and he heard people inside speaking Russian. One of the kids answered the door. He had a lightning-bolt earring in his nose.

"Segundo here?" Simon asked.

"Segundo!" the Russian kid screamed.

If there was anything funny, it was a Ukrainian kid screaming "Segundo." It sounded like something one says after a sneeze.

"*Gracias,*" he heard from upstairs. "Send him up."

Segundo's bedroom was tiny but meticulous. It had no windows except for a small four-pane square that let in some light but didn't open. The air in the room was stale, humid, and smelled like old socks. Simon walked in to find Segundo holding a steam iron to his harlequin pants that hung from the clothes bar that traversed the room.

"Jitters?" Simon asked.

"Professionals don't get jitters," Segundo said. He was focused on the wrinkles at the backs of the knees.

"Any messages from the blessed Virgin?" Simon asked.

"No." Segundo kept on ironing. "I think it's a sign."

"You think not getting any signs is a sign," Simon said. He shook his head. People could convince themselves of anything. "I'm gonna miss you when you go back," Simon said. "I feel like you just got here and now you're going."

"I'm glad to hear you say that. I'm not going," Segundo said. He didn't look up.

"What do you mean you're not going?"

"I realized the signs I was getting weren't really signs. It was the drinking. Soon as I stop, so do the signs. It was a test. A sign for me to stay here," Segundo said.

Simon cocked his head and looked at his friend. He couldn't follow the logic. "But what about Cuba?"

Segundo stepped back and inspected the pants. He pulled a loose thread at the leg seam. "Sooner or later, Castro's toes are gonna curl. Then all of the Cubans in Miami will dance in the streets. In the meantime, I like this place. I think I can help the people here. They need to laugh more."

"That may be true. But your lease is up at the end of the month. You'll have to find another place to live. And what about your family? They'll be disappointed," Simon said.

"I've already talked to them. I'm still going back for a visit. Jesús said he wants to come here to visit too. He's never been further north than Aventura." Segundo hung the pants on a hook at the back of the door. A red-and-yellow-striped shirt with enormous plastic daisy buttons was on the rod near the wall. He slid it toward him and started steaming.

"Have you thought about what you'll do?"

"Open a clown school. The trick is to get them little, before they have a chance to become jaded. It's the only way to break the vicious circle of clown abuse."

"Think clown *abuse* is a bit of a stretch?"

"Your nephew will be my first student," Segundo said. As he steamed the armpits, the smell of body odor was released into the room.

"Noel?"

"I saw him in the street and bought him a soda at the corner store. We sat on the wall and talked. He told me Eugene *somebody* was the last person to set foot on the moon," Segundo looked at Simon. He set down the iron. "What do you think made him that way?"

God's will, Simon wanted to say. "I don't know. Just his genes, I guess. Sometimes I wonder if I was given the chance to be really good at *one* thing—better than anyone—whether I'd take the talent, even if it meant I had to give up everything else. I mean how many people in this world get to do something better than anyone? That's how he paints."

Segundo resumed his steaming. "I had a red plastic nose in

my pocket. I showed it to him. He put it on and I had him look at himself in the store window. The people drinking coffee at the tables by the window laughed. Then he laughed. He liked it. He kept it on and walked up the street."

"Cooper must've loved seeing him come home with that."

"You think she laughed?" Segundo looked at Simon with eyebrows raised.

"I see your point. The people here could stand to lighten up a little." He was glad his friend was staying.

Segundo switched off the iron and set it down on the floor. He brought over a milk crate for Simon to sit on. "Please," Segundo said. He motioned for Simon to sit. "Something else is on your mind," Segundo said. "What is it?"

"Women." Simon had never told Segundo about Rose. By the time Segundo arrived, there was nothing to tell. Besides Simon wasn't the kind of guy who talked about his exploits, even to his best friend. But now he needed to get some of it off his chest.

"All of them?"

Simon held up one finger.

"What's her name?

"Rose."

Segundo produced a shoe box from under his bed. He opened the lid and took out two shot glasses. Then he poured some bottled water into each. "To Rose," he said.

Segundo handed Simon a glass, made a motion to toast, and threw back a shot of water. Simon sniffed the glass just to be sure, then did the same. He set down the glass upside down and wiped his mouth with his sleeve. Force of habit. Segundo righted the glass and filled it again.

"Never did water shots before," Simon said. "Not bad." He threw down another.

"So this Rose has broken your heart?"

"I don't know about that but I like her. Then today I found out she likes someone else. And if you knew the guy, you wouldn't know what to think."

"Let me give you some advice," Segundo said.

"As long as it has nothing to do with God or Jesus or Christianity in general." Simon glanced down and happened to notice the extremely worn red leather Bible on Segundo's bedside table.

"But it does have to do with Jesus," he said.

Simon started to shake his head.

"Or I should say, *Jesús*." This time he pronounced it like the Latino name. "My uncle. A long time ago, he told me a simple thing. He said women are like the mangoes. Each one is different. They ripen with age, become soft and sweet. But sometimes when you try to eat them, you get strings in your teeth."

Segundo poured another shot. He handed the glass to Simon. "So what's the point? If you fall for a woman, make sure you have dental floss?"

"Exactly."

Segundo threw back his shot.

Simon followed suit. "Maybe it's all the water going to my head but I don't follow you."

"If you want to taste the sweetness, you need to just dive in. Worry about the strings later."

"I'm afraid with Rose it might be too late."

"Only one way to find out," Segundo said.

• • •

Simon left Segundo's feeling buzzed from the water shots. Or maybe it was that optimism coming back. Maybe Segundo was right. There was only one way to find out if Rose was his mango. But it wouldn't be tomorrow. Simon knew there was a good chance he'd encounter Cooper and, if he did, the Tri-centennial fireworks would come a day early.

At least this time he was ready for her.

CHAPTER FIFTEEN

*One of the hazards of fireworks: Accidental
ignition due to human carelessness.*
—from Skylighter, Inc. Fireworks Safety Online Manual

By the time Rose left work, her ears were still ringing from
the phones in the office. The article about the time capsule and
Nauset has a secret had prompted calls from just about everyone
in town: people who were excited about the find and wanted
to know more, and people who swore the paper had gotten it
wrong, that there had to be something bigger behind it all. Devil
worship. Armageddon. Aliens. Terrorists. Republicans. Those
Hollywood liberals. The Catholic Church. There were some who
insisted *Nauset has a secret* had to do with the house going up on
the Point. And there were some who were just plain crestfallen,
the kids who'd gotten swept up in the craze to emblazon their
foreheads in a showing of solidarity over something, even if they
didn't know what, only to find it had just been some lame time
capsule. They'd been duped. After all, a time capsule wasn't the
latest Web craze or slick corporate teaser. It wasn't a new single
from their favorite rock band, or even a steamy celebrity sex
video. It wasn't reality TV or earth-shattering gossip. It was just
a box full of old stuff.

"Hey, don't shoot the messenger. Call the town administrator's office," Calvin had said over and over.

The irony was, the secret had only been half told. *Nauset has a secret* did have something to do with the house on the Point, at least to the extent that Zadie had never denied the fact that he'd been trying to divert attention from the whole controversy. According to most of the people Rose talked to, he'd screwed up in pushing that project through. He'd all but blown any chance he had of reelection. And for what? *Had* he taken money under the table as Cooper suggested? Rose had seen where he and Dorie lived. It was a comfortable home, a family place he'd inherited. After a successful career as an attorney, money had to be the least of his problems.

Tomorrow was the big day. From the athletic field came the smell of fresh-cut grass. From a tall locust tree, a bird swooped down like a hand opening and closing. It landed on one of the banners that traversed Main Street. The concessions were already set up in the field and were being stocked. In the common across the way, the kiddie rides were coming off the truck. Down the hill from the town hall, a stage had been assembled before rows of folding chairs. Here was the venue for most of the day's scheduled events, the kickoff prayer at 9 A.M., delivered by the town's Congregational minister, who'd won the match of rock, paper, scissors against the Catholic priest, and the Episcopal, Unitarian Universalist, and Methodist ministers. At ten, there would be a poetry recitation by the town's eldest citizen, Fred Wilcox, who attributed his rigorous health and clear mind to a morning tonic of one raw egg, a fresh-shucked Wellfleet oyster—*had* to be Wellfleet—and a shot of bourbon, so he'd confessed during an interview Rose had done with him several weeks ago to commemorate his 101st birthday. The time-capsule opening was scheduled for noon, followed by the Portuguese linguica–eating contest at 1 P.M., the logic being that seeing people stuff sausages into their mouths might somehow stimulate the appetite of the masses so that they would then venture out to the food concessions for two hours before heading down to the Point for the reenactment at three.

Rose had been assigned to cover Fred Wilcox and the time capsule. Calvin's girlfriend had the linguica contest and the reenactment, which was good because Rose was hoping for a chance to talk to Mike Eldridge, who was in charge of security.

Rose climbed the grassy hill to the town hall, an old white clapboard box with a mansard roof, tall windows, and a new front porch with benches where the old-timers liked to gather. As she passed though the heavy double doors, she was hit with decades of stale, recirculated air, the breath of town fathers from centuries past, mingling with the scent of aged wood and new carpet. The Snow Exhibit Hall was located at the front of the building and marked with a bronze plaque above the large oak doors, which were held open with worn needlepoint-covered bricks.

"Who cares where you put 'em as long as they're not crooked," Rose heard Cooper say.

"They should be chronological," Val said. "So they tell a story."

"Ladies, *please*. I think Milo is more than qualified to hang an exhibit," Dorie said.

Rose entered the room. "Hi, everyone."

Cooper nodded. She was standing in the middle of the room in her yellow slicker, arms folded tight across her chest. Rose could no longer make out the words *Zadie* or *ass* on Cooper's forehead, as she had been able to for weeks, though there was still peeling from the rash that had broken out on her skin after Cooper had taken someone's advice at the Legion Hall and tried nail-polish remover. Val was beside her, wearing a too-tight Jimmy Fund T-shirt, a former year's style, that barely made it to the top of her brown stretch-waist pants. She had a painting in each hand and was holding them out in front of her. The room couldn't have been more than sixty-five degrees yet her brow and upper lip glistened with sweat. Noel was sitting in a folding chair by the entrance, watching a spider crawl up the wall.

"Good, Rose is here. What do you think, Rose?" Val asked.

Dorie came up and took the paintings out of Val's hands.

"I think we already have too many cooks," Dorie said. She winked at Rose.

Dorie had on a green polo shirt, green chinos, green belt, green plaid cardigan, green flats, and a green headband, an outfit for which she'd probably dropped a few hundred in one of those preppy Chatham boutiques. The net effect, however, was that her greenness overpowered every piece of art in the room.

Noel's paintings were lined against the wall on the floor. Before them stood Milo Vanderloos, again in black, but this time wearing a belt of hammered leather with an ornate silver buckle with turquoise inlay.

"So what do you think, Milo?" Dorie asked.

Milo didn't respond. He seemed to be lost in his thoughts, so that at first he didn't see Noel pick up the painting of his mother on the floor with the goldfish and hang it on a nail on the wall facing the entrance, the best piece of real estate in the room.

"Noel, dear. We're going to let Milo—" Dorie started to say.

Milo snapped his fingers five times in a row. "That's perfect," he said.

Dorie turned red. Val looked at Cooper and shrugged.

"A little up on the left, Noel," Cooper said

Noel raised the painting a hair on the right.

"Nope, *other* left," Cooper said.

Noel raised the painting two hairs on the left.

"That's *perfect*," she said, mocking Milo.

Milo picked up the latest painting, the one of Simon. "Where do you think this one should go?" he asked Noel.

"In the trash," Cooper said.

Val shushed her.

Noel took the painting and held it about two-thirds of the way down a long blank wall.

"You're sure?" Milo asked.

Noel didn't answer. He just stood there holding the painting.

Milo picked up the hammer and a handful of nails.

"Sure you know how to use one of those?" Cooper said.

Dorie flashed her a caustic look.

Milo measured down from the wire on the back of the painting and hammered in a nail, then balanced the painting on the wire. He looked to Noel for approval.

Noel didn't say anything. He just picked up another painting and placed it on the wall. This is how it went until all the paintings were hung and perfectly spaced except for one: the portrait of Dorie.

Noel picked it up.

"Look at that. No more room," Dorie said. "Oh well."

Noel took the painting to a large dividing wall in the middle of the room, a wall that didn't go all the way up to the ceiling. It was a premier spot. The painting wouldn't be missed.

Dorie's forehead slid back. Her cheeks became inflamed. Cooper pressed her hand to her mouth to hold back her laughter.

"Yes, yes, yes," Milo said.

"Milo, I've been very patient with you—" Dorie said.

"Dorie, dear. This is about Noel, remember?" Val said.

"If it's *my* face up there, it is about me," she said. She took the painting out of Noel's hands. She started to walk out of the room with it.

Noel wailed. He flapped his hands.

"Give it back," Cooper said. *"Now."*

Dorie cringed. She turned on her heels and brought the painting back to Noel. She handed it to him.

With the exchange, the expression of anguish transferred from Noel's face to Dorie's. He lifted his chin. "The last angel to join *Charlie's Angels* was Julie Rogers," he said.

Rose heard footsteps coming up the hall. A moment later, Simon appeared in the doorway. It was the Simon she'd seen jogging down the street, the new and improved Simon with the trimmer waistline and the cleared-up face, a Simon who seemed to shine with confidence.

"Well, will you look at this," he said. He stepped into the room and spun in a circle with his arms out. "They look fantastic, Noel."

Noel was beaming. Milo looked up from his clipboard, then back down again. Val wore a nervous smile. Dorie's eyebrows were raised in surprise. Cooper just stood there, her spine frozen and her face glazed over. Her jaw slid from one side to the other in a move that made her look like she was chewing cud.

"Simon Beadle, is that really you?" Dorie said. "I heard you were back in town. Why look at you! I'd never have recognized you in a million years, except for the family resemblance, of course."

She went up to Simon and held out her hand. He shook it.

"Never mind that. Come here and give me a hug." She embraced Simon. From then on Rose would always have a soft spot in her heart for Dorie Nickerson. It was a kind thing to do.

"It's great to be back," he said.

Rose didn't think he'd seen her standing there until that very moment. He winked at her.

People use that expression that they *melt* when they see someone. Rose didn't know how better to express it than to say there was this warmth and tightening at the top of her chest, that seemed to originate somewhere between the base of her throat and the top of her lungs, the kind of feeling one might get going over a bump in the car. And then that tightening released and seemed to flow out to every part of her body, all the way to her fingers and toes, like warm honey. Like something solid becoming a liquid. Taking a deep breath only sweetened the sensation.

"Val, why don't you take Noel outside to get some fresh air. It's almost supper time. I'll just be a minute," Cooper said.

Val seemed relieved to be excused. As much as she liked to stir things up, Rose thought Val often preferred her make-believe world to the real one.

"Come, Noel, dear," Val said. She tugged on his sleeve and led him out of the room. "First thing tomorrow we'll come back and take photos. It's going to be so exciting. So many people will finally see your work . . ." She talked to Noel like that as they left the room.

"Well, will you look at the time. Poor Zadie must be wondering about dinner. Milo, we should be going too," Dorie said.

Cooper and Simon were squaring off like two pit bulls.

Milo was oblivious. "Not yet. I'm trying to assimilate the essence of the works," he said. He closed his eyes.

Dorie grabbed Milo by the arm and yanked. "You can assimilate your ass off tomorrow," she said. "Let's go. Nice to see you, Simon. Bye, all. Get a good night's sleep. Tomorrow's a big day."

Then there were just the three of them. Rose's turn. "Well, Simon, it was nice to see you. Cooper. I'll check in on Val later. So long."

"Rose, wait. I'd like you to stay," Simon said.

"Me?"

"You better stick around so I don't kill him," Cooper said.

Rose didn't think Cooper was kidding. Rose walked over to the chair where Noel had been sitting, an old-fashioned school desk with the seat attached. She sat there and made herself invisible.

"Look, Cooper. I don't want any trouble. I just want to set a few things straight," he began.

"You don't want any trouble. You've been nothing but trouble since the day you were born," Cooper said.

"I'm an alcoholic, Cooper. I'm not using it as an excuse. Just an explanation. But I've gotten my life under control and a big reason for that is my commitment to Noel." He paced a little, took a few steps in either direction, but came no closer to Cooper.

"Noel was doing just fine without you," she said.

"I know that. And I appreciate what you've done for him all these years," Simon said.

"While *you* were running around chasing whiskey and skirts, and falling off cruise ships," she said.

Chasing skirts. That much Rose could believe. And Simon had told her and Val about the cruise ship.

"You know about that?" Simon asked. He looked at Rose. He seemed nervous.

"The library gets all the big-city papers. Trust me, I know more about you than I ever wanted to," Cooper said. She looked from Simon over to Rose, then back to Simon. It was an accusation.

Rose wasn't going to let her get away with it. "Hey, wait a minute—" she started to say. She imagined Cooper in the window with her telescope having spotted them in the dunes that night.

"Lord knows what you see in him, Nowak. If you knew him the way we do, you'd be singing a different tune."

Simon said, "You're going to have to find some way to deal with me because, the fact is, I'm here to build a relationship with my nephew, and you can't stop me. You can try. If you want to do this every time we run into each other, we can. But then don't tell me you have the kid's best interests at heart because we all know what's best for Noel is to have his uncle back in his life and for the people he loves to get along."

"Sure, until you fall off the wagon and run again." Her words were an ice pick in flesh, cold, sharp, and indisputable.

"I'm not falling and I'm not leaving."

"And I'm not buying it."

"Suit yourself. Hell, I don't blame you. I'm not sure how I'd feel if the tables were turned. But sometimes you just have to take a leap of faith. That's what I'm asking all of you to do here. Give me a chance," Simon said.

He looked over at Rose.

"*Another* chance," he corrected himself. "I'm not going to let him down or anyone else. I promise," he said. He was still looking at her.

"You say he needs you in his life. What makes you so sure?" Cooper said.

Rose had to speak up in Simon's defense. "I was with him

the first few times Noel saw him. He knew his uncle right away and seems to brighten up when Simon's around. You saw him tonight. He was thrilled when his uncle walked through that door."

Cooper rubbed her chin. The silence was painful. Rose heard her stomach growl. Just then, she heard footsteps coming fast down the hall. Noel burst into the room. Val followed behind.

"I'm sorry," she said. "I tried to keep him outside but he wanted to see Simon. He wanted to say good night."

"The last 'Good night, Gracie' was in 1964," Noel said. He started for the door, then turned and said, "Good night, Uncle Simon."

Val gasped.

Cooper's jaw fell into her hand. "What did he say?" Cooper said.

"And he's said it before. Right, Simon?" Rose said.

"Twice," he said. Simon was proud.

"Good night, Noel," he said.

"Fantastic," Val said.

"I've got some thinking to do," Cooper said.

There was enough hope in the way she'd said it to give Simon something to hang on to. Noel had come through.

Simon smiled and gave his nephew the thumbs-up. Then he gave it to Rose too. She didn't know if he was goofing on her for when she did it in the car but she gave it back. This time it meant: *Way to go. I'm proud of you. I'm on your side.* And just a little bit: *Looking good,* though he didn't need to know that.

"Let's go home and have some spaghetti," Cooper said to Noel. "You like spaghetti. Can you say 'I like spaghetti'?"

The three of them left, Noel sandwiched between the two proud women.

It was just Simon and Rose. She got out from behind the desk. He walked over to her. "Thanks, Rose," he said. "That meant a lot."

"It was just the truth," Rose said. She slid her hands into her back pockets.

He backed up and looked around the room. He held out his arms. "Pretty incredible, huh?"

"It sure is," Rose said. "He has such a gift."

He took a step toward her. "So how've you been, Rose?"

Rose felt her heart beating in her throat. "Okay," she said. "I don't need to even ask you, do I? You've been taking good care of yourself. It shows."

He ran his hand over his hair and blushed a little. "I feel good."

"I hope it lasts this time."

He didn't hesitate. "It will," he said. His face was filled with determination.

There were so many things Rose wanted to say, that she missed him, that she was sorry for leaving him that night, and accusing him of lying about Val, but she just didn't have the nerve. She wanted him to say something first. Then he did.

"I've missed you." Then something happened, his face hardened. He took a step back and turned away. He walked over to the portrait of the old dying guy and just stood there looking at it.

"What's wrong?" Rose asked. She took her hands out of her pockets and moved a step toward him.

"I saw Mike Eldridge." He said it without turning around.

"Mike Eldridge? You must see him every day. Isn't he assigned to the site?" Rose said.

"I knew him years ago when we were kids," he said.

Why were they talking about Mike Eldridge? There was obviously something he needed to get off his chest. "So?" Rose said.

"Funny how people change, if you believe they really do," Simon said.

"Who's changed?" she said. She scratched her head. "You mean Mike?"

"Let me ask you." He turned to her. "What is it that women see in Mike? I mean I know he's good-looking but beyond that—"

He should be asking Val. Rose was still at a loss. "I don't know—"

"What did your old boyfriend do?"

"Martin?"

"I mean, is it a *uniform* thing?"

Uniform thing? "He's in advertising," Rose said. The conversation was getting more bizarre by the minute. "How did you even know about Martin?"

"I saw you at the Barnacle that night."

Rose stiffened. "So you were in a *bar,* were you?" He was right. People *didn't* change.

"And I saw him drive you home."

"You were *following* me? I heard you'd been outside my window but I refused to believe you were some kind of pervert. Is this something you do on a regular basis? Stalk your girlfriends? *Not* that I'm your girlfriend," Rose quickly added.

"I wasn't stalking you," he said.

"What do you call it, Simon?" she said. "I call it pathetic." She turned and started for the door.

"I've been working real hard to build a life I can be proud of. I wanted you in it. I thought maybe we had a shot."

Rose stopped and turned around. His face was dark.

"I shouldn't have looked in your window that night. But I'm not going to let you paint me as some kind of creep. You want to know why I did it? Because I'd taken Noel home, saw your light on, and—" He stuffed his hands in his pockets and looked down at his sneakers. "I couldn't get enough of you, Rose. After our night in the dunes, I just wanted to know more. I wanted to know the color of your walls and the last thing you see before you fall asleep at night." He cleared his throat and smiled. "And then I saw you standing there in your glasses and that silly yellow bathrobe, talking on the phone." He looked back up at her. His voice got softer. "And you were like some kind of angel."

Rose couldn't believe what he was saying. Her heart was racing. He kept going.

"And then I overheard some of what you were saying on

the phone and learned you were still involved with someone else, which, by the way, you'd never told me that night we were together." He walked over to the painting of his sister. He turned toward it. "I was in the Barnacle, *not* drinking. I'd been looking for a friend who was in trouble when I saw you there. With *Martin*. So I left. It was late. I took a walk. And while I was walking, the two of you drove past and pulled into the driveway." He looked at Rose. She could see the hurt in his eyes. "I heard you both laughing. I saw the lights come on in the cottage and waited for him to leave. Instead, the last thing I saw was him sitting on your bed." He adjusted the frame on the painting so that it now hung crooked.

He'd said he couldn't get enough of her. She walked toward the window. They were testing the Tilt-A-Whirl down on the Common. Rose felt like her head was on it. She could hear the music and see the spinning lights. "You're awfully quick to jump to conclusions. Especially for someone who wants everyone to believe in *him,*" Rose said at last.

"I don't judge you, Rose. I almost got myself thrown in jail for taking Mike Eldridge's head off with a crowbar when he made some wiseass crack about you. But when it comes to figuring out who to trust, I got my eyes and ears. They don't lie."

Rose kept looking out the window. "What about your heart?" she said, but maybe too soft. With the machines and the music outside, he didn't hear. She turned around, hopeful.

"Look, it's late," he said. "I'm real tired. I'll see you tomorrow, okay?" He pressed his hand to his forehead and let it slide down his face. He started to go and Rose didn't do anything. She just let him leave. She had too much pride. She hadn't groveled with Martin and she wasn't about to grovel with Simon. *Dignity. You could lose it if you weren't careful.* As soon as he was out the door, Rose regretted it.

CHAPTER SIXTEEN

Reactive forces, including kickback, can be dangerous.
—*from the Stihl Chain Saw Safety Manual*

Simon had never been one to turn down a free shirt but this was a true test of his own goodwill. The Jimmy Fund T-shirt Val had given him was a size XXL, so that the sleeves came down to his elbows and the bottom hit the middle of his thighs. Even worse, the neck was so loose it practically showed cleavage. Even if he was proud of his new chest muscles, this wasn't exactly the way he wanted to show them off.

On the shirt was the face of dark-haired little kid in a Boston Braves uniform. Simon had seen it plenty of times before and always figured the kid, like the Boston Braves, was long gone. According to the tag on the shirt, he *was* gone but not that long. And it turns out his name wasn't Jimmy either. It was Einar Gustafson and he'd died of a stroke at age sixty-five in 2001. Einar had beaten the cancer that almost killed him fifty years before and had gone on to live a full life. Nobody knew the truth until 1998 when "Jimmy's" sister outed him. The folks at Dana Farber had probably been afraid they'd lose the sympathy vote if people found out that their poster kid had actually survived. Simon figured the truth would have worked in their favor, on the logic that if you could cure one kid, you could probably cure more.

For Einer, and because it seemed to mean so much to Val, Simon now stood behind the back row of folding chairs facing the stage in his Jimmy Fund shirt. And if he thought it had looked funny on him, it looked downright ridiculous on Cooper, who stood to the right of the stage and practically had to hold up the hem so she didn't trip, and skinny Noel, whose whole body seemed like it might slip through the neck hole. As for Rose, standing beside the stage with her notebook and pen in hand, the neck slipping off one shoulder, Simon had yet to see her look silly in anything. He felt a pang of anger with himself for what he'd said to her the night before—anger mixed with relief that his feelings were finally out in the open. It was out of his hands now, though he could have at least stuck around long enough to see how it might have played out. Instead, he'd gone with his usual strategy. He'd run. Now, maybe it was just the breeze billowing down the neck of his too-big shirt, but he looked at Rose and felt a chill.

Old Fred Wilcox was nearing the end of his recitation of "Pete the Piddlin' Dog," his voice a thin ribbon unspooling over the crowd.

> ". . . He trotted in a grocer's shop
> And piddled on a ham.
> He piddled in a mackerel keg.
> He piddled on the floor,
> And when the grocer kicked him out
> He piddled through the door.
> Behind him all the city dogs
> Lined up with instinct true
> To start a piddling carnival
> And see the stranger through . . ."

After all the hype, this Tri-centennial celebration seemed no different from any other town event. In his younger days, Simon had seen his share. The same forever-old man reciting the same forever-old poem, people laughing in the same places as if they'd never heard it before. There was something awfully good-natured about that, Simon had to admit.

Simon looked out at the crowd. He spotted Val sitting a few rows back from the stage. Beside her was a young mother with a baby in her lap. For a few seconds, Simon allowed himself to think it was Eve and baby Rose. He wondered if Val was allowing herself to believe it too.

Zadie was already standing in the wings. Beside him, a platform on wheels covered by a red silk cloth and a banner rigged to it that said *Nauset Has a Secret.* Peppered through the crowd were people with the same words on their foreheads, even though the truth behind it, the story of the time capsule that had broken in Rose's paper yesterday, hadn't lived up to the power of people's imaginations. The truth almost never did.

The sun had broken the late-morning fog into patches of gray on a blue ground. Simon turned to the stage. He knew the poem well enough to know that Fred was winding up for the big finish. The old man's face was red and his eyes sparkled. At that instant, Simon felt happy to be home.

> "... And all the time the country dog
> Did never wink or grin
> But blithely piddled out of town
> As he had piddled in.
> The city dogs a convention held
> To ask, 'What did defeat us?'
> But no one ever put them wise
> That Pete had diabetes!"

The grown-ups laughed. The kids looked up at their parents in confusion. *I don't get it. What's diabetes?*

Someone helped Fred back to his seat as Zadie wheeled his platform onto the stage. He launched into his presentation with a long list of people he thanked for this and that. Then he put his hand to his eyebrows and scanned the audience. "My bride out there?" he asked.

People looked in the seats around them.

"Anyone seen Dorie?" he said.

They shook their heads.

"Late as usual," he said, and shrugged. People nodded their heads in sympathy.

Finally, he got down to business. "As you know, ladies and gentlemen, Nauset has a secret. And at long last, here it is." He yanked away the red cloth and there sat a plain copper box about the size of a large tool chest. People in the audience craned their necks to get a better view. "A time capsule discovered by the crew making repairs to the foundation of the town hall last fall. We decided to keep it under wraps until this special day. What better way to commemorate the three-hundredth anniversary of this town than with a treasured piece of its proud history?"

People cheered.

"Inside this box are things that haven't seen the light of day since 1879 when Grover Cleveland—who used to vacation right here at Gray Gables beach in Bourne, I'll have you know—was president of the United States. When this box was sealed, it would be thirty years until the start of World War One. At the time, Thomas Edison was busy working on his lightbulb. Folks were still living on the island of Billingsgate, which has long since given up her bricks to the sea."

"That man just loves to hear himself talk," a woman near Simon whispered to her friend.

"When this copper was forged, the Statue of Liberty was on its way to the United States from France. Why, Babe Ruth had not yet been born—"

"Yeah, and I'm gonna die soon," came a familiar voice. It was Cooper. "So get on with it, you old fool."

"Ahem." Zadie pretended to ignore her. "Our thanks to Fire

Chief Troy Miller, who has already snapped the lock, and so let's get started." He came around to the back of the box and wrapped his fingertips around the edge of the lid. "I'll just give this a good tug and . . ."

Zadie Nickerson tugged but the top of the box didn't budge.

Simon looked back out at the audience, to Noel, then Cooper. Their eyes met hers and he quickly looked away.

"Technical difficulties. Bear with me folks." Zadie moved around to the front of the box and tried to pry off the lid. No luck. Then he asked Ellen Feeny, who was with him onstage, to hold the box while he took off his sport coat, revealing a pair of whale-festooned braces which were most definitely holding up his pants, though a little too high. There were dark blue ovals under his armpits.

"Must've had some good glue a hundred and twenty-six years ago, I'll tell you that."

He set the box on the ground, spat on his hands, and clapped them together. He grabbed the lid and tried again. Nothing. "It's coming," he said. He whipped a handkerchief out of his pocket and dabbed at his brow. One more try.

Suddenly the top gave way and some of the contents went flying out into the crowd. Zadie stumbled forward to regain his balance and teetered on the edge of the stage. The audience gasped. He caught himself. "Okay, folks. Settle down. Anyone get clocked? Son, will you please bring that up here so we can take a look?"

A kid in the audience came up to the stage and handed Zadie a booklet.

"Ladies and gentleman, the *Farmer's Almanac* from the year 1879," Zadie said.

There was tepid applause.

"Let's see what kind of winter they were predicting," Zadie said. He started to flip though the pages. People in the audience groaned.

"Okay, okay. We can do that later. Let's see what else we have."

An older woman in the audience came forward and handed Zadie something with one hand, rubbing the corner of her forehead with the other.

"Sorry about that, Betty. And what do we have here? A cranberry scoop!"

"Got one like it in my kitchen," someone yelled.

More lukewarm applause. Zadie was losing them. He fished around in the box.

"Damn!" he said. He pulled out his hand, which now had a fishing hook embedded in the palm. Attached to the hook was a piece of old line and a lure.

"Excuse my French," he said. "Anyone have a Leatherman handy?"

"And a tetanus shot," Cooper said.

No fewer than ten men in the front row drew metal utensils from their pockets and began to fold them into pliers.

Zadie tried to shake his hand free of the hook and, in the process, hit the podium, driving it deeper. "Motherfucker," he said.

The crowd gasped. A young woman standing near Simon put her hands over her little boy's ears.

Mrs. Feeny, from the town's Historical Society, stepped up to the microphone. "Apparently, nineteenth-century fishhooks are as barbed as the town administrator's tongue."

The audience laughed as one of the fellows with a Leatherman and Fire Chief Troy Miller led Zadie offstage.

"Well, let's see what else we have." Ellen Feeny reached into the box and pulled out a slip of paper, which she carefully unfolded. "A tide chart," she said.

She set it down on the podium and went back to the box. "What's this?" She pulled out a leather-bound book, the pages edged in gold. "A Bible," she said.

Looked newer than Segundo's, Simon thought. He scanned

the crowd for his buddy. He must already be at his balloon station in the kiddie area.

She opened the inside cover, then held it up for all to see. "King James," she said with approval. She stuck her hand back in the box.

Simon yawned. He'd probably slept a grand total of three hours last night. Every time he closed his eyes, he saw Rose with Eldridge, Rose with Martin, even just Rose by herself.

"Now I feel something heavy and smooth."

Some kid let loose with a provocative whistle.

"It has a long neck." She pulled out a bottle. She peered at the label through the reading glasses on a chain around her neck. "We have a bottle of cranberry wine."

The crowd cheered.

"Crack that puppy!" came a voice from the audience. It was good old Fred.

"Says here: 'from the private collection of Jeremiah Beadle.'"

There was a hush over the crowd. People turned to Simon, who rolled back on his heels with the weight of the unwanted attention. He grinned and shrugged his shoulders.

The crowed laughed. Some groaned.

"Welcome back, Simon," Mrs. Feeny said.

He imagined he felt the eyes of Cooper and Rose on him but didn't want to look up to be sure.

There were a few more items that would be put on display at the Historical Society later in the day, a Civil War medal donated by a local soldier, an old tintype of a shipwreck off the coast, an ornate vial of French perfume containing whale ambergris, and a cast-iron toy train.

By the end of the presentation, Zadie was back onstage with his bandaged hand, thanking everyone for coming out. "And don't forget three P.M., down at the Point, we'll have the reenactment of the invasion of Nauset during the War of 1812, courtesy of Mrs. McGregor's high school drama club. Enjoy the day, be safe, and Happy Birthday, Nauset."

Most of the people had already gotten up and started to leave. Simon saw two teenage girls lick their hands and try to wipe the words from their foreheads. So far, were it to be judged for giving up Nauset's secrets, the morning had been a bust.

The crowd was spilling out onto the field in all different directions. Simon figured the best thing would be to go tell Rose he was sorry. He'd been out of line accusing her of being attracted to Eldridge. He suspected from the beginning that he was off base but he'd kept right on pressing, probably just so she'd tell him it wasn't true. But he'd pressed too hard, he knew.

Now she was busy talking to Calvin. Cooper, Val, and Noel were headed up the hill toward the town hall. Simon would eventually make his way up there too.

Some people next to Simon turned and pointed toward the hill. Simon turned too and saw a woman running down from the town hall. She had to be almost three hundred pounds. Simon watched her build momentum. As she drew closer, he could see her face was flushed and she was waving. At who? If Simon didn't know better, he'd have thought she was waving at him. But he didn't know her. At least he didn't think he did. He just stood his ground and hoped there was someone behind him, a movie star or a long lost beau. He imagined the carnage if she couldn't stop herself in time.

"Simon!" she yelled. "You're Simon, right?"

He nodded. She stopped like a dancer on cue. There was sweat dripping at her temples. She was a young woman, probably in her early thirties. Simon thought she had a pretty face. She probably got that a lot.

"It's about Noel's paintings. Two of them are missing."

"Huh?"

"I'm Molly Owens. Mrs. Nickerson put me in charge of watching the paintings during the time-capsule opening. I just left to use the john. I couldn't hold it." Too much information. "I couldn't have been gone more than four minutes. When I got back, there were two empty spots on the wall where Noel's paintings had been."

"Which paintings?" Simon asked.

"I don't know. I don't remember what was there," she said. She started to cry.

"Don't worry, we'll track them down. Maybe someone just borrowed them—"

"I could lose my job over this," she said.

"What *is* your job?" Simon asked.

"I'm on the culture committee." The poor girl was worried about losing a job that didn't pay a red cent.

"Don't worry, Molly," Simon said. "It wasn't your fault. You go on back up there and let Cooper know what's going on. I'll find a cop."

"I'm sorry," she said.

"We'll find them," Simon said.

She started back up the hill, a lot slower than how she'd come down.

Who would steal Noel's paintings? That Milo fellow had said it himself, how Noel was on his way to becoming an important artist and that his paintings might already be worth good money. Simon figured he should at least give the police a heads-up. And he'd just seen Mike Eldridge. Somewhere.

Simon headed toward the stage and saw Eldridge standing near the base of the podium in full uniform, gun holster and billy club secured to his waist, and a walkie-talkie that was making all kinds of noise.

Simon went up to him. "Hey, Eldridge," Simon said. "We got a problem."

The cop seemed distracted. Simon started to say more but Eldridge held up a finger for Simon to be quiet. He unclipped the radio from his belt and started talking into it. "What kind of boat?"

"Part of the hull of an old skiff, looks like," the radio voice said.

"Where was it?" Eldridge asked.

"About thirty feet from the finished part of the seawall. South side."

"They found something at the Point?" Simon asked.

"Shh," Eldridge said to Simon. Then he screamed at the guy on the radio. "I told them they weren't supposed to be digging this morning. Tell them to cover it back up. I don't want any kids cutting themselves up."

"Can't."

"How come?"

"Equipment's been cleared out like you wanted."

"Well, get it back," Eldridge said.

"Can't. Guys are gone and it's all locked up," the voice said.

"So there's just a wreck sitting there in a hole."

"There's a little water in it. And there are heaps of sand and other holes too. Guess they ran into some soft stuff this morning. They'll have to bring in some fill."

"Jesus Christ. Just mark everything off with police tape so no one enters the crime scene."

"Who said anything about a crime scene?" said the voice.

"Just shut your trap till I get there," Mike said.

He clipped the radio on his belt and started walking.

"Hey," Simon said.

"Not now, Beadle," he said.

"But something's happened. A couple of my nephew's paintings have been taken off the wall of his exhibit," Simon said.

"I said *not now*." He kept walking. "Got a safety issue."

"Hey!" Simon yelled, perhaps louder than he realized.

People turned around. Eldridge stopped walking.

"So you found an old boat. Big deal. This is important," Simon said. "There might be a thief running around."

A vein bulged on Mike Eldridge's forehead. "I'll send someone up there," he said.

"Yeah, right," Simon said, under his breath.

"What the hell is that supposed to mean?" Eldridge said. Another vein twitched on Eldridge's head. It was like Simon was watching a sci-fi movie, like next thing he knew some alien would be popping out of the cop's gut.

"You heard me," Simon said.

He stared Eldridge down. Unfortunately, it worked like it would on an angry dog. Eldridge grabbed the already too-big neck of Simon's Jimmy Fund shirt and more than a few chest hairs along with it, and drew Simon in close.

"Back the hell off, Beadle," he said through clenched teeth. Simon felt a drop of spittle land under his left eye. "And don't go mouthing off about the boat. It's police business. You hear me?" Then he shoved Simon away. Simon stumbled and almost hit the ground. While he was regaining his balance, Eldridge stormed off.

People were standing around. Some were shaking their heads, probably assuming Simon was once again living up to great-great-uncle Jeremiah's legacy.

Rose came up. "I saw that. Are you okay?" She helped adjust his shirt.

"That guy's wound," Simon said.

"I can't believe he did that. What did he say to you?"

"I was trying to tell him Noel's paintings had been stolen."

"What?" she said. Her eyes widened.

"Two of them. I just found out."

"Which ones?" Rose asked.

"I don't know. I was about to go up there," Simon said.

"I don't get it. Eldridge wouldn't help? That's what he's here for."

"While I was talking he got a call on the radio. Guess they found pieces of a boat at the Point."

Rose seemed startled. "What kind of boat? Did they say?"

"Think the guy said a dory," Simon said. "What's the big deal? There have to be hundreds of old boats sunk out there."

Rose looked out over the field and took a deep breath. She seemed a million miles away. "Let's see what we can find out about the paintings," she said.

In silence, they walked up the grassy hill toward the town hall, leaving the laughter, carnival music, and squealing kids, the smells of fried dough, onions and peppers, and fresh roasted peanuts behind them.

When they arrived at the exhibit hall, Noel was flapping around like a bird trapped in an attic, inconsolable. Val chased him as he ran in circles. Then he stopped, stood in the middle of the room with his arms outstretched, and wailed. It was a horrible sound, primal and raw. Simon cringed. His spine stiffened in a way that had become familiar.

"Which paintings are gone?" he said.

"You and Dorie," Val said between heavy breaths.

"Me? Who the heck would want a painting of me?" Simon said.

"Where's Cooper?" Rose asked.

"She went down to try to find a cop," Val said.

"Hope she has better luck than we did," Simon said.

There were four windows in the room that were open without screens, and an emergency exit with a crash bar that was supposed to sound an alarm if the door was opened.

"I'm going to take a look around outside," Rose said.

Noel put his head in his hands. Simon touched his shoulder. "We'll find them," he said.

CHAPTER SEVENTEEN

Sometimes the agitator will crack.
—*from "How to Remove a Washing Machine Agitator" on ehow.com*

Rose left the exhibit room and looked for signs of anyone in the building who might have seen something. The halls were deserted so she made her way toward the main entrance. The benches out front were empty. Everyone was down on the athletic field. The parking lot was filled with cars but there were no signs of anyone, thieves or witnesses. Rose walked around the right side of the building. It was a long shot but maybe someone was still hiding in the bushes, or at least maybe they'd left some clues. Beneath the windows to the exhibit hall were a row of old rhododendrons with heavy purple-tipped buds that were about ready to burst. Rose looked up at the windows of the exhibit hall and saw one of Noel's arms engaged in a rhythmic rising and falling. He was flapping again.

A boat had been found. A skiff. After almost thirty years, could this have something to do with Lino's disappearance? Or was it just that Rose been so preoccupied with finding out what had happened to him that now she was grasping at some random chunk of wood in the sand. Still, what she'd been able to find out about his disappearance kept leading her back to the conclusion that he'd never made it to shore that night.

Rose walked along the bushes, trying to see through the thick tongue-shaped leaves to the base of the foundation. She spotted something on the ground, a patch of color. She went in for a closer look, crawling under the lowest branches on her hands and knees. A thread of a spiderweb brushed her lips and she batted it away. There was an eye. A freckled nose and hair. Lots of hair. There, lying in the dirt, on top of a clump of damp, decaying leaves was the portrait of Simon. Rose tried for it but it was out of reach. She'd have to go deeper into the shadows. She inched her way forward and a large brown beetle that looked like a piece of chocolate crawled over her hand. She shuddered and shook it off. She reached out again and this time took hold of the frame, then backed out of the hole between the two bushes, careful not to tear the canvas. She stood up and did a little dance to get all the bugs and leaves off her. She brushed the mulch from her knees, then blew the debris and dirt off the painting and inspected the surface. Except for some scratches on the frame that must have happened in the fall, it appeared to be fine. Rose looked at the face. There was that kid she'd seen in the yearbook, those honest eyes, bright and vulnerable. A tiny curl at the corner of his lips. Rose wished she'd known Simon then. For a split second, she contemplated taking the painting for herself, hiding it in her closet. She would explore the origins of that impulse later.

The painting had landed just below the third window from the door. Rose retraced her steps to see if she'd missed the larger canvas of Dorie. With Simon under her arm, she walked around the entire perimeter of the building. Nothing. She went back inside.

"Look what I found," Rose said, holding up the painting.

"Look, Noel. It's Uncle Simon!" Val said. She fell back into an orange plastic chair.

Noel charged at Rose and grabbed the painting. He didn't

seem the least bit concerned whether it had sustained any damage. He just took it to the nail on the wall and returned it to its proper place. What did the paintings mean to him? Did he care about his works the way an artist does? Did he see them as a part of himself? Or as *children,* as precious things in and of themselves? Or were his paintings signs that pointed to something else? Did they represent the subject more literally, in which case, Noel would be happy to have his uncle back even if the latter was a little worse for wear. That's how it seemed, anyway. Once Simon was back on the wall, Noel went over to the empty spot where Dorie's painting had hung. He sat down beneath it and rocked.

"Someone must have tossed it out the window," Val said.

"It was right on the ground, at the base of the bushes," Rose said. "I went around the whole building but no sign of the other one."

Simon came up and pulled a twig (at least Rose hoped it was a twig) out of her hair. Then gave her ponytail a little tug. He smiled. "Nice investigative work," he said. Rose felt good.

"Suppose it was Cooper?" Val said.

"Cooper!" Rose said. "What would make you say a thing like that?"

"I know she's not my biggest fan but—" Simon started.

"I just remember last night Milo asked where to hang your portrait and she said 'in the trash,'" Val said. "I thought she was kidding."

Val knew better than to think Cooper would do such a thing. Rose believed she was just stirring the pot.

"Cooper *was* kidding," Rose said. "If she acted on half the things she threatened, we'd all be six feet under by now."

"True enough," Val said. "But Dorie isn't exactly her favorite person."

Rose could see Val would have liked nothing more than to see Cooper hauled away in handcuffs.

"Cooper wouldn't do that," Rose said.

"No?" Simon said. "You sure?"

"She wouldn't because she knows it would hurt Noel," Rose said.

Simon nodded. "I suppose," he said.

"Then who?" Val asked.

Cooper burst through the door so hard it rattled in its hinges when it hit the doorstop. "We've got him," she said. "They're taking him down to the station for booking right now." She clapped her hands like she was trying to dislodge the filth. That's that.

"Got who?" Simon asked.

"It was that clown," she said.

"What clown?" Rose said.

She continued: "I was trying to find a cop and spotted him making balloon hats by the merry-go-round."

"You've got to be kidding—" Simon started to say.

"Same one who was hanging around the house a few weeks ago. Same baggy pants, same makeup, though he did seem less scary than he was back then—maybe it's just that he wasn't popping out of the bushes in the middle of the night. This whole time he must've been casing the joint, looking into Val's windows, planning which paintings to take. Turns out he's a foreigner and living with *Russians*. Might be part of some big international art-smuggling ring."

Simon slapped his forehead.

"They don't know where he stashed the paintings, he wouldn't confess. But he sure seemed scared."

She stopped as soon as she saw Simon's portrait hanging right where it belonged.

"Where'd you find *that*?" she said.

"Someone had tossed it out the window," Rose said.

"We thought it was you," Val said.

"*Me?*" Cooper was indignant.

"I know that clown. He's a friend of mine. He had nothing to do with this," Simon said.

"The one we hired?" Val said. "He stole Noel's paintings?"

"No, he didn't—" Simon said.

"We hired a clown?" Cooper said. "Why would we do that?"

"Because Rose *loves* clowns," Val said.

"Actually, I'm not a big fan—" Rose started to say.

"I mean *little* Rose," Val said. "My granddaughter."

Simon looked at the clock on the wall.

Rose looked at her fingernails.

Cooper looked at her boots.

Simon finally broke the silence. "He'd been hanging around the boardinghouse looking for me. He knew I was back in town and only had Noel's address. He's not the thief."

"Well, Cooper, what do you have to say for yourself?" Val said.

Cooper sank down into the seat of the school desk. "Whoops," she said.

Simon shook his head.

"That's it?" Rose said.

"I'm sure the police will figure it out," Cooper said.

"So the question is, whoever the thieves were, why did they take two paintings and then leave one behind?" Rose asked.

"Maybe they got a good look at the subject," Cooper said.

Simon buried his head in his hands. He seemed too distraught about his friend to even register the snipe.

"So why would they want Dorie's portrait?" Rose said.

"By the way, has anyone seen Meeeelo?" Cooper asked.

"Nope," Simon said. He lifted his head out of his hands.

"Me either," Rose said.

"Think he had something to do with this?" Simon asked.

"Remember what a fuss he made over that painting of Dorie in particular?" Val said.

"*You* said he checked out," Cooper said. She glared at Rose.

"He *did* check out," Rose said. "There was too much there to fake." President of the Art Collectors Guild. Trustee of the Guggenheim. Guest lecturer at Harvard.

"You know, maybe you should just go back to teaching people how to screw in lightbulbs," Cooper said.

Just then, one went off in Rose's head. The boat. Obviously the cops hadn't told Cooper. Someone had to tell her, that is, if there was something to tell. Maybe Simon was right. There had to be hundreds of boats sunk out there. There was a huge chance it wasn't Lino's. It would be better to wait until they knew for sure. No need to bring the poor woman back to that nightmare, on this of all days.

"You know what it means. Milo *must* be the thief, the way he was drooling all over that painting, though God only knows why. I think it's butt ugly," Cooper said. "No offense, Noel."

Noel seemed like he hadn't heard a word of it.

"Well, he *did* make a fuss," Val said.

Cooper got up from the desk and started pacing. "Not only that but he's a nutcase," Cooper said.

Rose looked up and saw Simon staring at her. He raised his eyebrows. She smiled to let him know she was okay. "How do you know he's a nutcase?" Rose asked.

"He carries a pocketbook," Cooper said. She stuck out her knobby thumb. Point one.

"Lots of men carry pocketbooks," Rose said.

Simon raised an eyebrow. He smiled. "Rose has interesting friends," he said.

"He squeals at inanimate objects," Cooper said. She added her index finger. Point two.

"He's enthusiastic," Rose said. "Is that a crime?" She wasn't sure why she was defending him. She just had a feeling. One would think she'd have learned to ignore those by now.

"He wears a rat on his head," Cooper said. Point three.

Simon ran his hand over his scalp.

"Lots of men are self-conscious about losing their hair. So what?" Rose said. She looked at Simon and tried to picture him with a rat on his head.

"Oh, never mind," Cooper said.

"We're not accomplishing much just sitting here arguing," Simon said.

"Well, at least Dorie'll be happy," Val said.

"What do you mean?" Rose asked.

"You all saw how much she hated that painting," Val said.

Cooper lifted her head.

Simon turned to look at Val.

"Dorie?" Rose said.

"What'd I say?" Val said.

"Where *is* Dorie?" Cooper asked.

"Anybody see her at the time-capsule opening?" Simon said. "Zadie was looking for her."

"Maybe she wasn't feeling well. You know we've all been working so hard," Val said. "Might have gotten to her. She's been kind of high-strung lately anyway. Even more than usual."

Cooper, Simon, and Rose all looked at one another.

"We need to find her," Rose said.

Simon took charge. "Val, you stay here with Noel. Cooper, Rose and I will go," he said.

"But I've got to get down to the Jimmy Fund booth," Val said.

"The cans are out, right?" Rose said.

Val nodded.

"So what else do you have to do?" Cooper said. "I'll tell the people in the next booth to keep an eye on them."

"I suppose that'll be all right," she said. "Ask Seth the kite man and not Gert, who makes the shrunken heads out of apples. She's a little unstable. Oh, and make sure there are plenty of cans. There's another box of them under the table. And one more thing, if you see Eve and the baby, please tell her where I am."

"Sure," Cooper said. It seemed Val knew no one believed Eve and the baby existed, not even Rose. Val's expression was eerily vacant, like even she was just going through the motions.

"Hang in there, Noel," Simon said.

Noel looked up at his uncle. His eyes were swimming in their sockets.

As they left the building, Simon pulled Rose aside. "You okay?" he asked.

"Sure," she said.

"Something was eating you back there. Was it Eldridge?" he said.

"Not *that* again," Rose said. She jerked her elbow out of his hand. "Listen. The only reason I called him was to get the old police files on Lino and—"

Simon smiled. "I didn't mean it that way. I know I was wrong—" Then his expression changed. He got serious. "I mean you think the boat might be Lino's?"

"Cooper," Rose whispered. She was just a couple steps behind them.

Simon lowered his voice. "You think it is?"

"Might be."

"Jesus," he said.

After the time-capsule opening, Zadie had disappeared. No one had seen him, not even the people who ran the fried-dough concession, one of Zadie's favorites according to Cooper. He hadn't been by. Cooper suggested they check out the kiddie area to see if he was there "kissing babies." Simon kept his mouth shut but gritted his teeth as he passed the balloon stand with the abandoned air tanks. He was worried about his friend. There was no time now to go down to the police station and get him out.

In another hour, people would be making their way to the Point for the reenactment. They had to find Dorie before all that got under way. There were a few remaining concessions to check, including one for free blood-pressure screening. Beside it was the first-aid tent which had been set up like an old-fashioned army medical tent. Inside was a young beautiful nurse in an old-fashioned Florence Nightingale hat and costume. She had her fingers on the wrist of a patient, checking his pulse. Cooper, Rose, and Simon were so busy looking at her, they almost missed who the patient was. There on the white cot lay Zadie Nickerson.

Had he gotten more seriously hurt onstage than anyone knew?

"Asleep on the job again," Cooper said.

"Hello, folks," Zadie said. His voice was weak and his skin was mottled like wet paper.

"Are you okay?" Simon asked.

"Just a little overheated," he said.

The nurse looked at him and he winked at her.

"Yeah, wait till Dorie hears about *who* got you overheated," Cooper said. She nodded her head in the direction of the nurse, who smoothed out her skirt and glided to the far side of the tent.

"How are things going out there?" he asked.

"Great, mostly," Simon said. "Except we have a situation and we're hoping you can help. We're looking for Dorie and Milo."

"Those two get in trouble again? Can't leave them alone for a minute," Zadie said. He smiled. It was a sad smile. "Cooper, you have a little smudge," Zadie said. He took his own thumb, licked it, and pretended to rub a spot on his forehead.

Cooper licked her finger and brought it to the same spot on her forehead, then dropped her hand back down as soon as she realized Zadie was just giving her trouble about the writing that was still just barely visible on her skin.

"*Filho da puta,*" she said. Son of a bitch, Rose had finally learned.

"One of Noel's paintings is missing," Rose said. "It's the portrait of Dorie. We know she had a problem with that painting and we haven't seen her or Milo all day. We were just wondering if you knew anything."

"When I left the house this morning, she was already gone. Took her car when I was in the shower," he said. "Just figured she was up at the exhibit. You think *she* took the painting?" A little smile crept onto Zadie's lips.

"How's the hand?" Rose asked.

He held up his bandaged palm.

"That must've hurt," Simon said.

"His pride, more than anything," Cooper said.

The nurse walked over to a table and started straightening the bandages and rolls of gauze. Rose caught Simon staring at the girl and cleared her throat.

Zadie chuckled.

"What can you tell us about Meeeelo?" Cooper asked.

"You think he has something to do with this?" Zadie said. He laughed. "He's no art thief."

"What's so funny?" Cooper said.

"How can you be so sure?" Rose asked.

"Because he's a legitimate art collector," Zadie said. "And then some."

Rose folded her arms across her chest and looked at Cooper. The old woman shrugged.

"*And,*" Zadie continued, "he has enough money to buy this whole town ten times over."

"He's the one doing the building at the Point," Simon said.

Rose turned to him. How'd he come to that conclusion? Just because Milo was rich? There were lots of rich people in this town. "Why do you say that?" Rose asked.

"How many people do you know who are *that* loaded—"

"Lots—" she started to say.

". . . *and* oddball enough to want to keep it a secret?" Simon said.

They both looked at Zadie. His eyes told them they were right.

Cooper banged her hand on the tray table beside Zadie's bed. A plastic cup fell to the grass. "There goes the neighborhood."

"He's eccentric. No doubt about it," Zadie said. "But *he* won't be living there."

"Then who will?" Rose asked.

Zadie started to get up.

Cooper's eyes narrowed. "You have some explaining to do."

CHAPTER EIGHTEEN

Never attach yourself permanently to your kite.
—from the Flexifoil Blade II Kite Instruction Manual

"Anyone can live there," Zadie said. Simon helped him to his feet. "Thanks, I can manage."

"Anyone?" Simon asked.

"As long as they're dying." Zadie brushed off his lapels. "Let's find that wife of mine."

"I don't follow," Cooper said.

"It's a hospice," Rose said.

"Bingo," Zadie said. They left the first-aid tent, despite the protests of young Florence. Zadie led the way. He began to explain. "Milo's not just an art collector. He's a one-man charitable foundation. He inherited tens of millions, which he parlayed into *hundreds* of millions through art deals and smart investments during the high-tech boom."

"Jesus," Cooper said. "And he still dresses like *that?*"

Simon walked close to Zadie in case he needed support. Zadie had complained of heat exhaustion but for Simon that just didn't add up. For one thing, it wasn't that hot.

Zadie went on: "Back in the eighties, Milo learned an estranged lover had died of AIDS. He found out the fellow contracted the virus *after* he and Milo had split, thank goodness. But he also found out the poor guy had met his Maker in an abandoned fifth-floor walk-up in Manhattan, with no heat or running water, a penniless squatter surrounded by trash, broken glass, chipped paint, and filth, in the company of rats and roaches."

"That's horrible," Rose said.

"We get the picture," Cooper said.

"What's worse, his body hadn't been discovered for days, so that by the time the crackheads downstairs got around to making the anonymous call to the cops—thanks to the rats—there wasn't enough flesh left on the man to make a positive ID. Came down to dental records."

"Do you mind?" Cooper said. "I just ate a clam roll."

"Milo was devastated," Zadie said. "'Course it was too late to help his friend. But the whole thing got Milo to thinking maybe there was something he could do for people with terminal illnesses to ensure their last days, at least, could be lived out in relative comfort and with dignity. So he tried an experiment. He picked up a run-down Art Deco hotel on Miami's South Beach and converted it into his first hospice center."

"First? You mean there are more?" Rose asked.

They headed down a gravel road alongside the Common, down a well-known shortcut to Sea View Drive. Simon kept his eye out for Dorie as they passed all the fairgoers.

"Seven including Nauset," Zadie went on. "That first project turned out so well Milo set out to do the same thing in other coastal communities. He soon realized the biggest obstacle in his quest for waterfront property was wealthy people like himself, who seemed to be in a frenzy to gobble up coastal real estate for their trophy homes. Even if that was the American way, it didn't sit right with Milo, who's kind of a *socialist* rich guy, I guess. He thinks everyone should have the opportunity, at least once in their lives, to wake up to the sounds of surf and seagulls, to breathe in the salt air"—Zadie sighed—"to fill their hearts and minds with the divine power of the sea."

Divine power. God's will. Simon thought of Segundo sitting in a prison cell.

"Milo said *that?*" Cooper said.

"Okay, I paraphrased," Zadie said.

"I figured," Cooper said.

"But so far, the Vanderloos Foundation has built waterfront facilities in La Jolla, Seattle, Miami, Portland, San Francisco, and Puerto Rico. Turns out Nauset wasn't even on the short list. It was actually a family reunion that brought Milo back to the Cape last summer," Zadie said.

They turned left on to Sea View Drive. They had about an eighth of a mile to go to the Point. Zadie looked tired.

"Wanna rest a minute?" Simon said. There was a low stone wall in front of an old Cape like Val's.

Zadie sat. He took a wad of paper towels out of his back pocket and wiped his brow. Rose and Cooper sat on the wall. Cooper's feet dangled inches from the bottom.

"Milo's return to his old stomping grounds rekindled his love of the place. Not only that but the progressiveness of Provincetown had finally trickled down the arm enough to finally make him feel comfortable. People are much more accepting of alternative lifestyles now than they were—"

"*Alternative,*" Cooper said. "I hate that crap. Alternative to *what?* So you got a bunch of men shacking up with men, or women with women. Big deal. My idea of *alternative* is when you're not shacking up at all. In any case, get on with it."

Zadie just looked at Cooper as if he'd never seen one of her species in his life. Finally he had to blink. Then he continued: "At first, he considered Chatham. But he couldn't muster enough support there. In a town with that much money, no one wants to be reminded they're going to die. I'm good now." Zadie hoisted himself off the wall. "Ladies?" he said.

Rose and Cooper slid down too.

"One day I got a call out of the blue. Milo invited me to lunch. I'll have to admit, I was a little nervous, especially when I saw the spread of oysters and champagne. Thought he was aiming to make a pass at me."

"Something you want to tell us, old man?" Cooper said.

"Turns out, he did make an offer. The town would get a twenty-million-dollar state-of-the-art hospice and palliative-care facility owned and operated by the Vanderloos Foundation. All I had to do was come up with a waterfront site worthy of Milo's vision and convince the owner to sell. I knew that the Point had quietly been turned over to a real estate developer in the last six months by off-Cape relatives of Wendel Deschamps, who passed on eight or ten years ago. It was only a matter of time before something was going to go up on that property. I figured a high-end hospice facility was a more palatable use of the land. Thought it would serve the people of Nauset better than an enclave of private mansions."

"No beef there," Cooper said.

Zadie looked at Cooper. "If I did *anything* unethical in any of this, it was how I put the squeeze on the developers to get them to sell to Milo, though his offer *was* more than fair. I might have mentioned how the land happened to be long overdue for a tax assessment, and that it came with some pretty hefty zoning restrictions, including limits to the number of dwellings that could be built, the size of the septic fields, the number of bedrooms, the overall height."

Things Milo probably got speedy variances for, Simon thought. Hence the uproar.

Zadie continued: "No trees within a hundred feet of the wetlands could be touched. I also let them know the conservation commission would be monitoring their every step. And it was only fair that I warned them that most folks in town considered that land to be in the public domain and there could very well be easement issues and subsequent lawsuits. I told them they'd better brace for opposition from citizens, environmentalists, and the town's most celebrated gadflies."

Zadie stopped and pretended to tip his hat to Cooper. She shrugged.

"Just as I hoped, they backed off. Milo dug a little deeper into his pockets and the deal was done. And for my reward, well . . ." Once again, he looked at Cooper.

"Why didn't you just tell people what was going on?" Rose asked. "They would have understood."

"Brings me to Milo's last condition," he said, "that Dorie and I agree to keep the true nature of the project under wraps until it's completed. No one was supposed to know he was the underwriter."

"How come?" Simon asked.

Zadie laughed. "We think Milo prefers the clandestine role of 'run-of-the-mill kook' to that of 'multimillion-dollar kook,' which demands that people treat him with deference. Evidently, he prefers being written off and begrudgingly tolerated. He's a bit of a self-loathing millionaire."

"So why'd you tell us?" Cooper asked.

A tiny smile came on Zadie's lips. "Just tired of secrets, I guess," he said.

Simon took it all in. Until now, he'd felt some shame over his job at the site. When he told people he was in construction, he didn't hurry to tell them where. It had made him feel like a sellout. With this news, he was proud to be part of the project. The hospice center would be a boon for the town. It would bring jobs and draw visitors, relatives of patients who would need places to eat and sleep. Not to mention, as Zadie had pointed out, more than half of the town's residents were already over sixty. The upcoming decades would see people dropping like flies.

When Simon returned to work on Monday, he'd think of the

folks who'd take their final breaths within those walls, who'd experience their last days gazing out of the windows Simon had framed and installed. It made him feel good to know that the view from the Point, a place near to his heart, would be shared with those who needed it most. Not hoarded by a rich few.

Not only was Simon proud, he was relieved. All along he'd thought there was something strange about the design of the place. But he'd been out of the construction business on the Cape for so long that he wasn't up to speed on the trends and, therefore, didn't question the plans. Some decades were all about closet space. Others about professional kitchens. With seven baths on the upstairs floors alone, Simon had just figured the "day of the john" had arrived.

Zadie made Simon, Rose, and Cooper promise not to talk about the hospice until it was okay with Milo that the truth be revealed. He didn't want anything to jeopardize the project. They all agreed.

They walked in silence until they crested the dune and could see the foundation.

"Do you think we'll find Dorie at the Point?" Rose asked.

"She wouldn't miss the reenactment," Zadie said. "People will start making their way down over the next half hour. I need to see how Mrs. McGregor and her kids are doing too. I told her I'd give them a pep talk before the show."

Simon had been so caught up in everything Zadie had been telling them that he'd almost forgotten about Dorie and the missing painting. In the scheme of things, it just didn't seem that important anymore. Neither did the reenactment or the time capsule or the Tri-centennial or any of it.

Life at the Point was dictated by the tides. As a natural jetty sur-rounded on three sides by water, it fell victim to the same kind of flux and erosion as did the entire Cape. Sand had accumu-lated on the north side to create a level sandbar that remained relatively shallow, even at high tide. This was where the reenactment would take place. The south side was a different story. Here the seawall was really necessary. At low tide, water completely receded and the marked drop-off could be seen. Throughout the harbor the current was strong. It was on the south side that a tendril of that current would break off and become trapped, creating a churning whirlpool that gouged the sand in places. The reenactment had to be timed between tides so there'd be enough beach for the audience to stand on, and enough water for the boats to float, but not enough to put the kids in harm's way. The tide couldn't be outgoing or, if their anchors weren't properly secured, they'd be drawn out toward the mouth of the inlet. In the last hour, the tide had turned. For the next six, water levels would be on the rise.

At Zadie's suggestion, they took a shortcut across someone's lawn toward a private staircase that led down to the beach. From the top, they could see the kids setting up for the reenactment. Four boys from Mrs. McGregor's class were thigh-deep in the water, positioning several aluminum rowboats ranging in size from nine to twelve feet, anchoring them in place. Other students were slipping costumes on over their bathing suits.

About thirty feet from shore sat a stationary raft displaying a faded, two-dimensional plywood replica of the British frigate *Newcastle,* a three-masted, square-rigged fighting boat. The set had originally been made in shop class by a group of students who were, by now, going bald and having their prostates checked annually. On the beach in front of the boats, potted evergreens that had been strategically positioned on the sand were already sitting in water and would have to be moved farther inland. Once the invasion began, these would be the trees local militia used to block enemy fire as they drove back the Brits.

Simon had seen the reenactment plenty of times and it never changed. The British would row in from the frigate, their weapons aimed at the folks onshore. They'd fire. The people

onshore would scatter. The local militia would fire back, starting with just a few men behind the trees and slowly growing
in numbers. This would go on for however long the old people could tolerate the cacophony. Suddenly one of the British
invaders would be shot in the chest, spraying ketchup everywhere. (Thank goodness their coats were red, Mrs. McGregor
had said on many occasions. Meanwhile generations of locals
grew up with an unnatural association between ketchup and
the British.) The wounded Brit would stand, drop his rifle, and
clutch his chest, then lose his balance and fall overboard. The
onlookers would gasp. (Mostly in sympathy for the boy who'd
just plunged into fifty-five-degree water.) The gunfire would
stop. And there would be the fallen redcoat, lying facedown
in the water, trying to stay still while shivering and sneaking
breaths out of the side of his mouth. And depending on the
country's predicament and the prevailing sentiment toward war
at the time of the reenactment, the sight of the fallen navy man
might inspire cheers, or silence, or, as it had during the summer
of 1971 and perhaps this time as well due to the situation in the
Middle East, all-out jeers.

With the loss of their mate, the British would be paralyzed
with fear. They'd look at one another in disbelief, then retreat,
hauling up anchor and frantically rowing back toward the *Newcastle*. The kids playing townspeople from two hundred years
ago would erupt into cheers, which would radiate out to their
real-life descendants until everyone was on his or her feet, clap-
ping and hooting and whistling with pride at Nauset's nineteenth-
century insurgents. The militiamen and women would embrace
while Mrs. McGregor would step out of the audience and take
her fiftieth or sixtieth curtain call. Then the crowd would
disperse, on their way home the little boys obsessed over the
"wicked cool guns," the girls lamenting how unfair that the
wives and mothers didn't get to shoot anyone, and the old men
recalling the days when *they* played the militiamen, and how

the show—and everything else for that matter—had been much better back then.

As the four of them paused at the top of the staircase, Simon could see progress had been made on the south side of the seawall in the last couple of days. More sand and rocks had been set in place and a new delivery of boulders had arrived. They were scattered ten to fifteen feet from the base. As the tide went out, it had gouged large holes beside them, which were now filling with seawater.

The police tape stretched around the boulders was also hard to miss.

"What's all that about?" Zadie asked.

Rose looked at Cooper, then at Simon. "They probably just want to keep the kids away from the rocks," Simon said.

Rose nodded. "That must be it," she said.

Simon observed the pools beneath the rocks. One of them looked different. There was something light beneath the surface. Must be the boat, he thought, though he couldn't say how much of a boat or what kind. A jagged piece of wood was floating free above the wreck, perhaps experiencing the light of day for the first time in twenty-seven years. But Zadie and Cooper didn't see the boat. They were too busy looking at the woman who suddenly appeared on top of an island of boulder.

"Isn't that your wife?" Cooper said.

"Where?" Rose said.

"There." Cooper pointed.

All four of them looked at the less than graceful figure hoisting herself up on the twelve-foot boulder. She was easy to spot in preppy pink-and-green pants, her oversize Jimmy Fund T-shirt catching the wind like a spinnaker. And there was something she was dragging behind her. Something heavy.

"What in the world is she doing?" Rose asked.

"Almost thirty years and never a dull moment," Zadie said. He sighed.

Simon led the way down the staircase with Rose following fast behind. By the time Cooper and Zadie made it to the bottom, Rose and Simon had reached the reenactment set.

"There's Eldridge," Simon said.

The cop stood at the water's edge with his hands on his hips, legs apart in a state-trooper stance. Dorie was far enough away that he had to yell.

"See the police tape, lady? Come off those rocks right now or I'll haul you down to the station," he said.

"That how you talk to the town administrator's wife?" Dorie yelled back.

"Mrs. Nickerson?" He shielded his eyes from the sun to get a better look. "What are you doing up there?"

"Something I should have done weeks ago," she said, finally reaching the top. When she tried to sit, one of her kelly-green flats slipped off and fell into the pool just below the rock. It sank.

"Damn," she said.

Simon and Rose reached Eldridge at the water's edge.

"What are *you* doing here?" Eldridge said to Simon.

"Mike, what's going on?" Rose asked.

Simon spoke to the woman on the rock. "Dorie, need some help?" Simon asked. Her pants were soaked from about midthigh down from where the water got deep by the rock. She must have been out there awhile. Simon figured it had gotten deeper since she started out.

"No thanks," Dorie said. "I've got something I've got to do." She struggled to reach for the object she'd dragged up the rock. She swung it around and Simon saw it was Noel's missing portrait. A rope was tied around the frame of the painting, the other end of the rope secured around a cobblestone.

Zadie and Cooper had finally joined the party.

"What in the world are you doing, woman?" Zadie said.

Dorie saw her husband. "Just let me be," she said. "All of you." Simon thought she was weeping.

"Vindo para baixo!" Cooper said.

Dorie looked like a child being scolded. "I don't know what you said," she said.

"The hell you don't. I said come down from there! What do you think you're doing?" Cooper asked.

"I was doing just fine until *this,*" she said. She lifted the painting an inch. With the cobblestone attached, it was too heavy for her to raise any higher.

By now, it was pretty obvious to Simon what she intended to do. She was planning to drown herself, only not her real self. Her portrait. But why?

"Stop being such a vain fool. You should be proud of yourself," Val said. "You *and* your husband."

Dorie stopped moving. She looked up at the group onshore and listened.

"If you want to kill yourself, at least wait till the damn hospice is done," Cooper said.

Rose added, "Dorie, we *know.* Zadie told us."

Zadie raised his hands in protest. He shook his head no.

"Now you're the one being a fool. Are you that afraid of her?" Cooper said to Zadie. She turned to Dorie. "Did you think he could keep a secret like that forever?"

Zadie put his head in his hands.

Simon noticed the water was coming in pretty fast. Dorie couldn't get back on her own if she wanted to. It was flowing well over the tops of the holes now. He could no longer see the boat.

Dorie was looking wide-eyed at her husband. "You *told?*" she said.

"About the hospice," he said. "That's *all.*"

"What else is there?" Cooper said.

Dorie teetered on the rock. Simon worried she might lose her balance and fall. As for Eldridge, he didn't seem to care how this played out as long as people stayed away from the areas that had been taped off.

"You all think I'm crazy," she said. "It's just this painting. Noel must've seen me the day we got the results of Zadie's biopsy. I remember what I wore that day. I remember everything. Noel must've seen us."

Zadie's shoulders slumped. "I hadn't told them that part," Zadie said, too soft for Dorie to hear.

"What's she talking about. You sick?" Cooper squared off in front of Zadie with her hands on her hips.

Oblivious to the drama unfolding onshore, Dorie went on: "It's all right there in the painting. The pain, the lies, the secrets we had to keep. The poor man had just found out he was going to die and you know what we came home to? An answering machine full of hateful messages and threats."

Cooper seemed to lose an inch or two in stature. Perhaps she'd made a phone call that day.

"They were calling him names, accusing him of taking bribes. They didn't know he was trying to do something good for all of them. I couldn't bear it. His getting cancer was a divine kick in the gut. This painting"—she gave it a shake—"is another."

"You know Noel would never do anything to hurt you," Cooper said.

"I know that. He's just too good. He captures too much. It's a curse!"

"It's a gift," Rose said, nowhere near loud enough for Dorie to hear. Simon agreed. "What if we just take the painting and put it away so you never have to see it again?" Rose asked.

"Noel has lots of paintings. He doesn't need this one," she said. "Not as much as I need to know it's gone."

"Dorie, what are you doing?" came a voice behind us. It was Milo. In his black ensemble, he looked less like a millionaire than a waiter. The wind was blowing his hairpiece and Simon could see where it lifted slightly from his scalp.

"This is all your fault, Milo. You're the one who made us keep the secret, even after we found out about Zadie. And then you insisted we put the painting in the show, even though you knew how it made me feel," Dorie said. "You're a selfish bastard! And a coward."

Zadie staggered. He grabbed his forehead. "She doesn't mean it, Milo. You know how grateful we are," he said. "Why, you're the most generous person we—"

"And that's why I'm sinking this *here*," Dorie said. "So you can look out the window of your precious *project* and remember how you hurt us."

"*There's* the Portuguese." Cooper raised her fist. "Always liked that girl's spunk," she said.

Milo put a finger on the side of his cheek and sighed. "If that's how you feel—"

"No," Zadie said. He started toward Milo. "It's not how she feels," he reasoned. "Trust me. It's not how anyone feels. She's just upset. Between the project and the Tri-centennial planning and then my getting sick. A little rest and she'll be fine, really."

Milo appeared to be studying Dorie like she was an animal in a wildlife exhibit.

"Meeelo, over here. Mind if I have a word with you?" Cooper said. She put her arm around Milo's shoulder and led him away. They walked down the beach.

"What does Cooper think she's doing?" Rose asked.

"Look at Eldridge," Simon said to Rose. "He's freaking out."

Rose turned to look. Eldridge's fists were white. "He *knows*."

"Know's what?" Simon said. He took a step closer to Rose. "What do you mean 'he *knows*'?"

"Now you've done it, Dorie," Zadie said. His sank down on a large driftwood stump. He put his head in his hands. "What if he backs out? This was supposed to be my legacy. My last gift to the town."

"Zadie, I'm sorry," Dorie called. Zadie didn't look up.

Simon realized if they waited much longer, they'd need a boat to get her back in.

"Zadie!" she called again.

"Dorie, I'm coming to get you," Simon said. "*And* the painting. Sit tight." Simon took off his shoes and socks.

A crowd was beginning to gather down the beach. Some people were headed in their direction. One pointed to Dorie and clapped. What did they think? After all these years a new chapter had been added to the reenactment? The rescue of a militia woman who'd been kidnapped and compromised by the British? This *was* a new chapter, Simon thought. He was going in the water again, this time on purpose. And sober. Up the beach, he could see the kids had taken their places on the boats. The reenactment was about to get under way, that is, if there would be any crowd left to watch it.

Then the voice came, hard and slow. "You set foot in that water and I let go." Dorie stood and held the painting out in front of her. Somehow she'd found the strength to raise it on high.

From down the beach came a horrible wail. At first Simon thought it was one of those distress signals that came out of an aerosol can. Then he realized it was Noel. The boy was running toward them.

"Noel, wait!" Val yelled. Her face was bright red. She'd obviously been chasing him the whole way down from the town hall.

Simon looked back at Dorie, who had become so unnerved by Noel that she stumbled and lost her balance. It was as if the rest happened in slow motion: Dorie grasping the air in front of her, the cobblestone hitting the water, the splash, the rope disappearing, the canvas bobbing a few times, then slipping out of sight.

"Oh no!" she yelled. "I didn't mean to—" She pressed her hands to her mouth.

"Now, *that's* the biggest load of crap I ever heard," Cooper said. She and Milo had returned from their powwow.

Noel ran past Simon and started into the water. He tripped

and fell in face-first. Water went down his throat and he started to cough.

"Stop him," Val said. "He can't swim."

Simon grabbed Noel by the scruff of his Jimmy Fund shirt. With one motion, he pulled the kid out of the water and onto his feet. He grabbed Noel by the shoulders and spoke to him directly, forcing Noel to look him in the eyes.

"You stay here. You understand? *I'll* get the painting. You stay with Rose and Val," Simon said.

Noel took a step back and Val put her arms around him. He coughed some more.

"Keep him there," Simon said to Rose. "Don't let him follow."

Rose stepped up beside Val.

Simon pulled off his shirt and threw it onto the sand. He stepped into the water. The cold seeped though his pants. His jeans grew heavy. He waded out as far as he could. It wasn't too deep but the current was strong, and seemed to be coming at him directly and also from the south. Once the water reached his waist, he thought it might be faster to swim.

Simon plunged in and felt the breath snake from his lungs. He opened his mouth and tasted the salt, familiar, less briny, more metal. And colder. So much colder than down in the tropics. *Swim,* he told himself. His muscles responded to the cold with fits of flailing. He lifted his head and saw the rock had barely moved closer.

And the crowd, were they cheering?

Simon stopped to catch his breath. He spotted Eldridge on the shore. "Eldridge, get one of the boats and meet me at the rock," Simon yelled.

Simon took another breath, put his head down, and swam, this time at an angle to the current. Underwater, Noel's hollering sounded like cries of a humpback whale, reminding Simon of a relaxation tape Segundo used to play when they were hungover.

He thought of the whales and tried to slow his heartbeat. He was getting used to the temperature of the water now. He was almost there.

Finally, he reached the rock and grabbed hold. He stood at the edge of the hole. The water came up to his chest, the hole itself too deep to stand in. The current was wicked.

"I can see it, Simon. It's right down there," Dorie said.

Simon looked up. Dorie's eyes were ringed in mascara. There were scrapes on her arms and her pants were torn.

"You okay?" he asked.

"I'm sorry," she said. "I thought if I could just get rid of it."

"The painting?"

"How I looked, how I felt, all of it."

Simon understood. Her husband was dying. At least that's what she'd said. What would it be like to have someone capture your worst moment on earth? Immortalize it in oils. For Simon, which moment would that have been? Maybe the morning he'd gotten the news that his sister had died. He'd been passed out in the bed of a pickup truck that belonged to someone at the construction site he was supposed to be working. A cop had come and shaken him awake. At first Simon thought it was the foreman. Once he realized it was a cop, he figured he'd done something bad the night before. But the cop was being too nice to him. Simon even remembered the cop's mustache that was too long and had remnants of food caught in the bottom hairs. He remembered the cop's breath had smelled of cigarettes and oranges, and that he had a blemish on his cheek and a chicken-pox scar under his left eye. Time had slowed down for Simon in those moments when he got the news. And then his brain went back and underscored the details so he'd never forget, in the same way Noel had remembered the slippers and the bathrobe and the goldfish. And maybe that's what this painting brought back for Dorie. It underscored the *befores*. The outfit she'd chosen that morning, the tissue she had wadded up in her pocket, the roll of mints she'd bought for the trip to the doctor's office that she might have found weeks later in the purse with the clasp. The waiting room. The college ring on the doctor's finger when he shook Zadie's hand, before giving him the news. Simon could only imagine.

"Just sit tight," he said.

He tried to see down through the water but it was too murky. Dorie had a better vantage point. The current was kicking up silt. The only thing he could see was a faint patch of white, probably the back of the canvas. He'd have to feel his way along the bottom for the rest.

He took a deep breath and went under. As soon as he did, he heard gunfire. He thought of Eldridge wound tight as a drum with that gun hollering in his holster. His heart missed a beat. He scrambled to the surface. Everyone was still standing on the shore, except Eldridge. And then he remembered the reenactment. It must be under way. Hopefully Eldridge was commandeering one of the rowboats.

"See it?" Dorie said. She had her hands over her ears. More shots.

Simon felt like he was experiencing a flashback from 'Nam or, considering he'd never been there, a flashback from one of those 1970s war movies. "Not yet," Simon said.

He dove and kicked his way to the bottom. He felt around. He opened his eyes and through the haze saw what he thought was the canvas, and the rope. He grabbed it. The painting swung around and there, just inches from his nose, was Dorie, staring at him through the murk. He let out a cry, which was wrapped up in ocean and carried away by the current. He tugged on the rope but it wouldn't give. He needed more air. He kicked his way up.

"What the heck did you weigh it down with? A cannonball?" Simon said. He panted. "Can't get it to budge."

"Just a cobblestone," Dorie said.

Maybe it was that he had no leverage. This time he'd try to grab it and kick off the bottom.

Simon went down again. He caught hold of the rope, used it to pull his way down to the bottom, then adjusted himself feetfirst, grabbed the painting, and tried to use the power in his thighs to thrust his way to the top. As soon as he let loose, he felt a sharp pain on the arch of his foot. He let go of the rope and went back to the surface.

He dug his fingers into a groove on the rock and inspected his foot. Blood was oozing from a three-inch slit just above the heel.

"Simon, you're bleeding!" Dorie said.

The water was so cold that he barely felt the cut at all. But what had he gashed himself on? Whatever it was, the rope must have gotten tangled up in it.

Simon drew in another breath and went down again.

By now he'd kicked up so much sand, the visibility was zero. Carefully, he ran his hand along the bottom; there was something long and sharp protruding from the sand. Some kind of twisted metal. He followed the rope down with his fingers to try to find where it had become tangled. Meanwhile, the current was pushing him into the metal. If he wasn't careful, he'd be cut again. He needed more air. He righted himself and motioned for the top, only this time he didn't go anywhere. He was stuck, caught. Somewhere on his pants. He struggled and tried to tear free. He felt around his back to try to tell where he was ensnared. He planted his feet and used all his strength to push. Something shifted. His face became engulfed in bubbles. They tickled the flesh under his chin. Something brushed his arm in a rush to the top with the escaping air. He heard Dorie scream. He needed air. He was running out of time.

Come on, God, Simon said to himself. *Not now.*

Above his head, the distant surface of the water glistened like a shiny membrane, like a magic portal to the great all-you-can-breathe buffet. Simon tried to swallow back his thirst for air. A little seawater seeped into his nose and he coughed. When that happened, a thread of bubbles escaped his mouth. He watched what might be his very own last breath spiral like DNA up to the light. He saw it pierce the membrane and enter the living world. Then the sensation in his lungs changed from the feeling that they might explode to the even more terrible feeling of hollowness. His eye sockets burned. How much longer could he hold the ocean out?

Green drained from the water until Simon saw only black. And then, it was as if a piece of him broke off and followed his last breath to the surface. Once there, it didn't stop but lifted up, up into the air, then the clouds. He could see himself rising. And then, in a cinematic cut, a heavy-handed segue, everything shifted again and he was seated at a bar, before a giant plasma TV. On it, Simon could see the image of himself losing consciousness in the water. He patted down his chest to make sure he was really there. How could he be in two places at once?

He looked around. There beside him, one hand in the Anheuser-Busch pretzels and the other wrapped around the handle of a frosted mug, was God. He was wearing a David Ortiz Red Sox jersey and looked like He hadn't shaved in a few days. Still, Almighty that He was, He lifted the glass and shot back the entire beer in a single gulp.

"Impressive, Lord. But maybe You want to slow down a little. Now's not a good time," Simon said. He nodded toward the television.

"Is there *ever* a good time?" God asked.

A bottle of tequila and a shot glass appeared on the bar. God poured the yellow liquid into the glass and offered it to Simon. Simon shook his head. God picked up the glass and threw back the shot. Simon saw the worm at the bottom of the bottle. He wondered what God might see if He ate it.

"Stress gets to you, huh?" Simon asked.

"You have no idea," God said. He put his forehead down to rest on His arm.

"God," Simon said. He nudged the Lord with his elbow. "I hate to bother You but I was hoping You might help this guy out."

God raised his head and looked around.

"Up here on the TV," Simon added. "He seems to be stuck."

"Can we get the game?" God said to a bartender who, as far as Simon could tell, must've been somewhere cutting lemons. God looked at the TV. "Hey, wait a minute, I know that guy. I just rescued him a couple of months ago."

"Name's Beadle. Good guy. Means well. Maybe a little misguided—"

"A *little* misguided?" God said.

"But he's trying to set things right."

"Wasn't that the same guy I saw copping a bottle of Scotch from some kids in an alley less than a month ago?"

"Must have him confused with someone else," Simon said. He'd just lied to God.

". . . after he *swore* to Me he'd never touch the stuff again. And to think all those poor hungry sharks off Miami who went without supper that night."

"This time is different," Simon said. "This time he really means it."

God rolled His eyes and put His head back down on the bar. The image on the TV screen changed to a picture of Rose on the beach. She was screaming, tears streaming down her face. Her hands pressed to her head. "Save him!" she cried.

"You talking to Me?" God asked, like a kid coming to at a frat party.

"Still here," Simon said. He tapped on the bar. Time was running out.

God looked up at the TV. "Who's the girl?" He said.

"Rose Nowak," Simon said.

"One with the cheating boyfriend. You and her are a thing now?"

So that Martin guy had cheated on her. Simon hadn't considered that. "Sort of," Simon said.

Rose's eyes had gone ocher, or maybe the TV just needed a color adjustment. Simon couldn't help but be flattered at how distraught she was over the prospect of losing him. It made him feel happy and sad all at once.

Then the celestial station changed from Rose TV to Noel TV. There was his nephew at the water's edge, still in Val's arms. His face had gone dark. Under furrowed brows, his eyes fixed on the water in front of him. Simon knew what he was thinking. It was happening again. First his mother, now his uncle. If Simon left him, he didn't know what might happen to Noel, whether he might go so deep inside the caverns of himself so that no one would be able to reach him.

"I know that kid. I gave him something special. A gift," God said.

"He's an artist."

"Something else," God said. He snapped his fingers like it might help Him remember.

"No, that's it. *Really*," Simon said. "He's an artist. And if we don't save his uncle, he might stop painting altogether."

"Could've sworn it was something else," God said.

Anger boiled up inside of Simon. He felt rage and pain ripping through his lungs. "What else? There's nothing. You gave him a faulty brain, a deadbeat father, an alcoholic uncle. You took his mother when he was only five. And in spite of it all, he's a happy, decent kid who paints beautiful pictures, and who knows how to forgive a lot better than you—"

"*That's* it," God said.

"What's it?" Simon said.

"His gift. It has nothing to do with art. It's that he brings people together." God seemed proud of Himself. "See, I knew I'd remember," He said. "And by the way, Simon." He pointed toward Simon's feet. "Take off your pants. They're ruining the carpet."

Simon looked down and saw he was standing in a puddle of water.

Sight returned to Simon's eyes. He'd come to in time to realize he wasn't going to get out of this alive. His lungs were on fire. All he needed was to breathe in one good gulp of water and get it over with. What was that sound in his ears, that rhythmic splash and creak? The sound of the brain's engine room shutting down? Or might it be an approaching rowboat? Just maybe he still had a chance. And then, from nowhere, a thunderclap of inspiration. A flash of savantlike brilliance. It came to him. He didn't need to be saved at all. He undid the top button, unzipped the fly, wriggled out of his pants, and paddled with what little strength he had left as fast as he could toward the light. He was free.

CHAPTER NINETEEN

*Slew your telescope across the sky and track
objects as the Earth rotates beneath them.*
—from the Celetron NexStar JC Telescope Instruction
Manual

Unresectable adenocarcinoma of the pancreas. It was a
mouthful but Zadie said he liked the sound of it better than the
C-word. He told them it had started with him just feeling tired
and queasy. "Every now and then a funny little pain would well
up around my belly, nothing too bad. A little over-the-counter
Motrin usually did the trick. Just chalked it up to Dorie's pitiful
Welsh rarebit." Dorie elbowed him and he patted her knee.

"She's a fine cook as long as we keep her away from the Nickerson family recipes."

The others were so wrapped up in Zadie's story they didn't
see Mrs. McGregor marching toward the group, hands on her
ample hips in a painfully prolonged, "you're gonna get it" threat
as she stumbled over stones and tufts of beach grass in her sen-
sible shoes. The long gray braid coiled around her head seemed
to be keeping the top from blowing off.

Zadie continued: "The irony is, I found out about the cancer
after the deal had been signed on the hospice center." He winked

at Rose. "I told Milo the least he could do was let me pick the paint color for my room."

"Mrs. McGregor," Rose said. Everyone turned.

Rose could only imagine what thoughts ran through the woman's head as she encountered the tattered, one-shoed, half-soaked Dorie and her tired, greenish husband sharing a sea-smoothed stump; Val, with her eyes closed, spread-eagled in the sand; Noel, his legs crossed, rocking, gaze fixed on his uncle, who was also flat on his back, his hips swaddled in an oversize Jimmy Fund T-shirt, and who, every so often, would raise himself up on his elbows and spew seawater from his mouth. A few feet away was Cooper, sitting on her haunches and staring out at the bay, Milo, striking a meditative pose by the seawall, and Mike Eldridge, police radio in hand, chewing off his fingernails one by one. And Rose, her fingers laced with Simon's.

"Why, look at you," she said. "All of you. You ought to be ashamed of yourselves."

Mrs. McGregor directed the scolding at Simon. Rose suspected she either not so fondly remembered him or assumed he must be the one most responsible, seeing as he was the one most naked.

"Those children invested weeks on this show and for you all to spoil it is unforgivable," she said. She held up a gnarled finger that wanted to point back at her own shoulder no matter where she directed it. "Atrocious!"

Cooper kept her eyes on the horizon. "Save it for the kids, Clara. People are dying here. There'll be more reenactments, God help us."

Clara McGregor let out a little puff of air. The whole scene must have been too much for her. These weren't high school students, after all. Rose could hear the musical swoosh of her nylons, the zither of thigh against thigh, as she retreated.

"Why won't anyone believe me? It was a skull. I'm sure of it," Dorie said.

"For God's sake, Dorie," Zadie said. "It's been a long day. We all just need some rest."

Mike came over to Simon. "Do you want me to call for an ambulance or not?" he said.

"I think you should," Rose said.

He'd been out of the water for fifteen minutes, had a nasty gash on his foot that probably could use a stitch or two, and was still coughing up fluid from his chest. And his color wasn't so good, though he did seem pinker than he had been when he first came out of the boat.

"I'm fine," Simon said.

"Really?" Rose asked.

He looked at her like he only just realized she was at his side. The corners of his lips curled. Rose thought it was supposed to be a smile.

No one was looking so she unlaced her fingers and ran her hand up his arm, to his chest. Simon put his hand over hers.

"What's all this talk about *skulls*?" Val asked. She had her eyes closed and her arm thrown over her head.

"It came to the surface in a flood of bubbles," Dorie said. She fluttered her hands, raising them and then herself off the stump like she was doing the wave at a baseball game. Then she sank back down.

"What was down there anyway?" Cooper asked.

"Chunks of metal. Torn-up outboard, maybe," Simon said. He coughed to clear his throat.

Rose sat up and looked over at Eldridge, who stood with his shoulders hunched. It seemed like his eyes had migrated deeper into their sockets. His brows had become heavier. He slipped on his sunglasses.

Simon continued: "I remember the bubbles. When I was struggling to get free, I gave a good tug and something shifted. A bunch of air escaped. I felt something bump me on the way up but I couldn't tell you what it was." He sat up and tightened the shirt around his waist.

"Will you check the boat for something else?" he said to Rose. "Maybe a towel or a blanket."

Rose got up and walked over to the skiff Mike had hijacked during the reenactment. In the middle of the performance, he'd gone over and pointed to one of the kids in the water. *Who me?* the kid had gestured, pointing to his chest. Mike nodded. He ordered him to pick up anchor and row in. Then he stranded the kid on the mainland, hopped in the boat, and rowed to the rock to pick up Dorie and Simon. Unfortunately, the kid he'd shanghaied was the star of the show, the one who was supposed to take the plunge. At the last minute, another kid had to step up and improvise, only he hadn't rehearsed the fall and landed hard, getting the wind knocked out of him when he hit the cold water. Someone onshore with his kids, Rose's guess was a former lifeguard, sensing the kid was in trouble, tore off his loafers and his golf shirt, and dove in to rescue the British soldier, someone his ancestors had risked their lives to kill two hundred years before. History had come full circle.

On the floor of the boat was a plastic baggie filled with ketchup blood. Next to the mangled canvas of Dorie's painting was the British navy costume the crestfallen would-be star had abandoned when he was carted off by his irate parents. Rose picked up the red jacket, shook it out, and brought it over to Simon.

"What about the painting?" Val said.

"It got torn up when Noel's uncle was doing the cha-cha down there," Cooper said.

Rose handed Simon the red coat.

"Thanks, I *think*," he said.

She helped brush the sand off his back and he put it on. It was a little small but better than nothing. Actually he looked kind of handsome. Maybe there was some truth to that thing Rose supposedly had for men in uniforms.

"I'm sorry about the painting, Noel," he said.

"No, *I'm* sorry," Dorie said. "It was all my fault. I don't expect you to understand, Noel. But I hope you can forgive me."

"Temporary insanity," Zadie said. He squeezed her hand.

"Happens to the best of us," Val said.

Everyone turned to look at her. Evidently she missed the irony of her own words.

"And so, as Tiny Tim observed, 'God bless us, every one!'" Noel said. At least Noel had moved on.

No one said anything until Cooper finally broke the silence.

"I want to know more about this skull," she said. All this time she'd been staring out at the inlet. Now it was clear to Rose, if to no one else, that she had Lino on her mind. Rose glanced over at Simon.

"No skull," Mike said. He knelt down on his haunches, picked up a piece of seaweed, and tossed it into the breeze. "It was probably just an old mooring float."

Rose looked up at him. "How do you know for sure?" she asked.

His forehead was glazed with sweat. His sunglasses had slid down on his nose, so Rose could see his eyes. They were fixed on Cooper.

"But it sank again. Mooring floats don't sink," Dorie said.

"Could have been anything, a ball, a plastic bag, a horseshoe crab," Mike said. He stood up and brushed sand off his legs.

He was lying. Rose stood up too.

Val raised herself up on her elbows. "Oh, let it go, Dorie. Mike's a police officer. He knows what he's talking about," Val said.

"You think I can't tell a skull from a horseshoe crab?" Dorie said.

"What do you say we move this party back up to the field and call it a day," Mike said. He clapped his hands.

No one moved.

"I don't want to 'move this party up to the field,'" Cooper

said. "I want to know about what's out there." She pointed to the rock Dorie had climbed. The tide had risen so just the very top was visible.

Mike raised his eyebrows and his forehead creased like a Roman shade.

"Cooper, leave the poor fellow alone. It's been a long day. Come back to the house and I'll fix you something to eat, Mike," Val said.

"That would be nice, Val," Mike said.

He was looking for any way to escape, even if it meant going home with Val. Not so fast. Rose had a few questions of her own.

"Mike, remember when I asked you to check on those police records having to do with the disappearance of Cooper's son?" She looked over at Simon. His eyes told her he was with her. "What were you able to find out?"

Val shot up. She opened her eyes. "Lino?" she said. "What does any of this have to do with Lino?"

"I told you, I've been out at the Point. I tried asking around but nobody knew," Mike said. He took off his glasses, wiped the bridge of his nose with his sleeve, then put them back on.

"After you told me about that witness, I did a little digging myself and learned the only person who supposedly saw Lino after the accident happens to be blind as a bat," Rose said.

"Bassett? Maybe *now* he is. Who says he couldn't see then?" Mike asked.

"His wife," Rose said.

"Everyone knew as much," Cooper said. "Still, less work for the cops if they could say Lino was a runaway. Just another delinquent Portuguese kid." Cooper clenched her fist and ground her heel in the sand. "Pru should have come forward. She had kids of her own. I'll never forgive her for that."

Rose could see why Avery had defended his story. He'd become a laughingstock. Lino's disappearance had given him the chance to be an upstanding citizen again, a police witness, even. And like a good wife, Pru had stood by him rather than come forward and cause Avery any further embarrassment. Apparently, neither of them had stopped to think about whom they were hurting.

"I guess I don't really know what you're getting at," Mike said to me. "You're talking as if I have something to do with this."

"A kid gets news that's going to change his life. His girlfriend's pregnant," Rose said. Out of the corner of her eye, she saw Val lower her head. "He's upset. He goes out in his boat to clear his head, try to calm down, figure things out. And that's the last anyone sees of him. He never calls home. Never comes back to find out what happened to Val or the baby. This is a kid who got along with his folks. Had a good relationship with his girlfriend as far as anyone can tell. He loved boats, loved the water. Loved to tinker on motors. His dream was to open up a marina someday." Rose looked over at Cooper. Her eyes blazed. "Kids like that just don't run away. That leads me to the only logical conclusion that something happened to Lino out in the water that night. An accident. Foul play. *Something.*"

"What I've said all these years," Cooper said.

"*Foul play.* Come on," Mike said. His voice cracked a little and he cleared his throat. "Maybe something *did* happen. How would I know? I was just a kid myself."

"Exactly how you might know," Rose said. She realized she'd been pacing. She stopped and faced Mike. "Remember that day we went for a drive on the outer beach. As soon as I mentioned Lino, you started packing up. That felt weird at the time. And then there was your very public opposition to building at the Point."

"Me and half the town—" he said.

"And as soon as they started on the seawall, there you were, every day, watching," Rose said. "Like you were waiting for something to happen."

"Beadle will tell you. There was a rash of vandalism. I needed to be there. What's the big deal?" Mike said.

"What's the big deal about a missing shovel and a couple of broken windows? Nice to know the taxpayers can afford to put a cop on every construction site," Simon said.

"And then," Rose continued, "when Simon came to you earlier to tell you Noel's paintings were missing, you got that call on the walkie-talkie. Part of a boat had been found. Only it had happened when you weren't here to manage the situation. And that set you off, so much that you had them put police tape around the rocks to be sure no one would go near it. Then you shoved Simon out of your way so you could get here ahead of everyone else."

"Only Dorie beat you to it," Simon said. He tightened the Jimmy Fund shirt around his waist and stood.

"What's this about a boat?" Cooper said.

"You could see it before the tide came up. It was uncovered by the tractors this morning. I was there when he got the call," Simon said.

"We find wrecks out there all the time. It's no big deal," Mike said.

"It was a big enough deal that you couldn't help us track down Noel's paintings," Rose said.

"How come you didn't tell me sooner?" Cooper fired at Simon.

"We wanted to know more about it first," Rose said.

"We didn't want to put you through any of this until we were sure," Simon said.

She nodded. It seemed like she was softening toward Simon. She looked out toward the rocks.

"It's all starting to add up," Rose said. "I think you know something about what happened to Lino. I think you've known all these years. And now it's time for you to tell us."

Mike rolled his eyes in such a way that made it a blessing

he hadn't decided to go into acting. "Look, I don't want to hurt anybody's feelings here." He nodded at Val. "But this is the same *reporter* who fell for a tall tale about a family that doesn't exist. I'm not sure how much anyone should be trusting your instincts, Rose."

He had a point, Rose had to admit. What if this time, instead of ignoring clues, Rose was fabricating them, creating something where there was nothing? Only this time, with higher stakes, including the potential to devastate more than a few innocent people.

Simon jumped in. "Nice try, Eldridge. But Rose is a damn good reporter." He came between Mike and Rose. Then, in a lower voice, he said, "I also know what you came from and wouldn't put anything past you. You're no better than anyone else, Eldridge. Might even be a bit worse."

Mike's face turned the color of Simon's coat. Rose almost felt bad for him. She was surprised he didn't lunge for Simon's throat. She thought Simon was too.

She had to keep pressing. "Cooper, you know how Lino got in trouble for racing in the inlet?" she said.

"Kids think they'll live forever," Cooper said. Her voice sounded far away.

"Mike, you told me how you used to go fishing out there, sometimes even in the middle of the night," Rose said. "Did you ever race your boat?"

A drop of sweat from Mike's sunglasses fell onto one of his shiny buttons.

"Of course he did. Any kid who had a boat used to race it back then," Simon said.

Mike tightened his jaw. "You remember that, Beadle? Don't see how *you* could remember much of anything from those days," he said. *"Asshole drunk."*

Simon took a step toward Mike. "Who's calling *who* an asshole?" he said. All Simon had to do now was lose control and come after Mike. Then Mike could haul Simon down to the police station and this nightmare would end for him, at least for today. He'd have time to think. Cooper must've picked up on that too. She put her hand on Mike's shoulder. He flinched but didn't move away.

"Please," she said. "If you know, tell me."

Rose slipped herself into the sliver of space between Simon and Mike. "What happened that night, Mike?" she asked. Simon backed away. He was in no shape to fight even if he wanted to after what he'd been through.

"You were just kids," Cooper said. There was even a note of forgiveness in her voice. This was a new Cooper Rose was seeing. "Something happened. Whatever it was, you were scared and covered it up. You hid the truth for twenty-seven years. But don't you see? I have to know. Before I go to my grave, I want some peace." She pointed out toward the rocks. "Is that Lino's boat, Mike? Is he still out there? Were you there when he died?"

Mike stared out at the rock Dorie had climbed. The water was almost midway up it now, and there was a seagull perched on top. Everyone followed Mike's eyes out to the rock. The seagull cried, then lifted off and took to the sky.

"It was an accident," Mike said, almost too quiet to hear. He was trembling.

Cooper wilted like a peony that had suddenly gotten too heavy for its stalk. Simon saw her start to go down and grabbed her arm. She latched on to him for support. Her eyes filled, the way seawater rushes into holes dug by kids on the beach.

Val stood there with her hands pressed to her mouth. "My poor Lino," Val said.

Mike sank to his knees. He looked out at the horizon. He took off his hat and flung it onto the sand. Small waves licked the shore. The water seemed calmer now. At least on the surface. Who knew what was going on underneath. And there, in the shadows of the new hospice, Mike began the story of what happened on May 2, 1977.

"After my old man got sent away for the second time, being out in the boat was the only thing that seemed to clear my head. When the tide was low, I might haul up on one of the bars, plant a pole in the sand, listen to music. On rough days, I liked to crash through the breakers at the mouth of the inlet, feel it in my jaw, the slamming of the hull."

Mike stared out at the inlet. It was like he was out there.

"That night the water was smooth as glass. I'd been out on a sandbar having a few beers. The bar kept shrinking until the last ripple of tide erased where I'd been sitting. I got into my boat and started hauling up anchor. That's when I heard an engine. I knew it was Lino. I could tell by the sound. He pulled up along-side and I gave him a beer. We might have smoked a joint, I don't remember.

"You couldn't say Lino and I were great friends. At school we barely said hi to each other in the halls. 'Cause of my father. I got a lot of that. But I liked the kid. I'd see him out there and we'd hang out sometimes." Mike had a faint smile on his lips that flattened out. "That night, I could tell something was eating him. I asked but he wouldn't tell me. He said I'd find out soon enough."

Rose looked at Val. She was sitting with her hands folded over her belly, her eyes cast down. Simon leaned in to Cooper to let her know he was there.

"It was me who suggested it," Mike said.

"Suggested *what*?" Rose asked.

"That we race." His voice cracked. "The last time we had, Lino and another kid had wound up getting busted. But not before kicking my ass. I wanted the chance to redeem myself. Only by then, we were both pretty wasted. We cut our lights and glided without wakes toward the first green buoy. The races always started at the first channel marker, the one closest to the harbor. The straightaway would end at the red buoy at the Point."

Rose looked out at the water and saw a red buoy bobbing on the surface. She looked over at Simon. He nodded. From far away, it looked like one of those inflatable clowns that get punched down but keep coming back up.

"Had a six-cylinder, two twenty-five Merc on the skiff. That's a lot of engine. The flat hull gave me the edge in calm seas. Lino's dory sat low and cut deeper into the water. Didn't think there was a chance in hell he could beat me."

"So what happened?" Rose asked. Mike startled at her voice as if he'd forgotten there were people around. He turned and looked around at the group. His eyes lingered on Cooper for a moment.

"We were idling at the start. 'Let's chase one more,' I said. I tossed Lino another can of beer and held one up for me. I gave the signal and we tore the metal rings off the cans, put the beers to our mouths, and flung our heads back. I felt some of the cold beer trickle down my neck. Funny the stuff you remember. Anyhow, we chugged hard. I fought back the tears that came from the air bubbles rising in my throat. When the last of the beer was gone, I crushed the can in my fist and looked up in time to see Lino belch. He was already wiping his chin." Mike smiled and shook his head. "'On the count of three,' I said. I checked the trim of my motor. Lino was on my port side. I looked at him. He was grinning. Still see that grin like it was yesterday. On three, I plunged down on the throttle, opened it up all the way. We fired off in a cloud of gasoline exhaust. I'm pretty sure I got the better start.

"Seconds into the race, though, Lino closed the gap and pulled ahead. I saw the point of his bow slip ahead of mine. As we got close to the finish. I remember seeing something dark in the water. I swerved to avoid it. It was like the rocks had moved, but later I realized it was the channel markers that had been repositioned. They must've been off. Or somehow we'd veered off course. Before I knew what was going on, I heard it. The crunch of metal on rock. And then, for what seemed like minutes but could only have been seconds, I saw the entire hull of Lino's boat facing me broadside, airborne. And then the boat flipped and hit the water upside down."

Cooper let out a cry. She buried her head in Simon's red coat.

Mike fidgeted. He turned and looked at Cooper, then quickly turned away. "Must've—you know—happened on impact." Mike looked at Rose, then back out to the water. "I remember the sound of wood splitting. I cut the engine and swung around. I heard the gurgling of Lino's engine as it released air and sank to the bottom. And then there was silence. Just a horrible, eerie stillness. I looked everywhere for signs of Lino. I called out to him. I did that for a long time," Mike said.

"Why didn't you *tell* someone?" Cooper said. Her anger pierced the air. "Why didn't you get help?"

Mike lowered his head. "I was afraid," he said. "The way that boat hit, I knew Lino couldn't have survived. I also knew if I told people, I'd get blamed. I didn't want to end up like my old man, behind bars. No one in this town would have stood up for me. No matter what I did, people always treated me like it was just a matter of time before I turned bad."

He'd obviously grown up believing it too. "But if what you're telling us is true, it wasn't your fault," Rose said. "It was an accident."

"At sunrise, I went back to the scene. Tide was low. I decided I would leave it up to fate to decide what to do next. If I found Lino's body washed up onshore, I'd have to call the cops. But if Lino wasn't there, then maybe I could get rid of the evidence, whatever was left of the boat, pretend like it never happened. No one would ever need to know we'd been out there. We hadn't been seen by anyone else that night. It was crazy, I know."

"You had to think about his family," Rose said.

"I convinced myself early on that it had to be better for Lino's parents to live with the hope that their son was still alive than to know for sure he was gone."

"You still think that?" Simon said.

Mike looked over at Cooper, who was limp against Simon's chest. For the first time, she looked frail. He answered in a whisper. "No."

"What did you find when you got there?" Rose asked.

"I parked on the street and used the path to the Point. I took my shovel, a clam rake, and a steamer bucket." He turned and pointed to where the hospice now sat on the bluff. "When I got up there, I stopped and looked down. On the flats, there was nothing but a few pieces of shredded metal, the motor's prop, and a piece of the hull. I climbed down and started digging."

"Anyone who saw you would have thought you were digging for clams," Rose said.

"It was hard. The holes would close up as fast as I could dig. I started to feel like there were forces out there bigger than me trying to make sure I wouldn't be able to erase the evidence." He looked up at Rose. She thought she saw him shiver. "I covered up what I could and put the boat's prop in my bucket. I took it home and buried it next to the bones of my cat. I said a prayer for Lino." He stopped and looked at Cooper. Then he said, "For a long time, I worried his body would wash up. Right after the accident, I went out there every morning to scour the flats. But there was never any trace of him. No clothes, no keys, no shoes. When Avery came forward and said he'd seen Lino at the bus station, I almost started to believe maybe it was true. That somehow he'd survived. Maybe he'd swum to shore and then taken off, like everyone said. Because he didn't want to marry Val."

Rose looked over at Val. She wanted Val to defend her relationship with Lino. But Val wasn't the kind of person who defended herself. She just stared straight ahead. The hurt in her face was enough to forgive any lie she'd ever told.

"I let myself pretend I believed it on the outside. But never on the inside," Mike said. "I knew he was gone."

"I still don't get why you needed to carry this burden around with you your entire life," Rose said.

"He used to say he saw himself in me. My old man. He used to say it to piss me off. But he was right. You take away the uniform and the badge. You take away the gun and the good work done over the last few decades and you've got Mike Eldridge. Son of a felon. Only my dad never robbed someone of his life, not that he wouldn't have. He just never needed to. After the accident, I was as crooked as he was. The only difference between me and him is that he never took responsibility for anything. Sure he went to jail but he always claimed he'd been set up. He blamed everyone but himself. The only way to prove to myself that I was different was to not let a day go by without taking responsibility for what had happened. If I didn't have the courage to go to the cops and tell them what happened, at least I could make myself think about Lino's death every day of my life. For years I carried him with me, from the minute I woke up to the minute I lay my head down on the pillow. When I ate dinner, there was Lino, picking off my plate. When I took a girl to the movies, there he sat between us."

"That's not taking responsibility. That's torturing yourself," Rose said.

"Over the years, it sort of tapered off. I eased up on myself. Didn't think about it as much. The nightmares stopped coming. Until the building started out at the Point. And the damn seawall." Mike ran his hand down his face. "I knew there was a good chance they'd find something when they started messing around out there. When they did, I wanted to be there so I could try and manage things. So I'd go out there and sit on the dune and stare out at the place where Lino died, watching them dump boulders and move sand around. While I was out there, I started talking to Lino again too. Mostly begging him to stay put. Then that day when you brought him up on the beach, I nearly jumped out of my skin. It was like all of a sudden he was talking back. And I got this feeling like things were coming to a head. There was this terrible tension all the time." Mike rubbed at the back of his neck. "My father spent a good part of his life in prison. This is *my* prison." He pointed out to the rock. "No one can take it away."

Cooper broke away from Simon. Her eyes were blue fire. Slowly, she walked over to where Mike was standing. Then she reached way back with her right arm and, with all her strength, slapped him hard across the jaw, carrying his head to the side with the momentum. The sound vibrated out across the water. Mike turned to look at her. He was stunned. None of them had expected it. It was like she'd slapped away all the air too.

"*That's* for causing me the pain of not knowing what happened to my son all these years," she said. And then, to Rose's horror, she wound up and slapped him again, this time with the other hand across the other side of his face.

"Cooper, no!" Rose yelled. "Please."

"And *that* is for being a fool." She shook her hand. The blow must've stung her too. "The boy died. It was a senseless accident. Stop carrying him around. He was never *yours* to carry. He was mine. And Val's. Move on with your life, Michael Eldridge. Stop wallowing in self-pity." Her voice cracked. "That's all it is, for God's sake."

With that, she embraced him. He collapsed into her arms, the bulk of him disappearing into her yellow slicker. They both began to sob, their backs heaving up and down in an eerie syncopation. They stood like that together for a long time. Rose looked over at Simon and there were tears shining on his face. Rose wondered if Simon didn't take some of what she'd said about letting go of the past to heart for himself. It was good advice for every one of them on that beach.

Finally, Cooper pulled away and grabbed Mike's shoulders.

"If there's one person who can give you the key to get out of jail, it's me. I was his mother. If can I forgive, so can you."

Mike wiped his eyes with his sleeve.

"Now go," she said. "And get us some divers. I want what's left of Lino brought to McPherson's tonight." McPherson's was the funeral home.

Behind them, the sun was a yellow plate slipping into suds. Two hours had passed since Mike had told his story. Now, beyond the bar, the sea had kicked up so that it was roiling, creating a backdrop for the drama that was, piece by piece, unfolding onshore. Mike had gone and gotten the men Cooper had asked for but hadn't returned himself.

In the time that had passed, Simon had already left and come back again with Milo and another fellow, a small man with skin the color and texture of an aged wine cork. He wore his dark hair slicked back from his forehead and had on a black T-shirt over what looked like red-and-yellow jockey silks, only longer, and harlequinned. Rose might have believed he was a jockey, he had that body type, if not for the shoes. They were flat and red, bulbous at the toes, and twice the length of his feet. As he approached they reflected the clouds and the tops of the trees.

"Rose, Cooper, this is my friend Segundo Martinez," Simon said.

Segundo nodded, respectful of the circumstances. Simon must have cued him in to what was going on. Simon and Milo had taken Dorie and Zadie home in Milo's economical hybrid, then brought Simon back to his motel to get some clothes. They must have picked Segundo up at the police station. Val and Noel had returned to her house on foot. Rose had offered to take Noel so Val could stay but she didn't want to be there.

Rose wondered how Cooper might react upon seeing the clown who'd been loitering around her property, the man whom she'd helped put behind bars. Rose wondered whether Cooper might attack him or make a fuss. But this was a different Cooper from the one Rose was used to. This woman was resigned, too exhausted to put up a fight, a woman who was about to get what she'd been waiting for for twenty-seven years but never wanted.

Cooper raised her hand in a stationary wave. "No hard feelings?" she said.

"Of course not. My condolences," Segundo said.

With the sun going down, the no-see-ums were wicked. Simon brought back a blanket from his room for Cooper and Rose to huddle beneath as they watched the divers rise and dip beneath the surface, a head here, a flipper there, the occasional burst of air escaping from their tanks. From where they were sitting, the divers might have been seals, nearly as graceful, except for the eerie phosphorescent glow they cast with their underwater lights. They'd been at it for over an hour and had amassed a pile of debris that they'd deposited onshore, mostly small bits of wood and metal.

Simon stood at the water's edge. Rose was proud of him. She bet he'd even surprised himself today. To think how close he'd come to losing his life, how close Rose had come to losing him. She couldn't wait for the chance to be alone with him again so she could tell him how she felt, even though she had an idea he already knew. So much had been spoken between them today without words. Rose looked out at the boat anchored near the divers.

"Damn bugs," Milo said. "If I'd known about these, I'd have scrapped the whole project. Poor residents will be bitten to death before they have the chance to die." He sat down beside Cooper and pulled some of the blanket over his legs. "You know, this would be a lot easier in the daylight tomorrow, when tide is out. But I suppose you know that."

"I've waited twenty-seven years. That's long enough," she said. "Cops owe me." Cooper ran her fingers through the grooves she'd traced in the sand.

Rose stared out at the divers. "Milo, I've been meaning to ask you. When Dorie was up on the rock calling you *selfish—*" she started.

"Selfish *bastard,*" Cooper said. "Don't sugarcoat it."

"Right. Anyway, then later I saw you put your arm around her," Rose said.

"You want to know what I said to him to make old Meeelo here come around," Cooper said.

"Well, yeah," Rose said.

"Nothing," she said.

"How could I be angry with her? Zadie's the love of her life. And now she's going to lose him." Milo raised the blanket up to his chin. "I was in love like that once."

"I thought I was too." Rose was thinking of Martin now, and it occurred to her how long it had been since she'd even thought of him.

One of the men emerged from the water like the Creature from the Black Lagoon. He approached Simon. Milo saw where Rose was now looking. Cooper was still fixed on the sand.

The frogman spoke to Simon. Simon nodded. Then the man handed something to him, something small enough to fit in Simon's palm. He closed his fingers around it and dropped his hand to his side. Then he lowered his head and shook it slowly. Segundo put his hand on Simon's shoulder. Simon looked out at the horizon. Then he looked over at Rose.

"Sal and me were like that," Cooper said.

Simon was headed their way. The expression on his face was grim.

"Cooper," Rose said.

The woman looked up. And there it was. Rose saw all the air leave her chest. Cooper raised her chin to steel herself.

Simon sank down to his knees in front of her. He took one of the old woman's hands, pried it open, then dropped a piece of jewelry into her palm. Rose leaned in to get a better look. It was a Saint Christopher medal attached to a long chain. It was tarnished and had a strand of bright green seaweed affixed to it.

Cooper looked at it for a moment, then snapped her hand shut and brought the fist to her chest. Her hand was shaking. She looked up at the sky. Her eyes filled with tears. Simon hadn't even said a word.

She wiped her eyes with the back of her hand and looked at Simon.

"The skull?" she said.

"They found it. And a little more, not much. Enough for a proper burial," Simon said. "I'm so sorry."

Rose stood in Val's driveway. Segundo was in the front passenger seat of her car. She handed Simon the keys. The two of them stood by the driver's side door.

"Just give me a minute," Simon said to Segundo. He closed the door for some privacy.

"Think she'll be okay?" Rose asked. "I should check in on her later."

"She's a tough old bird," Simon said.

"I said I'd take her to the funeral home tomorrow. Val wants to go too."

"You sure you can spare the car? Segundo could take the bus to Boston tomorrow."

"We'll take Cooper's car." Rose flattened the collar of his shirt. "Just don't take off with my wheels," she said.

"It's tempting," he teased. "Sure you want to trust me?"

"I trust you," she said, so he knew she meant it.

"Don't worry, Rosie." *Rosie.* He twisted a strand of her hair. "I'm not the leaving kind."

"No?"

"Not anymore," he said.

Rose looked into his face. He was tired. It took more than a few hours to get over something like almost drowning. There were so many things Rose wanted to say to him. She wanted to tell him she was sorry, and that she was proud of him, and how grateful she was that he was alive. She wanted to assure him it was over between her and Martin. But the day had been too long and it was too late to get into all that. So she thought of a better way to say it.

Rose pressed her lips against his, gently at first, and just held them there, taking in the smell of his skin, the sound of the birds in the trees, the velvet of his lips. She imagined transferring her strength to him, her weakening, him strengthening, and felt it happen as her knees went limp. Then the kiss started to take on a life of its own. He wrapped his arms around her and spun her around until she was up against the car.

"Ay, caramba," they heard from inside.

They laughed into each other's mouth. Then his kiss got deeper, stronger. Rose realized something inside of her was still holding back. He knew it too.

"What's the matter?" he whispered into her ear. He lifted her up on the hood and stood between her legs. The car bounced again.

"Ay, papi!"

This time they didn't laugh.

"You and me." He pressed his forehead into hers. His voice was a hoarse whisper. "You and me."

It was as if he were trying to fuse their foreheads, to transplant the idea from his head into hers. And the next thing she knew it was there, an idea taking form, filling space, trying its new brain on for size. Or maybe it had been there all along.

"What if it's too soon?" she said.

"We can go slow," he said. He kissed her again, a long, languid exchange that was stirring things inside of her she never knew needed stirring. They came up for air.

"We've already passed *slow*, if you know what I mean," Rose said.

"We're starting over. Hi, my name's Simon. What's yours?"

"Rose." He kissed her again. Then he pulled away. "Slow is good," she said. She closed her eyes and waited for another kiss.

"Now I gotta go take Segundo home," he said. She opened her eyes. "He's got a big day ahead of him. A family reunion fifteen hundred miles away. We need to get an early start for the airport."

He was backing away, digging into his pocket for the keys. Rose realized her mouth was still open.

"Wait a minute," she said.

"Have to go." Simon grinned. He nodded toward Segundo in the car.

"When will I see you?" Rose asked.

"When I bring back the car," he said.

"When's that?"

"In three weeks. What do you think?" he said. *Tomorrow.*"

"I'll make us dinner."

"Too fast," he said.

"Dessert," Rose said.

"Still too fast." He reached for the car-door handle.

"Guacamole," she said.

"What was that?" he said

"I'll make guacamole." Rose didn't know why she said it. She didn't know how to make guacamole. It just seemed appropriately slow. "With chips."

Simon opened the door and slipped into the driver's seat. "Hey, Segundo," he said. "You got a recipe for guacamole?"

"That's Mexican, you idiot," Segundo said.

"Say good night to Rose," Simon said.

"Good night, Rose. It was a pleasure meeting you. And thank you for letting Simon take me to Boston."

Rose bent down and spoke to Segundo through the driver's side window. "You're coming back, right?" she asked.

"I'm just going home for a couple weeks. And then I'm

bringing my uncle back and he's going to help me get started," Segundo said.

"Clown school, huh? You really think you can make a go of it. *Here,* I mean?" Simon said.

"Have you ever met a funnier son of a bitch in your life?" Segundo asked Simon. He thumped his own chest. He was dead serious.

Simon looked at him. He laughed. "No," he said. "Not a chance." He slipped the keys into the ignition.

"Have a safe trip," Rose said.

Segundo smiled. She started to back away. Simon took her hand and kissed her palm. He let it linger there on his cheek.

"Good night, Rose," he said. He started the engine.

"Call me Rosie," she said.

"Good night, Rosie," he said through the open window as he drove off.

Coming back from the funeral home, Cooper asked Rose to drive. After they'd made the arrangements, the funeral director had given Cooper a Bible. Now she sat in the passenger seat with it in her lap. Val and Noel were in the back.

"There was a message from Eve when I got back last night," Val said.

Cooper didn't look up. She was running her fingers over the gold-embossed letters on the Bible.

"Greta Garbo's last movie was *Two-Faced Woman,*" Noel said.

Through the rearview mirror, Rose saw he had pressed his hands and face against the window. She caught the people in the next car pointing.

"She's going away for a while," Val continued.

"Really?" Rose said.

"She's moving to France," Val said. "She's fallen in love with a man with size EEEEE feet. Can you imagine?"

"Never been to France," Cooper said. "Never even been to Portugal."

"When will she be back?" Rose asked. She checked the rear-view mirror. Val was looking out the window.

"She probably won't," Val said.

Cooper looked at Rose. She raised her eyebrows.

"How does that make you feel?" Rose asked.

"A little lonesome," Val said. "But I have Noel."

"You'll always have Noel," Cooper said. She tapped the volume in her lap.

Val nodded and looked out the window.

"The last thing to escape Pandora's box was Hope," Noel said.

ACKNOWLEDGMENTS

With deepest gratitude to my editor, Trish Grader, and agent, Molly Lyons, and to the people at Florida International University: Lynne Barrett for your friendship and guidance; John Dufresne, Meri-Jane Rochelson, Les Staniford, and cherished pal Cindy Chinelly, to whom I'm forever indebted. Also, to friends and poets: Estee Mazor, Mary Miller, Malika Bierstein, John Camacho, and Jason Crespo for your encouragement during those "formative" years.

Thanks to Steve Cosmopulos for, among other things, writing *The Book of Lasts*. Thanks to wonderful lifelong friends—you know who you are—my Bonasia family, Uncle Fred and the "Piddlin' Dog," Lisa, Jeff, John, and with expressed gratitude to my mother, Lorrie Kiele, who lives on Nantucket and has been waiting for this day for nearly half a century.

Thanks, also, to the many who guide us through life, the writers of instruction manuals, the unsung heroes, many of whom either crafted or inspired some of the passages and chapter headings in this novel.

Finally, thanks to all the real, charming, wonderfully textured towns of Cape Cod that brought Nauset and its inhabitants to life.

Some Assembly Required

1. "Nauset has a secret" is a slogan invented by Zadie to promote the opening of the time capsule, but it seems to apply to other things as well. What are some of Nauset's other secrets?

2. Describe the two main characters, Rose and Simon. Why do you think they are attracted to each other?

3. "Instructions. Rose hadn't just written them, she'd followed them all her life" (6). How does being a reporter differ from being a writer of instruction manuals? What is the significance of Rose's decision to switch careers? How does leaving her "safety net" influence her development as a character?

4. Describe Cooper and Val's relationship.

5. "In the end, all Simon knew was this: he and Noel were damaged goods. Two peas in a pod. They needed each other" (97). Are there other characters in *Some Assembly Required* who might be considered "damaged goods" or who "need each other"? Why? What does the author suggest about human fallibility?

6. Discuss Simon and Segundo's differing views of God. What role does faith play in the novel?

7. Defining the term "washashores," Val says that it "just means people from away. Not born and raised here" (10). Like any small town, Nauset has its insiders and its outsiders. Who are the outsiders in *Some Assembly Required* and how are they perceived by the insiders?

8. Each of the major characters in *Some Assembly Required* is affected by Lino's disappearance. Describe the way this event has shaped the lives of Cooper, Val, and Mike in particular.

9. Loss is a major theme in the novel. Rose, Val, Cooper, Simon, and Noel each have different ways of coping with the losses they have

experienced. How did their various coping mechanisms affect your perceptions of these characters?

10. "It's all right there in the painting," Dorie says about Noel's portrait of her. "The pain, the lies, the secrets we had to keep" (290). What does Noel capture in his paintings? What role do the paintings play in the novel?

11. Discuss some instances in the novel in which characters are judged or misjudged by other characters. What conclusions do you draw from these instances? Which character(s) do you find most sympathetic? Why?

12. The past plays a powerful role in the lives of all of the characters in *Some Assembly Required*. What is the impact of the past on the present?

13. Discuss the major themes in the novel. Does *Some Assembly Required* have a central theme or message? If so, what is it?

14. Discuss the epigraphs at the beginning of each chapter. How do they relate to each chapter and to Rose?

Q&A with Lynn Kiele Bonasia

1. *You have spent many years on the Cape. How much of* Some Assembly Required *is drawn from your own experience?*

   In terms of character and story, the novel is entirely a work of fiction. That said, some of the "ways people are" in the book draw from my experience with locals. Cooper's feisty individualism, Zadie's Yankee pride, Val's eccentricity and the love they have for their town, how they bicker but eventually come together in support of one another, these things all have some basis in my own experience. I'd also say some of the lesser characters—the construction workers, the Bassetts, Fred Wilcox—are inspired by folks I've known through the years.

2. *Give us an overview of your writing career. Does* Some Assembly Required *grow out of your earlier work, or does it represent a break with what you've written previously?*

   I've spent my career as an advertising copywriter and had no aspirations to write a novel until my mid-thirties, when a switch went off and I suddenly became more interested in writing fiction. I used to think I had finally lived long enough to have something important to say. But I now believe it was more about my having gathered too many *questions* and realizing I had only the next half century or so to work out answers. And so I began writing more seriously, exploring themes and subjects that interested and confounded me. I sat down and wrote an entire novel. The book was terrible, but the exercise was a lesson in persistence. After that, I knew I had the endurance. I decided to go back to school and learn the craft.

As for comparing this with other things I've written, there are certain themes I am consistently drawn to whether or not I know it when I set out to write. Loss is one. And subjects like aging and substance abuse. And so I'd say this novel is consistent with some of the shorter pieces I've written.

3. *Was there a specific event or insight that inspired* Some Assembly Required? *What prompted you to write this novel?*

The novel began in a graduate novel writing course. I'd gone into the class expecting to revise the aforementioned terrible novel. But the instructor asked that we start fresh. So I began with a scene that had gotten stuck in my head. My mother, sister, and I had been apartment hunting on Martha's Vineyard. We'd landed at the home of a woman who opened the door and blurted out, "I'm a trapezoid." Not "Hello," or "Nice to meet you." Not only that, but it was a lie. She wasn't a trapezoid at all, though I knew she was talking about her property. I pondered that experience for days, the bizarreness of it. It went down in my writer's journal, and Val was born.

4. *How would you describe the town of Nauset? Is it typical of communities on Cape Cod?*

Nauset is an amalgam of towns on the Cape. I took liberties with architecture, layout, and geographic orientation so that there is no one town like it on the Cape. I think, too, Nauset is an amalgam of places in time, perhaps a bit of a throwback in its simplicity and quaintness. There's an innocence to the place that doesn't reflect the Cape Cod of today. I could be accused of sins of omission, I guess. I left out the CVS, the Papa Gino's, and T.J. Maxx.

5. *Two of your characters, Simon and his best friend, Segundo, hold dia-*
   metrically opposed views of God. While Segundo believes that everything
   that happens is part of God's plan, Simon thinks it more likely that God
   is a drunk who occasionally falls off the wagon and disappears or makes
   terrible mistakes. What is your view of the roles of fate and chance in
   our lives?

   I've always envied the Segundos of the world for their unwaver-
   ing faith and how through it they find meaning in everything,
   even suffering and death. For them it's all part of a greater plan. If
   they believe, they'll have all the answers one day. And then there
   are those of us who are less patient, and so we struggle. We see
   bad things happen to good people and have difficulty accepting
   that such things could be part of any master plan. So how do we
   manage to draw ourselves out of the fetal position? Maybe it's just
   to accept that things are what they are. All we can do during this
   short time on earth is to be students of life, live fully, be open and
   nonjudging, be grateful and kind because for some reason when
   we do these things, our own lives seem richer. There's not much
   room for chance or fate when you hold such views. Life simply
   unfolds.

6. *Each chapter of* Some Assembly Required *begins with an epigraph*
   taken from an instruction manual. Are these epigraphs invented or did
   you find them? How did you go about selecting the instructions for each
   chapter?

   In my acknowledgments, I salute these unsung heroes who direct
   us through life. I wrote none of the epigrams. I found them mostly
   online and in the big plastic bin where all the instruction manuals in
   our house get tossed. In fact, most of the manuals in that bin have
   outlived the products themselves. Proof that words endure.

7. *What prompted you to include an autistic character in* Some Assembly
   Required? *Did you research autism before writing the book?*

   I've always been fascinated with savants, which probably
   stems from a fascination with irony. Here are some of the most
   talented people an earth with the ability to touch strangers, and
   yet they lack the most basic capacity for human interaction. I had
   seen those *60 Minutes* episodes with the three-year-olds playing
   Mozart and the men who rattle off prime numbers ad infinitum.

As I did my research for Noel's character, I was stunned to learn we might all have such talent buried deep in our brains. What I wouldn't give to tap a little of that.

8. *Why does Rose choose the Cape as a place to start over? Why did you choose the Cape as the setting for the novel?*

Two reasons. When I started the book, I was living in Florida and feeling a little homesick. Writing about the Cape brought me back. But the more relevant reason is that the Cape is a haven for transients. In the summer, people come by the thousands. Some stay on, choosing to experience living by the sea for what can be a difficult but rewarding life. It's expensive to live there. Jobs that pay enough to cover living expenses are few and far between. The landscape is harsh and ever changing. In the book, I talk about the "quiet anxiety" of living at the water's edge. It's a trade-off. Some are fortunate enough to live in one of the most beautiful places on earth but, in some cases, all that they have could be swallowed up in one bad nor'easter. To sustain life on the Cape takes a certain toughness. Think of wind-battered seagulls, old cedars and pines and hardy beach roses. Maybe as a result of this struggle, there's a good deal of tolerance on the Cape for people from all walks of life and a spirit that we're all in this together. Most who live there are "washashores," meaning they come from someplace else. I wanted Rose to have to struggle to find home here and, as a consequence, become stronger. I also wanted some of the beauty Rose saw everyday to seep quietly into her own life.

9. *Did you begin writing* Some Assembly Required *with a clear picture of how it would end?*

Absolutely not, though in the back of my mind, I'm sure I had ruled out anything particularly dark. I would have had a hard time letting anything bad happen to Rose and Simon. They were filled with such hope. That's how I wanted the book to end—on a hopeful note. That's an important message. No matter how bad things get, there's hope.

10. *Describe your writing process. How long did it take to write* Some Assembly Required? *Did the novel go through several drafts? How did it change in the process?*

I can't even tell you how many drafts this novel went through. Because it ended up being my graduate thesis, the process was a bit drawn out and there was a lot of input to be gathered along the way from my professors. I'm indebted to them for helping me turn this into a cohesive book. But the editing didn't stop there. Once I signed with the publisher, there were subsequent drafts. On all counts, I'm grateful to have had such thoughtful feedback, though I hope to keep the next one down to a modest fifteen or twenty drafts.

11. *Does* Some Assembly Required *have a central theme or themes? What do you see this novel as being about?*

How do we move beyond loss? That's the central question. Do we attempt to start over in a new setting as Rose did? Do we drown our sorrows as Simon did? Do we become hardened as Cooper did? Do we make up lives and refuse to accept the truth as Val did? Do we blame and punish ourselves as Mike did? Do we act out as Dorie did? Do we speak in lasts as Noel did? For me, this is the central theme: processing loss and moving beyond it. And finding home. That's another key theme, whether that turns out to be a place or home within us.

12. *What is next for you?*

I'm at work on my second novel. It's about a woman who runs a seafood restaurant on the Cape. And I'm having fun revisiting my former waitressing days.

Enhance Your Readers' Group:

1. Learn more about autism and autistic artists. AutismArts.com and Autism.org are two good places to start.

2. Check out what's going on today on the Cape. Visit CapeCodVoice.com, the website of *Cape Cod Voice*, a local paper similar to the one where Rose works.

3. Hold your discussion over a seafood dinner! Try out some of the recipes at EdibleCapeCod.com.